Beyond the Stars:

KATARIA

KELLY BELTZ

Enjoy!

Kelly Betts

Dedicated to my family for their undying
support in all of my ventures. And to
all the dreamers out there with a love of
science, romance, and adventure.

CONTENTS

PREFACE

We can never predict how our lives will turn out. That's because tomorrow is always changing. Every day, we are forced to make choices—decisions that will ultimately influence what we create in our life. We can't be expected to know the best path to take without enduring a few mistakes along the way. It is the only way to learn about ourselves and what we really want. We discover our strengths, our weaknesses, and our desires. We might even uncover a skill we thought we were incapable of performing. Your reaction to what life throws at you can make all the difference. To adapt is to survive. We are all faced with our own set of challenges. I found that it is important to believe you will succeed no matter what the obstacle. It is imperative that you maintain your values and be grateful for what you treasure. Friendship, love, and family should never be taken for granted. It is through the kindness of others that we find the strength to prevail. This was made clear to me on my journey across the galaxy. How did I get there? Me, of all people—someone who never planned on leaving the surface of Earth? You might explain it by faith or destiny, but I call it an unforeseen set of circumstances. Most events seem to be random, but in truth, they are merely waiting for the right time to reveal their full connections.

CHAPTER 1

LIFT OFF

The day finally arrived. I just wanted this to be over with already. I had never planned on going into Space. Why go? Because my entire family was working on the completion of the Space resort, and I wanted to be with them. The Outer Space structure housed research and manufacturing facilities as well as a fancy hotel and zero-gravity sports arena. Although there was still a lot of work to be done, the resort was scheduled to start accepting guests early next year. I hadn't slept well ever since I agreed to go on the trip. I wished I could just hit fast forward and have it all behind me. The wait was grueling. I tried to picture my trip as a success. I reminded myself that my best friend, Noah, had been to the resort countless times and had always managed to make it home without a glitch. I crossed all the t's and dotted all the i's. I was as ready as I'd ever be. It was now or never. I even amazed

myself on how well I did on the mandatory Space training. There was no logical reason to back out now.

We were traveling to the Space resort on the newly-
built Space elevator. Although a whole new generation
of reliable launch vehicles capable of reaching Low Earth
Orbit (LEO) had long replaced the Space shuttle for most
of the transport into Space, they had drawbacks. They
fell short when it came time to deliver larger payloads
in the way of multiple passengers or numerous supplies.
They burned large quantities of fuel, adding to the cost,
and had a limited amount of space and weight they could
carry. The construction of the lift was the perfect solution
for eliminating issues like these. I was relieved that fuel-
burning rockets weren't lifting us off the ground. The lift
carriage was electromagnetically powered and capable of
traveling up and down its tracks at thousands of miles
per hour. The elevator launch pad was built on a floating
platform near the equator in the Pacific Ocean, which had
a lower risk of being hit by hurricanes or tornados. The
elevator carriage would carry us up five hundred miles
into LEO before docking onto a shuttle terminal. Once
docked, the entire lift carriage would be detached from
the elevator and reattached to a Space transport shuttle
for the rest of the journey to the resort.

Everyone on the trip had limits to the amount they
could pack because the majority of cargo space was
occupied with building supplies. We were required to

use the one standardized duffle bag and a small hand-bag handed out by the resort. *Ouch*, that was probably the hardest thing for me. The weight limit for each passenger's luggage was twenty-five pounds. I thought it sounded good until I started packing. It was challenging to adhere to both the weight and space limits. I kept thinking about what I absolutely needed to bring. The list changed daily. I couldn't remember a time when I'd packed and repacked so much before a trip. I think I must have emptied and refilled the bags over twenty times.

Leah, my nineteen-year-old daughter, arrived early to pick me up. I got in her car and asked, "Honey, are you sure you want to do this?" hoping for some last minute change of plans. She just smiled.

"Oh, Mom, we'll be just fine. Everything is going to go perfectly. You worry too much. I promise I'll take care of you," she reassured me.

"Thanks," I grumbled. I didn't care if she was my daughter and I was her mother, the thought of being taken care of sounded good to me. Leah was such a calming force for me. She had such a confident outlook on life. How in the world did I raise such a remarkable child? She was like a rock. Her poise made me feel safe. She definitely had her father Jack's courage.

Leah was always the world's best traveler. I remembered a trip we took to Europe for a science symposium when she and her brother Jackson were only five years old.

We traveled by train from Moscow to Warsaw. Our train did not have compatible rails for Poland and had to be lifted onto new rails at the Belarus border in the middle of the night. I was unable to sleep one wink after the disruption. It was also impossible to ignore the strong, howling winds that blew under the train car as we traveled. It felt like we were going to blow right off the tracks. Jackson kept waking up from the eerie gusts of wind, as well. My husband Jack and Leah, however, appeared to sleep soundly through the night. We arrived in Warsaw the next morning. Jackson and I were walking zombies. Jack and Leah looked great, even *well* rested. "That was fun. Let's do it again, Daddy," Leah had said.

Jack joined in, "Sure, honey." Argh! I couldn't believe them!

We checked in with a Space resort physician for a last-minute physical and got the green light to proceed. Surely, I could be infected with something that required me to go straight home to bed. No, I needed to stop whining to myself and hold it together before I had a full-blown panic attack. I planned to pretend I was only boarding an airplane in order to trick myself. "It's going to be a short ride," I told myself. "I will be with my whole family." I needed to be brave for them. That's it—I had an epiphany. Everything was entirely my fault. My parenting had led me here. I was getting just what I asked for: strong, fearless children. I knew I shouldn't have let them think

I was so brave over the years. I wished I would have verbalized my fears more to them. It was too late now. They were invincible, and here I was, about to be blasted off the planet!

The first part of our journey was to fly to the ocean launch pad. I was happy to see the lights of the runway come into view outside my window. Our plane landed smoothly on a navy aircraft carrier. We exited the plane and boarded a helicopter in order to transfer us over to the lift platform. There was no land in sight, only dark blue water in every direction. The ocean seawater filled the humid air with the smell of fish. It was still early. I looked at my watch and groaned when I saw it was only a few minutes after six in the morning. The orange morning sun was lighting up the horizon as it rose with the breaking of dawn.

Within minutes, our helicopter had reached the Space elevator platform. The entire platform was mobile and could be relocated if needed. This was a built-in feature designed to help avoid any accidental collisions with Space debris or storms that might threaten the structure's integrity. We exited the chopper as the loud, rotating blades still churned directly over our heads. *There's no turning back now*, I thought as I stepped out onto the lift deck. A gust of strong wind blew across the platform and wildly flung my hair out in all directions. I looked up at the cabled elevator track disappearing straight into the clouds. Its height was mind-boggling. My hands became cold and clammy. I wasn't sure if it was my anticipation of the ride or sea-sickness, but I wanted to throw up. I took a deep breath to maintain my composure and leaned into the strong wind. We naturally walked in pairs across the platform to the bottom of the elevator lift pad. I reluctantly grabbed hold of the metal railing and followed Leah and the others in order to climb up the open, latticed stairs to the elevator door and enter the craft.

Once inside, we walked along a stairlike ledge above the chairs before lying on our backs in our assigned seats. Before any launch, the carriage was rotated to always face in the direction in which it would travel. This was important to help its travelers avoid motion sickness. We all diligently strapped ourselves in like we were taught. I checked my buckles as well as Leah's for security ... *twice*. The seats were arranged like an airplane but had very little space in between the rows. The horizontal position made me feel like I was sitting on a ride at Disneyland.

The flight commander came on the speaker overhead and announced, "Welcome aboard, passengers and crew. We will be departing here momentarily to the Space Island Resort. The countdown will proceed once we are given the go," he announced pleasantly.

Sure, it's just like a plane ride. I didn't know why I was so nervous. We remained horizontal in our seats, ready to go, for another fifty minutes while the flight commander periodically informed us of some last-minute checks performed by the ground engineers. *Couldn't these details have been attended to before we boarded? Ahh*, what was I thinking? I thought about making a run for it as the grueling minutes painfully ticked by. *Hell, I don't even like roller coasters. What in the world was I thinking when I signed up to do this?* I struggled to ignore my escape plan and be a good passenger. I wouldn't allow myself to think of something going wrong. I had to have undying trust in the technology. Just then, I heard a loud, humming noise and felt our seats and floor vigorously vibrate as the electromagnets were rotated into place for contact. It tickled my entire body. I opened my mouth to keep my teeth from chattering together from the strong vibration. I looked over at Leah with terror. She managed to smile back at me with an exhilarated look in her eyes. She reached over to hold my hand, which I quickly snatched and squeezed tightly so that she couldn't let go. What was I doing? *I shouldn't be here. This sucks! Help!* I wanted to go home. I wished Jack was there. He always made everything seem easy. I could hear him telling me, "It's not a big deal. Everything is going to be fine. I promise. You can do this." Oh, wait a minute ... that was Leah's voice.

The countdown began: "Ten, nine, eight ... Blast off," broadcasted the ground control commander overhead.

It seemed like old habits died hard. The entire carriage unexpectedly jolted our bodies when the electromagnets were fully activated for launch. Suddenly, I felt a surge of strong downward pressure pushing me through the back of my chair. I could not lift my head from my headrest, nor did I want to. Our gaining momentum was undeniable. I slowly breathed in and out. Within a minute, the lift carriage seemed to reach its top velocity. Almost instantly, my body adjusted to the pressure as if I was riding in a fast car. I let out a sigh of relief after the pressing force slightly eased its grip against my body. I closed my eyes tightly and prayed silently that the ride would continue safely. I felt a little better, so I turned to my left and looked at Leah. She appeared relaxed. I quickly looked to my right to study the faces of the other passengers around us. Everyone was surprising calm and extremely quiet. No one seemed brave enough to talk. It was several minutes before the flight commander informed us that we would soon be weightless once we cleared Earth's gravitational pull. Just like that, the pulling sensation was released as promised. I knew that the harness seatbelt was all that kept me in my chair. It was the most bizarre sensation I had ever felt. It felt suddenly peaceful. I pictured us traveling away from Earth. We must have looked so small. Bad image! I felt queasy. I would rather have my feet planted safely on the ground. *Just get to the shuttle terminal*, I thought. *Then, maybe I can relax a little.* We would be arriving at the Space resort in about three hours. *I'll make it, right?* I had to. After all, there was nowhere to go but up.

"Mom, you're doing great," said Leah. "I'm proud of you!"

"It's not as bad as I thought," I grumbled.

"Are you done being afraid now?" she asked curiously with a half-smile.

"Yes," I lied. But how could I deny it? The worst part was over. "You know I wouldn't be here if it weren't for you and your brother," I ranted.

"I know, Mom, but I always thought Dad had a point when he said it was just a matter of time before you gave in and we got you into Space."

I sighed. "Maybe, but I don't know how I let you freaks talk me into these things," I said sarcastically. She laughed at my childish response.

How did I really get here? I thought. Memories flashed back as I remembered when I first started working for the Space Island Group over twenty years ago. It was how I became personally involved with the Space industry. Commercialization of Space was still in its infancy. It was a logical career choice. The growth in Space development was a booming market. Its expansion would be beneficial to our global economy and was expected to provide numerous jobs for the future.

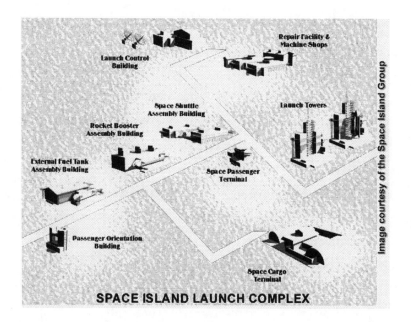

SPACE ISLAND LAUNCH COMPLEX

Launch Control Building

Repair Facility & Machine Shops

Space Shuttle Assembly Building

Launch Towers

Rocket Booster Assembly Building

External Fuel Tank Assembly Building

Space Passenger Terminal

Passenger Orientation Building

Space Cargo Terminal

Image courtesy of the Space Island Group

CHAPTER 2

MY CALLING

My first day working for the Space Island Group, otherwise known as SIG, was anything but dull. I was not sure how I landed such a dream job. The Space Island Group was a leading private company specializing in the commercialization of Space. They worked to incorporate technologies from NASA and other leading aerospace companies for the development of Space solar power and orbiting Space stations. The stations were to be used for research, manufacturing, and satellite repair centers, as well as Outer Space getaways.

Today would be my first time seeing the company's headquarters and meeting my new boss. Initial interviews for the position were conducted by the company's owners at my university's annual recruitment banquet. I was competing with numerous other applicants for their newly added positions. SIG said they would only provide a limited number of second interviews. Although I was unsure of the reason, I got the impression that they wanted to maintain the utmost security and only offered access to its facilities to those already on staff. While I was awaiting another interview, they called me out of the blue to tell me that I was hired. They told me that my recommendations spoke for themselves. The next orientation for new hires was scheduled to begin in two weeks. My new boss telephoned me and asked if it was possible for me to start with the group. I didn't dare say no. Besides, now that I graduated, what else did I have to do?

I had no time to drive, so I arranged for a moving company to bring my car along with the rest of my things at the end of my first week. But it didn't go as intended. My plan to catch the early flight into Los Angeles International Airport, get a rental car, and stop at my new apartment before my first day became a jumbled mess when my flight was inconveniently delayed by almost three hours. I called Dr. Tess Dixon, my new boss, to tell her that I was going to be unavoidably late. She was very understanding and told me to come in whenever I could get there. Upon arrival at the airport, I went to get a rental car only to discover that the flight delays had also caused a major backup in that department. There was an endless line of weary travelers standing impatiently, going nowhere. I didn't have time to waste, so without hesitation, I got in the first empty cab.

"My plane was delayed. I'm late for my first day at my new job," I told the cab driver, handing him a card with the street address.

He tapped on his GPS. "No worries, ma'am. I get you there," he replied in broken English.

Ma'am! What an insult! I was only twenty-three! How *old* did he think I was? He put his foot on the gas and took off like a bat out of hell. I held on tightly. "Hey, it's okay. My boss said I could get there whenever I could," I explained.

"No problem, ma'am," he said politely. He appeared to have no idea what I was saying.

"Really, you can slow down. The building will still be there," I complained some more.

"Yes, I get you to building." He looked back at me in the rear-view mirror and smiled as he swarmed in and out of traffic on the interstate. Clearly this was no time to work through the language barrier, so I decided it was better to remain quiet and endure the ride. At this speed, it would all be over with soon, anyway.

I took a deep breath and looked out the car window as the reckless taxi driver approached the Space Island Launch Complex. My neck jerked back when the car came to a screeching halt. I think I arrived from the airport in record time. Where did they teach these cab drivers to drive so fast? Now I was really feeling nervous. I'm not sure if it was due to all of the close calls on the highway or that I actually lived through the terrifying ride and had to deal with my reality. My anxiety soared when I realized how large the complex was. It was comprised of multiple buildings spread out across its industrial drive.

"That be eighty dollar, ma'am," yelled the cab driver, trying to gain my attention.

"Okay, keep the change," I replied and handed him one hundred dollars, despite the whiplash. The cabbie smiled back with a proud look on his face as he accepted the bill, probably because we'd arrived so quickly. I couldn't help thinking that he should have been the one paying me for having to endure his driving instead of the other way around. I grabbed my bags and got out of the car. "Here goes nothing," I said out loud. I walked down the sidewalk and into the building for the first time.

I entered into the two-story lobby and discovered it was nothing as I had imagined. It was large and practically empty. I approached the information desk with an older blonde woman sitting behind the counter, tapping away on her computer. "Hello, can I help you?" she said, taking a quick glance away from her screen.

"Hi, I'm Samantha Gerris. Could you please page Dr. Tess Dixon for me and tell her I've arrived?"

"Sure thing, Miss Gerris. You can have a seat while you wait," she said, looking up briefly with a smile. I let out a sigh and plopped down on the lobby's firm sofa with my heavy duffle bags. *I'm going to be sick*, I thought. *Why didn't I just wait until next week to start? I should have said no when they asked me if I could be here today. That way, I could have at least moved into my apartment first. No*, I argued in my mind. *It is time I stop acting like a student.* This was why I'd gone to school in the first place!

I kept watching for Dr. Dixon to appear. I remembered how she described herself on the phone to me as "one the best-looking women you'll see while you work in the physics department." Then she had let out a laugh on the phone and quickly clarified her remark by saying, "What I meant to say is that I've been the only woman in the physics department. It will be great to have some more estrogen around for a change." She sounded very welcoming on the phone. It made the plane ride much easier for me. I really dreaded flying. I was the kind of person who liked being in control. On an airplane, you are at the mercy of the pilot and the weather conditions. At least it was a beautiful, sunny, eighty-two-degree day, which left me no excuse to back out.

I patiently waited in the lobby while I struggled to contain my excitement. This was an opportunity of a lifetime. Here I was, about to learn from the best of the best. I loved challenges and was sure that the physics department here would not disappoint. Space development was growing by leaps and bounds. SIG had just begun launching solar power satellites and would soon be constructing its first commercial Space station. Blueprints for an Outer Space resort and elevator into Space were also in the making. It would demand the need for limitless designs. Besides, my new position would keep my feet planted firmly on the ground. Ever since I enrolled at Massachusetts Institute of Technology (MIT) for my doctorate in physics with a concentration in Earth and planetary sciences, I'd been surrounded by astronaut wannabes. I had to endure my classmates' endless enthusiasm, chattering on and on about how they wanted to be aboard the future expeditions into Space. I usually just nodded, hoping they wouldn't notice my lack of interest, and quickly changed the subject. Sometimes, though, I would pick their brains for ideas on things we should try to develop in the future. I took notes. Why not? I had a group of highly ingenious people at my disposal with imaginations more interesting than television. I tried to encourage the feasibility of their every fantasy, believing that it was just a matter of time before we figured out a way to do it. This only added fuel to the fire.

Minutes later, I looked up to see a beautiful, tall, shapely black woman approaching me. "Hello, you must be Samantha," she said cheerfully as she put out her hand.

"Yes, please just call me Sami. And you must be Dr. Dixon," I said, shaking her hand firmly.

"You can call me Tess," she reciprocated. "Martha, would you do me a favor and hang on to Miss Gerris' bags for her today while I settle her in?" Tess asked the blonde lady behind the desk.

"Of course I will, dear. Don't worry about your luggage, Miss Gerris. I'll be here all day and keep it safe for you," she said kindly.

"Oh, um … thank you. I'd really appreciate it. That's very kind of you." I quickly surveyed her trustworthiness and handed over my bags. It was a relief not being burdened with my stuff on my first day.

"She really will be there all day. I don't think I've *ever* seen her leave that desk," Tess whispered quietly after we stepped away. "The lab is quite a walk from here. I hope you'll enjoy the workout," she said jokingly. "'That's why I always wear my favorite hiking shoes," she said with a smirk. I followed her eyes to the three-inch black heels she was wearing.

"I didn't get to go for my run today, you know with trying to get to the airport on time and everything. So, I'm all for it." I looked at her perfectly polished ensemble and suddenly felt underdressed. *Maybe I should have worn a suit. After all, first impressions are lasting impressions. Oh, why did I wear my usual polo shirt and khakis?*

Tess didn't lie about her looks, either. She was stunning. She had long, silky black hair, golden-brown skin, a perfect body, and the face of model. She wore a crisply ironed white blouse and black skirt hitting right at her knee, which showed off her long, lean legs and heels. I'm not sure if it was the shoes or her height that caused her to tower over me. Perhaps if she didn't want to work in the physics department, she could have gotten a job as a supermodel.

We walked down the long hallway and stopped at a closed, unmarked door. Tess entered a numerical code on the key pad on the wall, pulled her ID from her blouse, and slid it under the sensor. "You'll get your password and ID before we leave today," she stated matter-of-factly.

The door quickly slid open, and we entered the lab. There were three men sitting at their work stations who never lifted their eyes when we walked into the room. I let out a sigh of relief. They were dressed casual, like me.

"Ahem," Tess cleared her throat to gain their attention. It worked. All three men jumped up and quickly sized me up and down as they walked forward to greet us. "*Miss* Gerris is here," said Tess proudly.

"Hello," I interjected politely.

"This is Josh Forester, Michael McCullen, and Noah Peterson. It is Noah's first day as well. That's why we were so eager for you to start today," Tess said in a professional tone.

They all shook my hand and welcomed me warmly.

Noah leaned down into my ear and whispered, "It's nice to meet you. I think they plan on orienting us together." He sounded excited by my arrival. He'd obviously arrived on time and sized up the schedule for the day.

"Sounds like a good plan to me," I said, feeling at ease, knowing I wasn't going to be the only one at risk for asking stupid questions.

Tess told us that Josh would be in charge of our orientation and briefing us on all of the current projects over the next few weeks. "I will join you once you are up to speed," she stated, sounding relieved that she was not going to be bothered with the break-in period of new hires.

Noah Peterson looked like he could still be in high school with his wrinkle-free skin and boyish face. He had tousled brown hair, bright brown eyes and cute dimples when he smiled. Oh yeah, he was downright adorable. Did he already have his doctorate? And here I thought I was young. I was considered a high school prodigy,

graduating at the age of fifteen. He must really be *smart*.
No wonder the SIG sucked him up.

Josh walked us down the hall into a bright window-
lined room. "Welcome home." He motioned for us to
sit down at the large wooden table in the middle of the
room that looked like it was a catch-all for the department. There were boxes piled up in rows that almost
reached the ceiling at one end of the room, three computer terminals on the other end, and piles of paper that
were neatly stacked on the floor along the room's border,
covering the carpet and leaving only a narrow walking
trail.

"This is the best room in the house, our multipurpose
room. I know it's a mess, but you should see our storage
room." He chuckled under his breath at his own joke.
"It's funny how we all used to believe computers would
completely eliminate the use of paper," added Josh when
he saw our faces cringe as we sized up the chaotic space.
"Anyway, it's one of my favorite spots. It's where you find
the coffee," he jested.

"Great," I quickly agreed. I didn't even notice the
coffee pot until I fully entered the room because of all
the piles of paper.

We all took a seat at the table. At least it was clean.
Josh handed us each a four-inch red orientation binder,
which he proudly announced he had put together.
He tapped each binder with his index finger. "If you just

memorize everything in here—you'll do just fine," he said with a smirk.

"Sure, no problem," Noah said confidently. He had a glint in his eyes that looked like it was going to be an easy chore. I just followed his lead and confidently nodded my head in agreement as if it was a done deal. How could Noah be so cocky and look so innocent at the same time?

The days turned into weeks as Josh went on and on about the successes and failures of the previous lab experiments. He was a man of great detail and could *really talk*. We focused on the current design of the solar power satellites and how they could be transported safely into Space. The panels were enormous and would span out once in orbit. Space solar energy was an untapped power source expected to provide clean energy for our planet. The solar power collected in Space was to be beamed back to a power grid on Earth by a microwave beam, which was no stronger than a cell phone. Noah and I diligently listened while we referred to the pages in the red binder. Occasionally, Noah would throw out possible solutions that we could try in the future to help ease the delivery of the satellites into orbit. Josh's eyes would light up in astonishment as if he never looked at things the way Noah did. I think baby Noah was holding back on just how intelligent he was. We spent every day together. I felt like I was being home-schooled with my little brother.

I really thought I knew Noah until I accidentally spilled my coffee across the table one day during break. I grabbed some paper towels and hurried to move our notebooks out of the way when I noticed some strange notes in the back of Noah's binder. I was alone in the room, so I flipped through the pages. The sheets were covered with complex diagrams and had text written in a foreign language. The lettering style was particularly disturbing. I didn't recognize it. The elegantly written cursive letters slanted to the right, taking on an appearance of penmanship centuries old. I heard his voice coming closer to the room, so I quickly blotted up the mess and returned everything back in its place. I wanted to ask Noah about the notes, but what if he was a spy? I had heard of people infiltrating developmental fields in order to steal their technology. Clearly, he had the mental and physical capabilities needed for espionage. I liked Noah and prayed he was good. He spoke with no trace of a foreign accent. Still, I could not think of a logical explanation for the bizarre writing. I was dying to take another look at the writing, but he didn't leave my side for the rest of the afternoon. The next day, I planned to take a picture of the pages when he stepped away, but the notes were gone. I kept looking for other warning signs. Nothing else seemed off, so I tried to forget about it. Days later, I was happily relieved to discover that Noah was a die-hard history buff in his spare time. Knowing him, he was probably memorizing a dead language. He could rattle off exact dates of historical events like a news anchor broadcasting the nightly news. Perhaps he should have pursued a career in the field of archeology.

We completed our orientation, and Josh announced, "Congratulations, class, you're both up to speed now. Tess and Michael will be joining us on Monday," he said, sounding a little disappointed.

"Great!" I blurted out enthusiastically. I couldn't wait to hear someone else speak. Josh got more dry and monotone the longer he spoke. If it weren't for the copious amounts of caffeine I ingested, the sound of his voice could induce me into a nice, sound sleep.

"Oh, wonderful, I'm glad you think we're ready to get to work," said Noah, smoothly covering my overreaction. I was grateful he had my back.

Monday morning couldn't arrive quickly enough. I walked into the lab and was immediately handed a new binder by Tess. "I hope you're up for the challenge. We have our work cut out for us," she said with a smile. "We have to fine-tune the regenerative environmental controls for the life support system of the future Space stations," she said like an advertisement.

"*Really?* We're not going to be working on the solar power satellites?"

"No. I would like you to concentrate your energy on something else. We have enough people working on the solar sats."

"Of course, I want to pull my weight around here," I said reassuringly. "What do you want me to do first?" I asked eagerly.

"Our job is to develop ways to make life in Space resemble life here on Earth, while considering the limits of available resources. The book is just a start. We need to come up with more ideas."

I looked through the binder. There were outlines for hydroponic food production, oxygen generation, and water recycling.

"Great, I know just where to begin." This was right up my alley and exactly why I wanted to work here in the first place. Where else could you make up the most outlandish ideas and have the people around you say, "Oh yeah, that would be great; let's build it"? I kept a list of ideas on hand for moments like these. If only I could call up my MIT classmates right now and tell them about this.

"I thought you might." She smirked.

"Where's Noah?" I asked when I realized he wasn't around. "Isn't he going to help us?" He had become my shadow.

"No, he is going to be working with the engineering department for a while. We need him to work on the alternate propulsion systems for the unmanned transport of the ETs," said Tess matter-of-factly.

ETs, or hollow external fuel tanks, were used as building blocks for the Space station. Normally, the Space shuttle is lifted off the ground by two rocket boosters that drop off and parachute into the sea after two minutes. The fuel needed for the next six and one-half minutes in order to reach orbit is provided by the ETs. Once exhausted of fuel, these large, empty tanks will become the modules that are outfitted by our construction crew once in orbit. They could be turned into living quarters or research labs, depending on the need. All the preliminary electrical wiring would be prefabricated in the walls of the tanks prior to launching to help facilitate the construction process.

"Why? Will you *miss* him?" said Tess, probably insinuating that there might be something going on between Noah and me.

"*Oh*, no, I'm just used to seeing him every day. That's all," I said flatly, as if I wasn't interested. Even though our relationship was disappointingly platonic, I liked spending time with him. I thought Noah was very good-looking, but he was just a friend. Besides, he treated me like I was one of the guys. He frequently told me about girls he had dated with little censorship. I could never tell if he was trying to get my opinion or if he was only bragging about his active social life.

"Do you have a boyfriend, Sami?" she asked softly.

"Currently, no ... not right now. I don't have time for that," I said defensively.

"Well, I enjoy being single, too," she quickly replied, sounding like she was sorry she had asked. "But, you do make time for fun, right? All work and no play isn't good for anybody."

"Sure, I love to read and knit, and I run almost every day," I said proudly, cutting her off. This was a touchy subject for me. I felt comfortable in my own little group of friends but never was much of a social butterfly.

"*Oh, good,*" she stated sarcastically. "I was afraid you might just go home every day and be a hermit," she surmised, as if she could read my mind. "You know—a night out on the town might be fun once and a while. I'll have to take you out with me sometime."

"Sure, sounds great," I answered without thinking.

What was it with people always trying to make me do something? I was happy living my life just the way it was. My parents had always made me try everything as a child in hopes it would make me a well-rounded person. They liked to take me horseback riding and taught me how to snow ski and water ski. Sometimes I think it was just to appease their personal sense of parental accomplishment. But I always agreed to oblige them in whatever they wanted me to do. I found it very hard to disappoint my parents. They had given me everything and more. I chalked it up as a drawback to being an only child. They both seemed to have an endless supply of energy and money when it came to me. Man—I'm glad I moved out.

CHAPTER 3

FRIDAY

Tess and I worked on many different projects at a time. It helped to keep our minds fresh and made the job exciting. Today, Tess and I worked on trying to design functional and practical living quarters for the Space station and resort with all the comforts of home, while utilizing the least amount of square footage as possible. We studied cruise ship schematics as well as hotel layouts. The development of an Outer Space paradise that mirrored a five-star hotel was not a new idea. It just wasn't feasible in the past. Previous Space companies failed to get the project off the ground due to the lack of funds and available resources required to support such an endeavor. The Space Island Group brought the idea to life by opening channels to private investors and utilizing existing technology. Physicists, engineers, and designers around the globe eagerly signed on to help make our quest a reality. Money was no longer an issue as public interest grew, and the budget became practically limitless due to all the investors. Problems were being resolved at incredible rates due to the sharing of information and the conglomerate of great minds. This was truly an exciting time to be privy to all the technological advancements taking place.

Friday came, and Tess seemed to remember our conversation from a few weeks earlier regarding my social life. "Sami, we're all planning on going to happy hour at the Honi Bar after work today. *You* must join us," she stated, as if it was an order.

"Really? Who all is going?" I asked curiously.

"Everyone. Josh, of course, and Michael will come for a little bit, but he always likes to get home before his son goes to bed. Noah and some of the guys from engineering are going to be there, too. Oh, it will be *so* much fun. My favorite band is even playing there tonight," she said with excitement, determined to make me say yes.

"Sounds great. I would love to see how Noah is doing." *I really could use a night out.* I hadn't spent anytime seeing the city. Plus, I'd be with the only people I knew in town. One of my greatest weaknesses was getting too wrapped up in work. I always found it hard to stop thinking about a project once I started something. I think my obsessive-compulsive traits tended to be overpowering at times. I could work for hours and hours without ever taking a break. I struggled with being a perfectionist. I tended to beat myself up until I got whatever I was working on right. Tess was right on target. I needed more balance in my life.

The day flew by quickly. Tess walked into my office to remind me it was almost time to go. I was busying leaning over my cluttered desk. I liked to spread out my projects for the day. I had been glued to my chair for the last four hours and didn't even realize that it was five minutes till five.

"Samantha, it's time to quit. Let's go. I'll walk out with you. Say, do you want to ride with me tonight?" Tess offered.

"That would be great. I have no idea where that place is, anyway," I said while I continued to clear my desk.

"Well, I've got to go home and get ready, but I can be at your place by six."

"Oh, I'm ready now," I replied. Just then, I heard Tess sigh in frustration when I looked over at her, only to meet her disapproving look.

"Sami, you really should turn it up a notch. I mean, those clothes are fine for work, but they aren't doing you any justice," she said bluntly.

"Fine, I'll change into my bar clothes," I replied, taking offense, although I knew that would please her. I could only plead guilty when it came to ignoring my wardrobe. I liked dressing simply. Wearing a polo shirt and semi-casual pants was a standard. It was easy to throw them on and took little effort on my part. I wished I could be as polished as Tess, but frankly, I really didn't care that much about how I dressed. Tess, on the other hand, took fashion seriously. She appeared to have a very expensive lifestyle and enjoyed taking care of herself. She was single but always had dates. She made it clear that she would never date anyone she worked with, even though the guys would be lining up and taking numbers. I'm not sure if she realized the way people looked at her. I needed to do my best to make her proud.

I rushed home to my apartment and hastily whipped open my closet door after stripping off my *boring* clothes. Argh! I had nothing to wear. Oh come on, I had to have something remotely sexy. I searched through the hanging garments and replayed Tess's words in my head. "Tell me you're not wearing that!" I pictured her saying as I flipped each hanger. Finally, my hand stopped upon a black tank that I usually wore under a blouse that was too sheer. Quickly, I pulled the hairclip, releasing my long hair, and let it fall loose before I pulled the low-cut, form-fitting tank over my head. I then slipped on a skin-tight pair of jeans, my black strappy heels, and a pair of dangly earrings. I touched up my makeup and gazed at myself in the mirror, feeling confident in my slutty ensemble. Tess would be pleased.

Tess arrived outside of my apartment exactly at six. I had never met a group of people who were so precise about time than the ones at SIG. "Hey, Sami, you look great," Tess cheered when I entered the passenger side of her bright red Porsche.

"Thanks, Tess. Nice car," I said. Of course, it would figure that Tess drove a car as impressive as she was. Without delay, she accelerated the vehicle with break-neck speed. I held on and had to brace myself when she stopped too suddenly at each red light leaving my apartment. I couldn't help slamming my foot down on the imaginary brake on the passenger's side floor. My attitude began to change after we attracted the attention of many onlookers. Riding in the car was exhilarating. Unlike other cars, you could actually *feel* the power of the motor. Now, I didn't even need to go to the bar. It was exciting enough just driving around town with Tess in her sports car.

We arrived at the bar in less than thirty minutes, partly due to Tess's driving. I had only looked down at the speedometer once to discover we were going eighty-seven miles per hour while on the highway. I thought it was better if I didn't complain about the speed ... after all, it was her license. Instead, I talked about last night's show on the Discovery Channel. It was Shark Week, after all. We walked into the loud bar looking for our friends. The place was busy, and the music was blaring. There were people lined up at the bar waiting for drinks, and every table was filled.

"Hey, you finally made it," said Josh, coming up beside us. He was wearing what he had worked in all day. Maybe I should have been born a man. "We landed the best tables in the house," he stated proudly. He pointed to a group of high tables literally five feet away from the bar that were positioned directly in front of the hallway with the restroom sign. "You see, Sami, as the night goes on, none of us like to walk too far to get to the bar or the restroom," he boasted.

"Great! You thought of everything. Do I know who to hang out with or what?" I acted impressed about their strategic location. Clearly, this wasn't the first time this group had gotten together for happy hour.

We walked over to the tables, where I saw Michael and Noah sitting with three other men I had never met. Noah quickly rose to greet me and gave me a friendly hug. "Sami, what have you been up to? I *never* get to see you anymore. Are they working you too hard in the physics department?" he said, sounding overprotective and sort of hurt. I suddenly felt a twinge of guilt for ignoring him.

"No, I'm good. Things are going great. I've just been really busy, that's all," I assured him.

Tess looked at the group of men at the table. "Let me introduce the rest of you. This is my friend, Sami. She's in need of some fun tonight. We need to show her how to leave her mind at the office," she said with an ornery grin, revealing her true motive.

Noah quickly introduced the others. "Sami, this is Brian, Roland, and Jack. I've been working with them in engineering."

They all said a quick hello, except for Jack. He stood up from his chair to shake my hand and smiled a crooked smile that made my heart jump. His welcoming gesture lassoed me right in. It also didn't hurt that Jack was ruggedly handsome with sandy blonde hair and a five o'clock shadow that he probably developed by noon. He was attractive in every way. I shook his large hand and glanced at his firm, muscular body, taking it all in. I caught myself staring and quickly raised my eyes to look him in the face. It was a mistake. His blue, smoldering eyes peered through me like I was the only person in the room. I dropped his hand and sat down awkwardly to hide my sudden mysterious onset of dizziness. I purposely looked away, trying to ignore my clumsiness.

"Sami, we should get together sometime. Hey, we are all going white water rafting next weekend if you want to come along," Noah offered enthusiastically.

"White water rafting, are you serious? You could drown or hit your head on a rock or something. Um …

I think I'll pass." My widened eyes clearly displayed a look of disbelief that he would find that fun.

"Okay, it's not for everyone. Maybe we could do something else," he said with a disappointed frown.

"Here we go," said Josh, coming up behind me with a handful of drinks. "Ladies, I took the liberty and got you the happy hour special, the house cosmopolitan."

"Thank you, Josh. You're the best," said Tess.

"Thanks, Josh. What's in it?" I asked.

"Hell if I know. It's a chick drink. I'm sure you'll like it." He smirked as the others laughed.

"*Hey.*" Tess nudged his shoulder for making such a sexist comment while giving him a stern look to control himself. Everyone quickly quieted down, trying not to offend her. I could tell that the guys were just happy that she graced their presence for the evening.

We were having a great time. However, I was definitely getting a little buzzed because I rarely drank alcohol. I always worried about it killing my brain cells. I did get drunk once before from wine at an Italian restaurant. It gave me such a terrible hangover the next day that I vowed never to drink that much again. It was a long time ago ... maybe it was just the wine. I tried to give myself a rational excuse to continue. *Surely a few drinks won't kill me.* Two cosmos later, I realized that I was undeniably drunk. It was getting late, and the band took over the music for the DJ for the evening.

"Good night, all. I'm gonna head out." Michael pushed himself out from the table. "My posse awaits me at home," he said, referring to his wife and son. He was proud that he had something better to go home to, unlike the rest of us. He was right. Roland was divorced, Brian's wife was out of town visiting her parents, and the rest of us were pathetically single. Michael was the kind of man who would never take his family for granted. He talked about his wife as though he had tricked her into marrying him. I was often shocked by his apparent insecurity. I searched for a reason. Maybe it was because his wife was ten times better looking than him. I never judged him by his appearance. But, physically, Michael was just your average skinny, nerdy, plain-looking guy. I overlooked his outward traits because his kindness, impressive intellect, and remarkable problem-solving skills greatly overshadowed his looks.

"*Ah*, you party pooper," teased Josh.

"Good night," the rest of us replied, understanding his urgency to leave.

Roland and Josh eagerly stood up and said in unison, "I'll walk you out." I watched as they walked all of ten feet, only to stop to talk to some women at another table. I wondered how long they'd been planning *that* move.

"I'll be right back," said Tess. "Do you want to come with me, Sami?" Tess offered before heading to the ladies room.

"No, thanks, I'm fine," I called after her while remaining safely in my chair.

Brian challenged Noah to a game of pool. Noah jumped on the game. I wondered if Brian realized how competitive Noah was. He loved to show me up when he could recite information he'd read from the red orientation binder without even opening his book.

"I guess this just leaves you and me." Jack smiled as he leaned across the table towards me.

"Yep." I sighed. I quickly hid my smile with a sip from my drink to cover up my excitement at being alone with the striking man. The alcohol took away my ability to think. Wonderful, I couldn't have picked a worse time to get drunk. *Ahh*, I needed to focus so I wouldn't make a fool out of myself. I sat up straight in my chair, tried not to fidget, and pretended to be in control.

The music was blaring, and Jack wasted no time before he slid over to the chair next to me. "I'm sorry. I need to move closer so I can hear you. It's so loud in here. I think I'm going deaf." He chuckled.

I nodded. "How long have you been working for the SIG?" I asked, saying the first thing that came to mind.

"Almost four years now," he answered. "What are *you* doing at SIG?"

"I've just started working in the physics department."

"Lord, *help me*, beauty and brains," he stated, staring up at the ceiling as if he were in prayer. "Where do they find them?"

"What do you mean?" I asked sheepishly. I couldn't help feeling flattered.

"You know, *people like you* … people who have won the genetic lottery." His smile and breathtaking eyes made me melt inside.

"You didn't do too bad yourself." I couldn't help flirting with him. I was feeling so relaxed and braver than normal.

"Oh yeah, I think I might have skipped a few lines when they were handing out bodies. I'm working with Noah right now, remember? That guy is freakishly smart—I can't even keep up with him sometimes. The kid has an answer for everything. And he seems buddy-buddy with you, so I know *you* must be one of them." He squinted his eyes while he leaned toward me, delivering his acquisition.

"So what if am? I can't change who I am." I decided to play along. "Being smart isn't a crime." I slid my hand up his thigh as I spoke. I immediately felt embarrassed by my forwardness. I thought I saw his lips turn up in a grin, but he pretended not to notice. Wow, I was definitely drunk. I fought to focus harder on keeping my hands to myself before I molested the poor guy.

"No, I guess not, but I'm just hoping you find me interesting enough." He watched me carefully for a reaction.

"You look like you can hold your own," I replied, flirting again. Why could I not control myself around this man? Fine, I guess I found his charm even more irresistible when he seemed so interested in me.

"Sure, I'm doing okay, but I got where I am by hard work. You know, the slow, *boring* way. I actually have to open books and even read them. They don't just enter me through osmosis," he continued to tease.

"Oh, what a shame. That must be really hard for you." I tilted my head empathetically.

"Yes, terrible," he said, looking at me with a frown and sad puppy-dog eyes.

Quickly, his face brightened up when the music changed. "Hey, beautiful girl, do you care to dance?" he said seductively, impatiently waiting for my response.

"Yes, I'd love to," I said without thinking.

He stood up and reached for my hand. I stood up too suddenly, causing the alcohol to rush directly to my brain. Oh, this was bad. I hoped I could walk, let alone dance. I reflexively squeezed his hand and leaned on it for support. He didn't even seem to notice, because he was much larger than me when we stood up. I couldn't help notice how rough and callused his hands were.

He must do a lot of work with them. I followed behind him as we walked to the dance floor, thinking how I must be careful not to embarrass myself. *Please don't trip*, I thought before I took each step in the dimly lit room. We reached the floor, and Jack spun me around to face him. The band played a song that sounded Brazilian. I had never heard it before. Jack naturally moved his hips, keeping in beat with the rhythm. He was a good dancer, so I just followed his lead. His confidence was enough for the both of us.

Jack smiled when the tempo of the Spanish guitar slowed. He pulled me softly into his body for the slow dance. Little did he know, I was grateful for his extremely close proximity. Now I could use his body to stay upright. He guided me across the floor with ease. The alluring music lowered my guard, making his moves even more captivating. "Who knew I'd get to dance with such an amazing woman tonight?" he said, looking down at me.

"Thanks," I responded and then turned my head to the side and leaned my cheek against his muscular chest. I spotted Tess back at the table. She was busy talking to someone herself. She shot me an approving look and gave me a slight nod.

"So do you want to go to Space someday, Sami?" Jack asked.

"Um … no," I admitted hesitantly. There was no use in lying. "I'm not crazy about flying, and just the thought of going up into Space … *no way*."

"What? *Really?* Amazing! Almost everyone I know is biting at the chance," he said, looking surprised. "You really are interesting." He stopped dancing and pulled me from his chest in order to look down at my face.

"I'm happy staying on the ground. So thanks, but no thanks." The fascination to travel into Space resided in everyone but me. I liked the challenge my job demanded in designing Outer Space living quarters but never felt drawn to experience it firsthand. He remained silent for a moment before he pulled me closer to continue dancing.

"Did you know that I was a pilot in the Air Force before I became an aeronautical engineer? Actually, I still fly with the reserves," he said, waiting for my reaction.

"Oh, really, that must be exciting." I tried to be convincing, but it was too late. It came out sarcastically. I had already let my true feelings be known.

"I fly an F-22 Raptor. It's such a rush. It's an amazing craft, packed with raw power. It has stealth technology, integrated avionics, and supercruise," he said, probably trying to impress me. If he wasn't so beautiful, his comment would have fallen on deaf ears.

"What's supercruise?" I faked an interest out of courtesy.

"It allows for sustained supersonic flight without the use of an afterburner," he answered happily as he succeeded in gaining my attention.

"Wow, you're kidding. You go *that* fast?"

"Absolutely. I live for it. Hey, I would love to help you get over your fear of flying. I could take you out on a small plane sometime," he said.

"I'd rather not." I shifted uncomfortably at the thought.

"I won't let anything happen to you," he said softly into my ear like he was making a promise.

"Great," I said sharply.

"Would you *trust* me?"

"Maybe," I said, wanting to keep him guessing. "After all, you are still here. You must know how to land a plane."

He laughed at my sarcasm and then twirled my hand and spun me around, only to turn me back to face him again. He smoothly pulled his arm in on my lower back and brought me into his chest. His moves had finesse. We continued dancing, but not speaking. I snuggled in closely to his body. I occasionally glanced up at his face a few times, only to have him look back at me with tender eyes. We danced until the band took their break.

We returned to the table. Tess was there talking to a man dressed in a business suit. He barely took his eyes off her to say hello to us when we sat down.

"Sami, we were thinking of going to get a bite to eat. Do you want to come with us or I could take you home first?" offered Tess politely.

"I could take her home," Jack quickly volunteered and then looked at me, awaiting my answer. I didn't know what to say. We'd just met. Our eyes met as I tried to determine if I could *trust* him.

"Oh, okay, sure. Thanks, Tess, but I'll be fine. I'll just get a ride with Jack. Don't worry about me." I didn't want to be a third wheel and wasn't ready to leave. I really wanted to spend more time getting to know this interesting man.

CHAPTER 4

MAGIC

Jack and I continued to ask about each others passions. "I want to know everything about you," he said with sincerity.

"What you see is what you get." I shrugged my shoulders.

"*Fine*, I'll go first," he responded, probably sensing my discomfort. He told me he was raised as a military brat. His father was in the Air Force and had moved around a lot when he was growing up. He sadly told me of how his mother died of ovarian cancer when he was only twelve. He and his little brother basically grew up in military school after that. I felt like he was carefully editing his past because he was embarrassed by his lack of family life. Jack graduated with a degree in aerospace engineering while he completed his military obligations for the Air Force. I could see that he would be an asset to his field and why he was offered a job by NASA after he completed his degree. He joined the SIG when rumors of budget cuts threatened potential layoffs at NASA. He said he loved the challenges his job offered him. His experience as a pilot proved ideal for designing structures that were both ergodynamically friendly and aerodynamically sound. He told me he was still in the Air Force reserves. He said he also worked as a test pilot, trying out new technology for aircraft at Mojave Air and Space Port. I must say, he was built for it, being both fearless *and* intelligent.

I was starting to feel tired and looked down at my watch. No wonder; it was hours past my normal bedtime. Jack noticed, grabbed my wrist, and turned my arm to glance at my watch, too. "*Jeez*, it's almost two in the morning, Sami. I should take you home. I'm sorry I kept you out so late," he said apologetically.

"Time really does fly when you're having fun." I smiled at him.

We walked to find his car and start on our way home. I hung on his arm so I wouldn't get dizzy and fall. I was relieved to see him open the passenger's side door of a black Acura for me. Sure, I was impressed by him being such a gentleman but even happier that the ride home had promised to be a little gentler than my journey in Tess's Porsche. Jack's driving made me relax even more. He didn't drive fast but not overly slow either. He seemed to be aware of everything around us. I imagined him maneuvering a plane in the sky with great skill. We talked in the car the whole way back to my apartment. Jack walked me to my door. Before I could put my key in the lock, he grabbed me as he had earlier on the dance floor, so elegantly, and kissed me delicately on the lips. He pulled his face away to check on my expression, carefully studying my eyes. I responded by running my hand through the back of his hair to pull him back down and kiss him again. This time, he pressed his lips firmly to mine. I got goose bumps and felt a rush when he responded to my advance. This kiss was much longer and passionate.

"Hmmm," he sighed. He easily pulled himself away from my embrace. "Beauty *and* brains." He stared at me, his expression unreadable.

All I could do was laugh. I had never heard anyone compliment me that way. "You're not so deficient yourself," I said, trying to say something witty. Great, I made it sound like he was lacking something. I wished I could take the words back as soon as they left my lips. Luckily, he didn't seem offended.

"Can I see you again, Sami?" he asked with hope in his voice.

"Yes, of course."

"Wonderful, I'll call you tomorrow," he muttered. He smiled and swiftly leaned in to kiss me on the cheek before he briskly strode away.

I walked into my apartment and headed straight to the refrigerator. I realized I was starving after eating only appetizers for dinner. I couldn't believe how much fun I'd had tonight. I had to remember to thank Tess on Monday. All I could think about was Jack. He was the most amazing man I had ever met. He exuded a confidence that was not conceited but reassuring. He had the body of an athlete and the bravery of a soldier. He was intelligent and absolutely *gorgeous!*

***

I covered my eyes with my blanket when I awoke to the bright light shining through my bedroom windows. I had forgotten to pull the shades before I went to bed last night. I lay there assessing my physical damages. My head hurt a little, but overall I might have evaded the dreaded hangover I'd hoped to avoid. I couldn't believe I'd slept so soundly last night. I got up and got a huge glass of water, just in case there was a delay in the onset of symptoms. My body jumped while I chugged down the liquid after being startled by the music of my cell phone's ring tone.

"Hello," I answered cheerfully, pretending I had been awake for hours.

"Samantha, it's me, Jack. Please tell me you remember me," he pleaded playfully.

"Jack … hmm, let me see … I think I might know someone by that name." I laughed. "How are you?"

"Great. I am guessing that you survived the night."

"Yes, I've never been better," I replied.

"Well, Sami, the reason I'm calling is to see if you would want to go gliding with me today. I wouldn't even ask you, but this is kind of a rare opportunity. My friend Regis just invited me to take his glider for a run. The weather today is perfect for it, so I already said yes. I would love it if you came with me," he said enthusiastically. I was allured just by the sound of his voice.

"You're just dying to get me in a plane, aren't you?"

"It will be *fun*," he said in an enticing manner.

"That sounds tempting, but I don't know—," I hesitated while considering his offer.

"Please, I won't let anything happen to you. *I promise*. You can trust me," he pleaded.

I sat quietly on the extension for a minute, just thinking about his words. I really wanted to see him. I wasn't sure if the alcohol made him so attractive last night or if he really was that hot. Plus, I couldn't let him think I was a big chicken. Oh, I hated saying no. "Okay, I'll go, but you aren't going to keep me up there for too long, *right?*" I ignored my temporary loss of sanity.

"No, of course not. We can just take a little cruise for some sightseeing."

"Okay, I'll bring my camera. I could use some aerial shots for my album," I stated, sounding pragmatic.

"Can I pick you up in an hour?" he asked.

"Perfect. I'll be ready. The sooner you get here, the better. It will give me less time to change my mind," I said. He laughed. Little did he know I was completely serious.

"Don't worry, you'll be fine. I'll see you at one o'clock then. Bye."

"Good-bye." I hung up the receiver and quickly looked up at the kitchen clock, which read five minutes till twelve. I couldn't believe I slept in this late. I hated drinking. I had already lost half of my day. I tore off my clothes and sprinted to the shower. I needed to try and look as good to him as I did last night. I got ready in record time. I left my hair down, just like I had worn it last night. I pulled on my black skort and a sleeveless coral sweater. I was grateful my mother brought me the outfit on one of our most recent shopping trips. It was my consolation prize for the torture I'd endured. The outing was the usual grueling day with my shopaholic mother. I generally tried to avoid getting in the car with her when she was in the mood to "run errands." I became her victim out of guilt. I only agreed to join her to get some mother-daughter bonding time. Tragically, it always ended the same, with me pleading with her to take me home. She could spend the entire day going from shop to shop. I didn't have the stamina or patience for that. I liked to go in a store, buy what I needed, and leave just as quickly as I had entered. I think that's why my father was so thrilled to have a daughter. He pictured himself being relieved of all his shopping duties. Unfortunately for him, I hated it just as much as he did. Once I got older, we would fight over whose turn it was to go. "I went the last time," we would each reply, trying to put the burden on each other.

CHAPTER 5

AMAZED

Jack arrived at my door exactly at one. What was with these people? I think it would be devastating if I stole all the atomic watches in the world. I swear they must hand out the satellite-controlled timepieces to every geek at birth. Although, deep down, I was happy not to have to wait one minute longer to see him. Jack declined my offer to drive, so we got in his car and left for our date. I couldn't help notice him turn to talk to me while driving, appearing to not even glance at the road as we made a sharp right turn. He seemed to be functioning on autopilot. He told me that it would take about an hour to get to our destination. I found myself scrutinizing his driving. I was still trying to decide if I was going to trust my life with him. *So far, so good*, I thought. He appeared to be competent. I carefully studied him when his eyes were safely on the road. He really was as attractive as I'd remembered him. Actually, he looked even better today. I couldn't help but feel turned on when I looked at his strong, muscular arms with prominent veins bulging when he gripped the steering wheel. I think I would have agreed to jump out of a plane with him if he asked nicely enough.

Jack asked me about my family. I explained that I was an only child and how my parents had me late in life. I told him about how much I loved my parents. I even felt comfortable enough to share how I used to pretend that my dog was actually my sister. I disclosed how my third grade elementary teacher was the one who brought me back to reality. She had asked my parents, during a parent-teacher conference, when my little sister Mikayla was going to be starting school. It wasn't until then that I had to drop the charade.

We traveled on an empty highway surrounded by thick forest on both sides. I looked at my watch. It was already two thirty. I was definitely lost and starting to get nervous. What was I thinking? I didn't really want to go up into the sky. Maybe I should have just stayed home. Why was it taking so long to get there? He better not be some psycho in disguise, planning to kill me and dump my body in some remote creek. Surely he would have had a thorough background check along the way to work for the Air Force and the SIG. I never had to answer so many questions in my life when I applied for the job.

It felt like I had nothing left to hide after that interview. But still, where in the world was he taking me?

"Where is this place? Shouldn't we be there by now?" I finally asked after we turned off the highway down a woodsy back road surrounded by thick rows of tall hemlocks.

He didn't answer right away and appeared to be concentrating on the road. He started to slow down and took a sharp right turn in between two tall brick pillars harnessing an open, thick black iron gate. It marked the beginning of a long tree-lined drive. "We're here," he said triumphantly. "I'm sorry—it took longer to get here because I'm driving a little slower than my usual."

"*Oh* my, what is this place?" I asked, trying to make out the structure peeking through the thinning forest trees. I quickly looked over at him and caught him smile at my reaction. We rounded the bend, opening up the obscured view. I looked ahead in the distance and saw what appeared to be a beautiful mansion with groomed flowerbeds and exotic plants rivaling a plush resort. We approached the circular drive in front of the stone façade and parked the car. My first impression of it being a mansion was an understatement. This place was a castle!

"This is my friend Regis's home. Well, one of them, anyway. It's amazing what you can do when you have a lot of money," he said with admiration as he raised his eyebrows.

"How do you know him?" I asked, sounding impressed.

"He took flying lessons from me for years, and then we just became friends. He's one of the nicest people you'll ever meet. He made his money in hotels and real estate. He lets me fly some of his toys now and then. I try to never say no. Regis is the kind of guy who is always on the go. You never know when he is going to take time off again to play."

"Did he ever get his pilot license?"

"Oh yeah, he's a great pilot. I taught him, after all. He will launch us off today," he said with a smile.

"Hmm," I sighed, suddenly remembering why I was here.

"Let's get going," Jack said as we got out of the car. "If I know Regis, he's been ready to go all day. There's nothing worse than keeping a billionaire waiting." He took hold of my hand.

We started up the herringbone-patterned brick walkway to the front entrance. Massive, carved wood doors topped with a leaded glass transom window towered high above our heads. The thing probably cost a small fortune. The craftsmanship was exquisite. I studied the patterned, spiral grooves in the wood while Jack rang the doorbell. A moment later, a man dressed in a black butler's suit opened the door to greet us.

"How do you do, Mr. Bennett?" the butler said formally to Jack. He motioned for us to come into the large foyer. I looked around. My eyes were immediately drawn to an elaborate crystal chandelier hanging above the central staircase that sparked like it had just been cleaned. The entrance's grandeur was undeniable and clearly well cared-for, *by staff*, judging by the fresh bouquet of starburst lilies adorning a high, circular table. An enormous bronze mirror and pair of hand-painted oriental chairs completed the showcase, making it picture perfect.

"Oh, very well, William. I couldn't be better," replied Jack politely.

Just then, a middle-aged man dressed in a white pilot's outfit strolled briskly towards us down the long, marbled hall. "Jack—it's about time! We're burning daylight! I was starting to think that you forgot about me."

"Never, Regis. We just got a late start, that's all," he reassured him before he shot me a quick glance, knowing what he had said about Regis probably growing impatient.

"*Well*, who is this young lady?" Regis smiled at me.

I reached out my hand to greet him. "Hello, sir. I'm Samantha Gerris," I replied in my professional voice.

He shook my hand as firmly as I would have expected from someone so accomplished. "Regis Coleman. It's a pleasure to meet you, Samantha. I was hoping that my boy, Jack, here would find himself a nice young lady like you one day. I was starting to get worried that he *scared* all the women away with all of his extracurricular activities."

Jack grimaced and looked carefully at my expression after the last comment. I thought I saw a glint of worry in his eyes, thinking I might actually be scared off and change my mind about being with him today. I stared back at him and just smiled, pretending not to care about any extracurricular activities. I'm not sure I really did care right now. I could only think about getting through today without losing my composure and looking like a wimp. Oh, what a turn on that would be. The memory of one plane ride in particular still haunted me to this day. Once, on a long flight home to New York, there was a lot of turbulence and a terrible snowstorm outside. I almost got in a fight when the lady sitting next to me actually had the nerve to ask the flight attendant to be moved to a different seat. She complained that I was making her nervous because I kept jumping and squeezing the armrest. I couldn't help it. I really thought we were going to die. In my opinion, I controlled myself quite well considering the circumstances. It's not like I was hysterically screaming or crying. How rude!

We walked through the long, shiny hallway into a formal living room. It was decorated with dark cherry furniture, Tiffany lamps, a colorful oriental carpet, and a massive white stone fireplace that was impossible to miss. It was all a bit ostentatious for me; however, it was a perfect fit for the style of the house. The tall, cherry-trimmed windows draped in billowy, burgundy curtains went from floor to ceiling. We exited the back of the house through French doors onto a large stone patio. Regis jumped into a golf cart that was parked right outside the door. "Come on, let's go have some fun. I had the planes readied this morning, so we won't have to wait."

We rode in the golf cart down a paved path through the trees. Through the clearing ahead, I could see a grassy field with an entire landing strip and metal hanger. I couldn't believe it—Regis even had his own runway. I must admit that this was possibly the most amazing thing I'd ever seen. I didn't think that Regis had the ability to ignore any detail. He looked like a man who knew what he wanted and had no problem making it a reality. He really did have quite a pad.

Regis stopped the golf cart. He jumped to his feet and waved to the two men awaiting our arrival. "You two are riding shotgun," he said with a smirk. An ornery look crossed his face as he pointed to a sleek white glider tethered to the back of a white plane. It looked so tiny compared to the size of the plane. I took in a deep breath when I saw the aircraft before me. My reservations must have shown on my face.

"Samantha, it's the smoothest ride in your life. You're going to love it," Regis explained reassuringly, probably to build my confidence in his fancy toy. I fought to control my anxiety and gave him a tiny smile.

"Regis, you've been holding out on me. When did you buy *that* baby?" Jack's eyes became bright as he looked at the plane parked in front of the glider. He walked back and forth to explore its design with admiration. His appreciation for the object was apparent. He even reached out and delicately stroked the glossy paint, making it appear alive.

"My wife, Tina," he said, towering over to me. "She got it for me for a Father's Day present. That woman has wonderful taste," he said with delight.

"Only the best for you, Regis." Jack smiled. "It's remarkable!"

"Yes, I'd have to agree." Regis nodded his head.

Jack helped me get buckled up in the front seat of the glider. "Are you sure you don't want to be up front?" I asked.

"No, it doesn't matter to me at all. Plus, you're the one with the camera. I don't want to block your view."

"Really, you can block it all you want. I'm not sure how much I am going to keep my eyes open, anyway."

Jack leaned back and lifted his sunglasses on top of his head. His light blue eyes squinted against the sunlight as he stared at me. It seemed as though he was trying to read my mind. "Well …" He contemplated for a moment. "You really don't have to do this if you're that afraid. I don't want to blow our first date by forcing you into anything."

"I'm still here," I whispered. "Let's go before I really do change my mind." I sighed deeply to summon up my confidence.

Jack smiled at me kindly. "I am *really* glad you came." He leaned down to pull me forward and give me a slow, gentle kiss. His rough, shadowy beard brushed against my face. I didn't mind. I found his rugged appearance incredibly sexy. He released my lips and leaned back to flaunt a beautiful smile. Then, he flipped his sunglasses down and nimbly climbed over to his seat before lowering the glider's roof around us. It was all the motivation I needed.

"Hmm," I moaned. "You're really hard to resist when you kiss me like that."

"I have no idea what you mean," he said with satisfaction in his voice.

Regis's voice came through our headsets, "We are all go for take off. Are you two settled in back there?"

"At your ready, sir," replied Jack in a military tone.

The plane took off effortlessly and climbed at an upward angle for what seemed like a heartbeat. I remembered I needed to breathe and took in a gasping breath of air. Jack must have overheard it and quickly asked, "Sami, how do you feel?"

"I don't know." I looked up at the sky and felt my head spin. I was prone to motion sickness. I could get car sick just from riding in the back seat and usually avoided amusement parks at all costs. "I'm just a little dizzy. I'll be okay in a minute," I said, feeling embarrassed by my weak stomach.

"Focus your eyes on the wood trim in front of you for a minute. It will help to orient your senses while you adjust to the altitude."

I tried to follow his direction. He was the pilot, after all. I slowly breathed in and out while the dizziness began to fade.

"Are you feeling any better?" he asked, sounding anxious now.

"Better than I imagined I would be." I gulped, praying the worst was over.

"Good." He chuckled under his breath, sounding relieved. "Then look out your window."

"*Oh*," I gasped. "It's amazing. You really can see everything from here."

"Exhilarating, isn't it?" he said, sounding truly excited by my response.

Regis came over the headset again. "Are you kids having fun yet?"

"It's wonderful," I answered.

"Glad to hear it; then I'll see you two back at the camp. Please take good care of her, Jack."

"Of course, Regis, I will land her like a feather," replied Jack with confidence.

"No, not the plane, you moron … Samantha. I would like it if you didn't scare her away. You need to start thinking about settling down before you lose all of your hair," he said with a laugh, since he himself was bald.

"Hmm." I chuckled to myself. If men only knew most women couldn't care less.

"Thanks, I will keep that in mind," Jack replied.

"Toodles." Regis's voice cut out.

The plane released the glider, and, as if by magic, we became instantly free from the drag of the plane's engine. We were floating—gliding effortlessly across the sky. It was the most soothing feeling I could imagine. I wasn't scared at all. We just drifted like a bird catching a strong breeze. I could see why Jack wanted me to go. This was the wildest first date I had ever had. Of course, I really didn't have that many first dates to compare it to.

"Sami, I am glad that you agreed to come with me today. You are not quite the coward you pretend to be," he teased.

"*Coward*," I protested.

"Well, what I mean to say is that you hold yourself together very well for a civilian. You should give yourself more credit."

"It's hard to be afraid when the ride is so peaceful. It's so quiet. I wish all plane rides were this smooth."

"Yes, it really is wonderful to glide without the weight of an engine."

"Okay, I wish you didn't just remind me of that fact. We are going to stay airborne and not just fall from the sky, right?" I groaned.

"Take it easy. We're safe. I know flying is an acquired taste. It will get easier the more you do it."

"I'll remember that next time," I muttered.

"Next time! You mean you'll fly with me again?" he said, sounding pleased.

"We'll see."

"I promise to bring you home in one piece," Jack replied playfully.

"That's nice to know. You make it sound so easy. I usually hate feeling this out of control. Aren't you just a little bit afraid of jumbling up a landing?"

"Some trust, Sami, *please*. It is a run in the park."

I took out my camera and snapped a few shots. The scenery was breathtaking. The clear blue sky and golden sunrays shined brightly through the window above my head, while the tree-lined landscape sprawled out widely below in every direction.

"Samantha, are you ready?" Jack asked.

"Am I ready *for what?*"

"It's time to go back. You have to obey your limits with these things. You might want to hang on."

Just then, he rotated us into a sharp turn. "*Ahhh*!" I screamed and held on to my seat. Jack laughed while our glider angled in the sky to gracefully bring us about. We returned to a level position for only a minute before he drifted us right over the treetops. His maneuver made us pick up speed.

Jack leaned forward, touched my shoulder, and whispered in my ear, "Do you want to drive?"

"No," I protested while partially closing my eyes.

"All you have to do is just take hold of the stick and steer," he encouraged.

"That's okay … I'll leave it up to you, Mr. Pilot. I can't make you any promises that I will return *you* home in one piece."

"As you wish," he said smugly as he leaned back in his seat. He was silent for a minute before he added, "Oh, and by the way—you smell incredible."

I thought I heard him sniff my hair. Jack continued to make the glider ride exciting by gently swooping us across the tree-lined ridges. When we got to the landing strip, Jack brought us down just like he had promised. There wasn't even a bump to complain about. We got out of the glider plane and returned to the house in an empty golf cart. Regis was outside on the patio, frying something on the grill in his outdoor kitchen. Just inhaling a whiff of the delicious smell made my stomach rumble.

"How was it? Wasn't it fantastic? Did you like it, Samantha?" asked Regis eagerly.

"It was great! Thank you so much for having me here today," I said graciously.

"Anytime, but don't run off. You have to stay for lunch. Wait until you try this," he said as he pulled some seasoned chicken from the grill. William quickly grabbed plates for us, each already filled with a crisp green salad for him to set the chicken on. I looked around at the sunny, beautiful, intricately-landscaped yard, the massive home with its amazing outdoor living space, and the charming men that surrounded me. It felt like I was in a movie. We sat outside on the stone terrace under a white umbrella and enjoyed the mouthwatering meal. Regis was an excellent cook. His enthusiasm for life seemed unwavering. I understood why Jack liked spending time with him.

"Jack, how are the schematics for the Space elevator coming along? Are you whiz kids getting any closer to launching that Space resort of yours? I have customers dying to go. I'm ready to go," Regis said zealously. I was surprised that he was so aware of our projects, the Space elevator in particular. It was purely hypothetical. We hadn't even determined if it was possible to build such a structure yet.

"I'm as ready as you are. Don't worry—we're still in the drawing phase but getting closer every day.

Your money is hard at work. Things are coming together nicely. It will be ready before you know it," Jack
promised.

I had discovered one hidden motive behind why
Regis befriended Jack. He was one of the investors of
the Space resort we were planning to build. He liked to
keep closer tabs on its progress than the SIG provided
him. He was anxious to get the place up and running.
He saw Jack as an inside link. It made me wonder how
much Jack had told him. Surely, he would keep the details under wraps.

"It's amazing how fearless you people are. We could
build any old contraption. It doesn't even matter if it's
five hundred miles off the surface of the Earth; people
will be lining up to go," I surmised. Other than the or-
bital distance, I knew the description "old contraption"
was a gross exaggeration from the truth. Safety was a top
concern. Every part of every structure to be launched was
a product of carefully engineered designs. It was our jobs
to tend to every detail.

"Tell me *again* how you got hired." Jack laughed at
my sarcasm. He looked at me with disbelief because he
must have underestimated my strong aversion to going
into Space.

"Funny, but you know I'm right," I said sharply. Jack
opened his lips as though he was ready to contradict my
statement but decided not to speak and let my comment

slide. We looked at each other silently for a moment. He seemed to be scrutinizing my face to determine what I was thinking.

"You know, Regis—Sami works for SIG as well," he said casually before he paused to take and chew a bit of food. "She is in the physics department. Perhaps you should work on her. She might even have more clout than me on attaining your goal."

"Wow, really? You don't say. I never would have guessed it. I love it when people surprise me." Regis winked at me. "So, how about it, young lady? Will I get to go into Space in this lifetime? Will you take me with you?" he said eagerly.

"I'll do what I can. But I'm not going with you. I'm quite happy to stay on the ground. I'll leave the Space walking to the two of you," I confessed.

"Aren't you excited about the Space resort?" Regis asked, sounding confused.

"Absolutely. I think it'll be wonderful for the people who *want* to spend time in Space. I love working on the design end of things. Also, the transport elevator would be a big improvement. It's going to be so much more economical and safer than strapping yourself up to a fuel tank and lighting it on fire."

"What's wrong with the rockets?" Jack frowned and held up both of his hands.

"I'm sure you see nothing wrong with them, but hopefully we can eliminate some of the danger," I explained. *Since when did self-preservation become a bad thing?*

"That's what I want to hear," Regis said joyfully.

Jack smiled. "I couldn't agree more. The trip needs to be satisfactory to even the most *discerning* travelers," he quickly replied. He raised his glass for a toast to imply that he was talking about Regis. "To the future!"

"Salute," Regis and I said in unison as we lifted our glasses to clink them off Jack's.

***

Our date was nearing its end. Jack thanked me for being such a good sport. I think he was trying to determine if I really had fun. He portrayed a genuine concern for my happiness. He brought me back to my apartment. I didn't want him to leave.

"Do you want to come in for a little bit?" I asked casually.

"Sure, I really could use something to drink. I'm thirsty all the time and need to drink a lot of water," he informed me.

"So I've noticed," I said, unlocking my door. He wasn't joking, either. I watched the man guzzle down what seemed like a dozen refillable aluminum water bottles on our trip today. It probably took him over a half hour just to load the cooler he brought with him in the

car. Maybe he was part fish. I went straight to the refrigerator and poured us two tall glasses of filtered water
from the pitcher.

"Thanks, Sami." He grinned when I handed him the
glass.

"Thank you. I had a great time with you today. I still
can't believe that you got me to fly in that glider. It's
like you have some strange influence over me. I usually
despise flying."

"I hope it wasn't too much for you," he responded,
sounding apprehensive.

"No, it was fantastic," I replied. I heard him exhale
in relief. "For some unexplained reason, you make me
feel safe."

"I'm glad, because if there's a job opening to make
you feel safe, sign me up." He smirked. He put the glass
down, took me by the hand, and pulled me into his
body. I looked up at his perfectly arranged face, feeling
excited by his sudden proximity. He gently brushed my
hair off the side of my face with his fingers before he
leaned down and kissed me. I couldn't hold back. I threw
my arms around his neck and kissed him back. His lips
were incredible—the perfect balance of softness with
power.

"Hmmm," I moaned as I came up for air. "You really
do have some unexplained effect over me."

"I'm having trouble holding myself back," he said. He looked at me tenderly while he stood with perfect posture, supporting my lower back with his arms.

"Oh well," I whispered. I took his hand and walked backwards in my small apartment, leading him into the living room. I tugged him harder, and he let me pull him down on the sofa with me.

"How in the world does a beautiful girl like you *not* have a boyfriend?" he said, staring at my face while he waited for an answer.

"I hadn't met you yet," I replied. There I went shamelessly flirting again. He leaned over me, carefully supporting himself with his arms, and kissed me again. I ran my hand through the spiky hair on the back of his head. He grabbed my right thigh and hiked it around his body. I felt a rush of excitement just being next to him and listening to his breathing getting deeper. I wanted to rip his clothes off right then. I'd always had a weakness for intelligent men. For me, a good mind-blowing discussion worked as well as foreplay. And after all the tantalizing conversation on our way home, I was more than ready to go. He stopped kissing me right after I had reached under his shirt and ran my hand across his firm chest.

"I'm not sure if I'm going to be able to control myself if you keep that up," he warned before the corners of his mouth turned down like he was in pain.

"Then don't," I demanded, but he removed my hand.

"I don't want to take things too fast and make you regret anything," he murmured. He pulled himself away.

I instantly regretted my assertive behavior. I felt my face flush with embarrassment. He noticed my reddened face and softly caressed my cheek with fingertips. I'd just met Jack, but he wasn't like anyone I'd ever known. When we kissed, it was magical. It was as though we were made for each other. My desire for him overpowered all rational thought.

"Fine, we'll take it slow," I conceded.

"Please, let's just relax for a minute. I don't want you to think that I have the wrong intentions," he said with his respectful military voice. This only made me want him more. If it was up to me, we would be between the sheets by now. I was fascinated by his coolness. Perhaps his being older than me made it easier for him to remain in control of his desires. He leaned back on the sofa and pulled me next to him so that I could lie across his chest. He kissed the top of my head and cradled me in his arms. I snuggled my body into his. He was so warm. Now I understood why he had consumed so much water. It was needed to replace all the fluid his body must lose through evaporation. I traced my hand up and down his arm and chest. "You can't imagine how good that feels."

He moaned. I thought I could. It felt unbelievable when he ran his fingers through my hair and down my back. The pleasure in his voice seduced me even more. I had chills!

"So, what do you dream of?" I asked, wanting to know him better.

"Changing the world," he said in a serious tone.

"Those are *bold* words, Jack Bennett." I sat up, surprised by his unusual answer.

"Why? You have to have goals, right?" he teased, as if it wasn't too big of a challenge.

"Yes, goals are definitely a necessity," I agreed. He really was remarkable. *He wants to change the world, does he?* Somehow I believed that he would. I cuddled back into his arms and let myself relax completely. We stayed there, silently losing track of time, while he snugly held me against him. I didn't want the evening to end.

CHAPTER 6

CHALLENGED

I returned to work on Monday hoping I might see Jack in the café or pass him in the long halls. I felt disappointed that the place seemed as vacant as it always did. It was rare to pass more than two or three people in the morning. The staff always seemed to arrive at different times and go directly to their own little department and get right to work.

"Good morning, Tess," I said, walking into the lab.

"Good morning, Sami," greeted Tess with a smile. "I see Jack got you home okay. Did you have fun on Friday?"

"Yes, Tess, it was great! Thanks for inviting me." I couldn't control the now-permanent smile that was plastered on my face. Tess looked at me after she caught the excitement in my voice, seeming pleased with herself. She liked making others around her happy.

"You deserve it. I appreciate all the work you've been doing around here."

"Thanks," I said humbly. I quickly got to work on my current project. I was trying to improve the efficiency and capacity of the current oxygen generator system for our research facility and future Space resort. An enormous amount of fresh air was needed to accommodate the numerous guests it was planning to house. It felt great to have something to help keep my mind busy. I worked diligently until the ringing of my phone awoke me from my trance.

"Hello, Samantha Gerris," I answered in my professional voice.

"Samantha Gerris," replied the man on the extension.

"Yes."

"I am calling to see if you would like to meet me in the café for lunch," offered Jack.

"That could be arranged. What time do you want to meet?"

"How about in three minutes?" Jack said in his alluring voice.

"Okay, see you there," I answered and then hung up the receiver. I was up for the challenge and made a quick bolt for the door. I shouted to Michael as I walked past his desk, "I'm going to lunch." He barely responded and looked to be in deep thought. I raced through the long hallway in a brisk sprint, only slowing down when I saw someone sharing the passageway with me. I got to the café in record time. I looked around to see if Jack had beat me there, but he didn't seem to be anywhere in sight. I stood still, looking down the hall to my right and took some slow, deep breaths in attempt to lower my heart rate and catch my breath.

"You got here fast," said Jack coming up behind me. Oh, how dense I must have looked. I had forgotten where the engineering department was located and was looking down the wrong hallway. I still got lost in this place. "Does the physics department have a transporter you're testing out?" he teased.

"I'll never tell." I smirked.

"Hi, Sami, I'm glad you could join us," said Noah, standing behind Jack.

"Oh, hey, Noah, thanks," I promptly replied. I had to lean around Jack to see him. I hadn't even noticed he was there until he spoke.

We all sat at lunch, talking shop while we informed each other of our most recent projects. Noah was part of both the physics and engineering departments and wanted an update on everything. I couldn't help notice Jack looking at me with his full attention when I was talking.

"Is something wrong?" I finally asked quietly.

"No, nothing," he said. He looked at me innocently and smiled.

Noah seemed to notice our exchange and quickly fought for my attention in order to hide his discomfort. He started rambling on about the white water rafting trip he, Jack, and Josh were going to take this weekend. "Sami, are you sure you don't want to come?" he asked hesitantly, since he probably remembered what I had said to him at the bar on Friday.

"Hmmm," I grumbled. "I don't know, Noah. I mean, isn't it really dangerous? I'm a good swimmer and all, but I'm sure that water is full of strong undercurrents." I decided to withhold that I was actually a certified lifeguard and worked at a local pool for two summers in a row. I took the job pretending it was for extra cash, but money was never an issue for a well-kept kid like me. I really did it to appease my parents' worry when they complained about me becoming a couch potato. They didn't like it when I spent too much time indoors studying or playing video games with my fellow nerds.

"It's really fun, Sami. We'll make sure you stay in the raft, and we'll do all the work. You can just go along for the ride," offered Noah. He nudged Jack's arm with his elbow as he summoned him for help.

Jack sat quietly, appearing to think before he spoke. "We would love it if you came along. The water isn't as high as it is in the springtime, so the rapids will actually be quite tame," he said in his harmonious voice.

"Well—if it's a good time to go …" I contemplated their invitation for a moment. I clasped my hands together and brought them to my mouth while I anchored my elbows to the table. I stared at Jack's eyes, and I thought about what he had said. I couldn't help but feel challenged when Noah insinuated that I could sit there helplessly while everyone paddled around me. I could carry my own weight. "I'll go. Just show me what to do," I muttered and then leaned my chin on top of my interlocked fingers.

"*Great*," they said in unison with a rise in their voices before they looked at each other with surprise. My answer shocked them both. Did they really anticipate that I would say no? I had no idea what I was getting myself into, but at least I'd have a reason to spend the day with Jack. Jack got up to get a refill on his drink. I watched him walk away.

"Are you going to eat that?" I asked Noah, eyeing up the leftover French fries on his plate.

"No," he answered.

"Do you mind?"

"Go ahead. You know, for a skinny girl, you sure eat a lot," he said. He pushed the plate my way and watched me eat for a moment before he spoke. "So, Sami, you like Jack, huh?" Noah leaned across the table, closing in on me while Jack was gone. He had an impish grin on his face.

"I do. *Why?*" I asked, confused by his sudden interest in my love life.

"You're acting different." He looked at me with a curious smirk. Okay, maybe he was right, but why did he need to know? It was none of his business.

"No I'm not. You're imagining things." I pushed his shoulder away from me. He pushed me back. Jack returned and caught sight of our playful tiff.

"I can't leave you two alone for one minute, can I?" Jack muttered. Noah snarled at me like an animal. I sneered back. Noah and I couldn't help but pick on each other when we were together. We all started laughing. Lunch was over quickly. Jack stopped and turned to me after we exited the café. "Do you really want to go with us on Saturday?" he said, appearing to study my body language.

"Yes, I'm game. I could use an adventure," I said playfully.

"Good. I have to go off-site for the rest of the week. I won't get home until late Friday night. I'm going to be dying to see you by then," he moaned.

"You make it sound so far away," I said, pretending not to mind.

"Can I call you later?" asked Jack, raising his eyebrows, looking like an adorable child.

"Of course. I'll talk to you after work." I waved and turn down the opposite hallway and strode briskly back to my desk.

The week went by quickly. I spoke to Jack every night on the phone. I loved that he was so easy to talk to and never seemed to judge me when I spoke. I admired the way he held himself. His motivation was contagious and made me want to be a better person. He was extremely optimistic about life. It appeared that he controlled any negative emotion he felt and easily dispelled it, instead of the other way around. I couldn't help notice how he managed to maintain his full attention in the present moment. He was thirty-one, eight years older than me, and seemed so composed and mature. The fact that he acted like a true adult was a complete turn-on.

***

Saturday morning had arrived. I got up and ate an abnormally large breakfast in hopes of building my stamina. The last thing I wanted was to have my stomach growling or develop low blood sugar while I was stuck on the raft. I knew how hungry I tended to get when I exercised. Jack and I arrived at the park to find Josh, Noah, and an attractive blonde-haired girl I had never met before standing near the shore of the river bed. The day was crystal clear. Sunlight sparkled across the water and made the surrounding pine trees appear a brilliant emerald green. I couldn't believe how loud the rapids were. I nervously looked at the fast-flowing water splashing up on the large rocks that jutted up intrusively in its path. I questioned my decision in participating. Had I completely *lost* my mind?

"Guys, this is Sarah. She wanted to join in the fun. Sami, I didn't want you to be the only girl."

"Thanks, Noah, that's very considerate of you. Hi, it's nice to meet you," I replied as I shook the girl's hand.

"And you." She smiled back at me.

"Looks pretty good today," said Jack while he and the others checked out the rushing river.

"Whoa!" I yelped when I accidently slipped after losing my footing on the rocky ground. Luckily, I was able to reach out and clutch hold of Noah's shirt before I landed on my butt.

"*Careful*," he said with widened eyes. He grabbed hold of my arm and lifted me back to my feet. I quickly glanced over at Jack to see if he had noticed my clumsiness. Fortunately, he seemed preoccupied with checking the height of the water.

"Thanks," I muttered.

Noah turned to me. "So, Sami, what do you think?" he asked, knowing we were out of earshot from the others.

"About what?"

"About Sarah," he said, tilting his head in her direction.

"I don't know. She's pretty." I shrugged my shoulders.

"Yeah, she is, isn't she?" he said, looking back at her with ogling eyes.

"Why are you asking me? Do you really like her or something?" I asked. Noah was always a little strange when he talked about the girls he dated.

"I don't know yet." He scratched his head.

"Well, when did you meet her?"

"Last night," he said smugly.

"*Oh*, I don't even want to know."

"Sure you do. She does this thing with her legs. Incredible!"

"*Ahh*, too much information."

"But it was fun. You should try it," he jested.

"Please, would you stop?"

"Look, I'm trying to help you out. You need to quit ignoring your sex life. It's such a waste to not use that tight body of yours."

"You're a slut," I teased, raising my eyebrows in disapproval.

"*Virgin.*"

"Humph!" I huffed quietly. Noah's appetite for sex never ceased to amaze me. I couldn't help but make fun of his promiscuity when he teased me about my inexperience. We both chuckled as the others approached. Jack gave me a peculiar grin but didn't ask what we were talking about. Curiously, I looked at Sarah, trying to figure out what she did with her legs.

I listened to the group while they shared in their excitement for the day. Then, as if by accident, I spotted Noah slip Jack a folded twenty dollar bill into the palm of his hand.

Noah spoke quietly to Jack, "I can't believe you got her here. Maybe you do know her better than I do."

"You highly underestimate her," Jack retorted.

I pretended I hadn't noticed and turned my face away from them to look at the water. I felt a wave of anger surge through me. Although I was happy to hear Jack's defense, those jerks had made a wager on whether I would show up or not! First, Noah poked fun at my lack of a sex life, and now this. I couldn't help wondering if he *wanted* me to see his bet, since he wasn't exactly inconspicuous in handing Jack the bill. Did he say those things to challenge me because he was so competitive? Either way, he knew just how to provoke me. That's it! I'd show those boys how to manage a raft. Now, with my adrenaline pumped, I could easily take on a few splashes of water. *Let the games begin!*

We all got dressed in our life jackets and helmets and boarded the raft. Jack realized that he and Noah were busted after I blatantly denied his offer to help me get ready. He slapped Noah across his life vest with the back of his hand and frowned.

"You're a jerk, Peterson, trying to get me in trouble," he muttered under his breath. I hid my smile.

Noah smirked. "Yeah, but it's all in good fun, right?" Jack gave him an irritated glare. Minutes later, I had all but forgotten about their bet when our raft surged through the rapids, bumping off rocks from both sides of the creek. It was exciting and nerve-racking all at the same time.

"There, push off there," Jack instructed Josh.

"I'm on it," he said with enthusiasm, using his paddle to push off the river's bottom.

Noah shouted at me, "*Sami, hang on,*" when our boat went crashing into a foreboding jagged rock beside me. The jolt from its impact lifted my body up from the raft and threw me airborne. A forceful wave of water furiously gushed up on my side of the boat immediately after. I would have fallen out if it weren't for Jack's super-human reflexes.

"Oh, *no you don't*. Come here." He quickly reached out and grabbed hold of my arm, securing me tightly to his side.

"Thanks," I said after the wall of water finished drenching us.

As we rafted, I watched the men with admiration. They seemed to be devising a strategy on the fly. Seeing Jack in action made the trip worthwhile. He functioned perfectly under pressure. His natural athleticism was impressive. His every move looked effortless. We finished our ride without a hitch. What a rush! I was amazed by my accomplishment. I didn't fall in, but I was all wet.

I had to sit on my towel during the car ride home. I couldn't believe that I was the only one who didn't bring an extra set of clothes.

***

Jack came into my apartment with me. I stopped to glance at myself in the entrance mirror. "I look like a drowned rat," I said. I pulled out my ponytail holder from my slightly dry hair and laid it on the little table beneath the mirror. "My hair's a mess." I tried to fluff it loose with my fingers.

Jack came up behind me and looked in the mirror with me. He smiled. "It looks good to me."

"Be honest. I've looked better." I looked up at his reflection and then back at my own.

"I like it that you let yourself get all messed up. You look sexy and wild. It's a turn on." He laid his hands on my shoulders and kissed the back of my head.

"Hmmm, weird," I jested. I stepped away to kick off my shoes and peel off my clingy, damp clothes. I stripped down to my red one-piece swimsuit, leaving my clothes in a crumbled up heap on the ceramic tile floor. I walked barefoot into the kitchen, grabbed two glasses from the cabinet, and poured us each some cold water from the refrigerator, knowing that Jack was probably down a few liters. He sat down on the barstool and watched me while I completed the mundane task.

"Nice suit," Jack complimented.

"Thanks," I answered. At least it was dry. "Are you hungry?" I asked. I took out a box of cereal and started eating some from the box.

"No," he muttered with his eyes glued to me. His expression confused me.

"Are you okay?" I finally asked after acknowledging his stare.

"Never better." He grinned.

"Hmm." I moaned after I chewed my last bite.

"Ah, Sami—could you make *this* any harder for me?" he asked. He squeezed the corners of his mouth with his hand.

"What do you mean?"

"It's hard enough that you are the most remarkable woman I have ever met. But how do you expect me to control myself when you look *that* good?" he said softly. He looked up from under his thick, black eyelashes.

"Well then, maybe you shouldn't," I said seductively. I leaned across the narrow kitchen island and looked at him intently. He gave me a smug smile. We gazed at each other without speaking.

"Hmmm," he moaned. It was all the invite he needed. Instantly he jumped off the stool, walked over to me, and took me by the hand to lead me into the living room. Jack guided me gently down onto the sofa. He leaned over me while keeping his weight on his arms. I sat up and gave him a short kiss. He didn't move. He stayed there, frozen in his disciplined position, and looked me in the eyes. "Not to complain, but it would be helpful if you could keep *some* clothes on. I'm not a saint after all."

"Actually, I was thinking that *you* are the one who's a bit overdressed. It doesn't seem fair, now does it?"

"No, I guess you're right."

"Would you mind taking this shirt off? It would help to even things up," I encouraged. I tugged at his clothes. He smiled back at me with a crooked grin.

"Sure, maybe that would help make things more even. I don't want to make you uncomfortable by being overdressed," he said, repeating my expression. I was happy he didn't object to my advance.

I helped him slip his T-shirt over his head and tossed it across the room. He seemed to like my carelessness. He smiled before he leaned back and pulled me on top of him.

"There, isn't that better?"

"You're amazing, Sami. Where *the hell* have you been hiding?" he said, looking up at my face with bright eyes. I smiled but didn't answer. He wrapped his arms around me and gently stroked my bare back with his hand. I was completely taken in by the feel of his skin against mine. Before I knew it, he reached out and held my head in his hands and passionately kissed me with a stronger force than I had ever felt him kiss me before. I loved how his fingers intertwined into the back of my hair as though he didn't want to let me go. I gave in to the sensation and allowed myself to be fully immersed in the moment. His lips were smooth and had the perfect softness. I could stay there kissing him for hours. I felt my body flush with heat after I let myself rest down into the contours of his flawless body. Was this what it felt like to be in love? Maybe it was lust ... I couldn't be sure. It was all too new. I had never felt this way about anyone before. All I knew was that I wasn't letting him go home any-time soon.

"You're driving me crazy. I can't take it anymore," I said in between kisses. I carefully explored his body, gliding my hand over his toned arms and abs. I felt con-fident he wouldn't stop my hand.

"You ... *good Lord*, if you were any hotter, I would melt," he said. He leaned up and kissed me more slowly before he gently worked his way down my neck while he cradled my head with his hands.

"*Oh*, you know just how to touch me," I moaned.

"I only want to make you happy." He kissed me on the lips once more.

"Well, you're doing a good job at that," I said, un-locking his lips while I clung to his firm body beneath me.

"Sami, I want you," he whispered in my ear.

"Good. Stay with me tonight."

"All you had to do was ask." He seemed pleased by my offer. I leaned in and kissed his neck and then made my way down to his collarbone before continuing down his chest.

He pulled me up to look me in the eyes before letting out a sigh as though he surrendered his guard. In an instant, he was on his feet and pulling me off the sofa to lead me into the bedroom. He tossed me onto the bed playfully. We made love. He was incredible! That sealed the deal. Let's just say, if I had to rate what I wanted in a man, he would get a gold star. Why should I be surprised? I already thought he seemed to be good at everything he did. Now I was certain. He was possibly the most talented man I had ever met!

CHAPTER 7

UNPLANNED

Jack and I continued to meet for lunch whenever possible, talk on the phone every night, and see each other
on the weekends. I didn't even attempt to keep it a secret that we were dating at work. I figured the office
masterminds would see right through me. Tess and
Michael seemed sincerely happy for us. Josh was nice but
appeared jealous at times when he saw how Jack and I
looked at each other across the lunch table. I was ecstatic
about my new job and new love. My life was perfect.

What goes up must come down, right? It's a simple
fact. For every action, there is an equal and opposite reaction. Life couldn't be this easy. I left work feeling sick.
I walked into my apartment and headed straight to the
toilet. *I think I vomited everything I ate this week. What's
wrong with me? Oh no*, I thought as I rushed over to my
wall calendar and started counting the days from my last

period. *What? No! I missed a month!* I stood in disbelief when I realized I hadn't had a period in four weeks! I sat down on the kitchen stool. I don't even think I needed to take a pregnancy test. I felt pregnant. *Stupid, useless condoms! How could I be so careless and irresponsible?* How in the world could I tell my parents? They always taught me that I should be married and financially stable before I started a family. I stared at the floor, only to be startled by the ringing phone. "Hello."

"Sami, hi, honey. I wasn't sure if you'd be home yet. How are you today?" said my mom cheerfully. Of course, it was my mother. Our mother-daughter ESP was working flawlessly today.

"Pregnant," I blurted out. There was dead silence on the other end of the extension. I listened attentively for the thud of her body hitting the floor but heard nothing. Finally, I spoke. "Mom, did you *hear* me?"

"Yes, of course I heard you, Sami," said my mother sharply. I braced myself for the unavoidable lecture that I was about to endure.

"What does Jack think about this?" she asked carefully, trying not to pry.

"He doesn't know yet. I haven't even taken a pregnancy test. I know I am, though. I'm four weeks late!" I shouted.

"Okay, Samantha—calm down. You're going to be fine. You are going to keep the baby, right? I mean, the way you talk about Jack, you have to—"

"Yes. I could never hurt any part of him," I answered without so much as a second thought.

My mother let out a sigh of relief. "Are you going to get married?" she asked in a faint voice.

"I don't know, Mom. *This* just happened. I haven't even told Jack. I hope he doesn't freak out." Jack was such a good guy. He was almost too good to be true. I hoped that my being pregnant wouldn't make him want to run. It would crush my view of him. I had never been so in love in my life. I couldn't imagine my life without him.

"It will be okay."

"Mom, are you sure you aren't mad at me?" I had to ask. Why wasn't she yelling at me? Shouldn't I be married and have money saved up?

"Sami, you can't always plan everything so carefully in your life. Sometimes you just have to be grateful when you receive such a precious blessing," she said reassuringly.

"Thanks, Mom. I love you."

"I love you, too, Sami. You're going to be a great mom. Dad and I will help you with whatever we can. Tell Jack. I think he'll be happy," she promised me.

I hung up the receiver and looked up at the clock. "Oh, no ... *Jack*," I screamed when I remembered I needed to get ready. I was supposed to go to dinner with him in fifteen minutes. I stood up from the kitchen stool slowly, in case I needed to make another run to the bathroom.

I was surprised by how normal I felt. I was fine. Amazingly, I didn't have one ounce of nausea.

I thought about my mother's reaction. I guess it shouldn't have surprised me. My parents had always supported me in my decisions. They had also suffered from infertility before they miraculously had me. They had tried fertility treatments and in-vitro fertilizations many times without success. They had all but given up on having children and spent their lives dedicated to their careers and taking extravagant vacations. My mother didn't get pregnant with me until she was forty-six years old. She thought she was in menopause. My dad was thrilled. Although he was nervous about being an older father, at fifty, he wanted me just as much as she did. I knew they would have liked to have had more kids. But being an only child had some advantages. The best one was all the adult conversations I was privy to because they would forget that there was a child in the room. It's amazing what you can learn. One thing I know for sure is that they secretly worried about never having the chance to become grandparents since they had me so late. To make matters worse, I never dated anyone who moved me the way Jack did. I had only a few boyfriends in the past. Usually, I was attracted more to their minds and ignored the physical part. I was never a smitten teenager in love. I think they worried that I'd become an old maid. But Jack, he was attractive both inside and out. I couldn't hide my excitement if I tried.

Jack arrived at my apartment exactly at six. I invited him in so I could deliver the news at home. Besides, my apartment was geographically closer to the nearest emergency room than the restaurant in case he went into shock.

"Jack, I'm late," I told him as he stood in my entryway. Why not just come out and say it?

"You look ready to me. Come on, I'm starving," he stated, not understanding the meaning behind my comment. I took his hand and led him to the kitchen barstools to sit down.

"Jack, I need to tell you something," I said. Maybe I could deliver the news with a little more grace. He sat looking at me with a puzzled expression.

"What, you hate Italian food? I don't care. We can eat somewhere else." He chuckled under his breath.

"I think … I think I'm pregnant," I blurted out. *There goes my telling him gently. At least he was sitting down.* I stared at his face to quickly survey his reaction. His expression was unreadable. His mouth opened a little while he processed what I had said. Without warning, Jack jumped to his feet, and before I knew it, I was in his arms. He held me tightly around my back and hugged me with an unbreakable grip.

"Oh—a baby, that's fantastic! Sami, are you sure?" he asked as he tipped me back to look at my face. He seemed a little apprehensive by my silence.

"So you're happy about this." I looked up at his face to see if he was truly glad. He wasn't stunned *or* running for the door. He was smiling from ear to ear with that beautiful, breathtaking smile. Could he be anymore handsome?

"Yes, *aren't* you?"

"I think so. I'm just nervous. I wasn't sure how you would feel about becoming a dad," I confessed.

"Are you kidding? Don't be foolish! Sami, I have always wanted kids, and I really want you! You are going to be the most amazing mother."

"You think so, huh?" I muttered.

Jack quickly dropped down on one knee and took my hand. "Samantha Gerris, will you marry me?" he asked with his engaging voice.

I looked at him, with his impromptu proposal. I'm sure I looked shocked. It wasn't how I imagined the moment. I thought that a marriage proposal had to be this carefully orchestrated event with a ring. I felt a rush of excitement. Tears burst from my eyes and ran down my cheeks. I couldn't move or speak. All I felt was how much I loved him. I looked into his bright eyes. We were making the decision to share our lives together, without all the hoopla. Just like that, right here, right now. It was perfect!

"Yes, I'd love to. I love you more than I've ever loved anyone." I smiled and pulled him up to my lips and kissed him. He lifted me up from the floor and spun me around like we were on a dance floor. He put me down after a few spins and hugged me tightly into his body.

"You make me so happy. I love you so much," he whispered passionately. His voice rang in my ear. I thought I had died and went to heaven. I couldn't believe I would get to share my life with someone so amazing. My mother was right. I should learn to be grateful for the good in my life and stop trying to control everything around me.

On the way to dinner, Jack told me that he was already planning to ask me to marry him. He said he was hesitant because we had only dated for a little over three months. He explained how he wanted to meet my parents first and ask my father's permission. This shouldn't have surprised me. Jack was a traditional guy. He was even too proper at times. My dad would have gotten a kick out of that. He always was a little overprotective of me. It would have played right into his parental ego. I imagined my dad enjoying his moment of power. He would have taken his time, making Jack sweat while he questioned him endlessly. Maybe it was better for everyone if it was a done deal.

"Oh, you wouldn't believe it. Tess gave me a bonus for completing my recent assignment at work. I almost forgot all about it."

"Well, then we must celebrate. We'll get dessert since you can't drink. Plus, I'm really hungry tonight."

"You don't sound surprised."

"Please, Sami, you have to know how good you are at your job. You're a breath of fresh air. I've heard that everyone is thrilled with your ideas. You're just what that place needed."

I was flattered by his perception of my job performance. I also felt relieved to hear that he understood my commitment to my career. I needed my independence. I could never tolerate someone who was overbearing. Jack gave me the impression that he would support me no matter what I did.

At dinner, we talked about the type of wedding we should have. Should we go to Vegas and get it over with? No, my parents would never forgive that. But it had to be soon. I didn't want to be huge, nor did I want to wait for the baby to be born before I could call Jack my husband.

"Jack, I want to meet your dad and your brother before the wedding." I couldn't believe I hadn't met his family yet, either. Our relationship was really moving fast.

"Oh, Sami, you mean my dad. I'm sorry. I didn't tell you that my brother passed away." He wrinkled his forehead with a stressed-out grimace.

"What ... *when* did he die?" I asked, stunned.

He bit his lip. "Six years ago," he said, appearing somewhat embarrassed.

"I'm so sorry. I didn't know. You always talk about him like he's still here," I said empathetically.

A solemn expression took over his face. "I know—it's complicated," said Jack, shaking his head. He looked down at the table before closing his eyes as he recalled his painful memory. "Peter was killed in battle by an incoming missile when he was only twenty-one. His comrades said he died the best way. He didn't feel a thing or see it coming. I know that this is going to sound weird, but I feel like he watches over me. Sometimes when I'm flying, I imagine he's my wingman. I can hear him in my head telling me what I should do. I like to talk about him in the present tense so I don't have to think about how much I miss him."

"Did you ever get therapy?" I asked sympathetically.

"No! Great, now you think I'm *crazy*, like I'm hearing voices," he said defensively while he shifted uncomfortably in his seat.

"I didn't say that! Oh no, what I mean is, did you ever get grief counseling?" I tried to clarify my remark.

"It wouldn't change anything. It is what it is. When you take a vow to protect your country, you know that you may have to sacrifice yourself in the process for the greater good."

"I understand that, but first you lost your mother and then your brother. The pain must be unbearable."

"The initial sting is gone." He leaned back in his chair, letting his arms fall limply at his sides. "I still can't believe Pete's been gone for six years now. Losing him really did both me and my dad in."

"How's your father handling it?"

"My dad's never been quite the same. It's like he shut down even more. He never got over losing my mother. He started drinking too much after we lost her. We were all a mess. My mom used to take care of everything. Women really do help hold a house together. You can only imagine three men trying to fend for themselves. We could barely function. I must say, things could get *pretty* ugly in the Bennett household." He frowned while he swirled his cup in his hand, making the ice cubes rattle.

"It would be terrible to grow up without a mom. Do you miss her?"

"I can hardly remember her now. All I remember from my childhood is taking care of my little brother. I had to grow up fast and act strong so Pete wouldn't cry so much," he said with sadness. I felt his sorrow radiating from him. He seemed to hold it close, like it was part of him. It was as though it gave him the strength to survive through anything. It was what made him so brave. I suddenly felt even more grateful for my cushy upbringing.

CHAPTER 8

DEVOTION

My parents were ecstatic with the news of our engage-
ment. They were flying in from New York this weekend
to help with the rushed wedding plans and meet Jack.
Our small families would make things easy. Our friends
would make up most of the guest list. Jack showed up just
before 10 a.m. Saturday morning even though my parents weren't going to be at my apartment until noon. We
couldn't wait to see each other since he had been working
off-site again all week. He walked over to me and pulled
me close to him.

"What are you up to, stranger?" I asked seductively.

"Missing you," he muttered. He drove his fingers
through his hair, uncovering a three-inch gash at his
hairline above his left eye.

"Jack ... oh my goodness, *what* happened to you?" I gasped and quickly lifted his hair back up to expose the sutured wound.

"What?" he said innocently like I wouldn't have noticed his injury.

"That! You know, the stitched area on your head," I snapped sarcastically.

"Oh—um ... I just had a little mishap when I was testing out one of the aircrafts," he murmured briefly. I quickly looked him over to discover that he was banged up in other places as well. Both of his hands had partly healed cuts all over them.

"*Jeez*, look at you. Are you sure you're okay? Why didn't you say anything to me about it?" I screamed. I couldn't help freaking out. It was shocking that he didn't mention anything about his accident when I talked to him on the phone this week.

"Really, it's no big deal," he muttered. He shifted his body as though my concern made him uncomfortable.

"Are you kidding? No big deal! What exactly do you *do* when you go away, Jack?" I asked bluntly, crossing my arms while I waited for an answer. I wanted to bombard him with a hundred questions. I didn't care if I was crossing the line here. Why the secrecy? How dangerous was this job? Was he doing something illegal? I suddenly realized just how little I knew about him.

"Well, I guess I have to tell you a little bit." He frowned and distanced his body from mine. "I help test prototype aircrafts for a specialized division of the military. They're experimental, one of a kind. You'd be amazed at how much headway we're making. Aviation will never be the same. It's all top secret, though, so I can't really talk about it. Great, I've already said too much. If I tell you more, then I'd have to *kill* you," he teased with a serious undertone, reminding me to keep my questions to myself.

"How did you get hurt?" I asked more casually, trying to pry for information.

"I sort of crashed. I dipped the aircraft nose a little too steep. It skimmed … no, really, it just grazed across the ground a little when I landed." He winced as if he were trying to lift the nose of the aircraft with his face while he relived the event in his mind.

"Wow, I didn't know …" I stopped myself and just shook my head in disbelief. "Why didn't you tell me?" The very thought of him racing across the sky at super-sonic speed made me ill. I wished he could work safely behind a desk every day and give up his work for the Air Force altogether. Of course, one job wouldn't be enough for someone with all of his ambition, and he probably wouldn't be satisfied without taking risks with his life. The whole world moved too slowly for him. I noticed his stiffened body language and somewhat threatening glare urging me to let the conversation drop. He didn't want to tell me more. There was no point, anyway. He'd be vague in answering any of my questions. I knew he couldn't tell me the full story since he was obviously sworn to secrecy. I wondered what other mysteries he kept hidden inside. I decided it was better if I looked the other way. Jack's love for adventure was what propelled him through life. There was no changing that. I tried to eradicate the worries from my mind. How else could I allow myself to love someone like him? I had to accept everything about him. No one was perfect. I just couldn't believe how he could talk so calmly about the whole thing. It was as if he could turn off his emotions at will.

"That's it, that's all you're going to say? Why aren't you yelling? Aren't you *mad* at me?" He sounded confused by my calm reaction.

"Yes, a little, but I'm just glad you're okay," I said coolly.

"Wow, you never cease to amaze me."

"Why?" I frowned.

"God, Sami, I never thought you would react so well to my crash. Most women would either scream at me till they were blue in the face or be running for the hills by now. But *you*—you're remarkable. Man, I must have done something right in a past life to deserve you," he said, sounding relieved.

"You know, you don't have to tell me exactly *what* you do, but from now on, will you tell me *if* you get hurt?" I decided to strike a deal.

"I will. I'm sorry—I should've told you." He gave me a quick kiss on my forehead.

"Mm-hmm," I agreed. He was already forgiven in my mind. My mind flashed forward as I thought about how many more mishaps I would have to endure with him in the future. At least life would never be dull.

"Hey, I got something for you." He smiled mischievously, breaking my sudden silence. His eyes held mine as he took my hand, led me to the sofa in the living room, and took a seat.

"What? Oh please, don't start buying baby stuff before the wedding," I demanded. I felt worried because, for all I knew, he could have a crib in the hallway. He was so excited about the baby. I knew he was dying to participate in any way he could.

"No, it's nothing like that. It's something for *you*." He smirked.

"I'm waiting," I said while my patience drew thin, unable to predict what he was up to.

He reached in his pocket, pulled out a small white box, and placed it in my hand. "Here, open it," he said. My face blushed with embarrassment at my incorrect conclusion. I opened the box and discovered a sparkling round diamond. It reflected rainbow facets of light across the room as it caught the morning sun shining through my living room window.

"Oh, Jack! It's beautiful!" I beamed.

"I thought you'd like it. I had to get something that was pretty enough for my stunning bride." He took the ring and placed it on my finger.

"It fits perfectly," I said.

"I used a ring guide to measure your finger while you were sleeping. I thought for sure you were going to wake up, but you slept like a log." He laughed.

"It's huge! How much did you spend?"

"Enough, but don't worry about it. I sold my car, and I even have some leftover for a down payment on a house."

"What, you *sold* your car? Are you crazy? You need a car more than I need this ring," I argued.

"Samantha, relax. Not my Acura," he sighed. "I've been restoring a 1957 Corvette convertible."

"I didn't know that!" What else was he hiding from me? His mysteriousness was alarming and intriguing at the same time. "Why didn't you ever show it to me?" I asked, puzzled.

"It was time to let it go. Besides, I don't think it would fit a car seat. Plus, it was really fast, and I know how you hate fast things."

"I never said that." I gave him a playful nudge on the arm. It hurt my hand without fazing him at all. He shrugged his shoulders while seeming to hold back a smile at my response.

"I'm just kidding. I didn't want to show it to you in case you liked it. Then, I could never sell it. I spent so much time rebuilding it. At this point, I was afraid to even drive it. I think a scratch would give me a heart attack. Besides, I just sold it for ninety-five thousand on eBay," he said proudly, with excitement in his voice and a joyful expression across his face.

"Wow, that's great! Forget the car, I'll keep the ring." I smiled with astonishment while I looked at my hand.

"Hmmm." He smiled widely before he took my hand in his and looked at the ring. "I thought you'd see it my way."

"I'll cherish it forever," I mused, looking up at him.

"I'll cherish *you* forever. Come here. I really missed you," he said before he gave me a passionate kiss. Our close proximity was all the foreplay I needed. It was almost impossible to control myself around him. Jack felt the same and wasted no time before he lifted me into his arms to carry me into the bedroom. I tipped my head back over his shoulder and quickly looked at the clock on the kitchen wall. My parents wouldn't be here for another hour and a half. Yes! We definitely had enough time to fool around.

Jack and my parents hit it off from the start. He had chemistry with them, as well. It made me happy to see them be so comfortable together. I think my parents understood why I loved him. Before they arrived, I had warned Jack about my mother's excessive enthusiasm about the wedding. He didn't fully grasp my mother's grandiose plan for the event until she started telling us about all of her well-researched ideas. He gave me a bewildered stare bordering on terror as she went on and on about how wonderful the wedding would be. We both decided it was all in her hands. Before the weekend was over, Jack was calling my mother "monster-in-law wedding planner" in a charming manner every time she brought up the wedding. She would laugh it off and continue explaining her ideas. She was not the kind of person who minded being teased for her extravagant imagination.

***

The wedding commenced exactly two months later. An unexpected cancelation opened up the perfect reception spot. It was phenomenal how quickly everything was arranged. I was truly blown away by the details my mother tended to. It also didn't hurt that she had friends in all the right places. I wore a soft ivory gown that had an empire waist, disguising my slightly distended belly. It didn't look like I was pregnant at all, just really fashionable. My aunt, Sarah, also from

New York, helped me to find the gown. Although I would have loved to have had a cousin, her and her husband chose not to have children. They both enjoyed their freedom and seemed dumbfounded by my parents' years of yearning for a family. I'm not sure if she still felt that way. I did know that she was more than happy to assist her only niece in finding the perfect dress.

At the reception, I introduced Jack to my old friends, and he introduced me to his. Every one of our friends from work flew into the Big Apple for the event. For the most part, I instantly liked all of Jack's guests. All except for one peculiar man who worked with Jack in the Air Force, test piloting aircraft. He wasn't married and came alone. He was so standoffish that he should have had "top secret" stamped across his forehead. I was surprised that Jack befriended him enough to invite him to the wedding. I asked him how he knew Jack, expecting to open up a conversation. My question was answered with uninviting eyes and a two-word response: "Air Force." It made me wonder what kind of duties Jack performed when he was testing the aircrafts.

Jack's dad gave me the biggest hug. "Welcome to the family, Samantha. I am so happy that Jack found you," he beamed. I could see the family resemblance when they stood side by side.

"Thank you, sir. I feel the same," I replied.

"Oh, please, call me John," he quickly corrected me.

Jack and I made our way across the room. Noah came up between us and put his arms around us both. "Hey, there you are. *Come here*, you two lovebirds," he said. Noah was our best man. "I need a picture with the lovely couple." He reached his arm around my neck to hold his camera out in front of the three of us.

"Noah, take the picture already," I pleaded. The weight of his arm was strangling me in a choke hold. I grabbed his arm with both of my hands and tried to lift it off my upper chest.

"Wait, it's not good. No, not yet," he said as he fiddled with the zoom.

"*Come on*, Peterson, just take the picture." Jack groaned.

"There." He finally snapped the shot and quickly turned the camera around to admire his work. "Oh, yeah, it's perfect. *Beautiful*, see." He held the screen up to show Regis and his wife, Tina, standing nearby. They held back a laugh.

"What, Noah? Let me see," I demanded and grabbed Noah's arm with the camera. He showed Jack and me the image. The picture was only of me and Noah. He had completely cut Jack out.

"You're such a dork." Jack chuckled and pushed him away like an annoying little brother.

"Thanks." Noah made a dippy smile and nudged Jack back. He was such a goofball. I couldn't believe someone so intelligent could be so immature.

Regis interrupted. "Play nice, kids."

Jack retorted, "Yeah, play nice Noah."

Regis leaned in to hug me and then Jack. "Congratulations. You two are great together. Take good care of her." Regis looked at Jack.

Jack's eyes met mine. "I will," he promised.

Regis smiled. "So, is there any news on when you're gonna launch the Space resort?

Jack grinned. "Not yet, Regis, but don't worry. You'll be the first person I call."

Tina rolled her eyes. "Oh you're just afraid you'll die before they get that place built."

Noah shook his head. "Well, have no fear, sir. I can assure you, it will be built. The future demands its existence," Noah said convincingly. His extreme confidence made me wonder if he knew something the rest of us didn't.

Regis laughed. "Yes, young man, it does," he agreed. Noah gave us a curious smile before he ran away. Regis sighed as he watched Noah walk across the room. "Ah, he's my favorite kind of person. Part of the so-called entitlement generation. Their high expectations and demands for a better life will make them our future's saviors," he said. We nodded our heads in agreement. "Hey, will you point me in the direction of your Space buddies? Maybe they will recruit me for their next mission," Regis said cheerfully.

"Sure, you want to talk with that group right over there," Jack said with a sideways nod directed towards our wedding party. Regis glanced over his shoulder to eye up his targets. "Look for the ones dressed in black," Jack added. All of our closest friends were somehow involved in Space development. They all either worked or went to school with us.

"Thank you. Now, if you would excuse me." Regis left, wasting no time while abandoning his wife with us.

"Once Regis gets an idea in his head, there's no stopping him." She quickly made an excuse for her husband's sudden disappearance.

"Tina," said Jack, trying to ease her discomfort. "Let me introduce you to Ryan and Emily, Sami's parents."

"That would be great," she cheered. We went to join them.

The whole night went by in a blur. I had never planned on being pregnant at my wedding, but it had its perks. Jack no longer invited me to go on any of his rugged weekend adventures. Noah and Josh were more than happy to take my place. He would only take me places with no risk of being injured. Our honeymoon was at a cabin in the mountains. We took a week off work and spent the days walking, swimming, canoeing, and making love.

It was at my next doctor's appointment when I discovered that I was pregnant with twins. I had Jackson and Leah four months later. They were a little early, but healthy and absolutely gorgeous. I didn't think it was possible to top the way I felt for Jack, but my love for them was indescribable. Jack was an incredible father. I couldn't have asked for a better partner to help raise them. My parents moved close by and took on babysitting when I finished my maternity leave. The two of them had recently retired and devoted much of their time to their beloved grandkids.

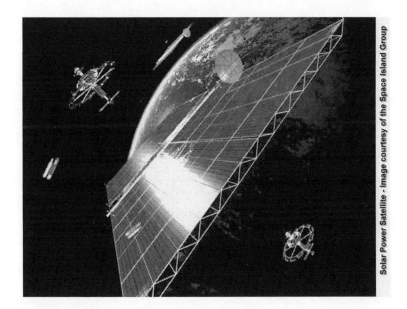

Solar Power Satellite - Image courtesy of the Space Island Group

CHAPTER 9

LEAPS AND BOUNDS

Days became weeks, weeks became months, and months became years. How could life pass by so quickly? I watched my children grow into intelligent, magnificent young adults. Life was different. The world had changed so dramatically since I was a kid. Leah and Jackson were born into a time of unprecedented advancement. Technology was growing at an alarming rate.

The boundaries of our moral compass were truly being tested. At first, society seemed to struggle with the implications of advancement. Some people fought for new technology and all it offered while others felt threatened by it. In general, everyone agreed it was important to proceed prudently. Over time, we all grew accustomed to the rapid changes taking place around us. We started to expect it, even embrace it. We realized we had an opportunity to make our world a better place after the benefits of each new discovery became apparent. Medical advances were taking place at a miraculous rate. Breakthroughs in human genetic engineering helped improve our quality of life and cure disease. Receiving a diagnosis no longer meant a lifetime of taking medicine or a shortened life expectancy.

One recent topic of controversy of was our ability to purchase knowledge. The desire to create improved humans seemed like an unstoppable milestone. We discovered a way to learn at an accelerated rate with implanted learning systems. It was now possible to obtain and retain information with the help of microchips interweaved into our brains. The computerized data interfaced directly with the brain, where all memory was stored. Information could be delivered wirelessly right into the microchip. To fully assimilate the lesson into one's knowledge bank, the participant would need to bring the concept into consciousness by an external trigger. Students could read, attend a class, or watch a movie to retrieve the information, depending on the subject matter. It was crucial to clarify any new downloaded information because the facts could become distorted and confused if the brain organized them incorrectly. Constructive learning only occurred if the person could obtain complete comprehension through personal experience. On occasion, a person's memory would appear fragmented and only be able to retrieve parts of the program. They would have to reload and review the information a second time. Despite the rare glitches, learning something new was easier than ever.

Jack and I disagreed on letting Leah and Jackson try the new technology at first. I felt it was too new. Problems could arise in the future. What if the chips were used for mind control? Brainwashing? How could I be sure of *what* was being infused into their brains? I conceded three years later when the microchips proved to be safe and became mainstream. Then, it was almost impossible not to give in. I didn't want my children to be inferior to their peers. They needed to be competitive to survive in today's world.

Jack voluntarily underwent the procedure first. He gloated about his ability to retain new information. He said he finally felt like he was on an even playing field with me. The rest of the family quickly followed his lead. We let the kids get chips for their eleventh birthday present while I reluctantly joined them. It took some time to get used to the eerie feeling of déjà vu that arose while I reviewed the data after receiving a new download. I must say, I enjoyed being able to retain the subjects I studied in their entirety. It also changed everything for the twins. Although they naturally excelled in everything they did, the microchip implantation helped them master their studies at a remarkably swift rate. They even graduated high school at the age of fourteen. They were scheduled to complete their undergraduate work at the age of sixteen and would finish their doctorate degrees and internships at nineteen. Leah majored in technological agriculture and resource renewal and Jackson in aerospace engineering. I only hoped their maturity could keep up. Their quick flash to adulthood made me uneasy.

At work, everything went as planned. SIG had successfully positioned five solar power satellites, which helped to satisfy the world's growing energy needs. The orbiting research and manufacturing facility had also been launched and was contributing to produce innovative pharmaceuticals and to support other scientific research. Components of the Space resort were now starting to be launched on an ongoing basis. Spacecraft capable of reaching Low Earth Orbit shuttled a limited number of passengers and supplies to and from the Space facilities regularly. But, we all agreed, in order to expand our colonization of Space, we required the development of a transportation system capable of delivering larger loads. With the advancement of nanotechnology, the drafted plans for the design of a Space elevator became a reality. Nanotubes were used in the construction of the elevator cables since they were about 180 times stronger than steel and capable of enduring the stress of orbit. The greatest minds of our times worked diligently to produce the durable material in a size that would be suitable for construction. Ironically, the gigantic carbon nanotubes were manufactured in Space. The absence of gravity allowed scientists to arrange chemical elements in new combinations to create it, along with dozens of other uniquely strong metal alloys that could not be produced on Earth. The development of the new alloys completely revolutionized the future of construction as we knew it.

The Space elevator carriage traveled from Earth to a shuttle terminal in Low Earth Orbit on a ribbonlike cable. The cable was anchored between a large counterweight positioned in the higher Geosynchronous Orbit in Space and an ocean platform here on Earth. It was stabilized by four floating platforms that were stationed every one hundred miles. The platforms were outfitted with thrusters and designed with an infallibly accurate positioning system to ensure that the lift's track was held in perfect alignment. This feature ensured the carriage a smooth, straight ride.

The lift was now complete and fully operational. It was one of the most amazing technological advances our world had ever seen, aside from the planned Space resort, of course. The two, however, would become interdependent. It helped solve one of the biggest problems: getting there and back. Its existence was crucial in providing an economical way to transport passengers and building supplies for its continued expansion. By eliminating the fuel needed for launching into Space, the elevator not only increased the safety of travel, but made Space development practical and affordable. The savings were phenomenal. The previous cost of Space transport, which averaged thousands of dollars per pound, had been reduced to just around one hundred dollars per pound.

Jack was busy working on the structural defense and propulsion system for the Space resort. Although most of the graveyard of orbiting Space debris left behind from old satellites and rockets had long been cleared, smaller objects could easily escape our existing collecting units. Even the tiniest of debris could be damaging if it crashed into something while traveling at speeds capable of exceeding twenty thousand miles per hour. He and others were trying to incorporate an encapsulating shield or force field around the resort to repel Space debris from haplessly crashing into its sides. The technology was already successfully utilized in our military planes but needed to be configured to accommodate the resort's larger, multi-level architecture. Jack also continued to test aircraft on occasion. I had hoped that after becoming a father, he would tame his reckless ways. It was wishful thinking. He liked pushing himself to the limit. One of his most recent stunts landed him in the hospital with a broken left collarbone and arm. We didn't even discuss what had happened. Did I *really* want to know? No. It would only leave me upset. He already put enormous pressure on himself. The last thing he needed was a guilt trip from me.

I spent my time participating in the worldwide collaborative effort to improve the design of artificial gravity for the living quarters of the resort. It was exhilarating to try and accomplish something that was once considered impossible. Although there was only a 2 percent reduction of gravity in Low Earth Orbit compared to Earth, the continuous motion created as the resort orbited the planet caused its occupants to experience a state of perpetual falling. The resort circled the Earth every ninety minutes, making it *seem* like there was zero gravity.

Currently, our Outer Space research facilities had a rotating wheeled station that provided the feel of one-third of Earth's gravity. It worked using centrifugal force. We wanted to see if we could do better. Artificial gravity was *absolutely vital* to the success of the project. Hotel guests would require a break from the aimless floating in Space. Space sickness, the detrimental effects of bone loss, and muscle atrophy were things that we hoped to avoid. Being weightless for long durations proved difficult for even the most experienced astronauts, let alone an inexperienced traveler. We also envisioned the ability to allow guests to function as they would on Earth. They could bathe, eat, and drink as they did on land. The original plans to increase the rotation speed of the resort to simulate higher gravity raised debate on whether a person might develop physical discomfort after an extended period of time. It might feel as though the body was being pulled in the direction of the spin. The body's equilibrium would also become disrupted from the continuous motion when one attempted to move about.

The solution to our problem came after a group of scientists developed a way to successfully detect gravitational waves. Knowing that light was not only a waveform, but made up of particles called photons, the scientists continued their search for the wave-particle of gravity. They found it! After they fine-tuned their instruments, they were able to isolate the once hypothetical particle believed to carry gravitational force, known as a graviton. Gravitons by themselves had little effect on surrounding matter. But, just as photons, the basic unit of light, exhibited electromagnetism when activated, gravitons exerted gravity when stimulated. We were able to develop a material that attracted gravitons like metal to a magnet. It caused the particle to mediate a force of gravity to all matter in its nearby proximity. We lined the resort floors with the material. The effects of gravity were inversely proportional to the distance from the floor. Its effects were weakest at the ceiling, but proved to be more than enough to serve our purpose.

***

Today was just like any other day at work until we were all called to the conference center for an impromptu meeting. I took a seat beside Jack and Noah and braced myself for the news. To my surprise, the meeting wasn't to deliver reports about material delays or other setbacks. We were pleasantly informed of a new group of investors and of a large manufacturing company joining in our quest. Their addition shortened our projected timeline for the completion of the Space resort dramatically. It was now estimated that the resort would be up and running in less than four years.

The construction would require the manpower of hundreds of workers on the ground and in Space. There was already a list of outsourced employees waiting to get to work on the Space resort. SIG also enlisted the help of its internal workforce to complete the task. A list of the hand-picked employees was then read aloud, and we all clapped, congratulating them on their new assignment. I felt happy about our accomplishments until I heard Jim Walker read the name Jack Bennett. *What!* My jaw dropped open in shock. I turned and looked at Jack as he smiled from ear to ear. I was irate. I grabbed onto the armrest of my chair to keep myself from hurting him. I think I could have shot laser beams out of my eyes, so I decided to turn away, as well. I fought to maintain my professionalism and sat quietly until the meeting's adjournment. I followed Jack out of the conference room before I took off briskly down a vacant hall. "*Ugh*," he moaned when I walked passed him once he realized that I was upset. He followed me and quickly strode up beside me.

"How could you take that assignment without discussing it with *me* first?" I said in a low, trembling voice while I marched down the hall.

"*What* are you talking about? Good Lord, Sami, you've known how I felt about this since the day we met. Opportunities like this are *exactly* why I work here to begin with. Unlike you, I actually like Space. You're a real fish out of water here," he lashed out angrily. Then, he turned his body in front of me, blocking me. I looked away angrily.

"There's plenty to do right here on Earth," I seethed through my teeth.

"Yes, and right now, there's even more to do in Space." He sighed and stared anxiously at me.

"So, that's it. You won't even reconsider?" I shook my head in disbelief. I knew he was looking forward to these missions, but I had hoped that this day would never come. I dreaded it. I could tolerate the stunts, the super-fast jets, but how could he choose this mission over his family?

"Sami, I'm sorry—I didn't ask you how you'd feel about this because I thought you already knew that I'd been waiting for this day," he said in a calmer tone, keeping his voice low because some of our colleagues walked past.

"I know … I guess I did." I bit my lip and closed my eyes, trying to make the conversation disappear. I took a moment to try to get a grip. "Jack, I *love* you. If anything *ever* happened to you—I would just die. I'm sorry. I don't want to hold you back. I'm just upset because the thought of you being up there worries me. I hate thinking about you working so far from home on a structure with no surrounding atmosphere. Call me crazy, but do you really think we can build this *thing* without making any mistakes along the way? The project is larger than anything we've ever built," I said convincingly. I didn't care if I sounded irrational. I was suddenly hit with overwhelming emotion, and tears filled my eyes.

"I love you." Jack loosely held both of my weakened arms as they drooped limply against my body with disappointment. He waited for me to speak. I looked up at his sparkling eyes filled with determination. Clearly, he saw nothing wrong with his decision. Was I being ridiculous? He could hurt me more than anyone. When did my heart become so defenseless?

I groaned in agony.

"I'll be okay. I will be extra careful. I will pretend I'm you. I promise, no risks." He held up his hand like he was taking an oath.

"Perfect. Then why don't you start acting like me right now and have some common sense and *not* go," I blurted out sarcastically. I wanted to scream, "Why don't you just leave me for good?" Then, I recalled my late mother's words of wisdom on how she and my father stayed happily married for sixty years. She told me that there would be times when either one or both of them would want out of the marriage, but if they hung in there, they could work things out. She would always say, "This too shall pass." This was definitely one of those moments for me, because leaving him might be easier than enduring endless worry.

"I want to go. I have to," he said firmly while he looked up the ceiling. He was disappointed when I didn't see things his way. We looked at each other for a moment without speaking. Jack held his hand to his mouth like an air traffic controller talking into his microphone. "I will be back before you know it. Do you copy that?" He knew I had a weakness for his humor.

I knew it was a losing battle. Jack always did what he wanted to do, regardless of my wishes. We both did. We'd both made sacrifices for one another to keep on common ground. I knew the beauty of our marriage was based on the power of unity. Together, we could accomplish anything. We had always supported each other's dreams at all cost. This was no different. I had to trust his decision.

"Fine, but you have to promise me you'll take care of yourself," I finally conceded. I swallowed my pride and tried to support his decision.

"I will. You're the best. I knew you would understand. Thank you. I'm going to make you and the kids so proud," he promised. A euphoric look took over his face.

"I'm *already* proud of you, and so are the kids," I said emphatically. "So, how long will you be gone?"

"Two months for the first trip," he muttered.

"The first trip, huh?" I shook my head nervously when I realized that I had no choice but to come to grips with this or I'd surely go insane.

"Yeah, I will be entered into a two-month rotation between the resort and here," he said coolly.

"Great," I moaned. I hung my head in defeat.

Jack pulled me towards him, lifted my chin, and stared into my eyes. "*Come on.*" He smiled irresistibly, which made it impossible not to love him. He supported my lower back with his left arm and gave me a quick kiss on the lips before he hugged me tightly. "Don't worry, honey. I'll be fine."

"I hope so." I sighed. He was glad to have my approval. I could hear the excitement return to his voice. I knew that he was anxious to participate in the construction. He also seemed exhilarated to be able to travel to and from Earth in the elevator he'd worked so hard on. But the thought of him leaving me for these missions was almost too much to bear. I tried to suppress my fears like I had done so many times before. I'd learned long ago that being married to Jack was not for the faint of heart. He did things that only someone so skilled and brave could survive. His actions both frightened and thrilled me at the same time. It made me question why I loved him so much. I would never fully understand him. He loved life more than anyone I'd ever met—yet he would risk it for the advancement of humankind without so much as a blink of an eye.

CHAPTER 10

BROKEN

Jack and I survived his new assignment. It'd been almost a year since he first started working in Space. He loved his new job and continued traveling to and from the Space resort, staying for weeks at a time. The construction project rapidly expanded as though it couldn't be stopped. Leah and Jackson had just celebrated their seventeenth birthday and were busy pursuing their graduate degrees at the university. I felt very alone. The house was incredibly quiet. I never imagined I'd have to face an empty nest so soon. I couldn't help but cling to Jack when he was at home. I think he found my yearning for him a turn-on. Although we had talked on the phone every day, I missed his touch, his smell, his body next to mine each night. I longed for him to scoop me into his arms and hug me in manner that only he knew how. We made love like it was the last time before he left on each trip. Whether it is was due to our anticipated separation or the fact that we had the house to ourselves, the sex was great. I cringed every time he left. I hated to see him go.

I found personal satisfaction in knowing that our separation also proved harder for Jack than he had anticipated. He was scheduled to leave again tomorrow. For some reason, it seemed harder than normal for him to leave me. Perhaps the novelty of his new assignment was wearing off.

"Come with me," Jack said, coming up behind me in the kitchen while I was cooking dinner. He pulled me into him, pushed my hair to the side, and kissed the back of my neck. I stroked down the sides of his firm thighs with my hands. I loved feeling his body pressed against mine.

"I can't," I moaned. I wasn't sure if I answered out of habit or because my resistance to change my old way of thinking had become part of me. Whatever the reason, it was easier to stay home than go.

"*Please*, will you reconsider?" He leaned me forward against the kitchen counter, lifted up my shirt, and kissed lightly down my back. His hands glided around my waist and down my hips, instantly exciting me.

"*Oh*, do you have to make this so difficult?"

"Yes, I'll use whatever weapon works." He turned me around to face him before he kissed me passionately.

"Not fair." I broke from his lips. He smiled and kissed me again. He was successful in achieving one goal. *Dinner would have to wait.*

Jack's words seemed to haunt me, replaying over and over again in my head when he left the next day. It made me miss him even more. He told me that he was going to kidnap me and bring me into Space. He said he missed having his better half. The pressuring didn't end there. Jim Walker, the operations manager of the Space elevator, constantly teased me about how he had an open seat on the lift reserved with my name on it. I was sure it was Jack who put him up to it. Jimmy was in charge of every transport to and from Space. He told me I should go to work on the Space resort with Jack instead of pouting every time he went away. I guess my misery must have shown on my face. I would tell him I appreciated the offer, but always answered with an emphatic "No thanks."

***

I poured all my energy into my work. I exercised daily and kept the house immaculate. I got used to the routine. The days mindlessly passed by. My life was completely predictable, making it a total shock when it was changed instantly. Everything I once knew suddenly came crashing down. My world ended when the phone rang. I had just returned home from a run. It was Leah. She was hysterical.

"Mom, *where* were you? Why don't you carry your phone on you?" Leah screamed frantically.

"I don't know. I was exercising. What's wrong?"

"Hurry, turn on the TV. There's been an accident on the lift."

"*What?* What happened?" I rushed to my television and turned it on. The news reporter was talking about an explosion. The camera zoomed in on a large hole blown out from the side of the Space elevator craft. I listened while he explained that two men on board were killed in the accident.

"Mom, is Daddy on that elevator? Wasn't he supposed to be coming home today?" She rushed through the words.

"Yes, Leah, he is supposed to be," I muttered. "Leah, please calm down. Don't jump to conclusions. Someone would have called me. Hold on. Let me check." I removed the phone from my ear and quickly scrolled through my messages. To my horror, the phone's screen displayed three messages from work, two from Jackson, as well as seven calls from Leah. Tears burst from my eyes. There was only one reason why I would receive a call from work. It was to deliver important news ... *bad* news. Just then, the other line beeped. "Hold on, Leah. It's work."

"Mom, wait. Put it on three-way," she yelled before I purposely cut her off.

"Samantha Bennett," I answered rapidly.

"Sami, it's me, Jim Walker."

I had never heard him so shaken up before.

"Jimmy, what happened? Is Jack okay?" I held my breath while I awaited the answer. I had to know if Jack was hurt.

"Sami—there's been an accident." He paused. "We lost two men. Jack was one. I'm *so*, so sorry." His voice broke.

"*No!*" I whimpered. I felt the blood drain from my face as I thought of our last good-bye. My whole body went numb. I crumpled to the floor, having to lean my back against the couch for support. This was a nightmare! This *couldn't* be happening.

"Samantha, it was a freak accident. Nobody saw it coming," he said tensely.

"What happened?" I could barely speak. I stared at the television screen. The hole in the side of the elevator lift had chucks of debris falling out of it. It blew around in the sky, floating slowly to the dark blue ocean below.

"There were compressed air tanks that broke loose on their descent when they slowed down at the last platform. They weren't properly secured. At that velocity, Jack and Nate never saw it coming. It happened so quickly. Sami, he wouldn't have felt a thing. He was gone on impact." He let out a sickened groan.

"Okay, Jimmy. Thanks for calling. I have to go," I whispered weakly. I tapped the phone to hang up. I couldn't bear to hear anymore. I had a lump in my throat. My worst fears had become a reality. I had spent years stressing over Jack's adventures. In a way, it shouldn't have been a surprise. I knew he'd been at risk for getting himself killed since the day we met. It felt as though time around me had stopped. He was gone. Just like that. I didn't want to accept this reality. I wished I could change the last few minutes of my life. Was there such a thing as a do over? I suddenly remembered Leah was on the other line. My trembling hands fumbled to get back to her.

"Leah, are … are you still there?" I stuttered. My heart broke even more when I had to tell her the news.

"Yes, Mom, who was that?" she moaned impatiently.

"Honey, it was Jim Walker on the phone. Your father was involved in the accident. He didn't make it." I tried to be strong, but hopelessness filled my voice.

"No!" Leah screamed and started to cry.

"It happened fast. He didn't feel anything." I tried to console her, as Jimmy did me. Truthfully, how could I know what he had felt? I only hoped he went instantly. I couldn't bear to think of him suffering.

"How could he die? Mom, how can he leave us like that?" she shouted angrily.

"I know—" We both started to sob uncontrollably. My perfect world that was supposed to last my lifetime was shattered. I felt empty ... less than empty.

CHAPTER 11

ADAPT

We all missed Jack terribly. It had been two years since the accident. Leah and Jackson were astoundingly resilient through it all. Jack's strong spirit resided in them. Despite their pain, they had continued with their studies and would be graduating in a few weeks. I wished Jack could be here to see them. He'd be so proud. I still remembered the bad days. I leaned on my friends at work for support. I was lucky to be surrounded by such good people. They were tremendously helpful. I think it wasn't only because that they knew Jack, but they realized that it could've been one of their loved ones standing in my shoes. Noah mourned as well. He was like a brother to Jack and seemed to recover as slowly as I did. At times, I even thought I was handling it better than him. I tried not to feel sorry for myself. Jack would be disappointed if I wallowed in my misery. He had taught me that I didn't have the luxury of thinking a negative thought. That, however, was sometimes easier said than done. Noah always visited me when he was on Earth. He spent more and more time working on the Space resort these days.

I learned that life went on whether you were ready or not. Time had taken away some of the pain. I was able to move from a place of complete devastation, anger, and sadness to being grateful for the time I had Jack in my life. He taught me how to live fully. If it wasn't for him, I probably wouldn't have had any fun. He was never a victim of fear. Just remembering all of the chances he continuously took with his life made me wonder how he lived for as long as he did. He wasn't perfect, but he was unique. He was wild and untamed by nature. I loved him unconditionally. I missed how he supported me endlessly, how he pushed me outside my bubble of comfort. I just wasn't prepared to lose him so soon.

I was busy working at my desk one day when I heard someone call out my name. "Samantha Bennett," a female voice said from the door. "How's it going, stranger? Working hard?"

"*Tess*," I said, surprised. I immediately jumped up from my chair when I saw my beautiful friend standing in the doorway and gave her a hug. I'd barely gotten to see her since she'd resigned from our department six years ago after getting married. She and her husband decided to start a family in their mid-forties. She was teaching part-time at Caltech, where Leah and Jackson attended.

"What brings you here? Did you decide to quit your teaching job and come back to work with us?" I teased.

"No, just visiting." She smiled as she pointed to the yellow visitor's pass stickered to her blouse. "I came to see if you want to go to lunch with me."

"Sure, that would be great."

"Is Noah around? Do you want to see if he can come?"

"Sure, that Space cadet is actually working here for the next two weeks."

We walked to engineering to ask Noah to join us. It was great talking with Tess. I knew she didn't miss the job, but I missed working with her. We entered the top floor of engineering. Noah was on the lower level, talking to two men who I didn't recognize. I thought I knew everybody who worked here. I looked down at them from the upper level with my bird's-eye view. It was loud in engineering. I couldn't hear what they were saying. I just saw all of them laughing and smiling. He looked like he was reunited with old college buddies. We leaned over the railing and tried yelling his name, but it was no use. Finally, Tess managed to get his attention.

Noah yelled up to us, "Come down here." He waved his hand, motioning for us to join them. We had to walk down the open metal stairs I usually fought to avoid. They scared me. It felt like I was walking on nothing but air.

"Look who I found wandering the building." I grabbed Tess's arm and pulled her to my side.

"Hey, Tess, it's been a long time. You look wonderful!" Noah leaned over and gave her a sideways hug.

"Thanks, Noah. You look younger than ever," Tess replied. We often teased Noah on his boyish looks.

"Oh, ladies—let me introduce you. These are two of our aerospace engineers." He smiled at the two men beside him.

"Samantha Bennett and Tess Morgan, this is Gaelan Liitanen and Pascal Saunders. They are our newest hires. It is their first day." I usually laughed when Noah introduced me so formally to people. I touched my lip to cover my natural reaction.

"Hello, welcome." I reached out my hand to each of them. Pascal quickly shook it, but Gaelan looked me in the eyes, took my hand, and firmly held it in his. I went to pull my hand away, but he held it for a few seconds longer before he released his grip. His lingering grip caught my attention.

"It is a pleasure to meet you, Samantha," he said in a smooth voice. I looked at his attractive face. *Oh, why did they have to hire such good-looking men?* I thought to myself. Couldn't they try and find someone a little homely?

"Mm-hmm, and you," I answered casually, trying to hide the draw I felt to the sound of his voice. He smiled at my reply. Noah declined our invitation to join us for lunch. He said he had to bring the new recruits up to speed. We quickly left them to their business. Tess and I proceeded to go to lunch at a Chinese restaurant nearby. Tess smirked at me after we walked away.

"Stop what you're thinking right now," I said. She looked over at me without saying a word. I could see her matchmaking mind at work.

"He was cute," she finally said harmlessly.

"Which one?" I answered, despite realizing I could only remember one name.

"You know which one. The *sexy* man who was staring at you," she said flatly.

"Yep, he was nice." I sighed. There was no denying it. Gaelan was incredibly handsome. He was physically fit, had light brown hair, sapphire blue eyes and a gorgeous smile.

"He wasn't wearing a ring."

"Uh-huh." I bit my lip. It's nice to know I wasn't the only one who looked.

"You should ask Noah to fix you up," she said with hope.

"Oh, *come on*, I can't even imagine being with a man right now. Just the thought of getting naked in front of someone for the first time is reason enough."

"That's the most *ridiculous* excuse I've ever heard. And since when are you shy? Besides, you're in fantastic shape. If you're that self-conscious, there's an invention— it's called a light switch!" she snapped back at me.

"Okay, fine, maybe it is a lame excuse. I just think it would be awkward. I was with Jack for over eighteen years. He understood me."

"Yes, and he's gone. You have your whole life ahead of you. You're far too young to be thinking like that. Just promise me you'll get out there. I know how easily you become a hermit," she said in a concerned tone.

"Yeah, I know, but I'm perfectly happy—"

"Upp, upp!" she interrupted. She held up her hand to make me stop giving her excuses.

"Fine, you're right. I should try to move on," I said, trying to appease her. Kindly, she let me off the hook. We talked about each other's work until we got to the restaurant.

"I see Jackson and Leah once in a while on campus. They look like they are doing great," Tess complimented.

"Thanks, Tess. How are your girls doing?"

"Wonderful. Haley is dominating kindergarten, and Marissa loves preschool."

"I can't believe how big they are."

"I know," she said after taking a bite of her eggroll. "Jackson and Leah told me they are finishing school this term. Did they find jobs yet?"

"No, I think they just want to graduate first. Why? Do you know of any openings?"

"No, I've been out of the loop for too long. I just wondered if Jackson has mentioned any opportunities to you," she clued. I remembered how she liked to approach difficult subjects in a roundabout way.

"*Why* do you ask? Tess, do you know something I don't know? You have to tell me. If it involves Jackson, I need to know." I looked her straight in the eye, pressuring her to tell me what she knew. Tess shifted herself uncomfortably in her chair.

"Sami …" She moaned. "I wish you already knew. I shouldn't be the one to tell you. But, I'd want to know if it was my kids."

"What is it, Tess? Just say it," I pleaded. This was obviously the real reason behind her visit.

"Jackson applied for a job on the Space resort, and he was hired. He's planning on leaving shortly after graduation."

"He did, *did he?*" I said under my breath. "I can't believe it—he still wants to follow in his father's footsteps and go up there," I huffed and let out a sigh in disbelief. I pictured him grabbing his bags to leave like Jack had and myself wondering if I'd ever see him again. "Thank you for telling me." I wanted to alleviate her guilt. "I'm glad you gave me a head's up. Otherwise, I might be at risk for killing him when he decided to break the news to me." I tried to find humor in the news and not lash out on the messenger.

"You know that it's much safer now. I heard that the entire carriage of the lift was redesigned after Jack's accident. There hasn't been an accident in over two years. He'd be okay," she reassured me.

I stared across the room, thinking about his decision. "I know. I'm just surprised he wouldn't have at least discussed this with me. I'm a reasonable person. Sure, I would have told him no, but I hate that he's *so* sneaky."

We spent the rest of our meal catching up on other things. I missed hanging out with her. She was clever and witty. I thanked Tess for stopping by and for keeping me informed. I returned to work and immediately called Jackson.

"Jackson, it's me, Mom. How are you?" I fought to control the tone of my voice. Our relationship had become strained ever since Jack's death. He made me feel like a consolation prize. I could never fill the shoes of his dad. I wasn't sure if his emotional distance was due to him trying to prove himself as a man or fear that he would lose me, too. Either way, he had become very secretive about his life.

"Great. I just got an A on my research paper."

"Oh, that's wonderful, honey. I'm so proud of you." For a minute, I forgot why I was calling. I wanted to tread carefully and give him a chance to spill his news. "Now all you need to do is find a job."

"Yeah— it's funny you mention that, Mom," he said with hesitation. "I just found out that I landed my dream job."

"Really, *doing what?*" I bit my lip.

"What makes you say it like that? *Doing what?*"

"Where are you planning on working, Jackson? It's a simple question."

"*Mom*, have you been checking up on me?"

"Maybe."

"You already know, *don't you?*" he yelled at me. "How come you know everything?" he hissed.

"Of course I know, Jackson. I'm your mother; it's my job. Besides, I work here, after all."

"Yeah, but that place is like a fortress on high alert. You're all bound to maintain strict confidentiality. You and Dad never talked about work at home."

"There are ways," I admitted impulsively.

"It's a great job. I will be working with some of the best engineers in the world on the Space resort. It's the opportunity of a lifetime," he pleaded.

"Why? Why do you have to go into Space? There are so many jobs right here on Earth. Can't you please consider one of those?"

"No, Mom! It's my dream to work on the station. I want to go. I'm not afraid. Dad wouldn't stop me. He'd want me to live my life—to go after what I want. He'd be right up there with me if he was still here. I'm sure of it."

"You sound just like him!" I shouted angrily.

"I am *just* like him!" he shouted back.

"Please, Jackson, don't get yourself killed."

"I'm not planning on it, Mom. It's perfectly safe."

"Okay, fine," I muttered. He was over eighteen. Legally, I knew I had no say. "When do you leave?" I conceded.

"In two months, right after graduation."

"Why didn't you tell me sooner?"

"Because, then you'd just have more time to worry about it. I didn't want to stress you out."

"I see."

"Mom, I'll see you at graduation. I love you."

"Okay, I'll see you then. I love you, too." I reluctantly hung up the phone and tried to finish up my work day. It was hard to concentrate. I'd already lost both of my parents and Jack. I would never survive if anything ever happened to *him*.

CHAPTER 12

NEVER SAY NEVER

I was fretting all night after talking to Jackson on the phone. Why was he so bullheaded? Why did he have to be so stubborn, just like his father? He was a carbon-copy of Jack—fearless, bold ... as if he were invincible. He couldn't get hurt. I couldn't bear it. I would have to be taken directly to the nearest psych ward. *That's it, he's not going. No! No way!* I was going to do everything in my power to stop him!

I went to work the next day with only one purpose—to see Jim Walker. I went straight to his department and walked into his office, slamming the door behind me. I was instantly hit with the smell of stale cigarette smoke. Although it was a smoke-free building, Jimmy secretly disabled the smoke detectors in his office the day he moved in. Physically, he was a walking time bomb. Despite being extremely intelligent, Jim did not take good care of his health. He was morbidly obese and smoked like a chimney. He was also a pack rat. His office was filled to the brim with stacks of books, magazines, and papers. Regardless, he always seemed to know exactly where to find something.

"Jimmy," I shouted, "how could you do this to me?" I scowled while I stared him down. He straightened his back in response and sat up defensively behind his desk.

"Sami, calm down. Let's talk about this reasonably," he said. A look of panic crossed his face. Clearly, he knew what I was going to say.

"Why didn't you tell me about this? You had to approve it. No one goes up in that *thing* unless you say so," I protested. He had the power to keep Jackson grounded.

"I just thought that it was better if Leah and Jackson told you they had applied themselves."

"What? Leah, too! You're planning to send both of my kids! *No way*!" I shouted.

"It's perfectly safe now. Really! What happened to Jack … that was a freak accident. We don't even bring the tanks up the same way. It's never been safer. We've been running the lift almost every other week now."

"Ahh …" I moaned. "I don't care. My kids don't have to go. Tell them that the space is limited," I urged.

"I can't. It's what they want, Sami. Don't hold them back. They are two of the most talented recruits we have.

I mean, with you're brains and Jack's determination, they're made for this," he said with conviction.

"Damn it! You just *don't* get it." I shook my head. Didn't he realize they were the only family I had left?

"No, Sami, can't you see? You're letting fear block your better judgment."

I moved a small pile of junk and dropped myself into a chair in front of his paper-covered desk, sinking into its worn leather upholstery. His voice seemed to fade in the distance. I sat, not speaking, and stared blankly at the wall while he continued trying to convince me. Why was I so worried? Jack's accident was the only major accident in the lift since its inception. Riding in a car was statistically more dangerous. Maybe I was being paranoid.

"Let them grow up. This is their life, not yours. It's an opportunity of a lifetime. They will get to be a part of the biggest creation in our history. I know Space exploration is risky business, but we don't give up because of previous failures or because of unknown dangers. We get smarter! If we quit now, we surrender all of our possibilities. You of all people should know that. Please don't try to hold them back. You would feel terribly guilty if you did, I promise you." He coaxed me on and on.

"Okay, please—*no* more. I've heard enough." I held up my hand to make him stop. "If they're going …" I sighed, taking in a deep breath. I shut my eyes to gather strength because I was about to say the most unthinkable thing. "Then, *so am I.*" I mouthed the dreaded words in a whispery breath. Even though I would rather go base jumping in the Grand Canyon, there was no way I was going to let my kids go up there without me. Being separated from them would be unbearable.

"*Really* ... wow, that's fantastic. *Thank you,* Sami. You're making the right choice," he said as though he didn't believe his ears. He leaned forward in his chair. "I was counting on your kids more than you know. And *you*—you'll be even more help." His expression brightened instantly, shifting from apprehension to relief.

"What do you mean?"

"Well, I might as well tell you now. You'll know soon enough anyway. I think they might be our best bet when it comes to understanding the Katarians."

"The Katarians?" I asked. "Who are they?" Geography was not my strong point, but I'd *never* heard of them.

"Sami, do you believe in aliens?" he asked matter-of-factly.

"I don't know. I mean sure, why not? In a universe so vast, it would be completely egocentric to think otherwise."

"*Well*, we have been working with aliens," he said hesitantly while he looked at me strangely. Maybe he was trying to decipher my reaction.

"You're kidding, *right?*" I let out a small laugh. I was shocked. "Are you toying with me?"

"I'm afraid not."

"Wow." I choked back. Where had I been? Why wasn't this front page news?

"They are friendly and technologically advanced beyond our years. You're sworn to secrecy, of course," he warned, looking up under his eyes in a threatening manner. I didn't respond. My body froze in disbelief as my jaw dropped while considering the implications of alien contact. "The Katarians have been docking their ship at our Space station. They have offered to share their technology with us. I don't know how they did it, but they managed to learn our language. Despite it, we are still struggling to understand their translations." He elaborated on their established working arrangement.

"Unbelievable! When were you planning on breaking this news?" I asked anxiously. It would be selfish not to share this information with the world.

"Oh, don't worry. We will get to it. We are waiting until we open up the Space resort to tourists. Actually, it was their only request."

"What was?"

"The Katarians asked us to keep our relationship a secret for now. They said they didn't want to be bothered with our media while we're working on the station. They asked if we would wait until our work together was complete."

"I can see their point. I could only imagine the stories that would follow."

"Sami, there's something else I want to tell you. It's about Jack. You've earned it," Jim said, changing the subject—signaling the alien topic was closed for discussion. He was offering me information in exchange for the future service of my family.

"What about Jack?" I asked curiously. He had caught my attention.

"Remember the test flights he did for us?"

"Don't you *mean* the test flights that he did for the Air Force?"

"Yeah, but we financed them with our subcontract."

"Yes, how could I forget," I said sarcastically.

"Well—the aircrafts he flew weren't always manufactured on Earth. Sometimes, they were something we found."

"Wait! You mean to tell me he was flying alien Spaceships?" I leaned my hands on his desk to keep myself from falling on the floor. I pictured the unexplained wounds my late husband frequently endured. No wonder he would come home at times looking like a crash-test dummy.

"Yep, and Jack was phenomenal. He was one of the only ones who could figure out how they functioned. *Hell*, he was the only one who could even manage to get the suckers off the ground. Man, I miss him," he said with admiration.

"He never said a word." I shook my head at the daunting task of trying to operate sophisticated alien technology. Reverse technology would be a huge under-taking, to say the least. Was it even possible to under-stand aircraft so complex it was capable of interstellar travel? I thought I knew everything about him.

"It was time for you to know the truth," he offered wholeheartedly.

"Hey, now maybe the Katarians will show you how to fly them," I concluded.

"They *might*," he muttered.

"Why? They don't want you using their planes?"

"No, that's not it." He chuckled under his breath. "I'm certain they would help us if they knew how. But the crafts aren't theirs."

"You mean there are *others*?" I covered my mouth when I gasped. I felt so ignorant. "How could all of this been going on around me without my knowing?"

"Need to know, Sami. Need to know," Jimmy re-minded me in a serious tone.

Obviously, he was done sharing, so I quickly got up to leave. The cigarette smell was making me sick, any-way. I could hear Jimmy yell after me to keep quiet from his desk. I just nodded and kept walking.

I left the office and called Leah on her cell phone. She knew the reason for my call even before I said hello. She was, however, exuberant when I informed her that I was going with her. Jackson was leaving two weeks before her, and she seemed thrilled to hear that I would be traveling with her. Or maybe, it was the other way around. I didn't want to go without her.

The next order of business was to attend the mandatory Space training. We had to be signed off on Space elevator lift transport and basic Space station safety precautions. We were also required to sign a handful of release forms. The header should have read, "Travel at your own risk." The forms absolved the SIG, the Space elevator, and the Space resort from virtually any legal responsibility. However, they *could* take us to court. We all had to sign a confidentiality form. It outlined the degree to which we would be prosecuted if we released any information about the existence of the Katarians. Basically, it gave them the right to repossess our assets and threatened imprisonment if we leaked a word. I saw Leah's eyes widen when they briefed us on the aliens and our harmonious relationship.

"Mom." She grabbed my arm in excitement.

"I know," I mouthed the words. I'd already had time to take in the startling news.

"This is so exciting. I can't believe it. Aliens! We get to work with aliens! It's going to be so much fun." She smiled brilliantly.

I shrugged. "Terrific." I was becoming overwhelmingly nervous as the trip neared.

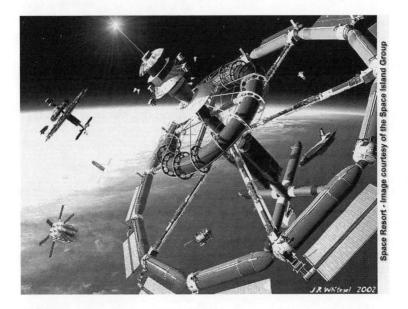

Space Resort - Image courtesy of the Space Island Group

J.R.Whitesel 2002

CHAPTER 13

ARRIVAL

Our lift came to a gentle halt once we reached the elevator terminal. I had made it! The entire passenger carriage was then effortlessly lifted from its tracks and attached to the Space transport shuttle by two long robotic arms. The shuttle was the transport system used to transfer guests and supplies from the elevator terminal over to the Space resort. The vehicle glided us smoothly across Space like we were sailing across the sea, making it safe to unbuckle from our seats. We retracted the seats into the floor to fully experience weightlessness. The sensation was indescribable. I felt light as a feather and as free as a bird. It was fun to float across the room. Gliding so effortlessly could easily become additive. Everyone gathered to the windows to catch a glimpse of the Space resort as we approached. We were like impatient children nudging each other out of the way to get a better view. I expected to see the Katarian Spaceship parked at the resort, only to be disappointed that it wasn't anywhere in sight. It figured that I would have to choose a time to come when they weren't around.

Our shuttle arrived safely at the Space resort. Our flight commander carefully docked us once we arrived. He announced overhead that we had capture, which confirmed that our shuttle's contact had been secured. The seal from our elevator cabin hissed as the hatch door flung open. Being dressed in my Space suit, I couldn't help feel like an astronaut when I exited into the shuttle bay terminal's air lock. We collected our bags and floated right out the hatch. There was more room to sail around than on the elevator car. Leah and a couple other people did somersaults to test out their Space acrobatics. It was surprisingly dark and cool compared to the elevator cabin. The cold seemed to pass right through my suit. There were only a few spotlights bordering the ceiling. It looked like a train terminal at night. We held onto a railing to keep from floating aimlessly as we entered through a hatchway into the heated corridor outside of the zero-gravity sports arena. The resort hosted various levels of gravity to meet the needs of its occupants. It was divided into zero-gravity, partial gravity, and simulated gravity regions.

We peered in through the windows of the arena from the passageway that ran along its perimeter. Zero-gravity games were just one of the highly anticipated attractions expected to bring hotel guests to the resort. The arena was so large that it had to be delivered into Space in pieces. Modified external tanks were built to open and expand once their position was secured to the station. The tanks expanded like an RV's side compartment to allow for extra square footage. It had three rows of stadium seating surrounding a central playing field. Each seat was outfitted with a harness-like seatbelt to help ground the audience. Currently, there were four people on the field playing dodge ball. We watched them push their feet off clear Plexiglas walls surrounding the inside ring of the arena, whizzing the ball at one another. They sprung around effortlessly. They were able to retrieve the floating ball into their hands with a glove that called the ball back to them. They all had giant smiles across their faces. It looked like a blast.

"Are they professionals?" I asked our flight commander, Michael.

"No, look at their uniforms. Those two are with a pharmaceutical company onboard," he answered.

"What about those ladies?" I asked, pointing to the two players who appeared to be winning the game.

"Mom, I'm *pretty* sure those are men." Leah chuckled and corrected me.

"Yeah, those guys work in our service department," he replied. "They do satellite repairs."

I took a second look only to realize my mistake. "Wow, sorry, I guess they are men. It was hard to tell with their hair floating all around," I said bashfully. We continued through the passageway to proceed to the resort's main lobby. We went through another hatched doorway and, almost immediately, my shoes firmly hit the floor. I couldn't help but smile. Countless hours went into perfecting the artificial gravity. It felt great to try it out firsthand. The station's simulated gravity made walking around feel like we were walking on Earth, only with a lighter foot. The sensation was sort of exotic.

We entered the resort's lobby to register for our rooms. It was simple. All that was required was one swipe of our identification tag across a scanner and the room number would be displayed and activated. The lobby looked similar to a fancy hotel, only it served to fulfill many purposes. Its large square footage was designed to function as a reception hall, conference room, movie theater, or any other activity requiring a large area. Here we sat down for yet another mandatory orientation session detailing station protocols. Michael explained that there were only two exits off the station—a shuttle bay at each end. After working so closely to the project, I couldn't help daydreaming because I found the information *painfully* redundant.

To keep entertained, I studied the people around me. It was amazing to see such a diverse group of people working together to complete a common goal. Our nations' borders seemed to disappear in Space. I admired the pleasantry of my surroundings. The resort aimed to provide the best of both worlds. It offered all the luxuries of being at home, with the added benefits of being in Space. The décor wasn't cold or stark, but rather warm and inviting. It was chosen to induce calmness and simulate being outdoors. The walls were painted a soft sky blue, and floors were made of a synthetic pale amber tile. Hydroponic planters of lush green air-producing plants lined the external walls of the room, adding to its coziness. The plants not only helped to provide for the resort's oxygen needs but helped to eliminate carbon dioxide and filter contaminates from the air.

To my relief, the review finished. We entered single file through another hatchway at the end of the room into an area even larger than the lobby. It was host to a large restaurant and gift shop and designed to accommodate many people at once. Its entire layout was fully built on Earth prior to launching into Space to ease its assembly. Michael told us to follow him and quickly led us on. He wanted to show us to our rooms to drop off our bags. We exited the area into a long corridor, passing windows peering into Outer Space along the way. Leah and I got to our room. We were staying in one of the hotel suites my friend Regis had purchased for his guests' future occupancy. The resort's suites were leased to multiple hotel chains and were scheduled to begin accepting guests early next year. I would love to see Regis's face the first time he stepped foot inside one. He would be ecstatic. I could hear his exuberant voice in my head. The image made me smile. I snapped a few pictures with my camera and e-mailed them to him. It looked just like the reproduction we had on Earth, but knowing it was in Space made it all the more impressive. I checked to see if everything worked. I turned on the lights, the water, and the television.

"Mom, *enough already!* Let's go find Jackson. I told him we would meet him for lunch, remember?" Leah reminded me as she frowned. "Can we go now? I'm starving."

"Yeah, of course. Call and see if he's ready." I continued to survey the room. "Leah, aren't you impressed by all of this?" I had to ask. I couldn't believe her apparent lack of enthusiasm.

"It looks just like a hotel room, Mom," she said, unimpressed, before she called Jackson on her phone.

"You're right, but we did it! It's real. A floating getaway. *Incredible*. We built this place in my lifetime." I was awestruck. It was amazing to see everything put together.

Leah seemed to take the accomplishment completely for granted. I think being born in a time of such rapid advancements made her believe that anything was easily attainable.

"We're here!" Leah said boisterously into the phone. "Well, you know. Yeah … yeah, no, fine. I'll tell you later. Okay, we'll see you in an hour." She tapped the phone off. I surmised they were probably talking about me. "He's right in the middle of something, but said he could meet us at the restaurant in an hour," she repeated as though I were deaf.

"Great." I smiled at her. Leah and I took the time to explore, but we didn't get far. We became enthralled with the miraculous view from one of the corridor's porthole windows. They were positioned every two feet on each side of the hallway. You could view different areas of the resort, look down at our planet, or see the surrounding galaxy depending on your location. Our view was of Earth. It was *spectacular!* The scene took my breath away. Our glowing planet was the most brilliant shade of blue with a bold, navy blue rim edging against the blackness of Space on its horizon. Fluffy white clouds drifted slowly across the surface, bringing the vision to life.

"Isn't it fabulous?" Leah said, pressing her hands against the glass.

"Yes, quite," I agreed.

"I love it!" she cheered.

"I love you," I said. I put my arm around Leah and gave her a hug. I was happy to share this once-in-a-lifetime experience with her.

"I love you, too, Mom. I'm so glad you came." She leaned her body into mine. I sighed.

"So am I. I can't believe I was missing out on all of this. It all seems kind of ridiculous now, you know, me not wanting to come up here." I looked at Earth. Seeing it from afar moved me in a way I never imagined it would. I couldn't help but be aware of the infinite universe surrounding me. There was no ignoring it from this view. Its majesty filled my soul, giving my humble life a deeper meaning.

"Mm-hmm," she hummed.

We spent longer than we thought looking out the huge window and were a few minutes late in arriving at the restaurant. Jackson was already there, sitting at a table with two other people.

"Jackson." I threw my arms around him when he stood to greet us. "I missed you!" I kissed him on the cheek.

"Hi, Mom, you made it! Isn't this place amazing?" he said with vigor.

"Yes, quite," I answered. I looked around the room. I was surprised to see so many people running around and sitting at the tables. It was buzzing with activity. The place wasn't nearly as crowded when we had come in.

"Leah." Jackson hugged his sister. "How bad *was* she?" I heard him whisper in her ear.

"Surprisingly, she did remarkably well. I still have all of my fingers and everything," she muttered back. I kept my mouth shut, pretending not to hear. Jackson turned to introduce the people at the table.

"Mom, this is Kylie, my girlfriend." He smiled at the pretty girl. "And Gaelan, my ... my friend," he stammered. "Kylie, Gaelan, this is my mother."

"Sami," I volunteered my name. "It's nice to meet you." I greeted them both. I immediately looked at the girl's innocent face and thought about warning her that she would need nerves of steel to be involved with my son. However, if she made it here, I was sure she could hold her own.

"I've heard so much about you," Kylie beamed in her sweet voice.

"Thanks," I replied. I didn't know what to say. I'd heard nothing about her. I sneaked a quick glare at my son. He just shrugged his shoulders. It would have been nice for Jackson to have told me about her in advance. Would it have killed him to mention her to me beforehand? Leah would have told me in a heartbeat if she had a boyfriend. I wondered how long they'd been dating. Jackson looked at her like he really liked her.

"Samantha Bennett," replied Gaelan, remembering my name. His voice was smooth and familiar. I turned my eyes away from Kylie to look at the man sitting across the table from her. His eyes flashed up at me. "I believe we have already met."

"Oh, yes, you're right," I quickly retrieved his image. "That day in engineering," I said with a smile. "It's nice to see you again." I blushed and slid across the bench to sit down. I hadn't forgotten Gaelan. He was the gorgeous man I had met two months ago in engineering when I visited Noah with Tess. Why is it that certain circumstances or people keep coming back into your life repeatedly when you least expect it? It's as though someone is screaming, "Hey, will you stop and pay attention to me?"

Jackson grabbed Leah by the arm and pulled her towards him. "Hey, let's not forget about this knucklehead. This is Leah, my older sister."

"Sure, by what, five minutes? It's nice to meet you both," Leah corrected her brother and plopped herself down on the bench beside me. Twin humor was something they never grew tired of. Before we could order, a waitress brought over a tray of glasses and a large pitcher of beer.

"Jackson, you ordered beer? You're only nineteen," I scolded.

"That's right, Mom. There's no drinking age in Space." He let out a wicked laugh and started to fill the glasses. "Besides, what am I going to do, steal the shuttle and go for a joy ride?" He and the others laughed.

"Funny," I said, rolling my eyes. I decided not to lecture about the dangers of alcohol and the young brain. I grabbed one of the mugs and took a large gulp. It was probably the best beer I'd had in my life. I could really use a drink after my day. "So, did you guys meet any of the aliens yet?" I wanted to talk about the taboo topic. "Do they have antenna coming out of their heads? Are they furry like a yeti? Or *maybe* they have superpowers?" Everyone laughed. Their attention urged me on.

"Mom, please," pleaded Jackson as he laughed.

"Do they walk on all fours? Do they have a tail or four eyes?" I continued while they all burst into laughter. "Are they giants or ridiculously small? Are they green?" I let myself get carried away.

Jackson held his side in pain. "Mom, come on, if you don't stop I'm going to drop a lung," he urged.

"I can't help it. I mean, we've made contact with extraterrestrials and can't even talk about it. This is the biggest news of our time. How can we pretend it hasn't happened?"

"Mom, before you say anything more, I have to tell you something," Jackson said with a chuckle and a strange look.

"What?" I held up my hands, feeling puzzled.

"Mom, Gaelan *is* from Kataria," he muttered softly.

"What? *Oh*—" was all I was able to reply. I covered my mouth and looked across the table at the stunning man and bit my lip. His flat expression was unreadable. I was mortified. "I'm so sorry—I didn't know." I wanted to disappear. If I could have crawled under the table and hid, I would have. Why did I have to open my big mouth? I kicked Jackson's foot under the table. He glared up at me and silently mouthed the word *Ouch!*

"No problem. We asked the same things about *you*," Gaelan said in a serious voice. A curious grin lit up his face as if he had found the whole thing amusing. He carefully studied my face. His clear, blue eyes went right through me. They pulled me in like a hypnotist's voice. I gasped at his perfect features before I turned my eyes away. We all became quiet while we sat and drank our beer. Gaelan excused himself a few minutes later.

"Why didn't you tell me *he* was a Katarian? You could have introduced him as such," I said.

"I didn't think of it. Besides, how was I to know that you would start bashing the poor aliens?" Jackson said, refuting blame.

"Mom, this is Gaelan. He is from Kataria. How hard is that?" I said sarcastically. He sneered at me.

"Hey, Mom, we should find Noah," Leah interjected before we got into a nasty fight. She liked being the peacekeeper of the family.

"Yeah, that's right. I didn't get a chance. I was supposed to tell you that he's planning to meet us later—after his shift at nineteen hundred hours. He's challenged us to a game of Space relay racing." Jackson joined in on his sister's deliberate change of subject. They always worked well as a team.

"It was really funny, Sami. Noah almost passed out when Jackson told him you were coming up here today. He said he was sure you would have backed out by now," Kylie chimed in cheerfully.

"Mom, if you would have seen the look on his face … *priceless,*" Jackson finished her sentence before they both started giggling about their inside joke.

Lunch went by without another mention of Gaelan. I think everyone wanted to forget my blunder, including me. Kylie was delightful. I could see why Jackson liked her. She was attractive, driven, and charismatic. Leah and Kylie chattered back and forth throughout our meal. They were in their own little world because they both specialized in agriculture and would be working together in the resort's hydroponic food production center. After dinner, Jackson needed to return to work to check on some experiments and complete his shift. Kylie offered to show us the greenhouse, but I decided to pass on the offer to join them. I felt completely drained and wanted to lie down before the evening activities began, so I excused myself and walked back to my room.

I looked at my watch. *How could it only be two o'clock in the afternoon?* The trip had disoriented my sense of time. The day seemed to be going on forever. Maybe I was suffering from sensory overload.

CHAPTER 14

PANIC

I walked down the long corridor to return to my room. I took time to admire every view outside of each of the windows along the way. Suddenly, an ear-piercing alarm and white flashing light boxes came to life, blinking every six feet along the passageway's ceiling. A computerized female voice announced overhead, "Attention all crew and guests. This is an emergency. Please proceed to the nearest shuttle bay for mandatory evacuation. This is not a drill. Repeat, you must proceed to the nearest shuttle bay for immediate evacuation."

My heart sank. I had just left Leah and Jackson's side less than ten minutes ago. There were only two exits off of the station, each at opposite ends. I'm not sure if I should go back to find them or go in the opposite direction to the closest shuttle. I looked up at the white lights and huffed in defiance when my eyes focused on the lighted arrows pointing *away* from the location of my kids. I stepped once in their direction, but jerked to a pause. *No, I'm sure they'd be gone by now.* I took in a deep breath and tried to remain calm. A man came running past me with no intention of slowing down.

"What's going on?" I yelled after him.

"Fire," he shouted over his shoulder without stopping. "Come on," he demanded without breaking stride.

"Fire!" I gasped. Although I knew the resort had several fire extinguishing systems in place, my body reacted to the urgency of the situation. I saw no option but to comply. I turned and walked briskly down the corridor to the nearest exit highlighted by the blinking arrows. I pictured being trapped in the enclosed space. My rising anxiety made the walls seem like they were closing in on me. The claustrophobia was overwhelming! Before I knew it, I was running frantically. Adrenaline surged through my veins as panic set in. The walls and lights in the corridor became a blur when I flew past them. I had to get off this structure, I told myself. I sprinted around the last corner to get to the shuttle and slammed my body full force into a solid object. It was hard, large, and a very good hit. Everything went black....

I looked up. Ouch, my head hurt. My eyes were blurry, and the passing lights had halos around them. My body was being jostled. Was I being carried? Yes. I looked up to see a man's face. It was Gaelan. He held me tightly in his arms as he ran. We entered a dark room. He turned in a rush and closed a door with the touch of a button. I saw him tap a light on what looked like a bulletin board on the wall and say, "All aboard—all clear for undocking." Gaelan didn't seem to notice my awakening. He carried me down a hall in a quick dash. We entered a large, well-lit room with people sitting at defined stations across the room. I squinted at the sudden brightness. Finally, he looked at me and saw I was awake. He sat me down in a chair. This was definitely not the shuttle. Maybe this was part of the station I hadn't seen yet. The crew sat at lighted tables with holographic computer screens floating above them. It looked similar to our Space station command center, but then I noticed the writing was foreign. A huge star map outlining the galaxy was floating in the center of the room. People seemed to be studying it attentively but made little movement. It appeared as though they were operating the controls telepathically. Oh no—it couldn't be. My body froze from the disorientation after I instantly realized I was sitting on the Katarian Spaceship! Although the aliens looked just like us, I felt a wave of fear surge through me from knowing I was surrounded by beings from another planet.

"Are you all right?" Gaelan asked, staring at me intently with a concerned expression.

"I'll be fine," I muttered.

"Good," he said firmly. He took his hand, placed it under my chin, and tilted my head up for examination. "We'll get that looked at in a moment, I promise. Just hang tight."

I reached up and felt a giant goose egg on my upper right forehead. No wonder my head was throbbing. I heard the Katarians talking around me in their native language. I couldn't make out a word. I tried to make out some of their actions. It seemed as though they were preparing to undock their ship from the Space station in order to follow the mandatory evacuation. I sat quietly and watched them work. After a minute, everyone seemed to pause from their duties. I noticed Gaelan and another man talking with serious looks on their faces. It seemed like they were arguing. I could tell by their non-verbal communication that their discussion somehow involved me. Gaelan gave me a quick, empathetic look. The stern black man he was fighting with motioned his hand to me and gnashed his teeth. He had a stiff, intimidating stance and looked upset by my presence. I sat helplessly. I considered asking what they were saying but didn't want to provoke any hostility. Instead, I waited patiently for their instruction.

Gaelan walked over to me. "Samantha, we cleared the station," he stated in a calming voice. "But we have a little problem."

"What?" I asked curiously.

"It seems that everyone is in agreement to travel home now. We had promised we would gather some supplies for the expansion of the station."

"Okay, that's great. Just drop me off at the elevator terminal."

He squatted down on his knees so that he could be at my eye level. "Well …" he paused. "That's what I need to tell you. We are already underway," he said, looking me directly in the eyes. I think he was trying to determine how much this would upset me.

"Really—no—you have to take me *back!*" I protested. My panic only irritated the man Gaelan had been talking with. He sighed and shot me an angry glare. He appeared to have zero tolerance when his orders were challenged.

"We can't, not yet," he said firmly.

"Oh," was all I could respond. I was almost too afraid to speak. I sat motionless for a moment, trying to digest the news. How could we be underway already? We only left a few minutes ago.

"I know you didn't sign up for this. It's just that, when I ran into you, I couldn't just leave you there *unconscious*. We'll have you back in no time."

"That was you?" I was shocked. I could have sworn I hit a wall. I wanted off this ship, but I got the impression that going back wasn't a viable option. I thought carefully before I spoke. I was clearly outnumbered here.

"I'm sorry. I didn't see you coming," he apologized.

"Are you sure there's room for me on board?" I quickly thought. Maybe this was a futile attempt, but it might have caused them to take me back.

"Plenty," Gaelan reassured.

Just then, the man he had been arguing with joined in. "Actually, Gaelan, we *are* short on rooms. We cannot use the lower east deck until it's been cleaned or for another three months. It's still full of radiation," he said, speaking perfect English. I guess he wanted me to understand him now.

"That's right, Tyden," he said, sounding grateful. "I forgot. Who has an extra bed?" Gaelan asked. He looked around at the crew members surrounding him, searching for a savior in the predicament. No one volunteered. I saw them shake their heads and shrug their shoulders as if they couldn't be of any help. "Fine," Gaelan said sharply. "She can have my bed. I'll sleep in my study." He turned back to me and reached out his hand. I took hold of it and let him pull me to my feet. "Come on, Samantha. Let's get you to the medic," he said, sounding upset by the apparent lack of cooperation from his crewmates.

As we left the room, I could hear the crew's voices murmuring behind us. It seemed they shared my belief that I shouldn't be here. "Why can't you just take me back?" I asked curiously.

"We choose our actions to meet the majority's needs," Gaelan explained as we walked. "You are only one person. We have to do what's best for the mission."

"I wish I could have told Leah and Jackson where I was going. I hope they made it off the station in time," I said nervously.

"Yes, everyone's fine. The fire was a false alarm. There was some smoke in the café's kitchen that set off a smoke detector. Your station's commander decided to use the alarm for a practice evacuation. I already had you off the ship before they had announced it was just a drill. They were bringing the shuttles back right before we left communication range."

"How do you *know* that?" I conveyed my confusion.

"We contacted your station's command center to check on the damages and to inform them of our plans to gather supplies. I told them that you were aboard our ship. Jackson and Leah will be notified."

"Thank you. I didn't know." I couldn't believe I had missed the whole exchange. "I don't get it, how in the world did your ship get there so fast?" Maybe it was the bump on my head, but I was really disoriented.

"What do you mean?"

"I mean, I didn't see it. You know, *all of this*, when I arrived at the resort. When did it get there?"

"Oh." He smirked with a small chuckle. "It was there—you just couldn't see it. That's because we cloaked it."

"You cloaked it? You made it *invisible?*"

"Yes, we wanted to keep it out of view from your satellites and telescopes," he said flatly. He smiled at me with satisfaction that they had the ability to render their large craft completely invisible. I couldn't help but be impressed. Optical camouflage for a vessel this big would require holographic imagery far beyond our current level of technology. We walked to the medic's office. The corridor was long and dimly lit. It looked like we were walking into a nightclub.

"Why is it so dark?" I asked, fearful of every corner we rounded. I didn't want to run into anything else and really appear to be a klutz.

"The corridors are a nonessential part of the ship. We have to utilize our resources very carefully."

The place felt like a maze. I was going to need a map so I wouldn't get lost. We arrived at the medic in a few more turns. We stepped into what appeared to be a doctor's office, hospital, and lab in one. There were four windowed partitioned rooms with empty beds lining the left wall. The room where we stood was large and furnished with an operating table complete with overhead lights hanging down above it. Lighted tables covered with beakers filled with colored solutions were randomly scattered throughout the room. A man quickly approached us as we entered. He was dressed in a navy blue uniform. He looked to be in his forties but moved around like a child on a sugar high. He spoke in their native language to Gaelan. His words meant nothing to me.

Gaelan replied, "Urit, this is Samantha Bennett. Samantha, this is Urit Lapinmaki, our ship's medic." He paused for us to nod hello. "She will be joining us on our journey home. Could you look at her head before you get her prepared for the trip?"

Urit raised his eyebrows and gave Gaelan a suspicious look. "Have a seat," Urit said, now speaking perfect English as he motioned for me to sit on the examination table. He picked up a thin, eight-by-eight-inch flat pane of glass or plastic. He slid his hand across the side, making the panel light up a deep violet. He brought it over to me, held it about an inch from my face, and looked through it. I looked up at the lighted object and was surprised to find that I could not see through it. I could only see the purple glow. I felt nothing. Maybe this was some sort of X-ray machine. Urit lowered the device and said, "You have a slight concussion." He tapped the side of the glass device again, causing it to glow aqua before he brought it back above the lump on my forehead. This time I felt a potent cooling sensation rapidly penetrating my skin. It felt like I had a huge ice pack draping over my entire cranium.

"Just a minute please," Urit assured me after I fidgeted when the coldness started to burn. He removed the device about forty-five seconds later. "Now, how does that feel?" he asked arrogantly.

I reached up and touched my head. The bump was completely gone. My head felt extremely cold. I gasped in amazement. "Better." I paused. "I mean, totally better," I replied in shock. I looked up at Gaelan by my side. He was smiling at me as if he was entertained by my response.

"Now, Samantha, your hand," instructed the medic coldly. The medic pulled out a penlike device from his pocket and pricked me in the finger.

"Ouch! You really cut to the chase!" I said. Urit was studying the reading on his pen and looked up at me with a face of confusion.

"No, there is no cut or *chase*," he replied defensively.

"Urit, it is just a saying. The people from Earth use them often," Gaelan explained.

"Don't you have sayings that that stand for something else? You know, metaphors?" I asked.

"No, we say *only* what we mean," Urit snapped back. Gaelan smirked at me, appearing amused by Urit's misunderstanding. I could tell that Gaelan must have spent more time on Earth than Urit had. Urit then got up and retrieved a three-inch cylinder from another table. This looked too much like a syringe. He pushed up my shirt sleeve without saying a word and hastily turned my arm while he held the device to a vein on my arm. Yes, it was a syringe all right, and the thing was going to my draw blood. I cringed and turned my head away to avoid watching.

"Go ahead, just get it over with," I conformed. I felt a prickling sensation. It was like my arm was being flicked with a rubber band. In seconds, it was over. "That's it?" I cried while I traced my arm, unable to locate the puncture hole. "Why didn't you tell me it was so easy?"

"I am not sure what you were expecting, so I didn't want to tell you the wrong thing," explained Urit. I heard a quiet beep. He turned the device and appeared to be reading the test results. "Hmm …you like to keep my job interesting, don't you, Gaelan?" he murmured.

"When can you have it ready?" inquired Gaelan in a serious tone.

"It's going to take at least three weeks—maybe more," Urit said. "Then, it will require another week to cool before I can safely inject it. Her DNA has limited exposure. She hardly has a trace of resistance built up," moaned Urit, sounding upset. "I will have to give her a dose of generic immunity for now." He seemed displeased with this option.

"Immunity? From *what?*" I shuddered. Gaelan looked at me kindly.

"We have to protect you from any organisms you may not have encountered on Earth, as well as any excessive cosmic and electromagnetic radiation you will encounter on our trip," explained Gaelan.

"Okay, give me whatever you can," I pleaded. My imagination soared. I pictured chickenpox for some reason. I always found anything that caused pus or skin lesions absolutely disgusting. I didn't even want to know what could happen to me out here. Ignorance was bliss. I was more than willing to do whatever was necessary to avoid getting sick with some bizarre alien virus.

Urit retrieved another device. "I can only give you a broad dose of immunity right now," he said through pursed lips. "I don't have enough time to tailor your personal vaccine since we are already underway. It won't fully protect you. I wish I'd had more notice. It's going to take me at least four weeks to get your vaccine to mature," he repeated sourly. "I will have to get started right away, as if I have nothing better to do," he mumbled under his breath. He tinkered with his electronic gadget before he looked me in the eyes with a vacant expression. "I will re-dose you as soon as it's ready. I must warn you—you might not feel quite like yourself for a bit. You may become gravely ill. Without the proper immunity, something that is completely benign to us may be lethal to you. The vaccine is absolutely vital for you to endure this trip," he said plainly. He scared me. He took notice of my widening eyes and nervously looked at me after he realized the bluntness of his remark. "Of course, everyone is different. You might be perfect," he said in a suddenly changed tone, probably to provide me artificial reassurance.

Urit quickly bolted across the room, opened what seemed like a cooler, and took out a handful of syringe devices. He came back to my side and laid the pile of cylinders on a nearby table. He grabbed my arm and turned it to eye up a new site. Before I could register his plan to inject me, he started shooting the syringes into the back of my arm with record speed. Snap! Snap! Snap! "Just a minute," he said when I attempted to pull my arm away from him because he was twisting it uncomfortably far. Snap! Snap! Snap! He continued injecting me, going through the entire stack. This approach to medicine was quite different from what I was used to. I guess informed consent wasn't something that was part of their regular routine. I rubbed the injection sites to assess for damages after the assault. My arm was sore to touch. I sat there stunned when I finally registered what he had said.

"*Four* weeks!" I blurted out. I became flustered. "What do you mean—four weeks? How far are we going? How long will we be gone?" I shouted.

"It will seem longer to us, but you will only miss a couple of days in your time," replied Gaelan in a soothing voice. "I will explain it to you later," he said, leaving no room for discussion. My mind began to race just contemplating the trip. Where in the world were we going? How fast were we traveling?

"Urit, you will also need to fit her with a language translator," he said like a demand rather than a request.

Urit shrugged. "I don't think that would be necessary, Gaelan. She will only be aboard for a short time."

"Yes, but Samantha will need to communicate with us," he argued.

"But mission protocol...." Urit gave him an angry glare. He seemed to be afraid of repercussions from his superiors.

"I assure you that it would be well within the guidelines. There would be no harm done," Gaelan said with a smile. "Samantha will frustrate everyone onboard if they can't communicate with her. Her understanding is crucial," he insisted. He spoke as though I was no longer present. I didn't mind his advocacy. A translator sounded good to me. I'd already had a taste of not understanding the Katarians. I would get extremely paranoid and wonder if the crew was talking about me if I couldn't understand them. I watched Urit while he paced impatiently around the room as he thought.

"She could become endangered if she could not understand the overhead announcements in an emergency," Gaelan stated boldly.

Urit crossed his arms. "Fine," he conceded. "Have it your way. You always did find a way to make the rules work for you. It's great to have you back aboard, old friend. Life is never dull when you're around," Urit said amiably. Gaelan grinned, knowing he had won the argument.

Urit opened a cabinet and removed some supplies. He emptied a white envelope of powder and poured it into a small silver bowl. He took out another syringe, squirted it into the bowl, and aspirated the contents before returning to my side.

"This will be hot," he warned. I looked at him with surprise. Had he already adjusted his bedside manner to what he thought I expected? I must say, these aliens were amazing when it came to noticing the small things. He parted my hair above my left ear to expose my scalp and injected a burning hot liquid into the roots of my hair. It felt like I was being scorched with a curling iron.

"*Ahh*," I screamed. "What is that stuff?"

"Please, Samantha—this will just take a minute," he reassured me. I looked over at Urit's hand. He lifted up what looked like a dime-sized metal battery. He took the object and pushed it firmly to the hot solution on my scalp while he cradled my head snuggly against his other arm. It hurt. I thought he was going to push it right through my skull. I felt smothered by his right hold but remained still in order to be a good patient. Although I was trying very hard to be brave, I felt a tear run down my cheek and winced in pain.

Gaelan ducked down under Urit's arms to see my face. "We're fitting you with a language translator, Samantha," explained Gaelan, trying to ease my distress. "It will train your brain to interpret our language. It's a bit uncomfortable, but you will only have to wear it for a week."

"Why will I need it for only a week?" I asked.

"Your brain will be done mapping the new pathways by then."

"How do I activate it?"

Gaelan looked at me curiously. "What do you mean? It is activated. You will be able to understand everyone aboard, even when we take it off. We use our *brains* to store new information, unlike your neural implants. There is no need to add any electronic hardware if you use the right neural interface. Your own brain has more than enough room. Your body is equipped with limitless inner intelligence. It has more cells than there are stars in the galaxy, all in perfect communication with one another," Gaelan explained.

"Wow, that's incredible … incredible and scary," I mused.

I saw Gaelan and Urit look at each other and smirk. I witnessed a glimpse of their vast comprehension of the world in their gaze. They seemed amused by our primitive ways. I was stunned by their advanced technology. I wondered how they governed their advancements.

Did they struggle with the conflicts of morality like we did? I remembered how I fought Jack when he wanted to let Leah and Jackson get learning systems implanted in their brains. I thought it was absolutely repulsive to mess with nature in that manner. I suddenly felt guilty, remembering my reluctance to give in. Here I was, having an alien language downloaded into my brain without *any* hesitation. I felt like such a hypocrite.

Urit released his grip and told me I was free to go. I stood up quickly before Gaelan could think of anything else I would need. I graciously thanked the medic and started walking towards the door. It opened before I could reach it, and to my surprise, in walked Noah! I couldn't believe my eyes! I wasn't alone. My lifelong friend came rushing through the door. I let out a sigh of relief.

"*Noah*," I beamed. "What are *you* doing here?" I asked eagerly.

Noah smiled and strode up to me. "I was already aboard—working in engineering, when the emergency evacuation took place. I just found out you were a stowaway, too."

I rushed to him and hugged him tightly. He put his arms around me and squeezed me back. My outlook on the trip suddenly improved. I knew someone on the ship! With Noah around, I felt far safer.

"I'm so glad that you're here." I clung on to his waist while verbalizing my relief.

"Me, too. Isn't this great?" His eyes lit up with excitement.

"It figures … you would be happy about this, wouldn't you?" I frowned.

"Sami, for someone so reluctant to travel into Space, I'm really surprised you've decided to go across the galaxy." He stood staring at me in disbelief.

I smacked his arm. "Thanks for the reality check," I muttered.

"Ouch," he flinched.

"I'm sure you heard it wasn't by choice," I said solemnly. Memories flashed in my head as I remembered all the conversations that Jack, Noah, and I had about how I would never leave the Earth. Boy, was I ever mistaken.

"I know, Sami. It's just funny that it's you of *all* people." He smirked as though he was suppressing laughter.

"Um, I know," I agreed. I looked at Gaelan and noticed he had a worried look on his face. I didn't want to make him feel guilty for bringing me aboard. He had been nothing but kind to me. "I guess I will just have to go with the flow," I said quickly. I plastered a fake smile on my face. It seemed to be somewhat convincing. I saw Gaelan's pursed lips relax.

CHAPTER 15

INDESCRIBABLE

Noah took the liberty of showing me all around the ship. He told me he'd been working closely with the Katarians and had their ship's blueprints memorized. Leave it to Noah to adapt so quickly. Gaelan had some work to attend to and planned to meet Noah and me in a few hours for dinner. I found out that the Katarians had been sharing their engineering technology with us for some time now, in order to aid in our advancement. Noah told me he had been practically living on board while he was stationed on the Outer Space resort. He said he felt so relieved to finally be able to confide in me since he wasn't allowed to mention a word of this when he was on Earth. He seemed to know everyone on board. I couldn't believe that all of this was taking place. It felt like a veil had been lifted from my eyes. The only information I was privy to was what the SIG had shared with us prior to our departure. I knew that we had contact with a friendly alien species and that they would be docking their Spaceship at the Space resort now and again. I found it challenging enough just keeping *that* news a secret.

The ship was much bigger than I'd imagined. It was difficult to grasp just how large it was. It had three different levels. Everything was connected by ramped corridors. Noah showed me hidden slides spread out along the corridor walls and from all of the departments. They were each marked with a tiny gold star that I never would have noticed on my own. They allowed for quick movement about the ship in case of an emergency. He said they were not well marked in order to provide the crew sanctuary in case the ship was invaded by enemies.

My favorite level was the ground floor. It contained all of the ship's recreation and resembled a food court at a mini-mall. It came complete with a gym, store, theater, sports club, café, and a circular park in the center with trees, grass, and a stream. Noah explained how the junglelike greenery produced fresh air for the ship. The ceiling above the park towered an amazing three stories in height. A waterfall equally high emptied into a pool below, which ran into a shallow stream. Its water trickled over round gray and beige stones, circling throughout the park. It functioned as a filter to clean and recycle water for reuse. The room was illuminated with a lighting system that mirrored artificial sunlight. The glistening white floors and walls surrounding the room were actually solar panels. Everything that was used had a built-in source of replenishment. I looked closer at the amazing mass of plants and noticed the Katarians were growing their own food, just like we had started doing on our Space retreat. Noah explained that the ground was slanted to collect the rainfall. My mouth fell open in disbelief when he told me how they made it rain on the little ecosystem.

Gaelan met us in the café for dinner. I had almost forgotten how attractive he was. He smiled at Noah and me as he walked towards us, accompanied by a beautiful woman.

"Well, Samantha—what do you think of our ship?" asked Gaelan.

"It's amazing. Your people seemed to have thought of everything. I had no idea it was so big. I really could get lost."

"I'm glad you like it," he beamed.

"Hi, Azil, have a seat," Noah greeted the woman at Gaelan's side.

"Samantha, this is my sister, Azil," Gaelan said. They each took a seat beside us.

"Hello, Azil. It's nice to meet you." I was deeply relieved to hear that she wasn't his wife or girlfriend. She was stunning as well. She had long brown hair, bright blue eyes, and a perfect body.

"Welcome aboard, Samantha. I will help you get whatever you need. I can only imagine how terrible it must be to travel without any preparation," she said graciously.

"*Thank you.* I'd really appreciate that." I certainly didn't want to wear the same clothes for the next few weeks. I only had my small handbag with me when I evacuated the station. It had a few essentials, but no clothing. It was almost comical how quickly all of my carefully orchestrated packing had become instantly irrelevant.

"Gaelan, I discovered that you had Sami fitted with a language translator. Why did you have to do that?" asked Noah.

"Noah, she needed it to function on board. I assure you that it was absolutely necessary," defended Gaelan.

"Yeah, but now we can't talk about her," teased Noah as he kneed me under the table.

I kicked him back. "Thanks a lot, Noah. Some friend you are." We sneered at one another. Gaelan and Azil laughed at our childish squabble. The night flew by. We talked about how well SIG downplayed their relationship with the Katarians. I admitted that I had no idea that Gaelan and some of the other engineers working at SIG were actually from Kataria. He didn't confess anything to me that day we met in engineering. Their secrecy was so well-guarded that I was still in shock. How could they be aliens? They looked just like everybody else. I must say, I agreed with SIG in keeping the Katarians anonymity while they worked on Earth. It was probably the only way to protect them and gain their trust. I could only imagine how bad the paparazzi would hound them if they were aware of their presence on Earth. The public might have panicked. The Katarians would be at risk for being harmed. It was so much easier to work in peace and avoid any undue mayhem.

It was getting late, and Noah said he was retiring for the night. I was hoping that I could share a room with him, until he told me he had a suite with three other men from engineering. Azil wasn't a viable option either. She shared her room with her husband, Zaric. I felt uncomfortable walking to Gaelan's room—feeling like I would be a major imposition. We entered his room and, to my surprise, it resembled an efficiency apartment. A queen-sized bed lying low to the ground dominated the center floor. Behind it sat a wall of shiny white cabinet doors, functioning dually as a headboard. To the right, there was a white wooden desk and chair facing the entrance of the room. There was a bathroom off the left side and a doorway straight ahead, opening into a study. I walked around, checking out the place, and entered the study. Gaelan followed. The room had a long, velvety brown sofa, one matching chair, and calming tiny spotlights that indirectly lit up the room. The sofa faced outward to an entire wall of curved glass windows that started three feet from the floor and continued to the ceiling. I looked out through the glass but could only see my reflection against the black sky. I turned to watch Gaelan while he reached back and dimmed the lights in the room.

"I want to show you something," he said smugly after he turned off the lights. "Look," he murmured. He laid his hands on my shoulders and turned me around to face the wall of glass.

"*Oh*," I gasped. "It's phenomenal!" The blackened window was suddenly aglow with colorful clusters of stars and nebulae. "I can't believe all this is out here, just lighting up the sky." I was at a loss for words. I gazed out at what looked like millions of bright, colorful lights. It was the first time I wondered how fast we were moving. I couldn't feel any movement, but it was clear that the stars were slowly gliding past the window.

"You look stunned."

I shrugged. "No, I was just thinking."

"About what? How far you are from home? How you wished I never brought you aboard?" he said, grinning.

"Yes—I mean, no," I stammered. *Was that a trick question?* "Actually, I was wondering how fast we were going. Are we traveling at the speed of light or faster?"

"No, we are actually traveling very slow right now. We are preparing for maximum acceleration. After we gather up enough energy for the surge propulsion, we have to activate it. We are still processing the harvested fuel. It takes time to remove the impurities."

"What do you mean, gather up energy? You don't mean you *use* energy from the surrounding universe? Do you?" The concept was something we had been researching for years. We could really learn a lot from the Katarians.

"It's hard to explain, but it's the most efficient way. Actually, it's the *only* way we've been able to cover vast distances. We collect our fuel. Otherwise, we would be too heavy, blow ourselves up, or run out of fuel before we got home."

"How does it work?"

"The universe is full of fuel-floating interstellar clouds. They are plentiful and could supply all of our energy needs for billions of years. The deposits occur randomly throughout Space."

"I've heard of them. You're talking about pockets of ethyl alcohol."

"Yes, precisely," he said, sounding surprised that I'd heard of them. "We also collect hydrogen for our fusion reactor as well."

"Free fuel ... *ingenious*," I said—completely enthralled by their discovery in being able to harvest it.

"Yes, all we have to do is collect it, filter out the contaminants, and heat the particles until they vibrate at high speeds for our jet propulsion. Does that make sense?"

"I suppose so, but I still don't understand how you can travel so far."

"We shorten the trip. We take shortcuts," he said smoothly. He gently brushed my hair away from my face. I jumped slightly by his soft gesture.

"You take a shortcut, sure. Why not? Sounds easy enough." I bit my lip. I knew I was about to become completely lost. I'd never felt so technologically inferior in my life.

"We cast a navigating beam to our desired location. It gathers up the surrounding space like a drawstring before it propels us to the end of our mark. Imagine folding up a sheet of paper; you sort of jump over to the other side before you release it. Therefore, you can skip all the space in between. Then the whole process repeats just like a surfer gliding over to the next wave."

"You mean you bring the universe closer to you rather than trying to go straight across it."

"Exactly," he said, turning up the corners of his lips.

Their advancement was astounding. I wanted to know everything.

"How don't you crash into anything?"

"We can only pull on empty space, those devoid of strong gravitational pull." He paused. "We also carefully draft our route. Our every move is perfectly calculated before it is executed."

"Remarkable."

"Then we also travel through port keys whenever possible."

"Tunnels to the other side," I surmised.

"Yes." He stared at me intently trying to assess my reaction to his explanation.

"That's … *that's* phenomenal." I tried to process the endless possibilities. I pictured climbing through a hole in a wall and entering into another room on the other side.

"I couldn't agree more."

"Where exactly is Kataria?"

"Well, look out right over there. Our solar systems are right across from each other," he said. He rotated my body to the left and pointed to a distant area of Space. "We live just beyond those stars."

"You mean to tell me Kataria is in the Milky Way Galaxy?" I asked with surprise.

"Yes, we are polar opposites," he explained. I knew the Milky Way had over a few hundred billion stars, with over six billion of them having the possibility of containing a planetary system similar to ours. Seeing Space travel through his eyes was thought provoking. I couldn't believe our worlds had been coexisting almost within reach of each other all this time.

"Oh—I can't believe I'm just standing here," I yelled. I bolted into the front room and grabbed my handbag that I had left on the bed in order to retrieve my camera. Without delay, I rushed back into the study and started taking photos of the breathtaking scene.

"What's your rush?" Gaelan laughed.

"Are you kidding me? I have to get some pictures of this." I aimed my camera randomly at the window and started clicking away. "Here, take my picture with this in the background. I have to get some proof that I was actually here." I put the tiny camera in Gaelan's hand and instructed him to press the button as he looked through the holographic viewfinder. He took at least ten pictures before I motioned for him to stop. I saw him smile. He seemed to be enjoying it. "This isn't a fashion shoot," I warned.

"You are more impressed with the view than I thought you would be. I would have shown you this earlier if I knew you would get *this* excited," he mused.

"I guess when you see it all the time, it must seem trivial," I said sarcastically. I took the camera back and took a few pictures of him to retaliate. He laughed at my harmless weapon.

"No, Samantha … I mean, Sami." He rectified himself after spending the evening with Noah. "I love it. I could stare out at the view for hours and never grow bored. That's one of the reasons I travel."

"I can understand why. It's so beautiful! I never imagined it would be so pretty."

"You know, you are quite beautiful, as well. You look amazing," he said. I wasn't even aware that he was looking at me. I looked up at him. His gentle eyes went through me. His lips turned up with a subdued smile. I let out a breathy gasp as I took in his perfect physical features. I was taken aback by how his skin glowed in the pink and golden light of the illuminating stars.

"Thanks," I muttered. Was he coming onto me? I had no idea how to respond. Clearly, I wasn't the only one who felt our instant connection. And yet our relationship was completely undefined. Was he a friend, a travel companion, or a potential lover? "You're very striking, too," I added casually.

He smirked at my response. I turned to look back out the window. We both stood in silence. I was suddenly uncomfortable. It was hard to suppress my attraction for Gaelan. Although his body left no room for improvement, he appealed to one of my greatest weaknesses—my love for inner strength and intellect. For me, deep sexual attraction always started with the mind. He possessed the ability to render me completely defenseless. I hadn't considered being in a relationship since I lost Jack. How could I allow myself to be so drawn to him?

"There is so much I could show you. Things you never would have believed existed," he said with excitement in his voice.

"No doubt … I can imagine that you've traveled a lot."

"I never miss a voyage."

"*Never?*" I asked with disbelief.

"No, it's what I live for."

"I can't believe how different we are," I mused. I continued studying the bright stars out our window.

His posture stiffened. "*Different?* Are you serious? Sami, our people couldn't be anymore alike," he said defensively.

"What I meant to say was that I've been living a sheltered life in my own little part of the universe while you're out here sailing around," I tried to explain myself. I didn't mean to insult him.

"That may be so, but it doesn't make you unlike me," he said, leaving no room for an argument. He seemed offended by my comment. I looked over at him, and our eyes met. He stared back at me intently with his gorgeous eyes. I sighed. I wondered if he noticed how he affected me.

"So, besides a room with a view, what are the other reasons that you travel across the galaxy?" I said, trying to distract myself from wanting to kiss him.

"*Freedom,*" he said with fervor. "Our planet has become so regimented, I feel like I am being smothered. The ship gives me a break from it. Plus, I like being able to explore new worlds. Traveling forces me to remember that the universe is only limited by our discoveries. Sooner or later, you uncover a path that opens a door and, with it, a whole new set of possibilities."

I struggled to grasp the challenge of exploring the infinite cosmos. The unknowns were endless. I felt incredibly small. How could he be so bold? "Aren't you afraid of what you might find?"

"Sure." He laughed. "But it's all worth it. We have encountered both good and the bad, but we exceeded all of our expectations when we found you. Discovering your people is indescribable. Humans … just like us. I still can't believe you exist. The union of our minds and sharing of ideas will only strengthen us both."

"But, you are light years ahead of us."

"Only in some ways," he said softly. "Your people possess many qualities we admire." I wondered what he was referring to.

"Do you have family at home or is it just you and Azil?"

"Sure." He paused to sit down on the study's long sofa and motioned for me to join him. "My parents, my brother and his family, and Azil and Zaric's children are at home."

"I presume you don't like them very much."

"*Why?* What makes you say that?" he asked, sounding confused.

"You're never home."

"Oh, no—it's not like that. We are *really* close."

"Don't you miss them?"

"Yes, of course I miss them, but we are secure in our feelings for each other."

"Do they ever come with you?"

"Well, Azil and Zaric's kids have come with us, twice. But my parents won't travel anymore, and my brother and his wife would never leave Kataria."

"What do you mean your parents won't travel anymore? Are they too old?"

"No." He shook his head. "It is not that. They stopped traveling after Azil's parents died," Gaelan said in a distressed voice. "They were too afraid to leave Kataria after that."

"Azil … *your sister*, Azil?" I asked, puzzled.

"I'm sorry, I'm confusing you. Azil is adopted. We have been a family for so long that I tend to forget where she came from." He laughed. "Her parents and mine were best friends." His serious tone returned. "They were killed on a Space mission, so she joined our family when she was twelve. My parents would have been aboard as well if it wasn't for my little brother. We were all at camp. The ship's expedition was short, planned to take one week's time. It was scheduled to return home prior to the science camp award ceremony. My parents were informed that my brother was a major contender for winning the highest honor award, so they stayed home at the last minute to help the little genius work on his presentation. He invented a way to accelerate the growth of food when he was only eleven. You know, just one of the life-changing discoveries he would go on to invent," he mocked.

"How were Azil's parents killed?"

"The ship was traveling through a port key when it collapsed on them," he said solemnly. "We were still in the early phases of learning how to stabilize the opening. None of us really understood how the port holes worked. We failed to consider all the possible variables that could alter its stability. I think the first few times we used them, the ships only returned by sheer dumb luck. Our society was becoming arrogant by our accomplishments. We thought we had successfully managed to create a port key to travel through the universe with no repercussions. It was a painful awakening to be so brutally humbled. We suffered such a great loss because of our blatant ignorance," he said regretfully.

I laid my hand on his shoulder to comfort him. "I'm so sorry for your loss." I knew all to well what it was like to lose someone in the name of progress. His saddened eyes filled with gratitude as I expressed my empathy.

"It was a long time ago. It was bound to happen. Call it a casualty of advancement, if you will."

"You and Azil seem really close. I can't believe you're not biological siblings."

"Thank you. I know what you mean. We are a lot alike. I am grateful to have her. My brother can be quite annoying at times, and Azil has made growing up in my family much more tolerable. We tease each other that neither one of us can die. Otherwise, we would only be left with Liam."

"Shame on you ... poor Liam," I scolded.

He raised his eyebrows. "You don't know Liam. He is a genius. *Obnoxious.*" He shook his head and frowned. "He has amazing observation skills. He notices things the rest of us tend to overlook. No—it is more than that. He sees the world in a unique way. I can't wait to introduce you. Maybe then you'll understand."

"Great, I'm so looking forward to it." I thought I saw him jump when he realized that I was still touching him. He leaned back, let my hand slide off his shoulder, and sighed. I thought my touching him made him uncomfortable.

"You can sleep in the bed. I'll sleep in here. Just make yourself at home. I can't be here to wait on you. I take a shift for nine hours every day."

"Please, Gaelan, I am more than happy to sleep in here. I don't want you to give up your bed," I said. I felt guilty enough intruding on his quarters.

"If you prefer," he hesitated.

"Yes, absolutely." I smiled. This seemed like the better room anyway. Gaelan was gracious and let me use the bathroom before him. He seemed determined to make me feel at home. I wished him good night as I slid the pocket door shut behind me after entering the study. I found what looked like a nightgown, a pile of Katarian clothes, cosmetics, blankets, and a pillow on the small brown chair. I thought I had heard Azil's voice while I was washing up in the bathroom. I imagined that she was responsible for delivering the goods. It was such a relief to get comfortable and slip into the silky gown. I usually changed out of my work clothes as soon as I stepped through my front door. I snuggled up on the sofa with a blanket and took out my camera. The gadget also functioned as a music player and phone. Well, two uses out of three weren't bad. I was happy to have at least some comforts of home in my possession. I viewed the pictures I took of Leah and Jackson at the Space re-sort. I wished I could be with them right now. I missed them already. I reviewed the photos I took today while I toured the ship with Noah. I had to laugh at the ones he managed to sneak into. He had the dippiest looks on his face just to taunt me while he destroyed my perfect shots. What a pain! Couldn't he ever be serious?

I finally scrolled through to the photos I took in the study. I flipped quickly to get to the ones I took of Gaelan. I dwelled on each picture of him and studied his face. He was gorgeous. It figured a man like him was from another planet. I wondered what it would be like to kiss him. I sighed as I fantasized about his lips touching mine while I traced the photo with my finger. I went back and looked at the photos of the stars. Wait a minute! What the *hell* was that? I noticed something I didn't see earlier. I sat straight up on the sofa—suddenly terrified. The picture caught a reflection off the glass window. It looked like a pair of glowing green eyes. It was on the right side of the picture, exactly where Gaelan had been standing. Was it Gaelan's eyes? I shivered as a chill ran up my spine. How much did I really know about the Katarians? Why did they look so much like us? Were they some kind of machine trying to infiltrate our planet? What was he? I remembered how hard his body felt when I touched him. I thought about the huge bump I got on my head when I collided with him earlier. He felt like a brick wall. I wanted to sneak into his room and check for a pulse.

I closed my camera and tried to put the image out of my mind. I tucked the covers in tightly around me for protection. I didn't want to know, I told myself. I remembered SIG's motto of how some information was on a need-to-know basis. Maybe they were machines. Who cares? There was nothing I could do about it. There was nowhere to run, nowhere to hide. I was trapped on an alien starship whether I liked it or not. I was at their mercy. I fell asleep shortly after trying to come to terms with the finding. I didn't sleep for long.

"Stop, no, stop," I said, sitting up in a strangled cry as I batted the covers away with my hands. I found myself awake in the middle of the night after having a nightmare. I was covered in sweat. I had dreamt that Tyden, the stern man from the flight deck, was reaching out to grab my neck to strangle me. Tyden's edgy demeanor scared me. I didn't think he liked me. Plus, I guess I was more freaked out about the eyes and being stuck on board than my subconscious could ignore. I needed to calm myself. I tried to focus on their hospitality—on my attraction to Gaelan, on Azil's pretty face, on Noah's immaturity. I still couldn't fall back to sleep.

CHAPTER 16

FOREIGN

In the morning, I got off the sofa and found that Gaelan had already gone. I decided to ignore the picture of the green glowing eyes. It felt nice to have some alone time. I figured I would give the bizarre shower a try. Gaelan had quickly explained how to operate it last night. I carefully hung my clothes on the hook inside the shower like he had instructed. They would be laundered at the same time. I stepped into the little stall and closed the door. I remembered how he told me to stand still when I pressed each of the three buttons. Everything was foreign. I wondered how mad he'd get if I broke the ship. But how hard could it be? I nervously tapped the first button.

My body was instantly blasted with hot, high pressured water in every direction. "*Ahh*," I screamed. I clumsily bounced back against the wall of the tiny stall and fought to maintain my balance so I wouldn't fall.

It felt like I was hit by a tidal wave. I took a deep breath when the tsunami finally stopped. I felt the walls to search for the shower's jets, but was unable to find where the water had sprayed from. To my surprise, I discovered I wasn't just wet, but covered head to toe in white sudsy bubbles. I let out a laugh. My kids would have loved this when they were little. I bravely hit the second button and was instantly shot with another powerful burst of hot water. This time I held on to the sides of the stall. Okay, that must have been the rinse. I stood there dripping wet like a drowned rat. What's left? I closed my eyes and braced myself as I hit the third button. *Oh, good.* To my relief, I was being blown dry with warm air. I had to hand it to the Katarians. They really had thought of everything. How economical—practical, and most important, what a wonderful way to eliminate laundry.

I put on the Katarian clothes and wandered out of Gaelan's quarters in hopes of finding Noah. Noah had invited me to join him in engineering last night. I looked for familiar landmarks to guide me through the dimly lit corridors. I knocked at the closed door where he told me to meet him. No one answered. Finally, I opened the door and entered a large room that looked like the power center for the ship. It reminded me of an engine room of a cruise ship. There were metal beams that extended to the ceiling and pipes that formed a maze through the entire room. I could also hear a low humming noise as the machinery surrounding me operated. There were a couple of people walking around. No one stopped to give me a second look. I grasped the fabric of my outfit at the sides of my thighs, feeling grateful for the inconspicuous clothing.

I had to ask a young lady nearby if she had seen Noah. She looked at me and smiled. "Noah, you have *company*," she shouted in a cutesy voice.

"Sami, you found me," he teased as he walked out from behind a large metal pillar. "She's just a friend, Karis," Noah said to the young girl while he walked over to greet me.

"Aren't they all, Noah?" she said with a smirk.

I shook my head. Ever since I knew him, Noah liked to date a lot of women but always avoided true intimacy. I imagined that the Katarian women were probably his latest targets. Clearly, being in Space hadn't changed him. Most women found him irresistible. I had to admit, Noah was incredibly charming and good-looking. He knew it, too. He should have come with a warning label. Noah purposely ignored her and led me to the back of the room—where a group of men fiddled around with tools on some of the pipes. The pipes hissed and released steam when they released the accumulated pressure from the pipeline. Every wall was adorned with digital control panels displaying the complexity of the starship.

I spent the day listening to the crew explaining their mind-boggling technology. At first, I listened enthusiastically but soon became lost when they described their breakthroughs in interstellar travel and jet propulsion. For some unexplained reason, I was experiencing difficulty maintaining my normal level of concentration. I might as well have thrown my education right out the window. Now I understood what Jim Walker had meant when he said they were having trouble understanding them. I'd never felt so intellectually inferior. I was completely out of my league here. They had things that we never even considered inventing yet. It became all too apparent at how primitive we were by comparison. After a while, I became saturated and started to tune out. I needed a calculator, a notebook, a tutor, or maybe just a brain transplant. Mostly, I needed time to assimilate everything.

I caught myself daydreaming and watching the young girl, Karis, prance about the room. She was hard to miss. I was getting tired just watching her continuous movement. I wondered if all the Katarian women were attractive. She was openly flirting with Noah and starting to get on my nerves. If she leaned down between Noah and I one more time, I would be tempted to pull her long hair when it hit my arm. Undoubtedly, she had fallen under his spell.

"Will you stop it?" I whispered. I elbowed Noah's arm when I saw him checking her out. Karis was petite and looked like she was about Leah's age.

"What? Pay attention," Noah scolded me and then smiled an ornery grin. We both returned our attention to listen to the engineer talking.

Within seconds, his eyes went back to staring at her. Lord only knew what he was thinking. *"Be good,"* I said under my breath. I studied Noah's face. He was in his glory. He looked ecstatic to talk to the Katarians about their technology and have the attention of the beautiful blonde.

He nudged my arm, prodding me to leave him alone. "I am being good. I'm *always* good," Noah said loud enough for Karis to hear. She smiled back at him. I took a deep breath and returned my focus to our discussion. I fought to listen intently while they explained how important it was to maintain everything in perfect running condition. The ship was a self-contained ecosystem. Everything was interconnected and could threaten another area if it was out of balance. I found comfort in their astonishing advancements. It helped me gain confidence in their ability to get me back home safely.

I hadn't realized how quickly the day had went until Noah told me it was time to go to dinner. I stood up to leave. Without warning, my blood rushed to my head, and I became dizzy. I had to hold onto the chair to steady myself. What in the world was *that*? The room's lights fluttered before my eyes as they morphed into floating, iridescent balls of light. I looked down at the floor to discover it also appeared to be moving in circles. Noah reached out to grab my arm to keep me from falling.

"Sami—are you okay?" he said urgently.

"I just got a little dizzy. Maybe I'm just hungry."

"The EMFs are probably too much for her," informed Karis arrogantly. I knew all to well what she had meant. Electromagnetic fields, or radiation, are caused by electrical currents, which are either man-made or from natural sources. At high doses, they're believed to have disruptive side-effects. "Your body isn't able to spend that much time in here," she said, flashing a big smile. It seemed as though this pleased her. Noah looked disappointed.

"Let's get you out of here and go eat." Noah escorted me out of the room after he gave Karis a second head-to-toe look. "Sami, I'm sorry. I didn't mean to make you sick. I just couldn't wait to show you how everything on the ship works. I knew you'd appreciate it more than anyone," he explained.

"Thanks, Noah. I'll be fine, but I don't think I want to come back again tomorrow. I've had enough after today." I developed a terrible headache radiating from behind my eyes.

"No problem. You're new to the ship. It would be safer if you waited until you had the full vaccine in you," he agreed.

"What about you? Don't you feel funny?" I asked suspiciously since Noah appeared to be unaffected.

"I'm fine. I think it's because I've had a lot more time to adjust to Outer Space living," he pointed out. I nodded in agreement.

"Noah," I said, once outside the door, "what's with you and Karis? You may look young, but she could be your daughter, you know?"

"At the very least," he muttered in a barely audible voice.

"What?"

"Sami, the way I look at it, age means nothing. You're either here or you're not. Anyway, she's hot and you know it. She's probably flexible, too. *Oh*, I bet I know just what she'd like. Yep, I would bend her and then I would … oh yeah," he said rubbing his mouth as he thought.

I plugged my ears. "Please, I don't want to know."

He smirked. "What about *you*? How was your night bunking with Gaelan?" he asked with an ornery grin.

"No-ah, as if." I acted insulted.

He laid his hand on my back and frowned. "Oh, darn, you could use some action."

"Well, unlike you, I have morals," I snapped back.

"Yeah, you do. What *a* shame."

"Hey, don't turn this on me. We were talking about you and Karis."

"You know I don't torture myself with all your crazy rules. If she's open, I'm willing. I'm not afraid to live and enjoy what life has to offer. You should try it sometime. Stop being so strict with yourself and have some fun."

I just bit my lip. I couldn't even respond. He was right. I liked seeing myself as being open for almost anything, but in truth, I was not. I had strong boundaries set for myself—made-up rules of what I could and couldn't do. I tended to be overly cautious and would live a mundane existence if it weren't for the persuasive influence of others around me. Remarkably, I had always managed to surround myself with such people. However, I think I buried all of my spontaneity two years ago, along with Jack. I turned and starting walking through the hall with Noah.

"Noah, have you noticed anything strange about the Katarians?" I asked, keeping my tone casual. I didn't want to tell him about the photo of the green eyes. I wanted to have more proof before I drew any wrong conclusions. I hated embarrassing myself in front of him. He'd never let me live it down.

"No, Sami." He laughed. "You know they're from another planet, so there are bound to be some differences. I am actually quite amazed at how much they are just like us." He seemed amused by my concern but revealed none of his own.

"Yeah, I know, you're right. I think I'm just a little freaked out about being here." The image of being on a Katarian Spaceship sailing across the universe flooded into my mind. The ship must look like a torpedo shooting across the dark sky. My imagination was spinning out of control. My leaving Earth was one thing, but this was just plain absurd. I didn't even know for sure that it was possible to travel such a mind-boggling distance. Not in my lifetime, anyway. Moreover, I had never planned on trying it. "Noah, why did I agree to go into Space in the first place? Why is my family so thirsty for adventure? Maybe I should have married a boring man. Leah and Jackson are just like Jack. I wish I would have just waited for them at home. I'm not brave enough for this." I grabbed Noah's arm for support.

"Sami, don't ever say that. I have never met anyone more determined than you. You *are* strong and braver than you realize. You can do anything. I think you're doing remarkably well, considering where we are right now," he assured me. Perhaps he was right. It almost seemed as though I'd been preparing for something like this all my life. My life with Jack had groomed me to survive such an adventure.

"Sure. And where *exactly* is that, anyway? Lost doesn't even begin to explain it."

"Trust the Katarians. They know what they're doing. We're going to be fine."

"Huh," I sighed, "like that's so easy. How do you stay so calm?" I studied his composed expression with disbelief.

"Sami, I think being aboard this ship is the coolest thing ever. I love it."

"You would." I almost forgot who I was talking to.

Noah and I walked to the café while I compensated for my extreme dizziness. I felt like I was drunk and trying to hide my intoxication. When we got there, we saw Gaelan and Azil already sitting at a table. Azil's husband, Zaric, also joined us. Zaric was an attractive man and looked like a nice match for Azil. They would finish each other's sentences and seemed deeply connected. I remembered how wonderful it was to have such closeness when I was married to Jack. I was happy to see them enjoying each other. Their joy was contagious. You could tell that they truly loved one another.

As the evening went on, I noticed subtle changes in the way the Katarians spoke to me. The more time I spent with them, the more they seemed like they were from Earth. They seemed to be adjusting their mannerisms and speech patterns to match mine. How did they possess the ability to adapt to their surroundings so effortlessly? Was this something they learned from traveling the universe? It was both comforting and disturbing.

Gaelan and I returned to our room after dinner. I still felt a lingering wave of wooziness when I moved.

I thought he noticed my sway when I walked into the study. Gaelan told me that we were on course for a quick trip. We had to make one stop in the Torra Galaxy for some supplies before we went back to Kataria. He said it was on the way. He told me that he would be working an early shift tomorrow and needed to get some sleep.

"Where do you work?" I asked curiously, when he was turning away to prepare for bed.

"I am working on the flight deck tomorrow. It's one of my favorite places. I help navigate the ship. We are constantly altering our course to take the shortest path. Today, I was essentially an electrician with little to do. I went around the ship and repaired two lights. Everything was up and running. Mundane," he said and rolled his eyes.

"You mean you have different jobs?"

"Yes, we all rotate duties in areas of our choice. It helps to keep the boredom down, and it is safer just in case …" He cut himself off and darted his eyes to my face to see if I had caught the last part.

"In case," I said, sounding slightly exacerbated out of fear, "*of what?*"

"Well, in the event that something would incapacitate some of the crew, we all need to know how to carry out several duties to keep things up and running." He raised his eyebrows and winced like he wanted to avoid answering the question.

"*Did* something ever incapacitate the crew?" I shuddered at all of the numerous scenarios my imagination quickly devised.

"Actually, yes." He paused for a moment. He seemed to be choosing his words carefully before he spoke. "We ran into a problem when some of our crew members were abducted and those who remained on board couldn't operate the ship correctly and crashed on the landing."

"*Abducted*, by whom?" I swallowed. I didn't want to consider the possibility that the ship could be boarded by enemies or its crew be taken hostage.

"Dreons. They are universe bullies. *Bugs* ... they have creepy black bug eyes." His eyes narrowed. My whole body stiffened.

"Dreons? Are they really bugs?" I pictured a monstrous insect.

His eyes shot me a dark glance. "No, just as annoying, though."

"What do they look like?"

"They're sort of human, sort of not. Some more buglike than others. Don't worry—we formed a truce with them years ago. They leave us alone for the most part."

"What happened to the crew on the ship?"

"The people they took were returned home after a few weeks, once they did their experiments on them," he hissed. "The ones who remained on board were killed on impact. None of them knew how to pilot the ship."

Gaelan stared across the room with a mortified expression across his face.

"I am starting to see that your planet's experience of Space travel has been no bed of roses. I can't even imagine what you've learned."

"A bed of roses?" He looked at me, confused.

"I mean, it doesn't sound fun. It sounds like you suffered some terrible tragedies. It must have been difficult to bear such a loss."

He looked at me wistfully. "Thank you, Samantha—I mean, Sami. I can tell you feel real compassion when you speak. You're a kind soul." He touched my hand before he told me good night and slowly exited the room.

CHAPTER 17

FIERY

The days went by much more slowly now that I could no longer spend the day with Noah in engineering. Azil let me tag along with her when she had free time. I went to exercise with her every day. Aside from using the general exercise equipment you would find at any gym, we attended the simulated outdoor exercise classes. The indoor park had rope climbing and zip lining challenges set up every morning. It looked fun. I decided to suppress my *moderate* fear of heights and give it a try. Why not? I could be more adventurous. *At this point, I'd do anything to keep myself entertained.* Despite the size of the ship, I was getting restless. It was time to take Noah's advice and break every rule I ever set for myself. Azil taught me how to maneuver through the course. I could see why her body was in great shape. She moved with such dexterity and flexibility. I was grateful for her enduring patience with me as she literally showed me the ropes.

Azil and I had quickly become great friends. What wasn't to like? Her cheerfulness and feisty wit were contagious. She could land a job as a personal motivator on Earth. I really enjoyed her company. She gave off such a calming vibe. She told me stories about her children. I asked her how old she was, and she told me she couldn't explain it in Earth terms. I guessed that she was probably my age, in her early forties, but looked amazingly young. Everyone on board was impeccably groomed and seemed to be in the prime of their life.

I looked forward to the daily exercise challenge. Unfortunately, I had to forgo the course one week later, right after I was getting good. I started experiencing spells of vertigo, headaches, and blurred vision throughout each day. It seemed to be getting worse. Sometimes, the dizziness would continue even when I was lying perfectly still. Urit assured me it was to be expected and that my vaccine would be ready soon. He gave me a daily shot for analgesia to keep the migraine headaches under control. It was only slightly effective. The throbbing behind my eyes seemed to linger regardless. I was surprised that Noah seemed totally unaffected. He had no problem waiting for his vaccine. I guessed everyone's tolerance *was* different. Of course, Noah was always a little super-human. I remembered how Jack bragged about him after the two of them would go rock climbing. It was the one thing Jack could never talk me into. Noah happily took my place. Jack was convinced that Noah was part monkey. He was always so impressed by his natural athleticism.

My impatience with being on board the ship grew worse with each passing day. I think I was suffering from cabin fever. I missed work and felt useless—trapped. I had always been terrible at sitting still. I couldn't tag along with Noah because my symptoms worsened any time I even got close to the engineering department. Normally, this would bother me more. Right now, I didn't care. My concentration was gone. I couldn't focus on what the Katarians were saying, anyway. I just had to get through the day. I couldn't stop thinking about home. It was amazing how many things I'd taken for granted. I realized that my life at home had been a virtual playground. I had an endless supply of choices of how I could spend my time. I felt so grateful for the charmed existence I had been living. It was irrelevant now. I wanted off the ship—*badly*. The never-ending confinement and inability to leave at will had become too much to bear. How could such a large ship make me feel so encaged? I wondered if anybody would mind if I slid down the emergency slides for fun.

I looked forward to Gaelan completing his shift each day. We stayed up late every evening talking—comparing stories about our different worlds. We both seemed interested in finding out everything we could about one another. It was great getting to know him better. At times, our conversation drifted into such a serious discussion that it seemed as though we were collecting data for a scientific research study. Although Gaelan was extremely hospitable, physically, he maintained his distance from me. Feeling as bad as I did, I didn't really mind. I was just happy to have his company. Looking at his gorgeous face would have to be enough. I imagined what it would be like to kiss his perfect lips. I loved how the corners of his eyes turned up when he smiled. Was he even aware of how I studied his every inch and hung on his every word?

I always sat at one end of the study's sofa, while he sat on the opposite. His body tensed up if I would accidently get too close to him, so I tried not to touch him. I found it odd that he actually never moved away—yet seemed relieved if I did. His signals were confusing, and his face gave away nothing. He acted desperate to spend time with me but appeared to maintain his distance at the same time. I couldn't tell if my being there made him uncomfortable or if he only wanted to be friends. Maybe he was starting to regret bringing me aboard. I hoped I hadn't said something that offended him. I tried my best not to be a burden.

Gaelan took me to watch a movie in their theater. When the film started, it was spectacular. The visual and auditory effects were flawless. It felt like you were actually on location with the holographic characters. Unfortunately, the realism became overwhelming. I became nauseated and had to leave in a hurry. I hadn't been that sick since I was pregnant with the twins. The cinema was now considered completely off limits.

Gaelan seemed to feel guilty for my failing health. His mood would darken instantly if I would so much as let out a whimper. My disastrous display of projectile vomiting after the cinema left him brooding for hours. I tried to appease his worry by not complaining. Urit graciously added anti-nausea medication to my daily regimen. Stopping in to see him became one of the highlights of my day as I grew undeniably bored. I had to find other entertainment. If only I had kept my computer in my handbag instead of leaving it in my room at the Space resort. That way, I would've had plenty to entertain myself with. I desperately wanted something to read. The language translator Urit implanted only worked on spoken words. The only words I recognized were the names on the signs I passed throughout the ship. I had to accept the fact that I was on foreign ground. I think this was probably the first time in my life I had no choice but to relinquish all control. Despite it, I maintained my belief that I was in capable hands and my torment would be short-lived.

Gaelan noticed my growing restlessness and arranged for me to volunteer in the café. It was much harder than I expected. Aside from beans, rice, and flour, I didn't recognize most of the ingredients. The cooks moved at great speed and timed everything with absolute precision. I couldn't read the recipes. I tried my hardest to keep up with the orders from the head chef. I could tell he was growing impatient with my need to have everything repeated. I licked the seasonings with my finger when no one was looking in hopes of identifying them so I could refrain from asking so many stupid questions. All that I could identify was cinnamon—*extremely* hot pepper flakes—possibly sugar—salt, maybe salt, could be salt—lemon and *grass?*

Hayden, a kind, sweet woman, was my only friend in the café. She also worked with Urit from time to time in the ship's hospital. She was a trained surgeon and usually had very little to do, so she spent her time cooking in the café. She moved at the same inhuman speed as Urit. I had never seen anyone so quick with a knife. Her moves rendered me speechless. Her ability to multi-task corrected all of my blunders. She would zip in out of nowhere and take something right out of my hand before I had the chance to destroy the food. The shifts were only four hours.

Although this was a relief, it left me without anything to do but wallow in my symptoms as they worsened.

I hadn't realized how sick I had become until the gravity of my illness struck me several days later. The day started out bad. I awoke with a grating headache and felt exhausted and weak. My hair seemed to be shedding at an alarming rate, as well. Thank goodness I had a lot to spare. I crawled back in bed only to be awakened by Noah pounding on the door telling me it was time to go to lunch. I was trying to be a good sport so I got up and got ready. While I walked to cafe with Noah, I suddenly lost my balance when something popped like a firecracker in my head. It was followed by a loud, roaring sound that echoed as if a plane was taking off overhead. A terribly sharp, stabbing pain surged out through both of my ears. The lights went black and I faded ….

"Sami. *Damn it, Sami* … come back to me." I heard Noah's faint voice calling out my name through my wavering consciousness as I lay helplessly on the floor. I tried but couldn't answer him.

I awoke to find myself lying in one of the windowed cubicle beds stationed in the medic's office. Noah was on the other side of the glass, talking to Urit. He looked like a concerned parent in an emergency room. They looked over at me when they noticed I was awake and came to my bedside.

"Sami, you scared me back there. Jeez, I thought you checked *out.*" Noah frowned.

Urit glared at him, showing his disapproval in Noah's choice of words. "Samantha, how do you feel?" he asked in a calm, professional voice.

"I'm okay. My head feels better, thanks." I rubbed my forehead.

"You ruptured a blood vessel in your head. I repaired it. But I also had to give you the vaccine early. I'm afraid it was the only way to keep you from getting worse. It will have to mature in you," informed Urit.

"Is that all right, to give it to me *early?*" I asked nervously.

"Well, there was no other option." His lips thinned. "You will live," he said nonchalantly. He sounded like he didn't believe himself and was unsure of the risks. "The only drawback is that you are going to have to drink massive amounts of cold water. The agent undergoes an exothermic reaction and produces some heat as it matures. But it has already begun to cool down and will not cause you any sort of internal thermal injury."

"Thanks, doc," I muttered. I leaned back against the back of the bed. I was not sure I totally understood. It didn't matter. He could do whatever he wanted to me. I needed no explanation. My life was spared, and my intellectual curiosity was all but gone. Urit and Noah talked on as though I was no longer there while they stepped outside my cubicle to further discuss the premature treatment. I lay there powerlessly watching them from my bed when Gaelan entered the office. He rushed right by them and was instantly at my side.

"Sami, I came as soon as I heard. Don't scare me like that! I'm so glad you're okay. I feel so terrible for bringing you aboard and risking your health." He took my hand and squeezed it with conviction.

"I'm sorry to be such a wimp." I tried to lighten his mood.

"On the contrary, you have been amazingly tolerant, resilient ... really. I was starting to take your perseverance for granted. Most people would have been incapacitated and bedridden much sooner." He shrugged.

"I haven't been at my best," I admitted.

"Don't worry. Urit's vaccine works remarkably well. Before he came up with it, this place was overcrowded. I think he devised it just to get some peace. He's a loner by nature," he joked, trying to elicit a laugh.

"Can I leave now? Will you walk me back to the room?"

"Oh, um, I don't think ..." Gaelan turned around to look at Urit. Their eyes met and they exchanged glances before he turned back to me with a serious expression on his face. "No, Sami, you have to stay here as a precaution," he said reluctantly, as if he had just read Urit's mind. Their faces scared me. *Jeez*, was there something they weren't telling me? "Urit needs to watch you for the time being since he has all the gadgets to cool you down quickly. The vaccine is going to cool down much slower in your body than it would have in Urit's freezer. Plus, the rest of the ship is going to get uncomfortably hot tomorrow."

"Why? What happens tomorrow?"

"We are opening up a port key," he explained.

"*What?* Say that again." I had difficulty focusing on what he was telling me.

"We're burning a hole through the fabric of Space. The conditions have to be just right. We have to position ourselves closely to the Ortara sun when we fire the laser beam. We utilize the solar winds produced by the sun to propel us through the opening. Plus, the heat from the sun provides a steady temperature while it generously expands the pathway for the passing of our ship. Our shields only work to a point. It will feel like, how do you say ... the tropics."

"Why heat?" I struggled to pay attention.

"To stabilize the space between the molecules ... to hold the door open, if you will."

I sat in disbelief. "You mean you actually *create* your own wormhole?" I said after a moment. Gaelan gave me a worried look. Apparently, I was still lagging behind in the conversation. "I don't believe it. We have been looking for wormholes that already existed for travel across the universe." Einstein's equations allowed for the existence of wormholes. Only a handful of scientists theorized that it was possible to create them. They were scrutinized by the rest of the scientific community as dreamers, so-called victims of the giggle factor, where scientists ridiculed their own kind. Most of them felt it was impossible to generate enough energy to create the distortion in Space. It was believed that the mass of a Spacecraft would instantly collapse the opening. But the energy of a powerful laser could do it, and the addition of heat could possibly prevent gravity from crushing the wormhole shut as long as you don't burn up. "Remarkable," I muttered as I pondered the idea.

"It's the only way to cover large distances. We like to skip across Space to save time. Zaric and I are constantly mapping new stars and galaxies. We target the best places for our port keys. It's exhilarating to find new shortcuts."

I rubbed my head. It started to hurt again. "I can't think right now." I shivered. The air around me became unbearably cold against my skin.

"Sami, rest. You need to get well. I will explain the port keys to you another time."

"Thanks. But how come I'm the only one who's sick? Why does Noah seem just fine?" I asked. Gaelan glanced through the glass at Noah and bit his lip.

"I think I better let Noah answer that one. Get some rest. I'll check back later to see how you are doing. I have to get back to work. I'm still on duty." Gaelan leaned over and squeezed my hand once more before leaving. I clung to the touch of his strong hand. The sensation seemed to linger—even though he'd let go. I watched him stop to talk to Noah after leaving my cubicle. Neither one of them looked happy. Each of them glanced over at me with a look of despair on their faces. This looked like a serious discussion. I saw Noah nodding his head, agreeing with whatever Gaelan had said. Why did this glass have to be soundproof? Noah gazed at me with a torn expression on his face. He walked slowly into my cubicle.

"Sami, you look better." He smiled.

"Thanks," I said. Seeing Gaelan could perk anybody up.

"Sami, there's something important I need to talk to you about. I can't bear hiding it from you any longer," Noah said with a somber look in his eyes. He sat down on the side of my bed beside me and turned to face me.

"What, Noah? Are you okay? There's nothing wrong with you, is there?" My heart stopped as I thought about how devastated I would be if something ever happened to him.

"No, Sami. I'm fine." He sighed. "I was trying not to hurt you. It would kill me if I ever lost your friendship."

"*Never!* What is it?"

"I have to tell you something I'm not very proud of." He gulped. "First of all, let me tell you how much I've always loved you and Jack, and Leah and Jackson. You are the closest thing to a family I have ever had. I feel terrible right now because I haven't always been honest with you. You know how I told you that my parents lived in Hawaii as an explanation as to why they never visited? Well, the truth is that they died. I lost everybody. My whole family was killed when I was thirteen," he said in a serious voice. He looked at me to assess my reaction.

"What? Why didn't you ever tell me this, Noah?" I blinked in shock as his voice echoed in my head. I felt a lump in my throat, making it difficult to speak.

"I couldn't tell you because ... because they didn't die on Earth. They were killed on a Space mission. Our people were just learning how to manipulate energy fields and open port keys. It was an accident. No one saw it coming." He frowned.

I braced myself and quickly put the facts together. I knew he must have been referring to the same disaster that killed Azil's parents. "No ... no way! Noah, you're from Kataria! You're an alien. Why didn't you tell me?" I was now shouting angrily. I felt my body heat up as the vaccine surged through me. My heart pounded in my chest. I could hear my racing heartbeat pulsating in my ears. I was sure my face was bright red. It felt so hot. "I don't believe you! After all these years we've been friends, you never said a word!" I lashed out at him—feeling betrayed. I never doubted my trust for him.

"I'm so sorry that I never told you. Please, calm down," he pleaded. "You look like you're going to catch on fire. Maybe this isn't the best time to tell you."

"No, it's not! We should have had this discussion years ago!" I huffed. I tried to regain my composure. I wiped my forehead when I felt a bead of sweat run into my eyes. "Did you have to wait until I almost died to tell me the truth? You could have trusted me."

"Sami, of course I could have. I would trust you with my life. I wanted to tell you so many times. I just didn't want to give you the burden of hiding my secret. You're the first person from Earth that I'm telling," he offered as a consolation. "You have no idea how hard it's been for me. I regret not telling Jack the truth every day, and here I was about to make the same mistake with you."

"When did you come to Earth? I've known you forever." I shook my head in disbelief. "I thought you went to college at Caltech," I ranted. A thousand images rushed through my brain. I remembered watching Noah listen to our colleague's ideas. It always seemed like he had something to add but was afraid to say it. Even more amazing, all of his suggestions always worked on the first try. Oh, yes, and then there were those strange documents I accidentally uncovered in his orientation binder that made me worry that he might be a spy. But he was so much more than that! He was an alien spy! Why didn't I notice this before? Wasn't he just incredibly smart? I thought I knew him. He was more than a friend. I considered him family.

"I did go to school at Caltech. Earth has become my home away from home. When I first got there, I felt a little out of place. We decided the best way to blend in was to enroll in college. It helped us to learn about your culture. It also didn't hurt that anything I did that might seem unusual or strange was instantly accepted and totally overlooked by my college co-eds. Your teenagers are the most open-minded members of your society."

"True," I agreed.

"I wish your culture didn't stifle your youthful habits. Your young have so much potential. Most people on your planet do nothing to stretch themselves, and waste away all their creativity instead of embracing it. They settle for mediocrity because they believe that's all there is. I think your people would be shocked by what they could accomplish if they stopped living just to earn a paycheck and acquire things," he preached. I couldn't believe my ears. He was talking to me like I was an outsider. He was judging the people on Earth. It seemed like he was trying to use his artful skill of changing the subject. I wouldn't let him. He wasn't getting off that easy. I needed answers—now!

"Noah, you said *we.* Are there a lot of *you* living on Earth?" I asked bluntly.

"There are a couple of us. Some of my friends came with me. They are living in other countries all over your planet. We thought it was best if we spread out."

"Why, so you don't stand out?"

"No, to be more effective," he corrected me. "We wanted to cover as many bases as possible."

"I don't understand. Have you been spying on us?"

"It's not exactly like that. My people are just sort of keeping track of your technological advancements over time. We are only slightly ahead of you. We felt drawn to you since we are so much alike. Finding a planet so similar to our own and, most imperative, people just like us was an invaluable discovery. Our society and yours are practically carbon copies. A parallel universe if you will. We thought about introducing ourselves, but your world seemed slightly unstable. We noticed the ongoing internal wars on your planet. We couldn't be sure how we would be received. You might see us as a threat. We decided to conceal our presence while we occasionally visited to see how you were progressing. Finally, you seemed to reach a pinnacle of discovery we couldn't ignore. A group of us concluded that, after all of our historical blunders, we should get more involved. We wanted to help you avoid making the same tragic mistakes we endured. It seemed like the only way to guide you was to join your engineers, scientists, and physicists."

I felt betrayed. It hurt to realize everything I believed to be true was a mirage. Of course, I had already believed in the existence of other intelligent life in the universe. It would be completely foolish to think otherwise. I wasn't even totally surprised when the SIG informed us about the Katarians visiting our Space center. But I wasn't expecting to discover that Noah was from another planet or that there were others like him living across our planet—right there, out in the open, blending in effortlessly. How could I have been so blind?

"What's your real name?" I snapped impatiently.

"Noah. Yeah, I was real happy when I didn't have to change it."

"Oh ...." I sat quietly for a moment and stared at my hands, thinking about what I wanted to ask next. Noah remained quiet, giving me time to accept the news. "Noah, weren't you homesick? Didn't you ever want to go home?"

"Well, actually," he paused, "I went home five times." Now Noah was the one blushing. "You know, the times I was supposed to be in Hawaii visiting my folks. I really went back to Kataria."

"But you always took such great photos," I said in disbelief.

"Fake. All of them. They weren't mine. I printed them from the internet."

I glared at him. "Liar! No wonder you never brought home any souvenirs, you little sneak."

"I don't blame you if you're mad at me," muttered Noah, "but I'm still glad I told you. It's like a weight has been lifted off my shoulders. Will you forgive me? Do you hate me?" He looked at me tenderly.

"Of course I forgive you, and I could never hate you. I love you, Noah. You're the brother I never had." I decided not to make this any harder for either of us and didn't have the strength to fight, so I leaned over to give him a tight hug.

Noah jumped back. "Sami … you're burning up," he said emphatically.

I wiped my brow. "No, I'm okay," I replied. Just then a burst of heat flushed throughout my body. Sitting up seemed to be more than I could handle. The heat surged up into my eyes, making them sting and water. I blinked to quell the burning. Without further notice, my arms and legs started to shake uncontrollably. I broke out in a full-blown sweat, like I had just finished running a marathon.

"Urit, hurry, *come here, now*!" Noah shouted frantically. He rushed to the door to retrieve the doctor. "She's getting worse!"

Urit was at my side in a blink. He had to have the quickest reaction time I had ever seen. He touched my forehead with a little metal probe. "Oh my, where's my Remi-Scan," he muttered to himself. Urit abruptly went to retrieve the same glass panel he had used on me the first day I was on board. He frowned as he frantically scrolled his hand along the side several times until it was a glowing deep blue hue. He lowered the device over me. I could feel a rush of cold rays penetrating my hot skin. It felt like I was standing in a freezer. My initial shivering at the extreme temperature difference was quickly converted into full body convulsions. Noah held me down so I wouldn't fall off the bed. Finally, the intense burning through my veins seemed to weaken. Urit wouldn't stop, despite my assurances that I was feeling better. I finally gave up trying and fell asleep during the treatment. I was in and out of consciousness while I endured several more treatments to extinguish the internal flames.

I thought I would never get better. The fever raged on and on. My temperature kept spiking to the point where I imagined my blood was boiling. Even my teeth felt hot. I stayed in the hospital for four or five more days. I lost count. I mostly slept, only to be reminded of how sick I felt when I awoke. Two other doctors, Bryson, who specialized in dentistry, and Hayden, my friend from the café, were there occasionally, but Urit seemed to care for me exclusively. He was there every time I opened my eyes. Once, I awoke to find him washing my hair. I remembered him pouring water through my scalp. Its coolness felt like heaven. I think he worried about prematurely injecting me with the vaccine. He seemed determined to see me recover. At last, the fever seemed to lose steam, and I was able to maintain 102 degrees Fahrenheit at rest. Urit finally agreed to release me as long as I checked in with him twice a day.

***

"You've escaped." Gaelan's face lit up when I walked in through the door of his quarters. He immediately jumped up from his desk chair and rushed to my side. He seemed truly happy about my return. He said he missed having my company. I missed being around him as well. I couldn't get him off my mind. I longed for his daily conversations. I wanted to tell him how I much I dreaded it when he left for his shifts and how I wished I could spend the entire day with him. He was amazing. He was beyond smart, but humble. It didn't hurt that he was incredibly sexy. It was difficult not to stare at his toned body or beautiful face for too long. I had never met anyone like him. I was able to totally relax when I was with him and be myself. He made me feel so safe, like he was my guardian angel aboard the ship.

"Yes, I've made bail," I answered.

"*Bail?*" Gaelan was confused by the term. "Urit was supposed to call me when you were ready to go. I was going to come and get you."

"He walked me over here," I confessed at the risk of sounding helpless. Gaelan pursed his lips in response. It was hard to ignore the unspoken competitiveness between them.

"Urit warned me that I had to make sure you drink enough water to keep your temperature down. He threatened to *take* you right back if you relapse."

"He did? So, did you tell him that I would drink gallons and gallons?" I muttered.

Gaelan grinned. "Yes—sort of. I told him I would make you drink and that I was planning to give you a cold shower every hour on the hour."

"Really? You said that to him?" My jaw dropped open in disbelief.

"Yeah, I did, and he wasn't too happy when I said it, either." He chuckled with an impish grin on his face.

"Hmm." I shook my head in disbelief.

"Well, he's been keeping you all to himself," Gaelan said jealously. "I was afraid that you've become one of his experiments. He really gets carried away sometimes. He should have released you days ago."

"Days ... oh no, how long was I there?" I rubbed my head, trying to reconstruct my gapped memory. I lost my concept of time. Everything was a blur.

"Ten days. You slept through most of it." He frowned.

"*Ten?* I can't believe it," I groaned. "I don't remember being there that long."

He took my hand. "Okay, let's go. You're looking kind of hot," he teased and motioned for me to join him in the bathroom.

I firmly planted my feet and pulled my hand away defensively. "Hmmm ... that sounds interesting," I mused. "Maybe later—I'll let you know." I fought to stop a smile from taking over my face. The proposition made my body flushed with heat. Just the thought of sharing a shower with him embarrassed me. I would never be able to control myself if his hands were touching me while I was naked.

"Fine, just say when." He raised his eyebrows. "A promise is a promise," he said playfully.

"Are you kidding? I really can take a cold shower?" I asked out of curiosity.

"Yes, of course. Why?" I saw his eyes perk up. "You've reconsidered?" He grinned.

"No—not yet. I just didn't know that it was possible to adjust the water temperature. I tried everything but couldn't figure out how. I've been enduring some really hot showers ever since I've been here. I wish you would have told me that before," I confessed.

He seemed amused by my apparent struggle with their technology and let out a quiet laugh. "You shouldn't have suffered like that. All you had to do was ask for help. I'm at your service." He bowed shamelessly.

Gaelan joined me in the study to watch the passing stars. It was one of my favorite things to do with him while we talked. Tonight's view was breathtaking. The stars appeared to be even brighter than usual. He sat down closely beside me on the sofa. His thigh *almost* touching mine.

"Gaelan, how do you feel about me?" I asked bravely. I held my breath awaiting his answer.

"I like you," he answered casually.

"I like you, too," I muttered back. We sat silently for a moment.

He winced and nervously licked his lips. "No, *what* am I saying." He ran his hands through his thick brown hair. "I feel much more strongly about you than that. You are *very* important to me. Sami ..." Gaelan grabbed both of my arms. His hands made me shiver; they felt like ice next to my feverish skin. "I could never forgive myself if you didn't get better. I hated seeing you so sick. It was like losing a part of me."

I looked into his eyes. They were bursting with determination. I could tell he was speaking with sincerity. Without delay, he leaned forward, reached up to my face, pulled me to him and kissed me passionately. I felt a surge of heat flow through my veins. I couldn't control myself. I pulled his hard body closer to mine and kissed him back. We barely came up for air. Gaelan released me when he noticed my face getting flushed. My cheeks were radiating heat and probably burnt the skin on his face. He excused himself for a moment before he returned with two large drinks.

"Drink," he insisted, handing me one of the glasses. "I meant it when I said I'm tired of sharing you with Urit. I want you all to myself." He sat back down and put his arm around me.

"As you wish. I think I like it better here, anyway." I happily obliged and gulped down the ice water. I put down the glass, leaned him back on the sofa, and rested my head on his chest. He smelled so good. Gaelan had an indescribable quality about him that was secretly driving me wild. Maybe it was the way he held himself or the way he saw the world. Whatever it was, it made him completely irresistible. "It's nice to know I wasn't the only one holding back," I confided in a whisper.

Gaelan shifted up onto his elbow and stared at me. He seemed to be searching for the right words before he spoke. "Sami, you ... you have been making me *crazy* ever since I met you. At first, I was worried that you were from Earth and wanted to stay far, far away from us aliens. You seemed so homesick. Then, you fell ill. I was afraid of letting myself feel this way about you. It's been a real struggle trying not to become too involved. But I can't control it anymore. I can't stay away from you."

"Good, then don't," I replied. He smiled brilliantly at my response.

I rose up on my arms and lowered myself down to kiss him gently. He exhaled strongly before he rolled me over, pressing my back into the soft sofa, and hovered above me. I looked into his intense blue eyes. He kissed my forehead and moved down the side of my face and neck before returning to my lips. I loved how he laid his lips delicately against my skin in an unhurried manner. His fingertips lightly brushed up and down my arm and then leg. Every stroke of his hand was filled with complete tenderness. His incredibly soft touches excited my whole body. I was really getting aroused, but he pulled away and leaned down next to me. He told me that he didn't want to push his luck and get me overheated. I couldn't argue. I could tell my temperature had risen. I was a burning inferno. "I think I'll take that cold shower now, please," I said with a laugh. He smiled back at me, pulled me into his arms, and held me lovingly against him.

CHAPTER 18

RENEW

I had to lay low for the next five days. Urit estimated the vaccine's reaction would burn out by then. I had no choice but to comply. Anytime I moved around too much, I would become immediately overheated. I had never been more aware of how my body was my number one mode of transportation. I'd never take it for granted again! When I sat perfectly still, I still had a 102-degree fever. My temperature climbed to 104 degrees Fahrenheit just from the walk from my room to the ship's hospital. Urit offered to visit me in my room, but I told him I would go crazy if I didn't escape for at least a few minutes everyday. He obliged but insisted on hitting me with a blast from his Remi-Scan the second I stepped foot through the hospital's door. I drank so much water. I couldn't help reminisce about Jack's insatiable thirst. Azil, Noah, and Gaelan took turns bringing me food from the café. The walk there was even farther. It was down two levels and took twice as long as it did to get to the hospital, making my going there totally out of the question. Gaelan and I seemed inseparable. We were becoming extremely close. I could imagine his face perfectly when I closed my eyes. It was difficult to keep our hands off each other. Although we were both trying not to push our luck with my health, he always seemed to be the one who pulled back first. I wished he couldn't feel how hot he made me. It probably felt like he was sitting too close to a fireplace when he was next to me.

I started to get very homesick. I missed Leah and Jackson terribly. My initial awe of the Spaceship had completely faded. The order, structure, and routine had become painfully predictable. The confinement of its walls seemed so limiting. I wanted to go home, to go outside. I couldn't believe how much I missed the stupid things. I wanted my television, my computer, my clothes, and my bed. I wanted variety. It was the small things in life that brought us pleasure. I eyed one of the woven blankets I had on my makeshift bed. I pictured unraveling it and knitting it back together again. After a few hours, I became weak, gave in to my yearning, and turned it into a giant ball of yarn. I spent all day knitting it back together with stirring sticks I had Noah retrieve from the cafe. Gaelan was speechless when he watched me. He just shook his head in disbelief as the garment grew. Gaelan told me how people on Kataria knitted with poppy fur. They were animals similar to our sheep but had soft fur like a rabbit. He told me about how he remembered watching his grandfather knit in the evening to relax. He said that, not unlike me, his grandfather found it physically impossible to sit still without doing something. It was one of his only memories of him since he died when Gaelan was just a boy. He said it was comforting to be reminded of him.

Day five had finally arrived. I awoke after hearing Gaelan close the door when he left to take a morning shift. Just as Urit had promised, I noticed that I wasn't hot at all. I felt normal—actually *great!* I jumped out of bed with exhilaration. Amazingly, I wasn't even weak from lying around. Instead, it felt like I'd just downed a cup of espresso. My body felt powerful and strong. I showered and got dressed. My clothes hung loosely on my body. I had lost some weight. Urit had explained that it was to be expected. He said the fever increased my metabolic rate by about 24 percent, a 7-percent increase for every degree my temperature was above normal. I looked in the mirror and I brushed my teeth. I wasn't sure if it was my imagination, but I thought I looked younger.

I thought about Gaelan while I got ready. I couldn't get him off my mind. Last night, he had fallen asleep beside me on the sofa. He had pulled an extra shift and seemed especially tired. I lay awake listening to the peaceful lull of his breathing. I pictured how he held me like a lover, the lingering sensation of his lips touching mine when he kissed me good night. I loved how his arms cradled me gently while his hand fell naturally on my breast. I'd never wanted anyone more. It took everything in my power to let him sleep. I reveled in the feeling of his body resting gently into mine. I couldn't wait till he finished his shift today. I had nothing to do until lunch. I got restless waiting around and left the room to go for my daily check-in with Urit.

I entered the hospital. I was two hours early but knew I would find him there. He rarely left the vicinity. Besides, his quarters were conjoined to the hospital.

"*Sam*, how do you feel?" he said eagerly after he magically appeared at my side in seconds.

"Great! Amazing! Nothing hurts. The vaccine really worked," I said with appreciation.

"Are you all right, Sam? You were *hurt,*" he said in a bewildered voice.

"No, I'm fine. I mean that my body feels great in general—no aches or pains," I explained.

"Oh, good." He sighed in relief.

"Urit, I don't think I ever thanked you for taking such great care of me."

"I wouldn't see it any other way," he beamed. I could only imagine what it took to care for my lifeless body.

"I can't believe how different I feel. You're a lifesaver. How do you accomplish so much?" I knew his treatment had spared my life.

"Just like everything else I do. First, I consider that anything is possible. Then, I always move in the direction in which I want to go. I am always learning from my research. Solutions arise in the most unexpected ways."

"Did this vaccine do anything else to me? I know it protects me from viruses and radiation, but I feel twenty years younger."

"Well," he smiled, "it's a cellular stabilizer. It will also correct any damage that has been done to your genetic code."

"Wait! You mean it repaired any previous damage in my body?" I listened to the words but didn't believe my ears.

"Exactly."

"You've found the fountain of youth!" I blurted out in excitement.

"The fountain of *what?*"

"Never mind. What are the long-term effects? Will it prolong my life?" I rushed through the words.

"Yes, how do you think I stay so fit at ninety-one?"

"No, Urit, you're not ninety ... you can't be." I shook my head in disbelief.

"Yes, Samantha, I am. Right now, I am testing out a new way to increase reaction time on myself. I felt like

I was slowing down, despite the cellular stabilization. I think it's working really well except for some mild hyperactivity. On the positive side, I only need about three hours of sleep to feel rested. Would you like to try it? Right now, it only lasts about sixteen weeks. I'm still working on a way to make the effects last longer." Urit went off on a tangent. Well, that explained his zipping around like a speeding bullet. I looked over at the counter covered with vials and beakers brewing multi-colored liquids. I could only dare to imagine what he had incubating in *them*.

"No, thanks, I think I'll pass," I graciously declined. I was happy to feel normal for a change. "Urit, our current life expectancy is already averaging 105 years. The vaccine …" I sighed after considering the consequences. "I can't outlive my kids. Will this ever go away?" I ranted. I was ready to scream at him. I wanted to ask him how he could do this to me. I stopped myself and took a deep breath as I stared at the floor while I thought about my potential longevity. It was absolutely astounding that the Katarians had created this marvel of medicine. Regardless, I was nothing less than grateful. Urit had taken such great care of me. I would have died aboard this ship weeks ago if it weren't for him.

Urit walked over and put his hand on my shoulder. "Sam, I'm sorry. I should have explained it better. I thought maybe you wouldn't be so aware of the changes.

Either way, I had no choice but to give you the vaccine. The effects will wear off with time. If you avoid future treatments, you will shorten your lifespan," he explained kindly as he tried to soften the blow.

"How long does it normally last?"

"I do not know. It depends on your environmental exposure. I wouldn't worry too much about it, though. Your people are on the brink of developing this as well," he reassured me.

"I know you didn't have a choice. Thank you for *everything*," I conceded. I tried to accept my new fate but couldn't help worry about outliving my friends and family. I suppose I would have Gaelan and Noah in my life, but I guess an early retirement was entirely out of the question.

"Samantha, now that you're well—would you like to join me for lunch?"

"I'm sorry, Urit. I already have plans to meet Gaelan."

"Okay, *tomorrow* then?" he asked in a hopeful tone.

"Oh, wow—I'm sorry, I can't, Urit." I paused searching for the right words. "Gaelan and I are sort of together," I explained. His offer completely took me off guard.

"Hmm." He looked away sheepishly. "Well then." He laughed under his breath. *"That* explains it." He shook his head while an enlightened expression drew across his face.

"Explains what?" I asked.

"Gaelan ... he would barely leave your side. I just thought he felt guilty about bringing you aboard and almost causing your death. Now I know why he looked like he wanted to *rip* my head off every time I asked him to leave while I cared for you." He chuckled with satisfaction at Gaelan's expense.

"He came to see me?"

"Yes, every day," he paused, "he hung out here for hours, waiting for you to wake up. I was hoping that you were only friends. I mean you and Noah, you two aren't together but are so close and always hugging. I can hardly believe you're just friends. I thought it could be like that with you and Gaelan," he said disappointedly.

"Oh," I said, feeling slightly embarrassed by my public displays of affection with Noah.

"Why hasn't it happened for you and Noah? I just cannot believe that he has known you for over twenty years and has not wanted more."

"No, it's different with Noah." I didn't want to explain that Noah and my late husband, Jack, were like brothers. In my mind, he was just part of our family.

"One day, I even asked Noah if he ever looked at you. I offered to check his eyes," he joked as he paced across the room. "I have developed a lens that can drastically improve vision. I coated the lens with a phosphorescent film that illuminates your retinal perception of your surroundings at night. It only takes ten minutes to insert," he said, cutting himself off after he managed to rein in his enthusiasm about his discovery on his own this time.

"Wait!" I said with excitement. Maybe this was the answer I'd been searching for. "Can the lens make your eyes glow green?"

"There is a *mild* reflective quality that can make them appear green in the right light. Why? Did Gaelan try to *impress* you by making you believe his eyes glowed in the dark?"

"No, it's just something I noticed." I purposely downplayed my reaction. I didn't want him to learn of my paranoid suspicions of them, especially after everything he'd done for me. But, oh, what a relief! The glowing green eyes of my nightmares were due to the implanted lens. Urit raised his eyebrows and looked me in the face. He seemed intrigued by my answer but didn't question me more. I hated the Katarians' annoying habit of *really listening* to you when you spoke.

"I wish you luck with Gaelan. Still, can I ask you to consider me if it doesn't work out?"

"I am flattered by your offer, but I don't want to ruin our friendship. Plus, I think you might be a little too young for me." I tried to lighten the rejection with humor. He made a small chuckle. I couldn't deny that his caring for me gave our relationship an intimacy of its own. I wondered if Urit liked having me around because he was lonely. He spent most of his time in the hospital or his quarters. He seemed to work in his lab at all hours of the day and night. The place was always quiet. It was rare that anyone ever stopped in. Everyone on board seemed to be incredibly healthy. Urit, along with Hayden and Bryson, the other doctors who occasionally joined him, spent their time working on experiments.

"But why wouldn't it work out?" I finally asked after an uncomfortable silence.

"I've known Gaelan for a long time. He has managed to sabotage every possible relationship he's ever had. If someone tries to get close to him, he takes off running. He's not the type to make a serious commitment."

"Thanks for the warning." I stared off across the room and searched my mind for clues to verify the accusation. Aside from our restrained physical contact, I hadn't noticed Gaelan maintaining any emotional distance from me. On the contrary, he had been more than willing to let me in. We had both shared our most intimate feelings with each other. It hurt to even think about letting him go. I had fallen in love with him. Why wouldn't it work out? After all, Noah had spent the last twenty-five years on Earth. My attention drifted when I pictured his handsome image in my mind. Mmm, just the thought of Gaelan turned me on. I thought we'd both die if we didn't make love soon. I couldn't wait to tell him I felt better.

"I don't want you to find disappointment."

"Thanks, that's kind. Well, what about you? Why haven't you found anybody yet?" I asked, trying to pull myself out of my unexpected daydream.

"I was in love once, for sixty-three years to be exact. Nadia died six years ago. You remind me of her in ways. *Oh, yes*, I was lucky enough to share my life with one *amazing* woman. There's not a day that goes by that I don't miss her. She gave me the greatest gift of my life, my beautiful daughter, Nia," he said, pondering.

"What happened?"

He closed his eyes and sighed. "Tragically, I lost her to a relentless virus. I tried to do everything I could to save her, but I did not discover a cure soon enough," he said in a defeated tone. I saw a tear well up in his eye.

"It's not your fault. You can't be expected to be able to cure everything you encounter," I consoled.

"I know, but I might have been able to save her if I wasn't away from her when she got sick. By the time I got home, it was too late—she was almost gone. The virus had shut down most of her organ function, making the damage impossible to reverse. Our medicines were useless. I didn't have time to find a cure. She died two hours later. There was little I could do to help," he said, sounding ridden with heavy guilt.

"I'm so sorry for your loss." I identified with the sorrow in his voice. I fought back tears as memories of Jack filled my head. I had to keep them suppressed, where they belonged. The pain still cut through me like a knife. I focused on my favorite coping mechanism: avoidance. To keep from crying, I always pictured myself riding a shiny, black, galloping horse through a field at top speeds. For some completely unexplainable reason, this bizarre, irrational thought gave me the ability to control my sadness. I wasn't sure if it the fantasy gave me peace by imagining a route of escape or by taking my mind off my grief, but it worked. I could relate to his guilt without being crippled by my emotions. I remembered beating myself up repeatedly after losing Jack. Maybe he would still be alive if I was a more demanding wife. I had learned that forgiving others was simple—but forgiving yourself was often easier said than done.

I approached him while he peered silently out across the room and stroked his arm. "Some things are beyond our control. I understand what it's like to lose someone close. Just try to remember how much joy she brought to your life while you were lucky enough to have her," I said softly.

His glum face looked at me. "Thank you, Sam. You bring light with your words. I really do wish you and Gaelan happiness," he said graciously.

CHAPTER 19

DECCA

Gaelan's and my path intersected on the way to lunch in the dimly lit, empty corridor. He stopped me in the hallway and pulled me under one of the spotlights illuminating the passageway.

"Sami, you look *fantastic*," he beamed. Seeing him look so happy sent a thrill of excitement through my entire body.

"I feel great. I was just with Urit. He said the vaccination is complete. I have a clean bill of health," I said cheerfully. I decided to leave out the rest. There was no reason to ruffle any feathers.

"*Finally.*" He smiled. "Come here," he said. He swung me into his arms. "Let me see. Wow! You're not burning up." He slid his hand under the back of my shirt to feel my skin.

"I'm just as relieved as you are, trust me."

"You have no idea how hard it's been to be close to you and have to behave myself. You've awakened a part of me I've been ignoring for some time now. But I've been worried I might accidently *kill you* if we got too carried away. In truth, I should've been worrying more about myself. You've been killing me slowly. I could self-combust at any minute," he said with a laugh. Then, without hesitation, he leaned down and kissed me robustly. He carelessly let my body push back against the corridor wall and brought himself in tightly against me. I could feel his excitement as he leaned his body into mine. I felt relieved when my temperature didn't soar. I ran my fingers through his luscious hair and relinquished my self-control—kissing him back with the same fervor. I couldn't stop myself. He gave me chills. I could never get enough of him. I hoped this corridor didn't have cameras. He ran his hand up and down my body, caressing my curves. I felt his hard muscles flexing across his back. I wanted to rip his clothes off right then and there. He had to look amazing under these clothes. We were starting to get carried away when we heard people talking while they approached us from around the corner. Gaelan stopped kissing me when the sound of their footsteps drew closer. He let out a giant breath and closed his eyes. He reluctantly released my right thigh, which he had wrapped around him in order to wedge himself between my legs. I didn't want him to let me go.

"Hmm, we need better timing. This shouldn't be *so* hard," he whispered. He rested his forehead against mine as he straddled his arms on both sides of my body to lean on the wall. "I can barely control myself around you." He groaned before he stepped away from me to fix his clothes.

"Me, either," I whispered back. I straightened my clothes as well.

"What am I going to *do* with you?" he said in a deep voice while he tucked in part of his shirt.

"I don't know. Why don't we go back to our room," I answered seductively. His eyes brightened.

He quickly gazed down at his watch. "Ahh, there isn't time," he moaned disappointedly.

"Fine, I guess we will just have to wait until later tonight … we'll pick up where we left off," I promised. Two crew members quickly walked past us without making eye contact. They looked uncomfortable in passing. I looked at Gaelan's face and grinned as they went by. I wondered how much they might have heard. I didn't care.

"Later it is," he said. His face held a dimpled smile. He was breathtaking.

"Hmm." I sighed. "I can't wait!"

"Come on, we should get something to eat." Gaelan motioned his head down the hall towards the café and hesitantly started to walk.

"Okay," I replied. I could feel the weight of his stare on me while we walked. I briefly looked over at his face and gave him a sideways smirk.

We sat down at a table with Azil and Zaric. Noah and Karis came in shortly after. Apparently, the two of them had become much closer while I was recovering. I was surprised at how friendly Karis was now that Noah was paying attention to her.

"Sami, I'm glad to see you back to normal. I missed picking on you," Noah teased.

"Life wouldn't be the same, would it?" I replied. I saw Karis possessively clasp her hands around Noah's arm. She was like a child grasping onto her new toy. Maybe she wasn't overly thrilled by my presence after all.

"Gaelan, did you tell Sami about Decca?" asked Noah.

"No, Noah, not yet—I didn't get a chance." He smiled at me. I knew he was referring to how we just spent our time on the way to the café.

"Decca, what's that?" I asked.

"It's a frozen rock," muttered Azil, sounding unimpressed.

"Come on, Azil, it's not that bad," corrected Zaric. "It's a planet we stop at for supplies on the way home."

Gaelan leaned across the table towards Azil. "I suppose you're not coming?" he surmised.

"No," she said sharply.

"Don't you want to get off the ship? Think of all the fresh air, the wide open space," he said, trying to coax her.

"No way, I've seen enough of that place after the last time. I had wind burn on my face for over a week!" she said, forging a viable excuse.

"Baby," Gaelan teased.

Zaric grinned. "I just came from the flight deck, and the weather report showed clear skies," he announced proudly.

Gaelan rubbed his chin. "You'll miss us when we're gone and wish you came along," he said, staring Azil down.

"Uh huh, you guys have fun; I'll pass." She shook her head to opt out of going on the trip.

Zaric leaned over and gave her a quick kiss. "Have it your way," he said. She smiled at his understanding.

Noah looked at me. His eyes lit up in anticipation. "Sami, Decca looks like a ski resort right after a snowstorm. It's really pretty. You have to go with us. We get to hike up to a cave. It's so much fun."

"Would you like to come with us?" asked Gaelan with excitement filling his voice.

"Okay, sure," I answered without so much as a second thought. "When are we going?" Snow or no snow, I was dying to put my feet firmly on actual ground.

"Right after we eat. We'll be there in less than an hour," Noah said enthusiastically.

Great, I thought, *Gaelan really did mean we'll pick up where we left off later ... much later.* This was disappointing. I was hoping he meant right after lunch. We finished eating and headed to a room I'd never seen. They called it the landing. The room was large and two stories high. It looked like a huge garage. There were six vehicles neatly lined up on one side: three white and three black. I walked over to check them out while the others talked. The surface of the vehicles had a matte finish. I stroked my hand across one of the black vehicles and watched in amazement as the surface took on the color of my skin and sleeve. Gaelan walked over to join me and explained that the alloy was capable of taking on the color of its surroundings in order to function as camouflage for their expeditions. They were triangular and the size of two Hummers put together. They didn't have wheels. I wondered if they could fly or if they slid across the ground. I would have asked more questions, but I had to get ready to go. Karis was waiting impatiently for me to join her in getting dressed.

Azil held to her decision to stay aboard and forgo the excursion. She seemed to have an aversion to snow. I briefly considered staying with her for one fleeting moment but decided not to back out. Who was I kidding? My choice was clear. I felt uncontrollably giddy to be getting off the ship, even if it was just for a little while. Karis shared my enthusiasm and was thrilled to be going. I think she would follow Noah anywhere. She grudgingly took me with her into a side room off the landing to get ready. We put on multiple layers. I copied how she added each piece. We topped them all off with a white snow parka and boots. How cold was it? I felt like a giant marshmallow. Just then, I felt the ship jerk. My body swayed to catch my balance. "What was *that?*" I was startled by the sudden movement.

"We just landed," Karis reassured me.

"That's it? Wow, that wasn't bad at all," I said in disbelief. I wasn't sure what to expect. "How come it was so gentle?"

"We have a self-regulating landing system. It's the latest technology. The landing gear surveys the land for irregularities and makes the internal adjustments to our speed and landing gear so we have a smooth landing," she informed me in an arrogant tone.

"Humph." I marveled at their ingenuity to be able to land such a large mass with such precision. I refrained from asking anymore questions. I didn't want to give

Karis the satisfaction. She didn't exactly hide the fact that people from her planet were undeniably technologically superior. On the contrary, she flaunted it.

"Let's go, Samantha—the *boys* will be waiting," Karis said exuberantly. I think she secretly enjoyed the unevenly exaggerated male to female ratio aboard the ship.

Waiting by the door were Gaelan, Noah, Zaric, and Tyden, along with two other crew members I'd never met. They were both dressed and appeared to be going as well.

We approached Noah. "Here you go, ladies," he said, handing Karis and me an empty backpack.

"Thanks," we said in unison.

"Sami," Noah said. "Pascal and Enos are coming with us as well. You remember Pascal—you met him the same day you met Gaelan," he introduced us again. Really, I met him? Pascal was a tall, muscular man. He had a bodybuilder physique, solid muscle, with shoulders as broad as an elephant is wide. He was definitely someone you would want on your side during a fight. How in the world did I forget meeting him? Enos was the complete opposite. He was a skinny, young kid.

"Oh, hello, it's nice to see you," I said politely to Pascal despite having no recollection of ever meeting him before.

"Samantha," Pascal replied, accompanied with a friendly nod.

"And that's Enos." Noah pointed to the young teenager talking to Gaelan. He paid no attention to us. They appeared to be in the middle of a heated discussion.

"No, no way. We can't," Gaelan argued with Enos.

"We're taking them," Enos shouted.

"*No*, Enos, we're not. We have to go by foot. The conditions aren't right. It's not safe. Decca is too windy." I was a little disappointed to hear that we were going by foot. I wanted to ride in one of the cool mystery vehicles parked inside the landing, too.

Enos glowered at Gaelan. "So what, you think it will be better for us to walk around without any protection in a harsh environment?" Enos challenged Gaelan's decision. Tyden looked at Gaelan with understanding and bit his lip. He appeared deliberate in keeping quiet to avoid getting himself involved in the fight.

Zaric leaned in between Gaelan and Enos. "If we crash, Decca doesn't exactly have a clean-up crew to remove your mangled body from the wreckage." He let out a small chuckle.

"This is absurd. You're afraid of crashing. Perhaps if you *knew* how to fly we wouldn't have to worry about hurting the precious Levitrons," Enos moaned as he pointed over to the strange vehicles. I saw Gaelan's eyes widen in disbelief at Enos's defamatory insult. He took a deep inhale like he was fighting to maintain his composure.

"We're walking," Gaelan shot back firmly. He quickly turned away, leaving no room for discussion. I couldn't believe how calm Gaelan handled the teenager's shoddy remark. Gaelan would make an excellent parent. He took my hand and led me down the wide metal ramp onto the snow-covered ground. Everywhere you looked, there was nothing but white—the landscape was barren. It was daylight, but there was no sun in sight. The sky was a clouded silver gray. I turned back to look up at the ship. My jaw dropped open in awe, letting the cold air hit my teeth. I was blown away by its mammoth size. The dark gray hull of the craft looked enormous against the white backdrop. It felt big on the inside, but seeing it in its entirety, it was even bigger than I ever could have imagined. The ship was shaped like a boomerang with perfectly curved, aerodynamically correct angles. Spotlights shined down brightly in a V-like pattern onto the snow below. The ship's lights made the snow glisten with rainbow prisms, like light shining off diamonds. Mist surrounded the ship as heat evaporated off its hull. It appeared to be cooling down after entering the planet's atmosphere. I would have loved to see the blueprints on something so extreme. Some of the other crewmen came down the ramp and remote-controlled a three-foot-wide metal pipe. The pipe dropped straight down from the ship and drilled right into the ground. It was practically silent but smelled like hydraulic fluid. I came back to reality and realized the others were already starting to walk away from the ship.

"Wait up," I called after them. I strode quickly to catch up. I instantly regretted not eating more for lunch.

"Do you like the ship?" Gaelan asked when I came up beside him.

"It's outstanding," I complimented.

"It *really* is." He smiled widely at my appreciation of the technological masterpiece.

"What is that?" I asked, turning back to point to the pipe coming down from the ship.

"We refill our water tanks here. Decca has fantastic water," explained Gaelan.

Noah pointed to a mountain range that was directly ahead. I gazed up at the tall mountain peaks in the distance. "That's where we're going, Sami. You are *mine*," he declared to the mountain.

"Great, maybe I should have stayed on the ship," I muttered as I looked up at the imposing wall of white. The land was completely untouched by habitation, as if no one would dare to venture up its tall ranges.

"Are you afraid of heights?" Gaelan asked cautiously.

"No, I just have a healthy respect for them," I lied somewhat convincingly. Of course I was afraid. What was I, stupid?

"Come on, Sami, are you scared of a little adventure?" prodded Noah.

"No, I'm game." I gave Noah a high five with my padded gloved hand. He smiled at my response.

"I'll show you adventure," Karis said competitively in an unbearably sweet little-girl voice as she cuffed her arm around Noah's. He leaned over and gave her a quick kiss on the lips. Her insecurity was draining.

We had to walk at least three miles across what looked like a frozen lake before we got to the bottom of the mountain. It was an easy walk since the snow was packed down smoothly by the wind. It also didn't hurt that the gusting wind was blowing against our backs, practically pushing us along. I worried that Enos's scrawny body would blow away. Maybe he knew the trek would be difficult for him. The wind circled him like a flag pole during a tornado. We stopped at the bottom of the mountain to tether our bodies together at our waists with climbing rope and grappling hooks. Before we could start our ascent, the planet rumbled and shook with a larger tremor.

"Watch out!" Tyden shouted loudly at Pascal and me. We were at the caboose of the line. Gaelan was directly in front of me and gave us both a yank, pulling us a stunning six feet forward before catching me in his arms. Luckily, Pascal brought his massive body to an abrupt halt before he flattened me like a pancake.

"*Ahh*," I screamed at the unexpected jolt. I turned to discover a large mound of dense snow had crashed down into a pile on the exact spot where we had been standing. It surely would have crushed us.

"Hey, beautiful," Gaelan said smoothly. I used his arms to stand up and gain my bearings. He had the ability to make a near-death experience romantic.

"Thanks," I replied quietly. It was uncomfortable having so many onlookers overhearing our exchange. I quickly suppressed my yearning desire to go somewhere where we could be alone. "What in the world was that? This whole mountain isn't going to tumble down on us, *is it?*"

"Decca frequently has shifts in its tectonic plates. They are usually mild and short-lived," Gaelan explained calmly, trying to dispel my fear. Without delay, the shaking returned as if it were summoned. Our eyes scouted the mountainside as the vibration rumbled beneath our feet. We stood in silence, gazing up at the snow-loaded slope towering high above our heads. It was terrifying to watch some of the snow roll down the hillside of the ridged terrain in the direction we were headed. A strong enough tremor would definitely sprout an avalanche. *I'd really like to avoid being buried alive here or anywhere else for that matter.*

"Let's go. We shouldn't waste time," said Tyden. He looked at me in a threatening manner before he turned around. He seemed to be saying, "Don't mess this up," only not so kindly. Everyone quickly followed his lead and started up the snowy route. Enos complained every couple of minutes. "How much farther do we have to go? Are you sure you remember where the cave is? Can we stop and take a break?" He whined on and on. No one paid any attention to him. I, however, found it hard to ignore and fought to control my urge to tell him to shut up!

For the most part, we followed a natural path carved into the sides of the cliff. Falling snow obscured our visibility the higher we climbed, making it difficult to see the stretch of trail up ahead. There was only one bend where I felt much too close to the edge. We had to wait patiently as each of us took turns stepping around a huge rock that jutted out in our way. I prayed that there wouldn't be another shake and tightly grasped the rope we had clipped to our waist that linked us all together. It was my turn. Pascal held my waist for as far as his reach allowed him. On my first step, I kicked off a clump of snow from the terracing edge and watched it fall down into the valley far below. "*Oh*," I gasped as the reality of where I was set in. *Do not look down*, I told myself before I made another move while I clung to the mountain wall like Velcro. The drop below was very steep. I didn't need to have vertigo right now. That same wind that had helped push me along the frozen lake had now become my enemy. It whipped around us forcefully. Each blast of wind blew my goggles painfully deep into my face. It felt like I could blow right off the cliff. I carefully secured my boot against the mountainside, nearly burying it in the snow. There was very little room to step as I shifted around the blocked path. It took six steps in all before Gaelan grabbed my hand as I came around the bend. I had made it! I exhaled in relief when I viewed the widened trail ahead.

Overall, I couldn't believe how effortlessly I hiked to the top ridge. Did Urit's vaccination enhance my physical abilities? I wasn't even out of breath or tired. I looked at the Katarians. They didn't seem to be impressed by their extreme skill. I guess it would be easy to take it for granted when you haven't experienced exertion fatigue. We entered a large cavern in the side of the mountain. It had a musty, dank smell. We undid the rope chaining us together.

The stone-walled cave was dimly lit compared to the bright white outside, but not completely dark. It had an amazing rosy glow, making the need for flashlights unnecessary. My eyes squinted as I adjusted to the darkness. It was also considerably warmer. We had to remove our gloves and unzip our jackets to cool off after we entered the rocky shelter. The ground was uneven, and I had to carefully plant my boots before I took each step. Pascal was so large. He took huge strides. Each of his footsteps resonated loudly throughout the cavern. Gaelan, Zaric, and Noah moved with grace. They seemed to float across the rough terrain with ease. Karis skipped around like a little elf. The group's natural ability was obvious. We moved deeper into the cavern before we reached a large opening that was entirely filled with the source of the glowing red light. I quickly surveyed the area. It was unbelievable! The cavern walls, floor, and ceiling were made up of huge rubies. The stones shimmered brilliantly. A snow-covered opening above us functioned like a skylight to light up the space. It looked like a jeweler had positioned a spotlight to shine on her display.

"Wow," was all I could say.

"Isn't it incredible, Sami? Aren't you glad you didn't chicken out?" Noah smirked. I gave him a nod.

I watched as Gaelan and the others took out pencil-sized laser pointers and began cutting free large chucks of gemstone with the laser's green beam of light. "We harvest the rubies and use them to line the hull of our ships. It adds incredible strength to the structural integrity," he explained.

"Those are really powerful," I said. The lasers carved through the thick stone like it was butter.

"Yeah, they're useful, only you have to handle them with care." Gaelan stopped cutting the stones for a moment to talk. He gave a little smile, turning up the corners of his lips, making him look even more desirable.

"Here, Sami, could you start filling up the bags?" He handed me his backpack, and I lifted the heavy pieces with two hands and stuffed them into the bag. Everyone was spread out all over the large room, diligently chipping away and filling their bags with the stones. I felt another tremor rumble through the ground and walls. Some dust and debris fell down on our heads, temporarily clouding the air. No one stopped working. Instead, they seemed to pick up their speed. "We'll be quick—we're almost done." Gaelan looked at me reassuringly. He must have noticed my fearful expression. My paranoid mind started to worry about a possible cave-in.

I was relieved when I saw Karis and Noah swing their packs onto their backs, signaling that they were finished. Zaric, Pascal, and Enos quickly joined them. They all appeared ready to leave. Before I could lift my bag, Gaelan grabbed my arm. "*Shh* ... did you hear that?" he whispered. The others all stopped dead in their tracks, standing like statues. His eyes were wide. His gaze met the others', but no one spoke. "We've got company," he said in a tense tone. I listened carefully, trying to hear what had alarmed him. Then, to my surprise, I heard something, too—faint sounds coming from the cave's entrance. He was right. We were not alone. I couldn't believe he was able to hear them over the noise we had been making. His senses were so keen to the surroundings.

"Is there another way out?" I whispered. My question was answered by a consensus of shaking heads. We were trapped. Carefully, everyone went into hiding. I wanted to run, but there was nowhere to go except deeper into the cave. Together, Tyden, Gaelan, and I slid behind a four-foot rock jutting up from the floor and ducked down on the ground. I was tempted to join the others since they were significantly closer to the exit.

"Don't move," Gaelan quickly instructed me, in a voice so low I could barely hear him, when he saw me re-think my hiding spot. The muffled voices and footsteps grew louder. The visitors approached and lit up the cavern walls with a bright white light as they drew closer. It was blinding to my night-adjusted eyes. Gaelan cautiously peered around the side of the stone to see who the visitors were.

"Dreons," he huffed quietly and slumped back down. He brought his hand to his mouth as he thought. I knew he wasn't happy by the irritated look on his face. His expression was somewhat terrifying. I recalled him telling me how they had abducted his people in the past for experimentation. I had never seen this side of Gaelan before. His was apprehensive. I was used to feeling so safe when he was near. His obvious anxiety only heightened my own. I looked at Tyden. He was leaning his head against the rock in front of us. He was so silent, I wasn't even sure if he was breathing. I tensed my entire body, trying to hold completely still and mirror his stance so I would go unnoticed. Gaelan looked at me as though he needed to tell me something.

"What?" I mouthed the words as I held up my hands in confusion. He slowly held up his hand to motion for me not to move. He carefully slid closer to me, looked down at me with saddened eyes, and bit his lip.

"I'm sorry," he mouthed back with his face drawn in agony. Tyden reached out his arm and clasped it around Gaelan's to get his attention.

"We need a plan," he said, more with his lips than his voice. Gaelan shrugged his shoulders as his eyes tightened in thought. Tyden concentrated as well, staring off into space as though he were trying to devise an escape plan. I could hear the Dreons moving the rubies around. It wasn't being done in the same manner we used. They were loud. It sounded like a noisy construction site. You could hear large rocks splitting before hitting the ground in a roaring crash. It was followed by the sound of gravel shifting under their feet as they walked past. I could see their thin shadows on the opposite wall. The narrow figures carried boulder-sized rocks out of the cave on their shoulders. How strong were they? These stones were heavy. It reminded me of the world's strongest man competitions on Earth. It never ceased to amaze me to see the contestants swing the 350-pound atlas balls around like they were filled with air.

Gaelan slowly reached down to lift the cuff of his coat and expose the metal bracelet on his wrist. It was a double-braided chain made out of a dull silver alloy. It was something most of the Katarians wore, aside from Noah. Once, I asked Noah if he had one. He said he did but didn't wear it because it might blow his cover on Earth since the metal wasn't native to our planet. Tyden shifted his eyes from the ground to look at Gaelan. Gaelan held out his arm to Tyden and motioned for him to remove it by tapping it with his finger. Tyden's mouth opened slightly, but he didn't say a word. He looked at me, the way he always did, seeming slightly upset by my presence. He unclasped the bracelet in the most bizarre manner. He had to turn it several times in different directions. It looked like he opened up the metal, separating the two strands. Then, he carefully handed one of the braids to Gaelan. He turned to me and held up a finger to my lips, barely touching them, to keep me silent. He lifted my left arm and laid the bracelet on my wrist. The ends of the metal attracted and snapped shut on my wrist. I let out a gasp. His eyes widened, knowing I was too loud. I prayed no one had heard me. Luckily, no one did.

We waited silently for the Dreons to finish their work. I wish I had sat completely on the ground instead of squatting on my knees. I was getting pins and needles in my legs and feet from the lack of circulation. Finally, the Dreons seemed to be done collecting the rubies. They were leaving. It became really quiet when the pain in my legs was becoming too difficult to bear. I couldn't hold still any longer. Before they were all gone, I carefully shifted my weight. Unfortunately, my numb left foot slid out from under me ever so slightly, kicking up a few small pebbles, causing them to roll across the cavern floor only to hit a Dreon's foot. I saw his shadow abruptly stop in front of us as he put down his load.

"Who goes there?" spoke the alien.

Tyden stood up, knowing our cover was blown. "The Katarians. We do not want to disturb you." He held himself with impeccable posture. His composure was admirable. Gaelan and I rose to our feet and stood behind him. I was alarmed not only to see the Dreon in front of us, but the enormity of the cavern when it was fully lit up by their lights. The alien was tall and lanky. He appeared somewhat human, aside from his solid black eyes, thin lips, and small chin. A white robe was draped over his thin body. He appeared similar to the gray aliens some people on Earth had been describing for years, except his skin was ghostly white and his shoulder-length hair was pale blonde. I couldn't believe his frail frame was able to lift the large gemstone resting at his feet.

"We had hoped to await your exit, Hyril," Tyden spoke with authority. I was surprised he knew the Dreon by name.

"Come out. We only seek some supplies ourselves," Hyril demanded in a non-threatening manner.

We stepped out from behind the rock. "Well then, we will be on our way," Tyden said, turning as he started to leave.

"Do not hurry, Tyden." The alien unclipped a long rod from a holster on his belt. *Great, he's going to shoot us. Why couldn't Gaelan have pulled out a gun or his handy laser cutter? What good was a bracelet going to do?* He held up the wandlike device to each of us and swished it up and down our bodies. I watched as Gaelan and Tyden stood perfectly still. They each had blank expressions on their faces. I immediately understood their reaction to the device when it was my turn. The tool emitted an invisible force that made it physically impossible to move. I struggled to shift my body again and again without being able to muster up so much as a twitch. My arms felt weighted and tingled, as if my molecular structure was made out of metal and stuck to a magnet, when I attempted to resist it. I stood there helplessly paralyzed as the creepy alien went up and down my body. It was hard to breath. I wanted desperately to run away but had no choice but to submit to the exam. Was he checking us for weapons? He didn't explain what it was, but he must have been satisfied with its readings and hooked it back to his belt.

"Introduce me to your friends," he seethed through his teeth as three more Dreons silently appeared out of nowhere. They stood quietly behind him, possibly awaiting orders.

"This is Gaelan and Samantha. They are part of my crew," Tyden said in a nonchalant tone.

"Gaelan, I know your father. Is he well?" Hyril stated as if he were a friend of the family's.

"Yes, he is fine," Gaelan replied flatly.

"And you, Samantha?" inquired the alien.

"She's with me," interrupted Gaelan defensively.

"Oh, I can see that," he sneered as he looked down at my wrist. The bracelet was a little loose, making it visible as it rested across the base of my hand. "Your name, Samantha ... that is something you do not often hear on this side of the universe. It is almost as though you are from another planet," he said, seething through his teeth. He moved his face very close to mine. His body was nearly touching me. Hasn't he heard of invading someone's personal space? My eyes met his gaze. He stared at me with his giant, glossy black eyes, waiting for my answer. Despite his somewhat human form, his eyes were definitely buglike. A chill ran down my spine. They scared the wits out of me. *Go to hell*, I thought.

"Oh, my dear, I did not mean it as an insult. I was merely curious," he said darkly. Did he just read my mind?

"Yes, I did. Is there *anything* else you want to share? Perhaps you will tell me where you are from?" He slithered the words out of his mouth like a hissing snake and brought his face in closer to mine. I concentrated hard on spending time with Gaelan aboard the ship. "Interesting." He gave a devious grin while he continued to stare me down.

Tyden and Gaelan stood in silence. I concentrated on preparing food in the café and exercising with Azil. I couldn't believe how hard it was to monitor my thoughts. It took all my energy and more to stay in the present. My reaction must have upset him.

"You want to be difficult, do you?" he sneered. He deepened his gaze. This time it hurt. His mind functioned as a weapon. It felt like he was cutting through my brain with a drill. I tried to look away—to shut my eyes, but I couldn't. He was holding them open somehow. The surrounding walls began to spin rapidly around me. I could hear a strange humming noise. The sound was unrecognizable. It sounded electronic. We were no longer in the cave.

We were *transported?* Was I dreaming? Tyden, Gaelan, and I were suddenly standing in the middle of a stark desert. The sky above us had a gloomy reddish hue, which reflected flatly against the blackened bark of some old, dried trees nearby. They looked as though they had been petrified for thousands of years. Brown dust whirred up in the hot air around us from the infertile ground. Everywhere you looked, there was nothing but brown, cracked dirt due to the droughtlike climate. Hyril suddenly appeared. He strode towards us, kicking up some sand with his feet, but did not speak.

Hyril stopped directly in front of me. "Samantha, what if I threatened to leave you on a planet such as this? Then, would you be willing to tell me where you came from?" he said harshly.

Gaelan stepped in front of Hyril and confronted him. "Stop this!" he demanded. Hyril glared but did not speak. Gaelan found his silence provoking and responded with a swift right hook that landed squarely on Hyril's face. He followed it with several blows to his gut. Hyril swung back clumsily, hitting only the air around him. Then, Gaelan delivered one hard blow to his jaw, causing Hyril to stumble backwards. Gaelan grabbed Hyril by the throat and lifted his thin body a few inches off the ground.

"Why can't you freaky low-lifes mind your own business?" Gaelan huffed.

"You are our business," Hyril sneered.

Tyden interjected, "According to who?"

Hyril glared at him. "According to this." Hyril had managed to grab hold of his paralyzing tool clipped to his belt. He aimed it at Gaelan. To my horror, it didn't just freeze him in place. Instead, it sent him soaring fifteen feet in the air, causing his body to crash down to the ground below.

"Gaelan," I screamed while trying run to him. Before I could reach him, Hyril fired the device at me and then Tyden. It stopped us instantly. We were unable to move anything but our eyes. Hyril looked at me with a sinister grin as he drew a long metal sword from his hip. *Oh no*, I thought in panic, he was planning *to kill us*. He approached Gaelan, who was stumbling to his feet. Without delay, he forcefully drove the sword through his gut. Gaelan winced in pain before sliding off the blade and dropping dead to the ground. *No!* I cried with anguish. Then, Hyril turned and drove the sword into Tyden to kill him as well. I watched whirls of dust blow over their lifeless bodies, sticking to their wounds. I stood beside them, unable to move or go to them as wide puddles of their blood traveled across the dry ground, seeping into the cracks and running into my feet.

"*Ahh*," I gasped, despite my petrified state.

"It's too late for them, but you can save yourself. You have a choice. You can go home. You will be safe there. *Tell me* where you are from," he demanded. His face was hard. His cold, dark eyes emanated evil.

I attempted to scream but couldn't make a sound. I was helplessly alone in the middle of nowhere with the murderer. I surveyed the landscape with my eyes, look-ing for an escape. There was nothing. It didn't matter—I was unable to move. He looked at me before he lifted the same bloody sword with two hands and impaled it right into my stomach and straight out the other side. I gasped for air as the horrific pain tore through me and brought me to my knees. With all of my power, I managed to resist the paralysis and grabbed hold of the sword with both of my weakened hands. I attempted to pull it out. Its sharp edges jaggedly cut into my palms, but it wouldn't budge. I felt my life force fading. Is this how it felt to die? *Oh no, I'm not ready*, I thought while I clung onto the embedded sword. I knew I shouldn't give up, but the wound was too great. I looked at my hemorrhaging abdomen and felt the warm blood soaking through my shirt. It was no use. There was too much damage. I thought about leaving Leah and Jackson. "No," I cried, "I can't! They need me. *I love them!*" I sucked in wheezing gasps of air. I fought to cling onto my life.

"Tell me about your planet," he persisted.

No, I thought. *I would* never. Instead, I said a prayer asking for a miracle. It seemed to give me strength. Before I knew it, I found myself surrounded by a warm, golden light and an overwhelming feeling of love. A peaceful, protective force encompassed me. I knew I was safe. This *couldn't* be real. I would be dead by now. It had to be the alien. He was putting the pictures in my mind to try to scare me, intimidate me. I took back control of my mind. I concentrated even harder on peaceful thoughts. I pictured the agility course aboard the ship. I thought about our walk across the frozen lake and climb up to the cave. "Please, make it stop," I cried out in desperation. Suddenly, Hyril's silhouette hovered above me, blocking out the red light from the sky above. He pulled out the sword, leaned down, and touched my abdomen with a glob of something wet and sticky. It closed the wound and caused the pain to instantly disappear. His hold on me seemed to lessen, my strength returned, and I regained movement in my whole body. I had won. Without warning, my body felt like it was floating and the desert scenery around me faded into the background.

"Well, I guess there is nothing more." Hyril's snarky voice echoed in my head as he backed away from me, sounding disappointed. I had mysteriously reappeared in the cave. How did I get here? Did I ever leave? I thought I was losing my mind. I shuddered at the revolting, deranged psychological torture he had planted in my head when he attempted to trick me into telling him where I lived. I felt him fully release his mental grip on me. I took a few steps backwards to maintain my balance when my body fell back as though I had been pulled off a giant suction cup. It was physically draining. My arms and legs felt numb and tingly while they regained their full strength. I immediately looked over at Gaelan and

Tyden. To my relief, they were standing there as they were before, alive and completely unharmed.

"Peace to you." Tyden stated to Hyril before he briskly turned to leave, ushering Gaelan and me ahead of him.

"And to you, my Katarian friends," replied the alien sarcastically in a slithery voice.

"Let's get out of here." Gaelan motioned with his hand.

"I'm way ahead of you," I said with urgency as I threw my backpack on my back. We walked swiftly towards the mouth of the cave. I led the way. Under pressure, I mastered the rocky terrain with ease. I stepped boldly across the stone beams and undeveloped landscape. My desire to distance myself from the Dreons took precedence over prudence. To my surprise, the Dreons were nowhere in sight. They seemed to have vanished into thin air. I didn't know how they were exiting the cave. They must have found another way in.

"Are you okay?" Gaelan called out wistfully from behind me. I continued rushing towards the exit.

"I'm fine," I answered in a faint voice. All my energy was focused on getting far away from the wicked Dreons. It was hard to forget the terrifying image Hyril had injected into my mind. It seemed so real.

We reached the snowy entrance in record time. Everyone was waiting for us outside. They had all managed to slip past the Dreons and get out.

"Sami, come here," exclaimed Noah when he saw me. He pulled me directly into his arms and squeezed me in a death grip. "Oh, thank goodness!" He sighed.

"You can say that again." The words could barely express my elation. "I'm not sure what the Dreons would have done to me if they knew I wasn't a Katarian."

"I was sure they would have taken you. Of course, then I would have to kick some major Dreon butt!" Noah threatened in a harsh voice.

Pascal joined in, "I hear you," sounding up for the fight. His voice rang with animosity.

"Take it easy now," warned Zaric in an authoritative tone. "Please don't start a war today."

I surveyed the white, barren landscape. "Where are they now? Did they come in another way?" I asked.

Noah shook his head. "They're not here. They use teleporters to return to their ship."

I looked up at the hazy sky, searching for a glimpse of their ship. I didn't see anything.

"You guys are masters at hiding," complimented Karis in a sweet voice as she glided up beside us. She seemed desperate for Noah's attention. I released myself from Noah's grip to ease her discomfort.

"We had a brief encounter," Tyden said grudgingly. My eyes quickly jumped over to his face. To my surprise, I found him looking back at me with a gaze much softer than usual.

Pascal's jaw dropped open. "*What*? They found you? How did you *all* get away?" he asked, sounding perplexed as he nodded his head towards me. "Did they perform a mind-sweep on you, Samantha?" he asked urgently.

"Yes, I think … if that's what you call it," I answered, unsure.

Enos rolled his eyes. "Fantastic, that's all we need. This is great news for them," he snapped sarcastically. "The Dreons will be ecstatic. The Katarians are harboring a girl from Earth. They will call us hypocrites. They will start taking liberties, all because of Sami. She'll put us all in danger," Enos complained angrily. I was starting to dislike him more and more. He could really get on my nerves. He was so cynical for such a young man. He had moaned about every little thing today. I liked him better when he didn't open his mouth.

"Don't overreact. They don't know anything, Enos," Gaelan reassured. "There is nothing to be concerned about." Gaelan's eyes tried to hold my gaze, making the comment seem as though it were meant for me.

"We took care of it," Tyden spoke calmly, trying to diffuse the tension. "Let us return to the ship and be on our way," he commanded, leaving no room for discussion.

I could see why Tyden, Gaelan, and Zaric held a high rank. All of them possessed incredible maturity. Tyden's order wasn't challenged. No one even asked how we handled the encounter once he spoke. Tyden's words clearly had authority. I could see that he was greatly respected by all members of the crew. One night, I had discussed my fear of Tyden with Gaelan. I told him how I found him incredibly intimidating. I remembered Gaelan laughing at me. He said that I would feel differently if I knew him better. He said he just had a serious demeanor. He explained that Tyden was the oldest crew member and that he had more experience than anyone aboard. Gaelan told me that Tyden could probably run the whole ship by himself if he had to. He spoke about him with such admiration. I was starting to understand why. Tyden held himself remarkably well under pressure. Maybe I was reading him all wrong. If it wasn't for him helping Gaelan, I wouldn't have been able to wear the Katarian bracelet and disguise myself in front of the Dreons. If he really didn't like me, he would have just let them take me. I would be a kidnapped lab rat right now. I was indebted to him.

***

We started on our way back to the ship. All traces of our footprints leading to the cave were already swept away by the frigid wind. It didn't matter. We walked farther along the mountain trail instead of returning the way we had come. Even if it was the wrong way, I wasn't going to argue. I think my being here caused more of a hassle than I was previously aware of. I relived Enos's words in my head about how I put everyone at risk. I didn't even ask for this. *Trust me, I would rather be at home right now*. I stomped my boots in frustration through the powdery white snow. I didn't feel like making the journey down the mountain with these heavy rocks in my bag. I wished I was already safely sitting on the ship.

Pascal stopped and dropped his bag. "This looks good," he said.

"Let's do it," cheered Noah.

"Do what?" I asked.

"Go back to the ship, Sami," explained Karis. "You don't think we're going to walk down, do you?" She scoffed at me like I was a complete idiot.

"How exactly are you planning on getting back?" I retorted, looking down at the steep snow-covered ravine. The snow was packed down into a slick slab of ice. It looked way too dangerous to survive. Plus, there wasn't a ski or snowboard in sight.

"We're going to slide down," Karis said proudly, with a snotty smirk on her face. "Our suits are designed for it."

"*No way*, are you crazy? It's suicide! We'll die!" Everyone started to laugh at my frantic reaction.

"Sami, it's okay. We'll be fine," Gaelan said, trying not to laugh. "I know that on Earth it would be extremely dangerous, but Decca has about three-fourths the gravity of Earth. Plus, our suit material will help act as a braking system." I suddenly understood why the hike up the mountain had been so easy. It wasn't so much due to my renewed body as it was to the lack of the planet's gravitational pull.

Noah shot me an ornery smirk. "See you at the bottom, Sami. Cow-a-bungaa!" he shouted before he stepped right off the mountainside. He was never one to delay. His fearlessness bordered on insanity.

I gasped. *"Noah!"* I peered over the edge of the extremely steep hillside to see him sailing smoothly down towards the bottom of the mountain, feet first. Karis enthusiastically followed after him. I watched as everyone else joined them without hesitation. They simply sat on their bottoms with the backpacks strapped to their backs and slid straight down the slope. They glided in a controlled manner instead of tumbling down in the giant snowball I had envisioned.

"Are you ready?" Gaelan reached for my hand while he sat down in the snow, letting his feet dangle over the side of the cliff.

"No, but whatever I have to do …" I bit my lip. There was no other option, so I bravely sat down next to him, closed my eyes briefly, and pushed myself off the edge. The initial sickening feeling of falling downward was quickly replaced with a smooth, gliding sensation. We descended side by side as though we were riding on

an elevator. A mound of crushed up soft snow gathered up like a growing platform, supporting my feet while I descended. I was at the bottom in no time. It was the best sled ride I'd ever had in my life. It was so much fun that I'd even do it again.

We trekked back across the flat landscape, but this time our faces were against the wind. It pushed against us as though we were in the heart of a hurricane. We had to lean forward and plant our feet firmly with each step to keep from blowing backwards. It started to snow hard. It also felt much colder than it did earlier. The vapor from our breath seemed to freeze as soon as it left our lips. The tremors seemed to be occurring more often now, too. I wasn't sure if there was a storm on the horizon or if the planet experienced night, but it looked really dark in the distance. The rolling gray clouds coming our way looked ominous. At last, we could see the lights of our ship arising through the thickening haze of giant snowflakes.

"This sucks!" Zaric complained.

"It's relentless," Pascal shouted back.

"We'll live. I've been in worse," Tyden added.

Gaelan pointed towards the ship. "Come on ... keep your eyes on the prize. We're almost home," he encouraged. Was that a metaphor I just heard? Perhaps I really was rubbing off on him.

We all moved at a steady pace, bracing ourselves against the powerful wind. Now, the ship had to be less than a mile ahead. Suddenly, a tremendous tremor shook the ice below our feet. The rumble spread across the terrain far and wide. The icy path we traveled across violently cracked open and split apart beneath our feet in a ferocious eruption. Large chucks of ice broke away and shot up through the frozen ground in massive blocks, exposing the deep lake below. Dark gray water rippled through the exposed cracks and gushed across the ice floor, splashing over our boots.

Before I knew it, the ground under Tyden and me was no longer stable and began to split apart. It broke loose from the ledge of solid ground where Gaelan and the others were standing and started to tear away. I fought to maintain my balance, afraid to make a move. Gaelan motioned for us to join them. Another aftershock brutally quivered beneath us, pushing our frozen landmass farther away from the icy shore. Tyden and I didn't hesitate any longer and leapt over to them. Gaelan grabbed my arm and pulled me onto the stable shore. I turned after I landed, sensing that Tyden didn't make it. He had slipped and hit the back of his head on a raised piece of ice. Bright red blood was splattered across the white ice on the spot where the back of his skull had struck. He rolled and barely made a splash as his lifeless body fell into the icy water and swiftly started to float away face down.

"*No!*" I screamed. I went to go after Tyden.

Gaelan held me back. "Samantha, no—you can't! *Stop!*" he shouted at me.

"Let me go." I struggled against him to break free. I succeeded, leaving Gaelan holding only my backpack. I ran and jumped straight into the icy water after Tyden. I glanced over at Gaelan and the others as they yelled and hysterically waved for me to swim back, but I ignored their demands. The current was swift and strong. It quickly pulled me away from the shore. I attempted to avoid the passing chucks of floating ice, but one pounded into my shoulder. Ignoring the painful blow, I swam with all my determination to catch up with Tyden. I stretched out my arm and finally managed to grab the hood of his coat.

Gaelan and the others kept screaming for me to swim back. They ran along the shore beside us to keep pace with the current. I tried to swim to the icy edge, where the group was frantically waving as I pushed Tyden's body to move him but made little headway. I not only struggled against the current but the weight of my water-logged snow gear. It was hard to keep afloat. Although I couldn't feel the coldness of the water through my snow-suit and boots, they must have become saturated with water and felt heavier on my body than the pile of rocks I'd been carrying. Their bulkiness made swimming difficult. If I were on Earth, they surely would have sucked me under.

"Sami," Noah shouted. "Get out of there before you get eaten!"

I could barely hear him with all of my splashing. What did he say? *Eaten?* I nervously looked down at the dark water, but couldn't see anything at first. Then I noticed something unusual. Thousands of tiny bubbles were rising to the surface. *Oh please, let it be my imagination.*

Gaelan was yelling, too. "Come on, it's dangerous in there."

Dangerous? *Oh no*, the bubbles were not my imagination. I shuddered to think what was below me. I started to paddle and kick harder. Gaelan lassoed the rope, which we had used to tether us all together on our climb, high above his head and threw it out to me. I desperately paddled over to grab it—its end quickly sank into the murky water. It was hard to hold onto with my gloved hand. He and the others swiftly pulled me in while I towed Tyden behind me to the ledge.

"Here, t-take him," I stuttered to Gaelan and Noah. They quickly pulled Tyden out of the water and rolled him onto his back. He was still unconscious.

"Let's go, Sami. Hurry up! Get the hell out of there," yelled Noah frantically.

I reached up, and before I knew it, he and Gaelan grabbed my hands and lifted me to my feet in one quick swoop. I couldn't maintain my balance and fell to the ground on my hands and knees next to Tyden, struggling to catch my breath. The cold wind instantly turned the water on the surface of my suit to a crispy, thin layer of ice. It froze my hair into icicles and burnt my skin as it whipped across my wet face. I would have frozen to death if it weren't for the miracle fabric inside my snowsuit. The suit's lining was radiating heat. The cold water must have activated some sort of built-in warming system.

"Come on, we need to move. We'll take care of him on the ship. There's a storm brewing," Zaric yelled out over the gusting wind.

I gazed up at the gray, darkened sky coming over us. The tumbling black clouds lit up with a huge flash of lightning. A deafening clap of thunder followed immediately after and seemed to resonate through the cracked ground. I crawled over to Tyden and leaned my ear over his face to check if he was breathing. I pulled off my gloves and felt for a carotid pulse. I felt nothing. He was motionless. His dark complexion made his lips look dark purple. I sucked in a deep breath, despite the cold air stinging my lungs and started CPR. Everyone stood around me silently.

"Sami, no, don't. Please, you have to stop," begged Karis. I looked up to see Noah hold her back.

"Wait, Karis, please. It's okay," he whispered. Within a minute, Tyden took in a couple of shallow gasps of air before coughing up an explosive fountain of water and sucking in one deep breath. He became semi-awake and bolted upright to take in a few more deep breaths while he continued to choke up mouthfuls of water.

Gaelan pulled on my arm. "Sami, come on—we have to go," he insisted.

"*I will!* Can you give him just a minute?" I answered, annoyed.

"No! *Not here,* we can't," he said urgently.

I followed his eyes and turned back to look at the water. While I was busy doing CPR, I had failed to notice that the currents that rippled across the water had changed. Large bubbles were now rumbling across the dark surface like a hot tub on full blast. Before I knew it, Gaelan grabbed me by the waist and pulled me up. Zaric and Noah put Tyden's arms around their shoulders and lifted him up together before breaking into a full sprint towards the ship. Gaelan and I ran directly behind them. Pascal, Karis, and Enos were already far ahead. They were about to start their ascent up the ship's ramp.

"What was that?" I asked as I ran. I could barely get the words out and gasp the cold air into my lungs at the same time. We were now in the midst of a full-blown blizzard and lightning storm.

"The Paramante," Gaelan replied while he sprinted beside me effortlessly.

"The *Para- what?*" I was expecting to hear that there was an underwater volcano erupting.

"The Paramante," he repeated. "That's what I was trying to tell you, but you wouldn't listen to me. You're *so* stubborn. Did you even stop to consider the risk? Are you trying to get yourself killed?" he said in an irritated tone.

"No, of course not. I was trying to save Tyden," I shouted back defensively over the howling wind. He looked at me with what looked like a tinge of guilt when he realized saving Tyden was more important to me than my own safety.

"The Paramante are ancient sea creatures that live here. They were swimming right below your feet. No one really knows that much about them. There are some horrific stories about them, though. The tremors must have disturbed them from their sleep."

My eyes widened. "Are they dangerous?"

"Oh yeah, they're enormous and can eat you in one gulp," he explained.

Suddenly, I acknowledged my rash behavior, realizing they could have swum up to get me. I turned around to look at the water. I couldn't believe my eyes. I saw what appeared to be a giant dragon head floating across the water. It looked prehistoric. The thing had enormous, yellow, snakelike eyes that seemed to be looking right at me. Then, I noticed several more swarming around. I gasped when I saw the scaly tail of one creature rise ten feet above the surface before it came crashing down, splashing a huge wave of water with its force. I shivered at the horrifying sight and the freezing wind pushing against my body. No wonder everyone was frantic when I jumped in to save Tyden. We reached the ship's ramp and ran through the open hatch. I exhaled in relief. As the ship's ramp closed, I turned back once more to look at the broken ice where the Paramante had surfaced. I could no longer see them, only big splashes of water hitting the icy shore.

Noah and Zaric laid Tyden down on the floor. Karis paged all available medical personnel to the landing. Gaelan and Noah helped me to pull off my sopping wet snowsuit. Zaric and Pascal undressed Tyden. He was conscious but looked stunned. Enos stood there helplessly watching us without offering any assistance. Two other men who were stationed there, awaiting our return, seemed to be getting the ship ready for take-off.

With the heavy, wet clothing off, I plopped down on the floor next to Tyden. Urit and the two other medics, Hayden and Bryson, entered the landing through the emergency slides. They were at our sides in a flash. Gaelan leaned down and tapped my shoulder. He murmured something to me about having to get to the command deck. He said he was needed to get the ship underway. Zaric, Noah, and he all ran out before I could say good-bye. A small crowd had formed around Tyden and me. I explained to Urit that I had to give him CPR. I told him about his head injury. I watched while Urit and the other doctors carefully examined him with the Remi-Scan and some other bizarre medical tools.

I sat quietly and was able to overhear what Karis, Enos, and several other crew members were saying as they stood around us. They were talking about how terrible it was that I brought Tyden back from the dead. Enos said I had no respect for an honorable death. I looked up to see him glowering at me. I turned away and watched Urit care for Tyden. Enos didn't stop there. I heard him say that I was completely out of bounds—that my ignorance disgraced the Katarian beliefs. The small crowd was growing around us and chimed in as well. Their comments became more disturbing. I could feel the weight of their stares bearing down on me. Enos continued to add to the disruption by grumbling about my encounter with the Dreons in the cave. He said it would endanger the entire crew. He said I might have started a war. I'd dealt with his kind before. He was a gossip-hungry naysayer who enjoyed getting a rise out of people by delivering some bad news. I knew it was pointless to try and defend myself at this time. It would only make matters worse. I could feel my lips thin in rage. I looked up at him. Our eyes met in an unfriendly glare. Then, as if that weren't enough, I saw his eyes widen and his jaw drop open when he noticed Gaelan's exposed bracelet on my wrist. He looked like he was going into shock. The angry murmurs of their voices were overwhelming. I couldn't take it anymore. I had to get out of there. I found my strength and quickly got up. Urit noticed my appalled expression and asked if I was okay. I falsely assured him that I was fine, to hide my fury. I quickly exited the landing and bolted full speed through the corridors to my room to escape from their hostile comments.

I finally made it to the safety of my quarters, slammed the door, and locked it behind me. I slunk down onto the floor in my wet clothes and leaned my head against the wall to catch my breath. My fingers were freezing. I rubbed them together, trying to generate some heat. I pulled my knees to my chest and put my head down, trying to stop my lips from quivering. Cylinders of ice melted off the strands of my hair and dropped onto the floor, forming puddles of water around me. What a mess this day had become. Thoughts of the gruesome details from the vision the sadistic alien had given me resurfaced. The feeling of looking death so close in the face was something I would never forget.

My eyes filled with tears. There was no stopping them. I started to sob uncontrollably. I twirled the metal bracelet around my wrist, looking for the clasp. The thing looked completely solid. I couldn't even see where the opening was. It had a swirly pattern engraved in the metal.

I tugged and pulled at it with all my might, trying to remove it. I whipped my hand back and banged it on the wall. It was no use. The bracelet was just tight enough to prevent me from sliding it off, and its clasp wouldn't release. I huffed in frustration as I tore my wet clothes from my body. I wished I could take back my decision to go to Decca in the first place. All this could have been avoided. I jumped into the shower and defiantly pressed the rinse button three times. It was the closest thing to therapy I could find. *Who cares about conserving water? They are probably going to kick me off the ship anyway.*

I slipped on my nightgown and slid into Gaelan's bed. It was comfortable and heated. I'd never slept in it before. Memories about the scary Dreon, Tyden's life-less body floating across the dark water, and the lurking sea creatures underneath me rushed through my mind. They seemed impossible to suppress. I remembered Enos's spiteful remarks and his judgmental expression. I clenched my jaw tightly, grinding my teeth. I didn't want the Dreons to endanger my new Katarian friends. "*Ahh,*" I groaned to myself. This was unbearable. I wanted to take the images out of my brain. I lay there wondering if they would've just let me die if I'd fallen in. I hoped that at least Noah would've tried to save me. My anxiety soared when Gaelan didn't come back to the room. He'd already worked his shift today. Clearly, we were already underway. I was sure I felt a nudge as the landing gear retracted when I ran down the hall. Gaelan was probably discussing my outlandish actions with the others. How was I supposed to know that CPR was such a repulsive act?

CHAPTER 20

EXPLANATION

Three hours must have passed before Gaelan came through the door. I had waited curled up in a fetal position on his bed, unable to sleep due to the torturous thoughts replaying in my head. He approached the bed and settled in beside me, before leaning up on his arm to look me in the eyes.

"Sami, how are you doing?" he asked cautiously.

"Better, now," I lied.

"I'm glad. You really had me worried. Urit said you looked really upset when you left the landing."

"Well, the truth is, I am very upset." I paused, searching for the main reason. I sat up in the bed. "Would you have saved me if I fell in the water like Tyden? Or would you have just let me die?" I cried.

He sighed. "No! *Never* ... how can you think that? Don't you trust me?" He sat up on the bed and rubbed his head with both of his hands. He was quiet for a moment before turning towards me and pushing a long strand of my hair behind my ear. "I would *never* let anything happen to you. You mean everything to me. I just thought I would be able to pull you out more easily when you swam back to me."

"The Paramante wouldn't stop you from jumping in?"

"No, Sami. If I thought you were in immediate danger, I would *never* hesitate. Look, I'm sorry I called you stubborn earlier today. I didn't mean it. I shouldn't have yelled at you. I had no right. If anyone is stubborn, it's me. You didn't understand the dangers. I'm sorry I put you in that position," he said regretfully.

"It's not your fault. I should have listened to you," I said remorsefully.

"Of course it is. I shouldn't have brought you on the expedition. It's my duty to protect you since I'm the reason you're aboard the ship in the first place. I just wanted to spend some time with you outside of the confines of the ship. Needless to say, *it didn't go as I had imagined.* I acted selfishly. It wasn't safe for you." Gaelan pulled me to his chest and gave me a warm hug. My body melted. He made me feel so protected.

"I guess you already heard that Enos, Karis, and pretty much everyone else aboard hates me." I pulled myself away from his embrace after a few seconds. I was still extremely anxious about their reactions.

"Yes, I heard some rumors. But it's all taken care of." His voice was calm and reassuring.

"Why? What's the consensus of the ship? Are you turning me over to the Dreons?" I replied sarcastically. I wanted to know everything they said, regardless of how much it hurt. I hated gossip, especially when it was about me.

"No, don't be ridiculous." Gaelan shook his head and appeared to be holding back a laugh. "Thank Urit. He held an emergency meeting and explained to the crew about your ancient technique of rescue breathing. He demonstrated how you stimulated Tyden to breathe by blowing up his lungs like a balloon. Now, everyone understands that you didn't bring Tyden back from the dead but just reminded him to breathe."

"But Karis was really freaked out."

"She's fine. She didn't understand before. Karis is young. She is accustomed to relying on our technology. When you used only your breath to save Tyden, it became far too personal for her."

"So, Karis and the rest of the crew are no longer angry with me?"

"Actually, now," he said with a rise in his voice, "you are sort of a hero. When word got out that you risked your life to save Tyden despite the icy water and the Paramante, their judgment quickly changed. Everyone is impressed by your self-sacrifice."

"How's Tyden?"

"He's okay. Urit is keeping him in the hospital for observation."

"Enos said I disgraced Tyden by taking away his honorable death. He seemed angry that I saved him."

"Enos doesn't even know what an honorable death is. For a young kid, his beliefs are outdated. He thinks everyone over three hundred should be dead."

"Tyden's over *three hundred?*" I was stunned. "Impossible! He looks *so* young."

"Yes, he is three hundred and then some. No one really knows for sure or is willing to figure it out." He let out a chuckle. "One thing I learned about living in Space is that you have to be willing to let go of some of the constant variables in your life. We all tend to think in black and white terms, but the universe is gray. Age becomes irrelevant. I think Tyden secretly knows how old he really is, though. He is meticulous about every other detail in his life. I just think that he prefers to keep it to himself."

"I can't believe it. *How* is that possible?"

"We've made serious strides in our ability to protect and renew our bodies. Urit alone has made some of the greatest contributions in the last fifty years."

"Urit gave me that vaccine." I gasped. "Will I be around that long?"

"No, but you will live longer than you would have without it. Your body will age more slowly. Does that scare you?" He had a look of curiosity cross his face.

"More than you can imagine."

"You don't have to worry about being alone." He smiled and looked me in the eyes. His face lit up with his offer. He looked amazing. I could definitely look at him for another two hundred and fifty years or so.

"Hmm," I voiced as I considered the bright side. "Tempting." Gaelan leaned over and kissed me gently. I closed my eyes and focused on his soft lips pressing mine.

"How old are you?" I asked as my face left his.

"Wow, um … by your measurements?" Gaelan hesitated before he looked down and bit his lip.

"Okay, not exactly, but approximately," I asked casually, bracing myself for his answer.

"Well, time varies around the universe. It speeds up and slows down depending on where you are and how fast you are moving. One second on Earth is not absolute in the rest of Space," he explained.

"Wow, Albert Einstein's theory was right again."

"Yes, he was one of your brightest. But, to answer your question, I have to consider the time I traveled as well as my time on Kataria and Earth. Then you must consider the fact that our body's age much slower when traveling in Outer Space." He looked perplexed by the question.

"We also have twenty-six-hour days instead of your twenty-four. Our year calendar is three hundred and seventy-eight days; yours is three hundred and sixty-five. Let's make it easy," he said, giving up. "If I just stayed on Kataria, I am four years older than Azil and five years older than Liam. I would be seventy-one." He looked me in the eyes. "Is that *okay*? How old do you want me to be?" he said in a precautious manner. He looked at me with a heavy stare, awaiting my answer.

"I don't care how old you are. It doesn't matter. I love you just the way you are."

"I can't believe I've lived so long without knowing you. To think all I had to do was hang out on Earth." He hugged me tightly in relief as I accepted his ambiguous explanation.

"Gaelan, I have to ask you something," I said hesitantly.

"Sure, anything," he said with a half-smile.

I bravely looked up at him. "Is it possible for us to continue seeing each other after I return home? Or will this be it?" I couldn't help remembering what Urit had said about Gaelan being unable to commit to a serious relationship. My protective armor had surfaced to guard me from the emotional pain I would feel if I lost him. I wasn't sure if I would survive.

"That's up to you," he said coolly.

"What do you mean?" I asked, fearful of his answer.

"If you will have me." He sighed uncomfortably. Gaelan leaned forward and put his elbows on his knees as he ran his fingers through his tousled hair, a nervous habit I noticed he reverted to whenever I asked him something that made him uncomfortable.

"You make it sound so easy. Did you even stop to think that maybe the reason our homes are so far apart is that we never should have met? Maybe we shouldn't have gotten so involved. Our relationship really complicates things. I can't help but worry about all the trouble I've caused you and will cause you in the future just from our cultural misunderstandings. What if it's a mistake trying to be together? Sometimes, I feel like I should've just stayed in my own world," I blurted out—regretting the burning words as soon as they left my lips.

"It doesn't matter what anybody else thinks. This is about us," he said adamantly. He turned his body back towards me with his eyes penetrating me deeply. "Are you *trying* to push me away?" he asked, sounding rattled.

"No." I bit my lip. I wanted to take in every part of him.

"Then, please, don't say that. I just found you. If we weren't supposed to meet ..." he paused, "it *never* would have happened. I don't care where you are from. I have never met anyone like you."

"I feel the same about you. I have fallen in love with you." I looked up at him and caressed his face. "But I don't want to live on a Spaceship or Kataria forever," I said sadly.

"Sami," he groaned, "I would never ask that of you. I would follow *you* to the ends of the universe. I would do anything for you. Don't you know that?"

"Gaelan, I never presumed that you would give up life as you know it for me." He put his hand under my head and pulled my face closer to meet his.

"Who says I'm giving up anything?" He looked at me seductively before leaning in to kiss me. His touch could instantly make me lose my train of thought.

"Gaelan," I pulled away, "there's more. I almost forgot. Enos saw your bracelet on me and looked really upset by it."

"He is *unbelievable*! Why can't he mind his own business?" His eyes squinted. "I *never* should have agreed to let him come aboard. The other commanders and I only conceded because his father is one of the primary contributors to our expeditions. His father begged us to bring him along. He said he wanted to broaden him. I don't think Enos even wanted to come. He doesn't seem to know what he wants. He is completely clueless." He huffed. I was pleasantly surprised to discover he shared my animosity towards Enos.

"Is he upset because I'm not Katarian? I'm guessing that the bracelet made the Dreons think I was, right?"

"Exactly." He paused and took a deep breath. "I put it on you to make you look like one of us. I didn't want them to know you are from Earth. I don't think they would have given us time to explain why you are traveling with us. I feared that they would have taken you."

"Why didn't the Dreons realize I wasn't Katarian when I spoke?"

"Well, our people have a theory on that. During one of our encounters, we accidentally discovered that most of the Dreons have very poor hearing. The ones that appear less human may even be completely deaf. Their interbreeding has given them the ability to understand many species on a deeper level. In other words, they feel what you are saying, not hear it. But their telepathy only seems to work if they are looking you directly in the eyes. We think, since they utilize their minds as their main mode of communication, biological advancement has caused them to lose their ability to verbally interpret speech. A natural occurrence of evolution—use it or lose it," Gaelan explained.

"Hmm." I pondered for a moment. "Well, what are the bracelets for?" I asked, trying to understand his culture.

"They are a display honoring our ancestors. We are given the bracelets at birth. Every family has a distinctive pattern encrusted in the metal. Only someone from Kataria could have one."

"How do you get it off? I don't even see the clasp," I said faintly. I studied the metal band around my wrist while tracing its embossed swirls with my finger.

"Sami, *please*." Gaelan grabbed my hand. "I would prefer that you would leave it on … for me. The Dreons are in the area. I saw them on our navigation. I want you to be safe in case we cross paths with them again. I can't risk them taking you. I can't lose you, not to *them!*" he said with his voice full of disgust.

"I see, only a Katarian is safe. So, me being from Earth, they could take me?"

"Yes, without a blink." He snapped his fingers.

The conviction in his voice alarmed me. The thought of being taken by the Dreons gave me a lingering shiver. I felt scared just thinking about their paralyzing device. It was impossible to oppose. It was even freakier when the alien read my mind. I could never control my thoughts for an extended period of time. Maybe I should take on a Katarian name as well for the trip since Samantha seemed to draw unnecessary attention.

"Fine, I'll leave it on," I answered abruptly. "Can I keep it forever?" I joked.

"Yes, absolutely. Nothing would make me happier. I feel for you intensely." His voice was filled with satisfaction as a smile lifted up the corners of his lips. He gently stroked his fingers under my chin and said, "If you want to wear it under your sleeve, I understand."

"Sounds good to me. Can you make it invisible like the ship?" I teased as I pulled my shirt cuff down, covering the jewelry. "I really don't want to make anyone else mad at me."

"Understood." He looked away. His expression turned into a frown after I probably reminded him of Enos.

"What is your agreement with the Dreons, anyway? Why don't they bother you?" I asked.

"We devised an agreement to meet both of our needs and end the war."

"You were at war with them?"

"Yes, unfortunately. We fought them about one hundred and ten years ago. Our weapons were not as powerful as theirs, but we managed to get their attention by the way of small victories. They sustained enough damage to their vessels that they decided to find another way to obtain their goal. They needed us. They were abducting our people to steal our genetic codes. It was a futile attempt to save their race. We suffered great losses. We needed them to stop blasting our planet and violating our people, so we negotiated an agreement that prevents them from abducting our people, in exchange for our DNA. It was the only way to ensure our safety at the time."

"Why do they need your DNA? For experiments?"

"No, they are *dying*, and rightfully so. They brought it on themselves. They've committed obscene violations in the laws of creation. I think the universe is trying to take them out," he said heartlessly.

"What did they do?" I asked as I pondered what he had meant by the laws of creation. Did he believe in a higher power or ethical boundaries?

"Who knows? We think they irreparably redesigned their genetics. It is alleged that they might have looked just like you and me at one time. In attempts to improve their physical and mental abilities, they purposely manipulated their genetic codes. To their dismay, they took it too far. Their additions permanently altered their chromosomes, creating a host of unforeseen problems. They lost their ability to reproduce, for one. Now, they have to grow their offspring in artificial wombs. And breeding with other species not only created characteristics that made them appear inhuman, it caused their cells to stop replicating and self-destruct at an accelerated rate. It has led them to suffer premature deaths and have sickly offspring. Their very existence teeters on extinction. Their will to survive has made them desperate and keeps them living in a vicious cycle. They live their lives repeating a harsh, never-ending lesson about not overly manipulating nature, but they are unable to see their errors of the past."

"Do they have souls?" I asked.

"*Hmm?*" Gaelan looked at me without answering and wrinkled his brows. He exhaled and looked down at the floor as he thought. The blood seemed to drain from his face as though my question had made him ill. I decided not to repeat myself.

"How does your agreement work?"

"We agreed to provide them with fresh samples from our people once a year in exchange for a promise that they will never take a Katarian again. But, in my opinion, we negotiated out of fear," he said with resentment.

"What do they do with the samples?"

"They crossbreed with our people. They mix our chromosomes with theirs. Our potential children become half-Dreon. Then, they use them as drones and continue the process. The very thought of it makes me sick." Gaelan squeezed his hands into fists as he shifted his body into a forward lunge. "I would like to put an end to the agreement. It needs to be stopped. I think our weapons could defeat them now. We've advanced immeasurably since the war." Gaelan raised his voice. "Their thirst for survival consumes them. I think their defense systems have become archaic while they have been so busy concentrating on their continued existence. No one wants to test the theory, though. Of course, then *nothing* changes, so here we are trying to keep the peace with the filthy, revolting bugs after all these years." He huffed in aggravation.

"If you knew you could win, would you start a war with them?" I asked hypothetically.

"Probably *not* … not at home, anyway." He took a deep breath. "Anyway, I think we would be successful. Our ship's lasers can obliterate matter with a single strike. But it's pointless. Our people believe that all of our actions will be reciprocated in some form. War is ugly. We try to use it defensively. There is a fine line in trying to achieve a desired outcome and blatant assault. Don't misunderstand me—we would engage in battle if it were necessary. We will protect ourselves and others from needless suffering, but the intention must be clear. We would need proof that they broke our arrangement and that the safety of our people was being threatened," he said in a dark tone.

I thought about his words. They haunted me. I could never bear having children I did not know, even if they were only half mine, being born into slavery. I felt his frustration. I admired his bravery in considering challenging the old arrangement. Our silence broke when my stomach growled loudly.

"Sami, I'm sorry. I did not realize that you haven't eaten! Ahh, I got all carried away with setting our course and dealing with those absurd rumors."

"I forgot myself. Are you sure it's safe to leave the room?" I asked sheepishly. I was in no hurry to see anyone else.

"You'll be fine. I promise. Come on, get dressed. We can get something to eat at the club."

CHAPTER 21

AMENDS

The club was a place the crew went for mingling and relaxing. It was dark and had music, just like our nightclubs. Soft black sofas were arranged in groups surrounding a central bar. I was only there a few times, because my weakened condition prevented me from going after that. Gaelan said he only went on occasion because he liked to spend most of his free time charting routes, exercising, or reading.

"Sami!" Karis ran up to me when we walked through the door. Noah followed behind her. They were there with Azil and Zaric.

"Hi, Karis," I replied cautiously.

"I am so sorry for what I said about you earlier. Urit explained that strange thing you did to Tyden. Sami, it really shocked me when you put your lips on his and he woke up. I had no idea that was even possible. Please, Sami, will you forgive me?"

"Of course I will, Karis. No harm done," I assured her. I looked over her shoulder at Noah. He was trying not to laugh. Apparently, he found her naivety amusing.

"Sami, you know I've been on Earth too long. I didn't expect such an exaggerated reaction to CPR." Noah shrugged his shoulders.

"I hear you."

"Sami," Azil yelled out to us from their seats across the room. We all walked over to join her and Zaric sitting on a sofa. "Are you all right?" She motioned for me to sit by her. I sunk down into the soft sofa next to her. "I heard about your adventurous day on Decca," she said. She stroked my back in a mothering manner.

"Yes, it was maybe a little too exciting."

"I hate that place," she confided.

"I can see why," I replied.

Azil nodded. "Zaric told me how you risked your life to save Tyden. He said you were incredible, that you didn't even hesitate," she said kindly.

"Yes, guilty."

Zaric leaned around Azil to look me in the eyes. "Sami, your bravery was admirable. And, hey, you must forget what Enos said." He twisted his nose and mouth in a nasty expression to look like Enos. "My mind is polluted with misery," Zaric grumbled in a perfect imitation of Enos's persnickety voice. "And sometimes it just reaches a boiling point where the poison has nowhere to go but to escape out of my mouth. Please—just ignore him—everything is understood." Gaelan and Azil burst out laughing at Zaric's impression of Enos.

"Thank you," I murmured. Having my friend's acceptance put me at ease.

"Besides, we've all had expeditions go far worse," Azil said, trying to downplay the events of the day.

"Really? Like what?" I asked.

The group answered in unison, "Contora," before they broke out in roaring laugher.

"What happened there?" I said with curiosity. I couldn't imagine it being much worse. They all laughed even harder when I asked.

Gaelan fought to contain his laughter. "Well, at first, we were all extremely excited when we found Contora. We thought we had found the perfect planet. It was sunny, warm, and breathtakingly beautiful … a paradise. We talked about making it a getaway spot," he explained.

"For vacation," Noah interrupted.

"Were you there, too?" I asked Noah.

"Yeah, it was on one of the trips when I went home," he answered.

"Anyway," Gaelan continued. "We were off the ship, exploring the land, taking samples, and measuring the atmosphere. Everything seemed to check out. We started celebrating our find and stopped paying attention to our surroundings. We became completely distracted by the sights. There was a beautiful clear blue ocean, warm sun, and soft white sand on the beach. But, while we admired the scenery—something had been admiring us. I went to take a step, but my feet felt heavy. I looked down and noticed this pink, frothy slime climbing up my boots. It was thick and about four feet wide and at least six feet long. It looked like it was coming up from the sand beneath our feet, so it could have been even larger."

Zaric widened his eyes. "Before we knew it, it was on everyone's feet and climbing up our legs," he said.

"We tried to shake it off, but it clung on like adhesive," Noah added.

"*Ewww*, gross," Azil and I moaned.

"Some resort," Karis said, sounding repulsed.

"It gets worse," Gaelan said in a disgusted tone. "In the few seconds it took us to notice the slime, we discovered that it was caustic and had started to eat away the outer shell of our boots."

"Oh my, what *was* it?" I asked.

"We didn't know," Noah said.

Zaric interjected, "When the stuff started corroding away the surface of our footgear and soon our suits, everyone panicked, knowing our flesh was next. We all took off in a mad dash to get back to the ship."

Noah stood in excitement. "We thought we were going to get eaten alive or be dissolved in the acidic slime. And it was hard to run because it pulled at our feet as we ran like some sort of glue sticking us to the ground," he said while pretending to move with sticky shoes.

"Yuck!" Azil, Karis, and I said together.

Gaelan continued. "We got back aboard. All of us were screaming to the landing personnel, 'Hurry, get it off.' The slime had traveled to our clothing. They grabbed the high-pressure washer we use to clean the floor and sprayed us down with a forceful jet of water. Our suits were left hanging on us like shredded rags."

"Did it work?" I said.

"*Hell no,*" Noah said with big eyes.

Gaelan shook his head. "It made matters worse. The water made the substance spew and bubble, doubling it in size. The bubbles started exploding, and slime was hitting all of the surrounding walls and dripping off everything. We were panicking. The stuff was taking over the room and soon the entire ship. Then, out of nowhere, Pascal shows up with a laser gun," Gaelan said as he pretended to hold a rifle.

Zaric chuckled. "Not just any laser gun. The biggest one we have on board. It could burn a hole right through the wall of the ship if you fired it too long," he explained.

"He started firing it all around us. I thought he was going to *kill* us! He went on a rampage. He was shooting beams in every direction, right over our heads and directly at our feet," Gaelan said with disbelief.

"It worked, though. He fried the slime!" Noah said with gratitude.

Gaelan shook his head. "Yeah, but I truly have no idea how he managed to miss hitting us."

"He probably didn't care if he did," Zaric added.

"The thing let out this high-pitched scream every time the laser hit it. It was vile," Gaelan said with his face crunched in disgust.

"Oh and it stunk!" Zaric added. "The stuff released a toxic gas into the air."

"The landing reeked of sulfur for weeks," Noah complained with a repulsed frown.

"Was anybody hurt?" I asked.

"No, unfortunately," Azil muttered sarcastically under her breath.

"Oh, Azil, get over it. We were lucky that no one was hurt," Gaelan added, looking at me. "We were all incredibly relieved to discover that the stuff only ate away at our clothes but didn't harm us at all. We were completely fine—*almost* naked, but fine. It was actually pretty funny. We all started laughing hysterically as we stood there half-dressed with the shredded remainder of our eaten clothes hanging off our bodies," Gaelan said.

"They *destroyed* the Space suits," Azil huffed.

"Yeah, and you were really mad at us. Do you remember how red her face got?" Gaelan asked Zaric and Noah. They nodded as they chuckled.

"Sure, you guys laugh, but do you have any idea how much work it was making those outfits? They were constructed out of the latest fabric, practically indestructible," she stated in an irritated voice.

"Apparently *not*," Gaelan snapped back at his sister. We all started laughing again.

"Stop it," Azil scoffed with a hint of a smile, trying not to laugh.

"We installed an arsenal of decontamination resources in the landing since then," Gaelan said reassuringly.

I looked at Noah. I couldn't believe he could keep stories like these to himself. So many things he never told me. How in the world did he not go crazy living on Earth?

It was great to be with all of my favorite people. Even Karis was growing on me. The group was discussing our arrival on Kataria in two days. Karis chatted on and on about the spectacular party planned to celebrate the ship's return home. You could hear the excitement in her voice. All but Gaelan seemed impressed by her enthusiasm. His face was distressed. He looked as though he dreaded the upcoming event. I wished I knew what he was thinking. While we were sitting there talking, I felt a light tap on my right shoulder. I turned to discover it was Tyden standing behind our sofa. He stood with his perfect posture and looked completely recovered.

"Samantha, may I have a word with you alone," he said seriously.

"Yes, of course, Tyden." I rose to walk with him, away from the others. "How are you feeling?"

"I am quite well. Thank you."

"You look much better, but it is surprising to see you here. I can't believe that Urit released you from the hospital so soon."

"Well, he did not have a choice. I told him I was leaving," he said stubbornly.

"Oh." I assumed Tyden wasn't accustomed to taking orders, only giving them.

"Samantha, I want to say thank you." He took my hand gently in his. I was surprised by his soft touch. "Despite what some of the crew believe, I am in no way ready to die," he confessed. "I still have plenty of good years in me. I am indebted to you."

"No, Tyden. Let's just call it even. You helped save me from the Dreons on Decca with Gaelan's bracelet. I never could have taken it off by myself."

"*Did* Gaelan explain to you what the bracelet stands for?" he said hesitantly.

"Yes, he told me."

"Would you like for me to remove it now or have you decided to keep it on?" His eyebrows rose curiously.

"Gaelan asked me if I wanted it. I told him, yes," I answered, puzzled. *Did he really want me to take it off?*

"Oh, I am happy to hear that. I wish I could be as bold as Gaelan at times. His actions are liberating," he said flatly.

"Thank you for understanding." I nodded.

"Samantha, I was wondering … do you remember when the Dreon, Hyril, did his mind-sweep on you?"

"Yes, unfortunately," I muttered. The sickening feeling of having the Dreon burrowing through my mind was something I'd never forget.

"What did you think about?"

"As soon as he asked if I was from another planet, I just thought about the ship and all the things I had been doing since I've been on board. I even pictured our walk across the lake and climb up the mountain today. Why?"

"You did not think about Earth?"

"No, I felt like that was exactly what he wanted me to do. He kept asking me to tell him where I was from. Actually, it was more like a demand than a request. He made me believe we were on a desolate planet. Gaelan was there, too, and he was kicking Hyril's butt."

"*That* doesn't sound so bad."

"No, there's more. He made me imagine that you and Gaelan were dead. Then he made me think that he killed me. At first, I thought it was happening, but then it didn't seem real. It felt like I was in a bad movie."

"It was a scare tactic. They've been known to show our people some very graphic images. He was trying to lower your guard. But I don't understand. How did you avoid answering him? They always know what you are thinking."

"True, but you can choose *what* you think. I wouldn't give in. I focused all of my thoughts on the present. Did I do the right thing?"

"Yes, without a doubt. I was pleasantly relieved when he believed you were a Katarian."

"That was my intention."

"Remarkable." He tilted his head sideways in disbelief. "I did not realize that it was possible to defend your mind so well against them. You possess a skill that may be helpful to us all in the future. Your mind is exceptionally disciplined for someone so young," he said graciously. I was surprised by his kind words. Not only was this the first time he wasn't glaring at me, it sounded like I had gained his respect. I wondered if maybe the Dreon's weapon didn't work as well on me as it did on the Katarians or if I really did possess a skill they didn't have. If so, the credit would have to go to all my years of living with Jack. He'd taught me that I was the master of my thoughts. He truly believed that you become what you think.

"It took a lot of energy to concentrate that hard. I'm not sure that I would be able to do it for very long."

"If you don't mind my request, I would like to suggest that you practice your technique for a few minutes every day to foster it just in case the need arises. You may be able to strengthen your abilities."

"Why, Tyden? Are they coming back?" I cringed. Being mentally violated wasn't something I'd hoped to repeat.

"Perhaps ... it is difficult to predict. The Dreons tend show up when you least expect them."

I shrugged. "Okay, I'll try."

Tyden gave me a nod and squeezed my hand before releasing it. He did not join the group after our discussion. He said he was tired and excused himself to retire to his room. I returned to my seat with the others. Gaelan gave me a satisfied smile when I sat down beside him. He seemed pleased to see Tyden and me getting along. I was relieved that the chaos I'd caused earlier was resolved. I was happy to see Tyden look like his indestructible old self. It felt safe to be around the Katarians again. I listened as the group continued telling funny stories about their adventures. It was astounding that I felt so good after feeling like I had wanted to die just hours earlier. It was getting late. Gaelan and I returned to our room.

CHAPTER 22

LOVE STRUCK

Gaelan wasted no time after we walked through the door. "Sami, you're not tired, are you?" He grabbed me by my wrist and naturally pulled me into his arms when I tried to walk into the bathroom. His body felt strong and amazingly hard.

"*Why?*" I smiled.

"I can't keep my hands off you any longer." He ran his hands down my back as he pulled me in tighter. I melted in his arms.

"I guess it is *later*," I said. He smiled as he pushed me against the wall and leaned in to kiss me. He hiked my leg up around his waist to position himself closer to me. He made me ache for more.

"I believe we left off here," he said in a deep voice.

"Hmmm," I moaned out with pleasure as his hand traveled down my body, caressing me. I responded by kissing across his chest.

"Mmm, you feel amazing. You *are* trying to kill me, aren't you?" Gaelan moaned as he stepped back. He scooped me up in his arms like I was a feather and carefully laid me on the bed. Then, he agilely glided next to me and leaned on his elbow to face me. He seemed to be moving at a deliberately slow pace. He put his hand under my head and pulled my face closer to meet his. His body felt so warm. We looked at each other silently. His face was breathtaking. He seemed oblivious to my stare. His soul shined through his gorgeous eyes. I could look at him all day. I didn't make a move—almost fearful of letting myself have the pleasure. He seemed to be aware of my body tensing up.

"What are you thinking?" I asked as he peered down at me. He looked so relaxed.

"About you. Why, what are *you* thinking?" His expression became confused.

"Just how different our lives are," I confessed. I thought about all the things he must have encountered. I was mesmerized, considering all the possibilities. My life seemed so dull and uneventful by comparison. I still felt traumatized by the day's events. I had been so oblivious and unaware of the world around me.

"Please, stop; don't overanalyze us. We're not that different. Where is this coming from? Did I say something to upset you?" The inflection of his voice rose with concern.

"No, it's not that. I just wondered what it is you see in me," I muttered. His eyes widened with disbelief as he shifted his body uncomfortably.

"How can you question me? Don't you see, you are *everything* to me! I can't get enough of you. You have this ability to accept people as they are. It makes you irresistible. I'm sorry I am not able to explain it very well. I have never wanted anyone more in my entire life. I am grateful for your existence."

"Um, wow, thank you," I said humbly. I was flattered by the remark. Every word drew me in closer. But before I could completely surrender myself to him, I had to be sure. "I guess I just needed to hear it."

He let out a big sigh. "We observed how your people tend to have this disconnect between your consciousness and the energies surrounding you. I'm sorry. I thought maybe you were more aware of the vibrating field around you than you actually are. But if you were, you would already know how I feel and wouldn't be asking these ludicrous questions. Did you know that I can tell when you are bored, restless, angry, scared, happy, excited, or in love? Your every thought creates an intense force of energy that radiates out from you based on what you are feeling. Once you focus on what you are releasing or registering, it becomes something you can't ignore. I know you have this ability as well. You should try to focus in on it and allow yourself to embrace it," he said in a serious tone.

"No, I understand what you're saying. I can feel it, but I don't always trust it," I admitted hesitantly, even though it revealed my weakness. Great, he had a finely tuned sixth sense and could read me like an open book. Had he been aware of my emotions all along? No doubt I was probably frustrating him with all of the signals I must have been missing. What else was he capable of and not telling me? I looked at his face with sadness while thinking about how his society was light years ahead of us. It felt like we would never catch up. He nervously looked back at me as though he had said too much.

"I want to be with you. If you don't believe me, maybe I can *show* you how I feel," he said as he slid his body closer to mine. He leaned down and kissed me passionately for a few minutes, causing my heart to pound out of my chest before he abruptly pulled himself away, easily unlocking my lips from his. Yes, kissing him could cure any inferiority complex I had. His lips were the perfect balance of softness and strength. When I was touching him, nothing else mattered. He had the ability to make everything around us disappear.

"How can you ignore that?" he asked before he hovered above me and kissed me once more. "Is *that* a mistake?" he leaned in and whispered in my right ear in a provocative voice. I gasped but couldn't speak. He then placed one slow, gentle kiss on my neck, giving me chills through my entire body. "Or that?" he said quietly. He lightly swept his fingertips across my upper chest and pushed my shirt collar open, barely touching my exposed skin before he slowly kissed down my body.

"Ahh," I moaned but remained still, enjoying the sensation. He paused to smile a crooked grin, realizing he had gotten my attention, before he returned to my lips. He kissed me more tenderly this time before stopping to look me in the eyes. Each kiss left me wanting more.

"Can you feel how much I care for you?" he said in a deep, sensuous voice.

"Oh, Gaelan, *yes*," I moaned as I flung my arms around him and kissed him back. I ran my fingers through his hair and down his back. I couldn't contain myself. I stroked my hands across his firm thighs. His muscular body pushed down on mine. Then, as if he could read my mind, he leaned back and lifted his shirt up over his head to pull it off, exposing his hard, muscular chest. He looked even better than I'd imagined. He took me in his arms to kiss me once more.

"Good," he said softly when he momentary lifted his lips from mine, sounding relieved, before he kissed me again. He stopped for a second to give me a mischievous smile and look me in the eyes.

I gasped for air.

"Sami, can I have you?" Gaelan whispered into my ear in his beautiful voice.

"I thought you'd never ask."

Gaelan stroked his hand across my collarbone and shoulder before he opened the front of my shirt with its zipper and kissed me tenderly down my neck and chest. After he undressed me slowly, we made love. Wow, he had the moves. He handled me lovingly. Being able to read my emotions made him an excellent lover. What a gift! There was no turning back now. It would break my heart to let him go. I would follow *him* to the ends of the universe. He moved me to the depths of my being. I couldn't believe someone like him was real.

***

The next morning, Gaelan had to work an early shift. I felt him kiss me on the cheek before he left. I got up to get ready for breakfast. I was only meeting Noah this morning. Azil was going to catch up with me later for our exercise class. I couldn't hide my smile. I felt alive. I felt ecstatic. I was hopelessly in love. Noah was definitely going to notice. He knew me too well.

"Sami," Noah greeted me at the café.

"Good morning, Noah," I replied cheerfully. "It was fun last night, huh?"

"Yes, it really was. It's great to see you smiling. You look happy, like your old self again," Noah said, looking down at me while we grabbed our food from the buffet line. I knew it. He'd noticed already.

"What do you mean, again? Did I look miserable?"

"No, not really miserable, but after Jack died, I hadn't really seen you look truly happy. Don't get me wrong—you put on a good front. Most people wouldn't even notice what I'm talking about. But now, I think your zest for life has *finally* returned."

"Oh, thanks," I murmured, understanding exactly what he meant. I'd been functioning on autopilot. Although I learned long ago not to rely on others for my happiness, losing Jack had left me feeling depressed. I sadly couldn't say I'd been truly happy for the past two and a half years.

We sat down and started eating. I thought about what Noah told me. I noticed that Gaelan's bracelet was showing from under my sleeve. I quickly pushed it up under my cuff to hide it.

"Sami," Noah shouted out before he leaned across the table and firmly snatched my wrist in his hands. He pulled my arm closer to him to investigate his finding. "*Where* did you get that? What are you wearing?" he asked in disbelief as he pulled back my shirt cuff to get a better look.

"It's Gaelan's. It's how he kept the Dreons from taking me on Decca. He asked me to keep it on in case they came back."

"Sami!" his mouth dropped open. "How in the world did he get it off? I had to have the Katarian council take mine off before I went to live on Earth. These things are almost impossible to remove." Noah tugged at the metal.

"Trust me, I know," I muttered sarcastically.

"Only a few people even know how to do it. They are like those annoying brain teasing puzzles that Michael always got for Christmas from his wife." I remembered the puzzles all too well. He would bring them to work and put them on his desk for the rest of us to play with after he had already figured out the solution. He liked watching everyone struggle with the frustrating toys while he sat piously, knowing the answer.

"He didn't open the bracelet. Tyden took it off him. Why?" I asked.

"Tyden," he said shockingly. "He could do it! Sami, do you know what it means?"

"Yes, Gaelan told me it honors your ancestors. That only Katarians wear them. I know it might upset people. Why do you think I'm trying to keep it covered?" I whispered. I pulled down my sleeve and looked around the café to see if anyone had noticed. Luckily, the people around us were all enthralled in their own conversations.

"You're right, a few people on board might be of-fended if they saw you wearing it, but that's not the en-tire meaning." He raised his eyebrows.

"What, Noah? You have to tell me. What else does it mean? Why can't I wear it?"

"Sami, to put it bluntly," he paused, "you're mar-ried! You and Gaelan are now lifelong companions." He grinned at my apparent ignorance.

"I am? No, really, *we are?*" I gasped. "I don't believe it."

"Well, theoretically speaking, of course. Tyden is ca-pable of marrying Katarians. Therefore, if he removed the bracelet and gave it to Gaelan to give to you, then yes. You are married. But you would have to consum-mate the marriage for it to be standing," he explained.

I huffed, pursing my lips as I sat there silently, recall-ing my passionate night with Gaelan. I wouldn't have changed it for the world. He was a remarkable man. But why didn't he tell me the real meaning of the bracelet? Did he give it to me intending it to be a wedding band or to mask my identity? Couldn't he trust me with the truth? Was he afraid of scaring me away?

"Hey, Sami," Noah prodded, awakening me from my daydream. "You didn't, *did you?*" He raised his eyebrows as he waited for my answer.

I looked at him and put my hand through my hair, as I must have been picking up Gaelan's nervous habit. "Um, I don't know what to say." I shrugged.

"*Jeez* ..." He bit his lip. "No wonder you look so happy. Well, at least I'm not the only one having fun." He smirked. "I must say, though, I never met anyone who meets someone, falls in love with them, and marries them faster than you do."

"You know how I feel about him?" I said defensively. Deep down, I knew he was right. When I fell in love, it always happened hard and fast. Truthfully, what was there to think about? Feelings like these could not be denied. If I had to decide whether to love him or not, the choice was simple.

"I'm not a fool. Sami, I would have to be blind not to notice," he snapped. "And he obviously feels the same way. I mean, the way he looks at you—he couldn't hide it if he tried." He shook his head. "If I didn't like him ..." he balled his hand into a fist and punched it into his cupped hand.

"Noah, Gaelan didn't tell me it was like a wedding band. Why do you think he would keep that from me?" I asked with all seriousness.

"Well," he looked up to the left and thought for a moment, "probably because no one has ever married someone who wasn't a Katarian."

"*Ever?*" My eyes widened in shock.

"Nope, never. Gaelan and you would be the first," he said sourly. "Our people pride themselves on being pure-blooded. It is something that we feel strongly on maintaining ever since our encounters with the Dreons. We find them repulsive. Their crossbreeding with different beings is unscrupulous. Our people took a stand to not interbreed with other species."

"But, Noah, I'm *exactly* like you," I retorted. I couldn't help but feel offended by the discriminatory comment.

"I know, but no one ever considered that we would find people identical to our own. I guess that changes everything. Nonetheless, Gaelan would take some heat for it if anybody found out. There are still a lot of Katarians who would be extremely upset by this. Old traditions are difficult to break."

"What are the repercussions? Is Gaelan in trouble?"

"No, don't worry too much about it. He'll handle it. He's tougher than anyone I've ever met. Even though he's been known to ruffle a few feathers along the way, he somehow manages to come out squeaky clean in a controversy. Knowing him, he's probably already thought of a way to explain his actions. He's skilled in debate and can devise a convincible loophole in a heartbeat."

"Enos knows. He saw it when we returned to the landing. Maybe I should get Tyden to take it off."

He frowned. "Great, of all the people. He's such a complainer. I wouldn't take it off just because of him, though. I heard that the Dreons are still showing up on our scanners. Leave it *on*," he blurted out as a demand. "I would give you mine to wear if I knew how effective it was in protecting you. Unfortunately, I don't have it with me. It's at home in my sock drawer. I must say, Gaelan is probably one of the most resourceful people I know under pressure. He's ingenious to outsmart the Dreons with the Katarian band."

"Why aren't you wearing yours, then? Won't they take you?"

"Maybe, but not for long. They would return me. My genetic code is already registered in their database. The freaks have our individual imprints numbered in a catalog."

"What do you mean, not for long?"

"They would have to return me once they realized I'm Katarian. But you ..." He gulped. "If you were taken from open Space, they would feel no obligation to return you. You would become a drone, enslaved to them forever."

"Wow!" I said, feeling gracious. I thought about how the band on my wrist saved me from a terrible fate, and I shoveled a large bite of food into my mouth. I worried about Gaelan upsetting his people. Why was it so wrong to marry someone from Earth? We're human beings.

"Yeah, just picturing being stuck living with the Dreons is nightmare scary," he responded to my anxious expression.

"Noah, is that why you never got married? You are expected to marry and have children with another

Katarian?" I asked, trying to understand their adversity to uniting with another kind.

"I don't know. I guess so. That may be part of the reason." He paused. "No, that's not it. If I wanted to marry a Katarian, I would have stayed on Kataria."

"Why not then? Clearly, we are not anything like the Dreons. You know that. You've been living on Earth for all these years. "

"It's your fault, Sami." He huffed.

"*What?* How is it my fault? Noah, what are you saying? You know I love you, but please, not that way. I never meant to cause you any pain. I have always wanted you to find happiness." I couldn't help jumping to conclusions. I panicked out of fear that I had somehow led him on.

"Relax, that's not what I mean, not that I haven't thought about it."

"Noah!"

"You're an amazing friend. You never hurt me." Noah took both of my hands in his and interlocked our fingers.

"Oh, *good.*" I sighed deeply in relief.

"Besides, I could never be with you. I loved Jack just as much as I love you. He was my brother. I could never betray him like that. You have been my family all of these years, the only family I remember now." He looked at me with tender eyes.

"I know," I muttered. I felt Noah's pain of losing his parents so young. In a sense, we had adopted each other to become family.

"Of course, you are the kind of woman I should want, but it would never work out anyway. You're way too stable and independent. I like women who aren't clear on what they want. You know, kind of messy, needy. They're more fun."

I leaned my finger against my lip as I looked at him in bewilderment. Despite his intelligence, he always seemed to gravitate to women with the least compatibility. How could he be so aware of his dating trends yet unable to change them? "And you don't see that as the problem?"

"No." He smirked.

"I don't get it. Then how am I to blame?"

"I think it was from watching you and Jack. It's just that the two of you set the bar so high. Your devotion was evident. I wanted to find someone I could love like that, but I never felt that way about anyone. I have *never* loved anyone with such intensity. And here you are, doing it all over again with Gaelan. The two of you look inseparable. How do you do it? How can you fall in love so easily?"

"Oh, Noah, hmm, I don't know. It just happens. It will happen for you, too. You need to be willing to let someone in." I didn't have an answer. I wished I could magically give him his ideal woman. But how do you

help someone who seems incapable of making good decisions when it came to choosing a partner? I thought
about his impression of my relationship with Jack and
now with Gaelan. He was right. I had been blessed twice
in my life. I could hardly believe my own good fortune.

***

I went to exercise with Azil later that morning. I could
have sworn I saw her notice the bracelet as well. The thing
seemed impossible to hide. I was relieved that she never
mentioned it, though. I'm not sure how she would have
felt about it. She was her usual bubbly self. I wished I could
have told her, but after what Noah had said, I decided
not to. Instead, I repeatedly tucked it under my sleeve.
That's when I first noticed something strange about the
bracelet. When I touched it with my fingertips, the metal
gave me an unexplained feeling of being connected to
Gaelan. It was bizarre. The sensation made it impossible
to doubt the bracelet's origin. I *knew* it was Gaelan's. His
essence seemed *preserved* in its metal. It made me wonder
what it was made of. I couldn't wait to speak to him. He
had some explaining to do. I waited in our room for him
to finish his shift.

"Hey, gorgeous," Gaelan said, pulling me into his
arms when he walked through the door.

"Hey, yourself. How was your day?" I smiled.

"Uneventful," he said flatly before he gave me a quick kiss. "How was yours?"

"Good. I went to breakfast with Noah and exercised with Azil. Noah saw the bracelet you gave me today," I said casually as I freed myself from his embrace.

His cheerful expression quickly faded into a nervous frown. "Oh yeah ... and what does he think about it?" he asked hesitantly.

"He said he's happy for us."

"*Really?* He said that. What a relief! I wasn't sure what he would think. Sometimes, he's really hard to read." He exhaled. I knew he was referring to Noah's brotherly over-protectiveness of me.

"With Noah, what you see is what you get," I explained.

"Yeah, but he still tends to look at me like he hasn't decided if he likes me being with you."

"No, it's not you. He's just been a really good friend and doesn't want to see me get hurt."

"I can see that. He's very loyal to you."

"Gaelan, is there something you want to tell me?" I asked.

"Yes." His face looked anxious. "First, tell me *what* you know," he said reluctantly as he let out a huff of air.

"Well, apparently, we're married." I held up my arm with the bracelet.

"Yes, technically," he muttered.

"Technically. What is that supposed to mean?" I held up my hands in frustration. "When were you going to tell me?"

"I would have explained about the band yesterday, but you had already been through so much. What more could I burden you with? It just wasn't a good time."

"What about last night? Wasn't that a good time?"

"Please, Sami, let me explain. Last night, *ugh,"* he said with a small grin lifting the edges of his lips. "Last night was great! I wanted to tell you, but it was late. I just wasn't totally sure of your reaction. I didn't want you to get upset with me. I couldn't ruin the moment. I was afraid you might insist I remove it at once. It felt fantastic to be so close to you."

"I need you to be truthful with me," I pleaded while I maintained my distance.

"I wanted to ask you formally," he said in a soothing voice.

"Really? You mean you didn't just give it to me as a decoy to protect me from the Dreons?"

"No," he stressed the word, "I would never give it to someone unless I meant it."

"Then, please, by all means." I crossed my arms, awaiting his next move.

"Sami," he pulled me towards him and gently unwound my arms to hold my hands, "I have never met anyone like you. I never want to hurt you. I want you. I never want to let you go. I hope that you desire the same.

Would you please consider being with me forever?" he asked as he kept his eyes steadily on mine.

I reached up and hugged him. "I will. *Yes*, Gaelan, I will." He embraced me tightly. I should've been angry for the initial deception, but, instead, I felt even more drawn to him. I couldn't resist my feelings for him if I tried. He leaned down and kissed me tenderly. I pulled off his shirt and kissed his chest. The rest of our clothes soon followed. He laid me on the bed. Before I knew it, we made love. His movements seemed so deliberate yet delightful. He touched me as if he could anticipate my every desire. His kisses left me breathless. Extreme passion emanated from his strong body, making it impossible not to fall straight into a state of bliss. My body *shuddered* with intense pleasure when I rested peacefully beside him. He scooped me into his arms and pulled me to his chest to hold me close.

"I will love you forever. We will have the best life together. Your happiness is my happiness," Gaelan whispered softly.

"I love you, too. I'm so lucky to have found you," I said with sincerity.

"*You?* I'm the lucky one."

I couldn't help myself. I was completely taken in by him. I had never wanted anyone more. He seemed willing to sacrifice everything to put me at the top of his list. Unlike with Jack, his job didn't seem to have quite the hold on him. My head filled with memories recalling the resentment I had felt when Jack first accepted his assignment to work on the Space resort, leaving me behind. Today, I couldn't keep his memory from popping into my mind after talking with Noah this morning. Gaelan made me believe that he would give up everything to be with me. I trusted him with all my heart.

"Ah, you're amazing. You make me so happy," I replied. I closed my eyes and snuggled into his body. We stayed there comfortably for another half hour before Gaelan quickly sat up, jumped out of bed, and started pulling on his clothes.

"I have to go. I lost track of time. Tyden and Zaric will be wondering where I am."

"Why? Where do you have to go?"

"I have to finish some last-minute reports before we land. And to make the task even more grueling, we are required to submit them in formal Katarian hand."

"*Really?* I can't even remember the last time I wrote something by hand."

"Uh-huh. It's absurd." He let out a huff. I could tell he wasn't pleased with following the old tradition. I couldn't believe they were forbidden to use dictation. *Who's the more advanced society now?*

"What kind of reports do you have to prepare?"

"Reports on you, of course." He smirked. "We have to describe how your people are progressing, your current level, and the success of our instruction."

"I see. You know it sounds sort of creepy when you put it that way. It makes us sound like a charity case."

He stared at me blankly. "A charity case? I do not understand."

"When you say you are measuring the success of your instruction, it makes us sound helpless."

"No, you're anything but. We're impressed by your quick advancements. Your society is progressing faster than we had anticipated. However, it has been decided that we will not disrupt your natural timeline of discovery. It is important that you reach each stage on your own. We are only allowed to intervene in improving your current technology and helping you avoid catastrophic events. Our goal is to guide you. We cannot jump you ahead before you are ready. That may hurt you more than help you."

"You sure have a lot of rules to follow."

"More than you know."

CHAPTER 23

HUNTED

Gaelan returned later that evening, and we had another amazing night together. I'm not sure if my heighted desire was due to having Gaelan as my partner or my vaccine-renewed body. Either way—this could be dangerous. I felt more relaxed being with him than ever before. I think I had secretly been fearful of losing him. I let down my guard. I was exhausted from the excitement of the past few days. I fell asleep in his arms, only to slip into a terrible nightmare ....

I was standing in the study alone when each of the ceiling lights started to burn out one by one. The room was suddenly freezing as the temperature seemed to plummet at the same time. I ran into the bedroom and watched in horror as the energy was sucked out of each of those lights as well. I reached to grab a small flashlight

I had in my bag and flicked it on. Within seconds, its beam of light dimmed and went out. I had no idea what was happening. A power failure perhaps, some sort of interference with the electronics? I felt around in the dark room, fumbled upon the ship's communicator, and quickly called Gaelan. To my relief, his face appeared on the screen.

"*Gaelan, what's going on? The room went completely black*," I told him anxiously.

"*Everything's okay here. Don't worry, I'll be there in a few minutes to check it out*," he said. That's when I felt it. *Whoosh!* A whirling rush of wind flew by my arm as something went past me in the darkness. I wasn't alone. Goosebumps rose on my arms from the coldness and unexpected presence. Whoosh! There it was again.

"*Gaelan, help, there's something in our room*," I shouted. His image faded as the power from the communicator went dead. "*Who's there?*" I frantically asked. I reached my hands out to feel for the intruder. *Whoosh!* The thing whipped by me once more. I swung my arms out, trying to catch it, but came up empty-handed. Then, without notice, something grabbed a hold of me. "*Ahh! Let me go!*" I screamed. It dragged me across the room by my right arm with its squeezing grip. A flash of blinding light suddenly shined upon me. I fought to open my eyes against its brightness.

I found myself lying on a hard, cold table with bright operating room lights suspended directly above me. The room surrounding me was almost pitch black. I saw shadows of ghostly figures moving around the perimeter of the large room in the blackness. The fabric of their light-colored robes picked up some light. Dreons dressed in the same long, flowing white gowns surrounded me on all sides and hovered over me but did not speak. I fought to get up with all of my might but couldn't. Their long, clawlike fingers, with sharp, jagged fingernails, were clenched tightly around my arms and legs, pinning me down. Their faces stared down on me, watching my every move. I heard a woman scream out in terrible pain in a nearby room.

"What are you doing to her? Stop it! Leave her alone," I demanded. I listened to the sound of the horrific torture coming through the wall. Her screams could only be caused by severe suffering. Clearly, I wasn't the only one being held captive against my will.

"Oh, you do not like what you hear? Perhaps you should worry more about yourself," said a tall, thin Dreon in a sinister voice, approaching my restrained body. *"Now, tell me where you live or you will find out why she is screaming,"* he threatened me. He leaned his sunken, emaciated face over mine while holding a forbidding glare. I swore I could see his bony skeleton shining through his paper-thin skin. His matted hair resembled gray, twisted rope. He looked more like a bug than a man. His giant, glossy

eyes were bulging out an inch from his head, and his pasty white skin made him look severely anemic.

"Get away from me!" I shouted back in a shaky voice.

"You told us you are from Kataria, but we have no record of you on file. Why do you think that is? Are your people hiding you for some reason, or are you from someplace else?" His mouth was so close I could feel his hot, stinky breath blow against my face when he spoke.

"No, I am from Kataria. Your records are wrong. You've made a mistake," I retorted.

"Tissk, tissk, mistakes; we do not make mistakes. We are not burdened with your flaws," he scoffed before he leaned back and started pacing around the table where I lay.

"Well, if I am so beneath you, why do you even bother with me at all?"

"It is not of your concern." He paused and wrung his hands together. *"Where are you from?"* He asked, waiting only seconds before he abruptly surged his face down over me.

"Get away from me!" I shouted. He was so close, I thought about biting his nose, but the other aliens quickly pinned my head down when I lifted it up from the table.

"I should kill you right now for your defiance." He clenched his hand tightly around my neck, pushing my head forcefully against the hard table. *"You will tell us*

what we want to know. We have ways to make you comply," he seethed.

"Let me go!" I screamed, despite my crushed throat.

"Show me your home," he said in a roaring voice. His black eyes loomed closer to mine. He looked as though he was ready to do a mind sweep on me. I prepared myself for the intrusion. I would die before I gave him what he wanted. Nothing—I would think of nothing to shield my memories. I pictured a blank white room in my mind. I focused my thoughts on its emptiness. It was easy to do with the bright lights shining in my eyes. Soon, I felt the burrowing weight of his eyes on mine. The invisible force was trying to worm its way into my mind. I fought back by harnessing my attention on my vision while I matched his glare and didn't move. I held my stare firmly on his eyes to compete in the showdown. He seemed caught off guard when I looked directly at him. He hesitated for a moment before he released his hand from my neck and backed away.

He was unable to penetrate my mind. He looked too frail to summon the energy required to complete the task. He had to alter his interrogation technique. *"We can take you home. We only want to meet your people. It would be beneficial for us to become allies."* I remained perfectly still, not saying a word. *"You insolent woman,"* he huffed impatiently at my silence. He reached his hand back to a table full of metal instruments and held up a stick with a glowing orange tip. Without warning, he sadistically delved his tool into my forehead while the others restrained my head. It felt like a hot lead weight was sinking through my skin like quicksand. I yelled out in agony. My body jerked in response to the pain it caused as it penetrated through each layer of my face like a burning coal.

"*I will be listening to your every thought, invading your mind, knowing your every move. You will be powerless and begging for my mercy when I am through with you. Then, you will help us.*"

"*Stop*," interrupted a screeching voice from the darkness. I couldn't see where it came from with the bright lights hovering above me. The interrogating alien turned to face its source.

"*You are lucky. You have made a friend. Hyril seems to think you will be a valuable addition to our kind. He believes you possess unusual capabilities unlike our own.*" I could tell by the length of his explanation, they were speaking to one another telepathically.

"*Hyril*," I said. Wasn't he the enemy? Surely, he was a bad guy. His pale face came into view as he approached the table when I called out his name.

"*Samantha*," Hyril answered me in a detached, unemotional tone. He walked up silently and stood stiffly at my side. Hyril looked remarkably human next to the Dreon trying to hurt me. "*Leave us. I will talk to her*," he demanded to the others. The surrounding Dreons let me go and left the room. As a defensive reflex, I sat up on the table and quickly hopped down on the floor. Ouch, I thought. Its surface was so hot it felt like it would burn holes through the soles of my feet. Hyril rushed in front of me in order to block my body with his. His strong, hypnotic stare easily permeated my mind like a tractor beam on its target. *"Are you ready to talk?"*

"I've already told you everything."

"Look, for your sake, you must cooperate. Your life depends on it. They are planning on torturing you to the brink of death."

"I don't understand. Why are you helping me?" I asked, afraid to trust him.

"Do you not understand that I only follow my commands? Haven't you figured that out by now? Did you not realize I never physically hurt you on Decca? I could blow your mind apart—shattering it into a million pieces if I wanted to. I was merely trying to get information out of you," he lashed out angrily. He let out a gruff moan as if it was obvious.

"Oh yeah, it was so much fun. Let's do it again," I replied sarcastically. *"Where am I?"* I asked. I looked around at the unfamiliar surroundings. The walls were smooth, windowless, and appeared to be made out of sheets of gray metal. The doorway the other aliens exited blended evenly into the surrounding room, making its location a mystery.

"You are on our ship."

"What? How did I get here?"

"We brought you aboard. It is your fault you are here. Your fresh DNA and mental capacity to resist me has made you an interesting commodity," Hyril said forcefully.

"How do you know that?"

"We took a sample."

"No, the other thing. How did you know I resisted you?"

"We know everything," he said, walking ponderously around me. I turned and watched him closely as he kept his eyes glued to mine. *"When I was in your mind, I could feel and see everything you were thinking, your fear and your pain. But you would not answer my question and show me your home. I am curious, though. You pictured a boy and a girl."*

"Yes." I remembered thinking about Leah and Jackson when I thought I was going to die.

"When you saw them, you had this feeling, this feeling of joy, of warmth? I do not know why you were happy to see them."

"It is called love."

"What is love?"

"Ahh, I can't say."

"No, please, I do not mean you any harm. I want to know," he said, sounding sincere.

I reluctantly answered. *"Love is a good feeling. It is something you have when you care deeply for another person or creature."*

"Would you consider me a creature?"

"No … I would consider you a person, I guess." I studied his body in search of human traits. They outnumbered his unnamed terrestrial features. Perhaps a makeover and some contacts would help him look more like us.

"So you love the boy and the girl."

"Yes, they are my children. I brought them into this world, raised them, and care deeply for them." I was careful not to reveal too much information. I was taking no chances. Perhaps this was some roundabout way of getting me to picture my life.

"Is it common to feel that way about children?"

"I believe so, yes. I think all parents love their children. Do you love anyone?"

"No," he said shortly.

"What about your parents?"

"I do not know them. I was born aboard the ship in order to serve," he said with a feeble huff. I suddenly realized that he must have chased the others away for his own personal agenda. I had sparked his interest when I thought about the love I felt for my family, and he wanted to know more. It was something he'd never experienced. I looked at him more closely. He appeared depressed, almost completely devoid of all happiness. He was unclear of who he was and even what he was. The Dreons had entangled themselves into a real mess when they took creation into their own hands. I couldn't help but feel sorry for Hyril

after seeing this side of him. He was a victim of circumstance. His life was not his own.

"Can you find them?" I asked empathetically. His face turned defensive.

"No, it is forbidden." He looked away with a saddened expression and then walked silently around the room.

"Are you okay?" I asked. He didn't answer me, because he must have missed my question. Gaelan was right. The Dreons' ability to communicate seemed dependent on eye contact. *"Why are you doing this?"* I asked when his eyes returned to mine.

"It is our purpose."

"What, to take people against their will and perform experiments on them? It's morally wrong. Don't you have rules against that sort of thing?"

"Yes, we have rules, and you broke them by not complying. Now, you can end this right now. Just tell me where you live," he pleaded.

"Kataria," I answered.

"Fine, I can wait. We are out of time. I have to send you back now, but know that I can only protect you for so long. They will be back for you, and you will have no choice but to obey," he said in an echoed voice.

***

"Ahh, ahh, no!" I screamed. I bolted straight up in the bed, awakened from the horrible dream.

"What's wrong? Are you okay?" Someone stroked my back.

"Don't, don't touch me!" I shouted and pushed away the figure.

"Hey, it's okay; it's only me," Gaelan said with alarm.

"Huh … where am I?" I moaned, confused by my surroundings. "Oh, I just had an *awful* dream."

"About what, having to live on a Katarian starship? Oh, wait a minute, that already happened," he teased.

"No, I was on the Dreon ship. They took my clothes off and were examining me on a hard, cold, metal table. I couldn't move. I was struggling to get away, but they were holding me down or I was paralyzed or something. They were trying to make me tell them where I was from. Hyril, or whatever his name is, was there, too, but he was nice in a weird way. For some strange reason, I felt like I knew him before Decca. He gave me a déjà vu feeling. I can't explain it. Oh, I don't know. I can't remember now."

"I'm sorry. This trip must be very hard on you. Stress is causing your imagination to be overly active. It's okay; it was just a dream. Those disgusting creatures give *me* nightmares. Let's go back to sleep." He wrapped me snugly in the covers and rested down next to me. I tugged on the neckline of my shirt to keep it from strangling me.

"Gaelan," I sat back up suddenly, "if it was a dream, then why is my nightgown on backwards?" I asked, mortified. Gaelan jumped up and flicked on the light beside the bed. A look of horror spread across his face.

"What!" He quickly inspected my clothing. "This can't happen. I'm going to *kill them* if they touched you!" he said through clenched teeth.

"What are you talking about? You don't think it really happened, do you?" I trembled. His alarm frightened me. I questioned his rationale. But knowing I never would have put my clothes on wrong, his conclusion seemed almost logical.

"I don't know. Let's try to remain calm." He sighed. "Your dream may not be your imagination. The Dreons are known for giving people amnesia. It's how they justify their actions. They believe they cause no harm if they can keep people from remembering what happens to them. But maybe you're able to remember something. I have no idea how you managed to keep your wits about you during the mind sweep. It might be hard for them to suppress you. Your mind is amazingly strong, as though you were born with a natural immunity to resist their methods."

"How could it be them? I was just dreaming," I offered. My mind filled with flashbacks. I tried to sort out the confusing dream.

"I'm not so sure. I *know* your shirt wasn't on like that. I would have noticed. The only logical explanation isn't a good one. We have to find out if it was them. Pascal's on duty." Gaelan reached for his ship's communicator and called the command deck.

"*Please*, Gaelan, I don't want to bother anyone. This is silly. It's three in the morning," I pleaded.

"*Shh*, just let me check on something. We have to be sure." Gaelan motioned for me to be quiet.

"Hey, Pascal, it's Gaelan. I took off my watch earlier today, and I think I left it at my station. Could you check to see if it's there?"

Pascal's image bounced around on the screen while he searched. "Hmmm … mmm-hmm," he hummed. "Nope, no, nothing. It's clean."

"Thanks, I guess I'll just keep looking. It's got to be around here someplace."

"Good luck finding it, because apparently you really need it. You shift doesn't start for another four hours. You should be asleep right now."

"Yeah, I know, but I can't sleep. How's your night going?"

"Good, except for the Dreon ship that has been tailing us for the past three hours."

"What do they want?" Gaelan asked causally.

"Who knows? I tried to lose them, but the suckers keep chasing us. They're maintaining an uncomfortably close distance off our stern. I'm not sure where they are going. Perhaps they are trying to follow us home."

"Well, try to get rid of them for me, would you? I want to have a good day tomorrow," he said with a chuckle.

"I'll do my best."

"Thanks. See you in a couple hours." Gaelan tapped off the communicator.

"So, is that bad? The Dreon ship nearby?" I asked.

"Hmm, I don't know yet. Those vile creatures are capable of anything." Gaelan moaned as he tapped on the communicator to call Zaric. "Zaric."

"Ahh, come on, Gaelan, can't this wait until morning? What's wrong?" he said drowsily.

"Hey, how long did you have to wait for us to come out of the cave on Decca the other day?"

"I don't know. It was something like thirty-five or forty minutes. Why?"

"Sami just had a nightmare that she was on the Dreon ship, and Pascal just verified that they are in our airspace. I think she's been tagged," he hissed.

"*Oh no*, is Sami all right?" he asked, panicky.

"Yeah, she's okay. She's right here."

"You don't think they *took* her, *do you?*" The inflection of his voice rose with trepidation.

"Yes, I'm starting to believe so. You said we were in there for over thirty minutes. I thought it was ten, at the most. They would have had *more* than enough time to do it." I could see every muscle in Gaelan's body become tense.

"We need to get her to Urit," Zaric said urgently.

"We're on our way." Gaelan rushed to get off the communicator.

"What's going on?" I demanded an answer.

"Come on, hurry—you need to get dressed." Gaelan scooped up my clothes from the chair and threw them at me before he pulled on his own with record speed. I started changing, hurrying to keep up.

"Can't it wait until morning? Urit is sleeping right now," I protested.

"No, it *cannot* wait," he demanded.

"I don't understand. Hyril never touched me. Aside from glaring his big black eyes at me, the images he showed me weren't real," I said, feeling confused. Was I missing something? I sat to put on my shoes.

"No, it might only appear that way to us. They had *more* than enough time."

"If the Dreons wanted me so badly, then why didn't they just take me earlier?"

"They may have. For all we know, all three of us may have been taken on board. None of us would remember any of it. But it would explain the loss of time." Gaelan stood by the door, ready to go.

"Why would they take me again?"

"The bastards probably didn't get everything they wanted from you and needed more. If they put a tracer in you, they would wait until you were sleeping to take you. It's when they like to strike. They don't like to have any witnesses. It's their style."

"How would they know that?"

"We discovered that their tracers monitor and transmit your brainwaves back to their ship. They wait for theta waves to appear on their analyzers, notifying them you are asleep." I had heard of the term *theta wave* when I underwent mandatory Space training. Our Space helmets for our trip featured monitors to record our vital signs as well as provide an electroencephalogram (EEG) to analyze our brain activity. Theta waves would appear if a person was asleep, under anesthesia, or hyperventilating.

"Where is it?" I patted frantically around my body to search for the device. A wave of terror tore threw me. Could this really be happening? All sorts of questions shot through my mind as I recalled every clouded memory I could fester up regarding the Dreons. My recognition of events seemed to blur together. Now, I wasn't sure if anything had happened or if it was all a dream.

"You won't find it. They hide them *inside* your body."

I looked at him with disgust. "Ugh! You're kidding me."

"Let's go." He grabbed me by the hand and rushed me down the corridor behind him. I had never seen him so panicked.

"Stop it! I'm coming. I can walk by myself." I fought back, trying to yank my hand free. It was no use. His grip was too strong.

"We have to get it out … now!" he shouted while he momentarily stopped to turn around to look me in the face.

"Ouch," I whined and pulled away, taking back my hand to rub my bloodless fingers.

"Sorry," he muttered.

"Why? Will it hurt me?" My voice cracked with panic when he took off racing through the corridors once more. I sprinted behind him to keep up.

"It's the only way I can protect you. They can teleport you right off the ship with that thing *anytime* they want to. Our hull won't even keep you safe," he said with apprehension.

We knocked at Urit's door. To my surprise, Urit was wide awake, tending to some experiment in his room. He seemed completely unbothered by the time.

"Sam, Gaelan, and *Zaric*," Urit greeted us as he stood at his door holding a breaker filled with green liquid while Zaric rushed in directly behind us. He furrowed his brow. "Well, this can't be good. You slackers are usually asleep right now. So, something must really be wrong."

"Urit, I think Sami's been tagged. You have to check her for a tracer," Gaelan ranted hysterically.

"A tracer, are you sure? I mean, we haven't had a problem with one of those for *years,*" Urit said. He shook his head in disbelief while he put down the glass beaker on a nearby table.

"Please! Just to be certain." Gaelan gave Urit a look of desperation. Urit motioned for us to join him in the examination area.

"Sam, do you remember anything out of the ordinary?" Urit asked calmly in his professional voice while we all walked across the room.

"I just had a bad dream. I dreamt I was on the Dreon ship. I was captured, kidnapped, and held down on a hard table with people dressed in white robes walking all around me. The room was very bright, or maybe it was dark. I can't remember." I felt too humiliated to mention my turned around nightgown.

"Oh, I can see the reason for your concern." Urit got a rattled look on his face. He sighed and gave Gaelan and Zaric a silent glare of despair.

"Get it out of her. If they touch her again, I'll make them regret it. I swear I'll *blow up* their damn ship," Gaelan threatened through his teeth.

Zaric's eyes widened. "*Uh-oh*, time to lock up the hull-piercing lasers," he jested.

"Gaelan, no, *you can't*," I warned. Now I really would be responsible for starting a war.

"Why not? They are clearly out of line," Gaelan snapped back.

"Please, Gaelan, be reasonable. If it's there, I will find it," Urit said confidently, retrieving a long wand from his cabinet.

"Here, give it to me." Gaelan huffed impatiently as he reached to take hold of the wand and fought to take it out of Urit's hand.

"No." Urit held his grip.

"Yes," Gaelan demanded. I watched them impatiently struggle against one another.

"Hey, take it easy. I can do it. Will you stop?" Urit swiftly snatched his hand away to defend his tool. Gaelan abruptly released his grip at the same time, causing Urit to fall backwards unsteadily. I thought I saw a glimpse of a smile cross Gaelan's face at Urit's fumble. He seemed to get pleasure in taunting Urit at times.

"Is it going to hurt?" I asked wearily.

"No, but I need you to hold extremely still. The tracer gives off an almost undetectable signal. It vibrates at a higher frequency than your natural biofield. That's why people can walk around with them for years and never suspect a thing," Urit instructed. I had no idea what he was saying. I listened to his request and stood completely motionless as he slowly swooped up and down my body like I was going through a security checkpoint. "There ... that's the mark. I think you're right. There is a subtle vibration coming from right there," Urit concluded, pointing between my eyes.

"Oh, no," I cried. "Can you take it out? Did they put something in my brain? Get it out, now, please," I pleaded. Urit bit his lip and didn't answer me. His prolonged silence horrified me.

"Sam, I just need to take a look to see what we're dealing with." Urit pointed to his examination table. "Could you hop up and lie down please?" I got onto the table and laid back for him to put a long, thin scope up my nose. I took in shallow breaths through my mouth, too afraid to move. "Yep, I found it. There it is. The bugger's right in there. Just as you feared." He frowned as he pulled out the scope.

"Unbelievable! Will they stop at *nothing*," Gaelan scoffed in disgust. I've never seen him so enraged.

"I can't believe they're up to their old tricks again," Zaric retorted.

"Don't worry, Sam. I can take it out," Urit comforted me.

"Urit, you're going to need help," Zaric demanded.

"No, it's not that deep," Urit explained. "Besides, it's better if we are the only ones who know about it. I'm not so sure that the crew will be as understanding when it comes to this." I could only imagine what it took for him to convince the crew that CPR wasn't a crime. He seemed eager to avoid any more controversy.

"Urit, get help." Gaelan urged. "Call Bryson, he's a good guy, or Hayden. I'm sure we can trust them. Anyway, it doesn't matter. I don't care what repercussions we'll face."

"Hayden, call Hayden," I interjected. Hayden was my friend. She would help me.

"I won't need to. You two can be my assistants." Urit pointed to Gaelan and Zaric as he took out a tray of surgical instruments. Our requests were ignored.

"Oh no, is this going to hurt?" I worried.

"I'm going to give you some anesthesia to numb your face," Urit explained before he sprayed a cool mist up my nose. "It will help a little." I felt my forehead and the roof of my mouth become numb as if I'd just gotten a big shot of Novocain from the dentist. "Gaelan, Zaric, would you two scan each other for tracers while Sam's medication takes effect?" he said, handing the wand over his left shoulder to Gaelan, motioning for him to take it while he maintained his eye contact with me.

"We should check Tyden, too," Gaelan said, coming up behind him to grab the tool.

Urit glanced at him briefly. "I'll do it tomorrow when he stops in," he replied.

"Thanks," Gaelan said with gratitude in a calmer voice. He appeared to have regained his composure in dealing with the situation.

He and Zaric walked into an open area of the room to check each other.

"Sam, you are going to be okay. I've done procedures like this many times before." He took my left hand in his, only to discover Gaelan's bracelet adorning my wrist. I saw his loving expression quickly fade into a frown.

"Thank you," I said nervously when I noticed his reaction. Urit turned and glanced across the room at Gaelan as he stood motionless while Zaric was passing the wand over him. Then he quickly looked back at me. Gaelan took notice. He looked at us and squinted as though he was trying to decipher what we were saying. I knew he was out of earshot by the curious expression on his face.

"I ... I don't know what to say. I didn't know." Urit paused as if he could barely form the words and hesitantly lifted the bracelet with one of his fingers. He stared at it while remaining speechless. He looked heartbroken. I think he still fantasized about the possibility of us becoming a couple. At that moment, I wished I could give him more. He was a good man. After all he had done for me, his disappointment was killing me.

"Urit," I pleaded for his understanding.

"Humph." He shook his head in disbelief. "I guess I was wrong about him. You must really mean something to him. I never thought I'd see the day … oh, what am I saying? I'm glad for your happiness. If Gaelan gave you this, he surely has good intentions," he kindly gestured, as he didn't seem to want to say anything derogatory about Gaelan. He was a true gentleman and able to swallow his pride. I respected him even more knowing he was able to accept our relationship with grace.

"Thank you. You are a good friend," I said gently.

"As are you," he agreed with a fragile smile.

"We're all clean," Zaric and Gaelan said together, sounding relieved while they came over to join us.

"Hmm, good. Let's get this thing out," Urit said after he cleared his throat. "Now, you might still feel this, but it will only be uncomfortable for a minute." Urit laid his hand softly on my shoulder. "Here, Zaric, you hold this and give it to me when I ask for it." Urit gave Zaric a thin pencil-like stick.

"What is this thing?" Zaric asked.

"It's a cautery. It will stop the bleeding," Urit explained.

"I'm going to lose blood? How much?" I hesitated.

"You may. I'm just taking precautions to be safe." Urit clarified. "Gaelan, I want you to hold Samantha's head very still. Sam, are you ready?"

"Sure, just get it over with," I urged. Urit put the long scope back into my nose, turned the scope on suction, and yanked. It felt like he was going to pull out my sinuses. "Ahh," I gasped. My eyes watered as I struggled to hold back my tears.

"Hold still," Gaelan whispered in my ear. "You're doing great."

"Now, Zaric," Urit directed as he reached for the cautery. It felt like an electric shock crossed my forehead. I nearly jumped off the table. I would have if it weren't for Gaelan's death grip on my head. "That's it. We got it, Sam." Urit exhaled in relief as he laid the scope down on a table with the tracer still attached to its end.

"Let me see it." I sat up to see what he'd removed. It was a silver ball the size of a marble.

Urit stared at the tracer. "Well, that's new. I've never seen one like that before. Probably more advanced."

Zaric looked over Urit's shoulder. "What should we do with it? Destroy it? I could only imagine the crew's panic surrounding this news," he surmised.

Gaelan pulled the metal ball off the scope and picked it up to study it at eye level. "No, I think maybe you should put it in me. Let the low-lives bring me aboard their ship. I would like to see who's responsible," he said angrily.

"Gaelan, please, no. I don't want them taking *you*," I cried.

"Fine, forget it … it was just an idea." He exhaled in frustration.

"We could dump it." Zaric smirked. "You know, shoot it off the ship and send them on a wild goose chase."

"No, I don't think that would be wise. It may draw some attention if we have an unscheduled dump," Gaelan cautioned in a serious tone.

"We could just wait for them to retrieve it on their own," I interjected quietly.

Gaelan looked at me while he thought. "No, it's not safe. Someone might find it in the meantime. If we're really going to keep quiet about this, we have to find a way to get rid of it. I don't want anybody seeing it accidently," he said with conviction.

"He's right." Zaric agreed adamantly. "We need to destroy it. We should dispose of the evidence."

"Well, I could try to dissolve it in some acid, but that would be a waste," Urit said, unconvinced about demolishing the object. "I mean, think of it ... this is our only chance to study their latest technology. Perhaps we could develop a way to protect ourselves from them," Urit proposed. I already knew what he was thinking. I could see the gears turning in his head. He was not someone to let a prime opportunity to learn something new pass him by.

"Urit, you can't study it here. Someone might find it," Gaelan scolded.

"No, I agree, not here—but we'll be on Kataria tomorrow night. I can hide it until then. I would love to show it to my daughter, Nia. She is gifted when it comes to designing technological instruments. She could analyze it, break it down piece by piece, and uncover what makes it tick," Urit explained to me proudly.

"She could really do that?" I asked.

"Oh yeah," Zaric interjected. "Take Urit here for example. He's a smart guy, right?" he said, putting his arm around Urit's shoulders. Urit shrugged uncomfortably at his unwelcomed touch.

"Absolutely," I agreed. Urit relaxed a little and smiled back at me.

"Well, take that and *multiply* it by a hundred," he exaggerated.

"Wow," I mouthed the words.

"Thank you, Zaric. That is really kind, but I can't argue with you. She is truly amazing," Urit said humbly.

"Okay, here. Just hide the thing before I change my mind." Gaelan huffed and tossed the little ball in the air, making Urit jump to catch it before it hit the floor. "Where are you going to put it?"

"I have just the thing." Urit opened his cabinet and retrieved a small jar from a shelf. He unscrewed the lid and dropped the metal tracer into a red, gelatinous liquid. "Hand me those tweezers, please, Sam." Urit carefully pulled out the tracer with the tweezers and let the excess red liquid drip off the ball into the jar. The tracer was now covered with a red, rubberized material. It looked like a little toy bouncy ball.

"Great, you turned it into a toy," Gaelan said sarcastically. "Is that your idea of hiding it? Here, kids, I got something new for you to play with." Urit shot him an irritated glare.

"Actually, that's precisely what I am going to do ... give it to my kids," Urit defended as he walked over to his aquarium full of lab mice and dropped the ball into their cage. "Here you go, my little friends. I got you a new toy. You'll keep this safe for me, won't you?" He talked baby talk to the furry critters. Gaelan and Zaric looked at each other and chuckled under their breath by his cutesy display of affection towards his pet mice. I thought his solution was brilliant. I thanked Urit for removing the tracer before the three of us left.

"Do you think he'll keep quiet?" I asked Gaelan and Zaric. I wanted to determine if we could trust Urit to keep the news about the tracer a secret.

Gaelan smirked. "Don't worry, the man's a vault. Besides, I think he would do just about anything for *you.*"

"You think so?" I acted unsure of what he was insinuating.

"I've never seen him act that way with anyone else before," Gaelan explained casually while we walked through the corridor.

Zaric nodded in agreement. "It's true. Wow! You said he was different. I don't know what's gotten into him."

"I know. Like I was telling you before, he's been super nice. He's a changed man." Gaelan held up his hands in disbelief.

"Yeah, I mean normally he hates to be bothered, and … and he's even *gentle*," Zaric said, sounding surprised.

"Oh, please, Urit's a great guy. He's always been very kind," I defended him.

"Yeah, *right*," Zaric muttered. "If that was me or Gaelan in there, he would have been like, *come here*." He grabbed Gaelan's hair and yanked his head back in a headlock while he snarled to make his teeth look like fangs. Gaelan joined the act and pretended to grimace in pain. "Stay still," he demanded firmly while he pretended to forcefully pull out a tracer from Gaelan's nose. "There," he said sharply. "I got it. Now off with you," he teased as he jerked Gaelan's head away forcefully.

"*Ahhh* … that hurt," Gaelan moaned and covered his face with his hands, continuing to act out the skit.

"No, that didn't hurt me at all. Now go. Leave me," he sneered like a mad scientist, "I need to return to my laboratory. My mice children are waiting for me," Zaric mocked.

"Stop it." I laughed at their humorous charade. "He's sweet. He's not like that." I tried to defend him.

"Yeah, to you, *Sam*," Gaelan teased. "I'll do *anything* for my new playmate, Sam."

"You're just jealous," I jested.

"Yep, of course I am," Gaelan conceded.

Zaric smiled. "Actually, we should be thanking you. You've changed him for the better. Now going to the hospital is safer for everyone."

"Good night, Zaric. Thank you," I said gratefully. We returned to our quarters and went straight to bed. Neither one of us wanted to talk about the Dreons kidnapping me. Besides being dead tired, I think we both wanted nothing more than to forget about it.

CHAPTER 24

KATARIA

Gaelan reluctantly left me to report to duty the next morning. I assured him that I would be fine. Despite my reassurances, he repeatedly called me on the ship's communicator every two hours. I asked him if the Dreon ship was still around. He happily reported that they were nowhere in sight.

I spent most of the day looking out the study's large window as the ship approached Kataria. I stared in disbelief as the planet appeared to grow in size the closer we got. The blue, glowing planet suspended in the black sky looked so much like Earth. I had to remind myself that I was not going home. To my surprise, the ship did not land directly on Kataria as we did on Decca. This time, we docked onto their orbiting Space station, called Spaceport. I almost had a heart attack when a man dressed in a blue Space suit appeared outside my window. He was the Spacecraft's window washer in a sense. He sprayed down the entire hull of the ship with a bubbly foam, which appeared to dry on contact. Gaelan had told me how the ship had to be cultured and cleaned after every trip as a precaution. They worried about possible contamination from unknown organisms. He explained that they once discovered a microbe on their hull days after landing. The strange organism was so hearty it had managed to survive the heat of re-entry and disintegrated the grass and soil beneath the ship's landing pad. He told me it created a sink hole that was over ten feet deep and thirty feet wide before they could identify the cause. Luckily, they managed to wipe it out before it spread.

Spaceport was gigantic. It housed roughly ten thousand and functioned so independently, it had almost become its own planet. I wondered how long it took to build. Gaelan told me I should go explore while he completed his shift, but I decided not to. I would have to go alone and didn't want to encounter anymore unknowns.

"Sami, Gaelan, hello—it's me, Azil." Azil was knocking outside our door later that evening.

"Hello, Azil. Are you ready for this or what?" Gaelan moaned and invited her in. She hugged a small pile of clothing and accessories with her left arm.

"Oh, Gaelan, it's not going to be *that* bad. Just try and have some fun. You'll be fine," Azil reassured him, nudging his shoulder with her free hand.

"Sami," Azil shrilled as she walked past him. "I'm so glad that you're okay. Zaric told me that you had a busy night. I would have checked on you earlier, but I just found out." She hugged me delicately.

"Thanks, I'm fine," I reassured her.

"So much for it not leaving the room," Gaelan mumbled.

Azil scoffed. "Please, brother, like you can keep a secret from me. I'm usually the first person you confide in. Besides, there are no secrets in this family."

"Well, Miss Nosey-pants, just remember, I know where you live," he joked.

"Funny." She shrugged before she quickly snapped back, "Hey, you have no room to judge. I heard that you wanted to blow up their ship." She walked up to him and waited for an answer. I couldn't tell if she was upset by his comment or merely teasing him.

"I considered it." Gaelan rubbed his forehead.

"What stopped you?" she said curiously.

He crossed his arms defensively. "The lucky bastards brought her back unharmed."

"*Careful,* Gaelan, you must be rational," she warned in a serious tone, with all of her attention on him.

"I know. I'm not *unreasonable,*" he said trying to disregard her concern. He seemed insulted by her threat. It was as though they were talking in code. Was Gaelan *really* serious when he said he wanted to blow them up? This whole thing about saying what you mean was hard to get used to. I was accustomed to people being dramatic and words not holding their full value. Azil seemed worried about her brother's judgment and the repercussions of his actions. Neither of them spoke for a moment. She turned away from him to face me, putting an angelic smile across her face. Her mood went from threatening to cheerful in a blink.

"Sami, the other reason I'm here is because I brought you a dress and shoes for tonight's reception." She draped a gorgeous red gown across the bed. "Our homecoming gala is considerably formal compared to our everyday attire," she explained excitingly. "I was hoping that you would consider pulling up your hair. It is considered more appropriate for the occasion," she explained as she continued to unload a handful of accessories from her arms. It seemed impossible for her to miss out on any detail.

"Of course, Azil. Thanks for thinking of me. The dress is very pretty, but it's just so bright and vivid," I moaned.

"Yes, I think the color will be just beautiful on you." She sounded thrilled. My sarcasm was lost on her. I couldn't help feeling like her Barbie doll at times.

"Will you be wearing something similar? I would prefer to blend in as much as I can." It's not that I wasn't grateful for her help. She was most considerate, but *bright* red?

"Don't be concerned. This is perfect. You'll fit right in. Let me know if you need anything. I am going to be in my quarters." She turned to leave. Obviously, she didn't plan on giving me any other options and left before I had a chance to complain.

"You should trust her. It's her specialty, after all," Gaelan chimed in after the door closed behind her.

"What is?"

"I know Azil spends her time in the gardens, but she is actually an accomplished clothing designer," Gaelan explained.

"I thought she specialized in agriculture. She knows everything about the gardens here."

"Well, that's sort of a given when you grow up on a farm. Her main duty is to clothe the crew. It's the ideal job for her. She can't control her creativity. Her usefulness was discovered by accident. She always took it upon herself to make sure everyone aboard was perfectly outfitted for our travels. She did it so well that it became her designated duty aboard the ship."

"Really, and to think, I thought she just liked me."

"She does. You should see what she would give you to wear if she didn't." He crinkled his face up in a disgusted look.

"Stop it," I scolded. Gaelan just laughed. Truthfully, I knew she provided clothing for the crew, but I thought it was because she was in charge of keeping track of it. I never realized that she was the one who actually designed the clothing. She never told me. She was too humble to mention it to me.

My mind drifted to the previous topic of conversation. I couldn't help wondering about his remarks to Azil. "Gaelan, I have to ask, you weren't seriously considering blowing up the Dreons' ship, *were you?*" He didn't answer me at first. He furrowed his brow and looked at me as though he was trying to decide if he could tell me the truth.

"Mm-hmm. If they hurt you, yes, I was contemplating it."

"Wow," was all I could reply.

"What? The universe would be a better place without them."

"True, but that's not for you to decide."

He looked at me with a forbidding glare. "You are *really* starting to sound Katarian."

"Hmm." I shrugged in response. I didn't know if he meant what he said as a compliment, but it sounded like an insult. He seemed to have a deep, underlying resentment for his society's submission to the Dreons. I could see his point with them being as intrusive as they were. The temptation to eliminate your enemies would be a challenge when you have such powerful weapons at your disposal. Still, I was glad he acted prudently. He walked past me to avoid any further inquisition.

"*Well*, I wouldn't mind seeing you in this." Gaelan raised his eyebrows as he sat down beside the dress and slid his hand across the silky gown. "Maybe the party won't be so bad if you're there." He sulked.

"Gaelan, why are you so unenthusiastic about going home?"

"It's hard to explain. No, actually, it's easy. There are a lot of reasons. For one, the gala is obnoxious and completely unnecessary. I don't know why it's mandatory to have one after every trip. The other reason is the guilt trip from my family. They never want me to leave after I'm home. They would be happier if I would stay with them. They think I'm lonely, that I isolate myself. 'You should start a family and live on Kataria,' I hear over and over," he whined. "It gets old. *Maybe*, they'll leave me alone after I introduce you to them." He smiled a little and looked at me with a glimmer of hope in his eyes. "But then there's the whole bureaucratic nonsense. We are required to explain in detail our success in meeting our mission objectives. The council constantly threatens to cut our future support if we do not obtain their preset goals. It's just to demonstrate their power. They like to tell us what we can and cannot do. I would just like to avoid the whole thing."

"Great, I can't wait." I sat down next to him on the bed. "Are you still sure about me keeping the band?"

388 ✫   BEYOND THE STARS

"Sami, I have never been surer of anything. Just let them challenge me on that. I will *not* let them dictate how I choose to live my life."

Gaelan leaned over to me, stroked his hand across my back, and gave me a long, intense kiss. It felt incredible. He reminded me of how easy it was to love him. I followed Azil's instructions and got ready for the homecoming. I couldn't believe I was about to step foot on yet another planet. I wished I had a stamp in my passport showing where I had been since leaving Earth. I hadn't been this nervous since my wedding to Jack. I hoped that the rest of Gaelan's family accepted me as easily as Azil and Zaric had. Gaelan seemed confident that our intergalactic marriage would be openly embraced. His bravery to stand up for what he believed in seemed unfaltering. I, however, wasn't sure how it would be received. I knew how crazy people on Earth could be when old traditions were challenged. Being the first of anything increases the risk in any event.

***

The ship was cleared for landing, and we effortlessly reached the planet's surface as we did when we landed on Decca. Again, I couldn't help but be amazed at how smooth the ship lowered itself to the ground. There was hardly a bump. I came out of the bathroom dressed and ready to go.

Gaelan gave me a huge smile. "You look stunning," he said with his smooth voice.

"Thanks, as do you," I replied. He looked fantastic in his elegant suit. His magnificent body conformed to his clothing perfectly. We followed a crowd of crew members down the corridors to the landing. I hardly recognized everyone in their formal dress.

"Sami," Noah beamed when he saw me, "you're a Katarian goddess." Karis looked across the room, pretending not to hear him.

"Thanks, Noah. I'm nervous," I moaned.

"Don't worry. You'll be just fine. If I survived on Earth after all these years, surely you can handle a few days on Kataria."

"Let's go, my love." Gaelan linked his arm in mine as he escorted me down the ramp.

We stepped out onto a plush, grassy, green field. It was early evening on what appeared to be a warm summer's night on Earth. A large, coral-colored sun was beginning to set in the distance over the trees. You could see bright stars and two moons, one full and one crescent-shaped, appearing in the clear twilight sky. The air felt clean and fresh, so I took in a few deep breaths. A mellow breeze carried the scent of flowers and freshly cut grass. I couldn't believe their planet was so similar to ours. Ahead of us was a long stone patio hosting the reception gala, elaborately decorated with strings of tiny white lights canopying over the crowd. Spanning out directly behind the patio was an enormous stone castlelike building illuminated with shining gold spotlights. It was five stories high and appeared to be centuries old. Its colossal size was breathtaking. The entire scene was absolutely beautiful. I felt like I was crashing a millionaire's wedding. Our group walked up to join the swarm of eager people rushing forward to greet us. I felt Gaelan's grip on my arm tighten protectively. Festive music grew louder in the background as we approached the group.

"*Gaelan*, over here," shouted a man, popping his head up while he cut his way through the mass of people.

"Liam!" Gaelan smiled after spotting his brother. They happily embraced each other when they met and patted each other's backs. Liam was every bit as attractive as his siblings.

"Azil, Zaric," Liam cheered as he quickly hugged his sister and brother-in-law as well. "I was worried you explorers would never come home. I thought maybe you forgot your way and I would have to send out a search party," he teased. I was glad to find that he had a sense of humor.

"Where are Mother and Father?" Gaelan asked.

"Oh, they are around here somewhere. They were with Gallina and the kids the last time I saw them," he said absently.

"How are the little geniuses? Getting big, I imagine," Gaelan said kindly.

"They are wonderful. I learn something new from them every day. You are really missing out, Gaelan. When are *you* going to start a family of your own?"

"I do not know the answer to that, Liam. Could you please stop asking me that?" Gaelan turned and looked at me for empathy. I gave him an understanding look.

"Liam, I want to introduce you to someone," Gaelan said, changing the subject. "This is Samantha Bennett." Gaelan pulled me closer to him. "Sami is from Earth." Liam paused and stared at my face. His mouth opened slightly like he was stunned. It was as though he didn't even notice me before. He stepped back and brazenly looked me up and down.

"Hello, it's a pleasure to meet you." I reached out to shake his hand. He grabbed my fingers and squeezed three of them, unsure of the appropriate response. I was accustomed to the Katarians knowing our normal greeting. Apparently, the people aboard the ship understood me better.

"Hello, Samantha. I would have thought my brother could have told us of your arrival ahead of time. Tell me, how did you end up on a Katarian starship?" he asked smugly.

"It's a long story. It was sort of by accident," I answered meekly.

"Take it easy on her, Liam," Gaelan warned.

"Well, welcome," he said boisterously, loud enough for people standing twenty feet away to hear. "You are the first person from Earth to reach our land. This is a historic moment," he continued. I glanced over at the crowd around us and was met with curious stares after the people overheard Liam's exaggerated reaction.

"*Please*, Liam," begged Azil, "enough with the theatrics. Don't draw attention. Can we just go and join the party?" she attempted to hush him.

"What? What did I say? Oh, you are all *too* modest," he refuted through pursed lips.

"Liam, *behave*," Azil scolded through her teeth. She meant it like a threat.

Liam smiled as though it gave him pleasure to get a rise out of her. "Certainly, we must introduce our guest to Mother and Father immediately. They love surprises."

Gaelan and Azil ignored his comment and continued walking to the decorated patio. I could already see why Gaelan said I had to meet Liam to understand what he was like. His personality was overbearing, to say the least. I looked across the grass and saw Noah with Karis and what looked to be her parents. She was introducing them enthusiastically. He gave me a wince as if he were in pain. I smiled back, trying not to laugh. He looked like a sixteen-year-old boy meeting a girl's parents for the first time.

We stepped onto the stone patio, where the music and crowd were considerably louder. There had to be over five hundred people in attendance. People were eating, socializing, and even dancing on the central dance floor. They danced a dance that resembled an Austrian waltz. I couldn't believe the similarities our people shared. Aside from some of the clothing, it felt like home. I had to remind myself that I was on another planet.

We quickly found their mother, Miria, and their father, Colin. They looked shockingly young. I didn't know why I was so surprised, having already been aware of their discovered longevity. Gallina, Liam's wife, and their daughters, Mia and Liana, were all together. Azil and Zaric's children, Ariana, their adult daughter, and her husband, Zander, as well as their teenaged son, Maric, also joined us. Ariana and Azil's resemblance was uncanny. The way Azil and Zaric embraced them made me long to see Leah and Jackson.

Each of them gave me a simple nod as Gaelan introduced them to me. I copied their mannerisms. Here, I was the outsider trying to behave with acceptable social graces. The group greeted me with open arms. They were almost too nice. It was as though they didn't want to do or say anything to scare me away. Regardless, I was just happy to receive such a warm reception. I was starting to relax with the tightly knit group when Gaelan had to excuse himself, leaving me alone with his family.

He promised to return in a few minutes. Liam wasted no time. He quickly approached me and backed me away from the others. Everyone was enthralled in their conversations and didn't notice his advance.

"Samantha, I am curious. How did you meet my brother?" he asked bluntly.

"Please, call me Sami. We met while working on our Space resort." I decided to keep my answers brief.

"Do you think it is wise to become so involved with someone from another planet?"

"As long as it's a good relationship, I see no harm."

"How long have you been *in love* with my brother?" He turned to face me straight on and looked me directly in the eyes, awaiting my answer.

"Oh, what makes you so sure I'm in love with him?" Talk about being put on the spot. I was grateful for my maturity. Direct questioning like that would have had me in tears in my twenties. Gaelan had warned me about his ability to notice everything. He wasn't kidding.

"Oh, so do you *deny* having feelings for him?"

"No. *I do.* I'm just surprised that you're asking." I tried not to get defensive.

"Well, I was just wondering. I am concerned for my brother's happiness. After all, if you are companions, then I would hope that you loved him. I can imagine he would only risk giving you *this* if that were the case."

He lifted my wrist and touched the metal band with the tip of his finger. Was he the only person that noticed it in all the excitement? "You know, in wearing this, you are making the greatest commitment. You've become an inseparable addition to our family. Are you planning on staying here on Kataria?"

"No, I'm not. I have to return to Earth. I have a family of my own at home."

"I am wondering how that will work. The two of you are from different worlds. You are from opposite sides of the universe," he stated dramatically.

"I understand your concern, but I just want to be with him. I love him with all of my heart. We belong together. I've never been so sure of anything. Plus, Gaelan has been working with us, on our side of the galaxy, anyway. We can be together there. We'll find a way to make it work."

"Your determination is enlightening. I am pleasantly surprised. I did not think my brother was capable of having an authentic relationship. Thank you for being so open with me, Sami. You have given me exactly what I needed to know."

"Gaelan," I blurted out when I saw him returning. I wanted this conversation to end. Liam turned away and quietly rejoined his wife.

"Sami, let's get something to eat. You should see the selections." He smiled.

"Sure." I quickly took his hand and headed to the large buffet of food. I now felt paranoid about being from Earth. I wasn't sure if it was just my imagination or if the people surrounding us were actually staring at us on purpose. Either way, Gaelan and I were definitely getting noticed. I wondered if rumors of me being here had spread. I couldn't help remember the nasty gossip Enos had started about me aboard the ship. I tried to push the bad memory out of my mind. We filled our plates and retreated to the corner tables to sit with Gaelan's family. Liam stood up quickly and stared out across the room. He seemed to notice something that sparked his interest.

"Come on, my dear, it is time to mingle. There is someone I need to speak with, if you would excuse us for a moment," Liam said as he took Gallina by the hand and left us in a rush.

"Gaelan," I whispered, "Liam asked me about us when you were gone."

"Oh, I'm *sure* he did." He laughed under his breath. "Don't worry. You must have said something right. Otherwise, he would have made some sort of spectacle." He reassured me with a grin before he took a bite of his food.

"He seemed particularly alarmed by your bracelet on my wrist."

Gaelan looked down at his plate while he tore off a piece of bread with his teeth. He appeared to be preparing what he was going to say. "Liam is only concerned because it involves him. You are now conjoined to our family's bloodline. He was trying to determine if you're worthy. The band is constructed with genetic samples from our living and deceased family members infused within the metal. The alloy's molecular structure carries our family's specific energy vibration. It provides its wearer strength. That's why it is considered a gift. The blending of life forces gives the individual the group's unified power. Over time, it takes on the wearer's personal signature as well, which contributes to its potency while retaining the strengths of the whole. It has the ability to link energy fields to its counterparts. Now that I've given a part of it to you, we will grow more in tune with how the other is feeling."

I took the band in my right hand, held it between my fingers, and thought about what Gaelan had said about it being linked to his family. Then, as if on cue, Miria and Colin halted their conversation and turned their heads to look over at me. Our obvious connection could not be ignored. I gasped, releasing the bracelet from my fingertips. Gaelan noticed but didn't comment. Instead, he gave me a reassuring nod.

I felt a little uncomfortable and wanted to talk about something safe. "It seems like your sun has barely moved since we got here."

"Ah, you noticed. Our sunsets take longer than Earth's because of our longer days," Gaelan explained. He seemed impressed by my observation.

Liam and Gallina returned to our corner about thirty minutes later. Liam leaned down and whispered something into Gaelan's ear. I watched as Gaelan's face fell into a frown as he seemed upset by his message. Gaelan sat there glowering blindly ahead, appearing to be forming a plan. Liam went on to say something quietly to his parents, Azil, and Zaric. I could not hear what they were saying over the music.

"Is there a problem?" I asked, suddenly alarmed as the once joyful expressions of the people around me crashed and burned.

Gaelan stood up. "Word travels quickly. We need to go … now!" He moaned. The rest of the family gave each other a discerning look and seemed in agreement. Gaelan was a natural born leader, so we all followed his command and walked around to the front of the building. The entire front lawn was full of white, green, and black vehicles parked in rows. They resembled the ones I saw parked in the landing on the ship, only much smaller. They were all so similar, I wondered how they could tell them apart, until I noticed red reflective numbers etched on the front and back of each car. Despite our rush, I was excited to finally have the chance to ride in one.

We piled into a white vehicle with Gaelan's parents and Liam's family. Gaelan and I hopped in back. Its interior looked similar to our cars at home. Before I knew it, it levitated from the ground, rising about ten feet into the air, and took off. Gaelan saw my dazed reaction as we gently glided across the sky, and he quickly explained to me that people on Kataria used levitrons as their main mode of transportation. Even though we were flying, it felt more like we were riding in a boat. The air-car seemed to rise upward before leveling out and had a bit of a drag whenever Liam accelerated. I looked out the window twice, expecting to see water beneath us. It was an impressive design and had everything I ever wanted in a vehicle, primarily the ability to pass anyone, anywhere.

"Gaelan, what happened? Is something wrong?" I asked as we rode.

"Yes." He bit his lip. He had a terrible expression on his face.

"What ... what is it?" My heart sank.

"It's the council, our government," he explained. "Liam overheard that rumors got out about you being here and our relationship," he said as he looked at me with saddened eyes.

"I take it they're upset," I muttered. I felt terrible. The last thing I wanted was to cause him any trouble.

"Oh yeah, and they are not too happy about our run-in with the Dreons, either. They feel it may cause problems in the future," he said vaguely.

"Can I be of help? Maybe I could explain how my being here was just accidental."

"You can." He squeezed my hand. "Look, Sami, that's our home and farm over there. Those are the fields we grow our produce in." He pointed out the window, never missing an opportunity to share his experiences with me. I loved how he could remain so level-headed under stress.

"You own *all* that land?" I gazed down at the acres and acres of fields.

"Yes. This is our headquarters. Actually, this is now the smallest plot we grow in. We own bigger fields in the other six territories, but this place will always be home," he said.

I could see a large white structure illuminated by the moonlight in the far distance. It resembled an old chateau. "What is that on the crops?" I asked. The ground looked like it was covered with dark green netting. It was difficult to tell what it was as the darkness set in.

"Oh, that's Liam's doing. Remember when I told you that he discovered a way to speed the maturity of crops?"

"Yes."

"We cover the plants with the augmentation wonder net. The netting feeds the plants, enhances photosynthesis, retains moisture, protects from insects, and accelerates the entire growth cycle." It sounded like he was conducting an infomercial. I looked down at the crops that seemed to stretch on for miles. I finally understood the full scope of Gaelan telling me about his family producing a large percentage of the country's food supply. They had to be indispensible to the agricultural market. Not only did they supply massive amounts of produce, they supplied revolutionary growth products to other farmers.

"Remarkable. How old was he again when he came up with this?"

"Eleven—hence the name." He smirked as if he was holding in a laugh and raised his eyebrows.

"Hey, I heard that," Liam shouted back from the driver's seat to us in the rear row.

"*Good!* I meant for you to. Just drive," Gaelan snapped back at his brother.

"It's a good name," he defended.

"Uh-huh," Gaelan mocked. Liam's daughters found their bickering funny and giggled in unison with their sweet little voices. "You should have seen his bedroom when he was developing it. It looked like a greenhouse and smelled like one, too. I remember my mother sweeping the dirt from the hallway into his room and shutting the door." I heard the rest of the family chuckle quietly as they listened in. Apparently, Liam wasn't the only one eavesdropping on our conversation.

We landed in front of the large white stone house that glowed against the dusky evening light. Azil and Zaric's children's vehicle came in directly behind us. We entered through the arched front door. Liam and Gallina's girls took off running to their rooms. Inside, the home's floor and walls were made with the same white stone that covered the house. A huge round glass skylight took up most of the ceiling of the foyer. I imagined they must utilize the same solar energy techniques in their homes as they did aboard the ship.

We all sat in a large, formally decorated living room once inside. It was beautiful, with décor that looked centuries old. There were several large, carved wooden chairs and two sofas with soft navy blue cushions, big paintings of landscapes covering the walls, and lamps with shades made out of dangling clear crystals. The room's tall ceiling was trimmed with a plastered crowned molding, which was both visually inviting and impressive. I could imagine its photograph on the cover of *Architectural Digest*. Miria and Gallina cordially served everyone by pouring each of us a glass of wine. It was red and sweet. I wondered if they had grown the grapes themselves. We weren't there even ten minutes before there was a loud knock at the door. Colin answered it and returned with a letter in hand.

"Gaelan, this came for you," he said resentfully as he handed him the envelope.

"And so it begins." Gaelan sighed and opened the letter.

"What is it?" I asked. Gaelan's eyes quickly moved across the page as he read the document.

"They are putting us on trial," he muttered. Silence swept across the room as everyone froze.

"What does that mean?" I asked. Gaelan continued to read the paper.

"What grounds do they list?" Colin said, sounding perturbed.

"It states here that the council is requesting an explanation for my involvement with Sami and for my actions on Decca. We have to defend ourselves in front of the council," he scoffed.

"When?" I muttered.

"We'll have to go in tomorrow morning." Gaelan huffed.

"You're in trouble because of me. I didn't mean to cause such pandemonium," I said with exaggeration to show my sincere remorse.

"I would like to know who complained about you and Sami," Azil mused.

Gallina looked at Gaelan and me. "I am not sure why this is a surprise to anyone. We have had friendly relations with your people for years. Did they not think that it was possible for our people to fall in love with one another?" she interjected. Clearly, Liam wasn't the only one to notice our union. I now realized that everyone in the room was already well aware of Gaelan's Katarian band on my wrist. They probably felt something was up the moment it clasped itself shut around my wrist.

"I'm sorry." I bit my lip.

Miria put her hand on my shoulder. "Sami, it's not your fault. You do not have to apologize. I am grateful that Gaelan has found you. People just need to get used to the idea of you entering our world," said Gaelan's mother.

Liam joined in. "Sami, our people are reasonable. I have many friends on the council. They are expected to investigate every complaint. It is their duty. Gaelan will seek justice."

"He's right. It is just a formality," Colin agreed. "We will not give you up without a fight," he said adamantly. He looked Gaelan in the eye as if he were conveying a hidden message to his son.

"From what I heard, I think they are more concerned with your inconvenient run-in with the Dreons than with you two being together," Liam hedged.

"Why does it matter if the Dreons know about me? How does that put you at risk?"

"They are just being cautious," Colin explained. "Some people believe that the Dreons only stopped their exploitation of our people because we explained our strong beliefs against inter-species breeding when we made our agreement with them. If a Katarian has a relationship with someone from another planet, it would make them assume we believe otherwise."

"Oh, please," Zaric scoffed. "The Dreons are *anything* but noble. They are only concerned with their own agenda. Our feelings mean nothing to them. In their view, we are only prey for the taking."

"I think the real reason they agreed to the truce was our unexpected success in resisting them," Liam exclaimed. "Our weapons hurt them more than they cared to disclose. We should have demanded that they leave our planet, never to return." He seemed to share his older brother's view.

"Easier said than done, Liam," Miria interjected. "I can only imagine how hard it must have been for our council to keep their thoughts in order. I am certain that they distorted their thinking with their mind control."

"Sami, don't worry. Everything will be all right," Azil comforted me. "Try to get some sleep. I'll help you get ready in the morning." She anxiously went off to her residence with Zaric and their children, in the left wing of the home. I could tell they were desperate to spend time alone.

"Thanks," I muttered.

***

Gaelan and I wished the rest of his family good night. He led me to his side of the family home. He explained that each of them lived separately within the massive estate. I could have gotten lost. Gaelan's suite was decorated much more simply than the elaborate living room we had just been sitting in. It was also considerably more modern. He didn't have a lot of furniture. There was one wide black sofa, an overstuffed chair, and two square, lighted acrylic end tables in the living room. Taking up the far left side of the room was a sleek slate-green kitchenette. The place was neat but unfussy. He had things set carelessly across the kitchen countertop. Three doorways led to other rooms. I could see a low bed through one of the doors. I saw him trying to size up my reaction as he showed me around.

"I don't spend much time here. I live more on the ship than anywhere else," he said, sounding embarrassed by the somewhat vacant space.

"*No,* don't explain. You have a great place," I assured him, despite the sound of my loud, echoing footsteps resonating throughout the almost empty room. I looked around. It made me realize how materialistic I had become. His minimalist lifestyle carried a freedom of its own. I suddenly valued my voyage to Kataria even more.

It had forced me to adapt to living with less and place value on what truly mattered. I smiled while I happily took in the simplicity around me. "I'm just surprised by how old-fashioned Kataria is compared to the ship."

"That's because our society has become two-sided. Those who want tradition live and work on Kataria, while those seeking modernization reside primarily on Spaceport or the ships."

"It's like two different worlds." I thought about his words.

"Yes, and that's something we find interesting about Earth. You don't seem to be experiencing such a split as you become more technologically advanced. It's impressive how gracefully you've been able to accept change." He looked at me curiously for a moment before his eyes brightened. "Come, I want to show you something. It is my favorite room," he said enthusiastically. He took my hand and led me into a large, barren room. The ceiling was twenty feet high with a wall of cathedral-like windows at one end. It was furnished with two stools and a long, dark wooden table covered with colorful jars. There was a large painter's easel with a crumbled gray canvas tarp underneath it stationed below the room's tall windows. The bright moons were shining brilliantly through the uncovered glass, vividly illuminating the vast array of paint jars strewn across the table below. The remaining walls were covered floor to ceiling with the most amazing paintings, each illuminated by tiny spotlights shining down on them from above. I gazed up at the colorful masterpieces of stars and breathtaking landscapes.

"I like to spend my time in here, painting, when I'm at home," Gaelan explained.

"Wait! You painted *all* of these?" I asked in disbelief.

"Yes," he said humbly.

My jaw dropped in awe. "Gaelan, they are *fantastic!* You are so talented! They're beautiful." I wandered around the room, peering up at all of the canvases covering the walls before I looked over at him. He had a wide smile across his face from my positive response.

"Thank you. I enjoy it. It relaxes me. Being in here is the thing I miss most when I'm away."

"Do you ever paint on board?"

"No, and I don't know why. I guess it is something that is sacred to me. I like to do it in private. Also, the lighting isn't ideal. I prefer to paint in natural daylight, leaving only the commonly shared areas of the ship as acceptable locations, so again privacy becomes an issue."

"Hmmm ... I never pegged you as the eccentric artist type."

"I am happy to share this with you." He half-smiled.

"Thank you; it's an honor."

"Everything I have is yours. Please, make yourself at home," Gaelan said smoothly as he walked over to me and pulled me into his arms to embrace me. I looked up into his loving eyes. He wasted no time and kissed me with one of those succulent kisses. I felt a warm rush. He could stop time and make me feel like we were the only ones in the world. The transcending sensation pulsed through my lips and awakened my inner desires. I came back to reality when he released his lips and held me snuggly against his body.

"Hmmm," he moaned, "you feel great."

"So do you," I replied while I felt his muscles across his back. "*Enticing.*"

"*Ahh*, Sami, you are really hard to be around sometimes," he murmured through my hair before he kissed the top of my head.

"Tell me about it," I agreed, understanding exactly what he meant. I loved feeling his body next to mine.

"Hmmm," he sighed again while he caressed my back with his hand.

"Gaelan, I'm worried about tomorrow," I admitted.

"I know. I am sorry you have to deal with this on your first visit to Kataria," he muttered casually.

"*First* visit?"

"You caught that, did you?" he chuckled quietly.

"You plan on dragging me across the universe again, do you?"

"If you so desire, yes."

"What should I expect tomorrow? How does it work? Do you have an attorney, you know, someone to help us?"

"No, but we can call upon witnesses. The council's document stated that they already summoned Tyden and Urit to testify. They would be my first choice, anyway." His smile faded as his voice took on a serious tone.

"Noah could help," I offered.

"No. He is considered biased. He's been too close to you all these years. You've made every one of his reports."

"Really, I did? I would like to see those. Wait a minute." I gasped in horror. "I thought that the reports were strictly professional. You mean they cover *more* than just our technological progress?"

"Well—we also mention our success in building relations with your people."

I started pacing around the room. "Has the council read those reports? What do they know about me? Did *you* know about me before we met?" I vented.

"Yes, I knew some things about you. Noah has commented on you throughout the years," he admitted hesitantly.

I clenched my fingers through my hair. "*Oh*," I groaned. "This is just too strange. I feel invaded. This is a violation of privacy. I can't even imagine what things Noah may have said about me over the years. I confided in him completely. I told him things I *never* would have told anyone else. We've been so close. What *exactly* has he written?" I ranted, demanding an answer. Gaelan shifted his body nervously.

"Please, Sami, don't get the wrong impression. Noah's reports mostly cover your technical advancements. He had always been very professional when he mentioned you and Jack."

"*Arrgh*, you know about Jack?" I stood motionless with widened eyes.

"Yes," he said flatly.

"Why didn't you tell me?" I raised my voice in anger. "I can't believe it. You never said a word," I responded abruptly. Although I knew it was something I should have told him about myself, it felt easier to put the blame on him. I'm not entirely sure why I didn't just say, "Oh yeah, and by the way, I was married to another man for almost eighteen years." I guess it seemed only fair that I kept some secrets of my own. He already appeared to know more about me than I did him.

"I'm sorry, I know this is awkward. I should have told you, but I did not want to remind you of your pain. I thought maybe you would tell me about him when you were ready. Besides, it makes me uncomfortable. I am not sure how I would compare."

"I would never compare you. How could I? I didn't mention him because …" I took a deep breath and shook my head as I searched for an acceptable answer. I thought about how I loved both men. But they were from two different eras in my life. Jack was gone, and Gaelan held the key to my soul now. He was my present and my future. I pulled myself together and finally answered, "It makes me feel helpless when I think about it. It was a hard time in my life. I need to distance myself from the pain. Block it from my mind. I wasn't prepared to lose him, and I did." Truthfully, there were few people I could talk to about Jack, usually only those who shared in my suffering. It was private. I didn't like to expose my out-of-control emotions. It made me feel weak. I wanted to tell him that I couldn't handle it if anything happened to him. That no one could ever compare to him. He was everything and more. He was so easy to love. I hated being so vulnerable.

"He sounded like a good man."

"Yes, he was," I said solemnly. "What did you hear about him?"

"I knew he worked for SIG and was a test pilot. By the way Noah described him, he sounded like someone I would have liked to have on board."

"What do you know about the test flights? I just found out that Jack wasn't only flying our experimental aircraft but alien vessels as well."

"Yes, we've been following those for a while now. Your people are in the possession of several Garmite and Farni ships."

"Who are they? They aren't dangerous, *are they?*"

"No. They aren't going to ask for their ships back if that's what you worried about." He paused and studied my face for a moment. It was as though he was deciding if I could handle the truth. "The Farni are beings that reside in oceanic regions. They are nice for the most part. Harmless. They make their homes wherever there is a lot of water. They not only live on Earth but all over the galaxy. They've got more colonies than we can keep track of. Besides being a little careless, always getting spotted entering or exiting the water, they try not to interact with other species and usually never leave a vessel behind. It's extremely lucky that you managed to get a hold of one."

"And the Garmites. What about them?"

"Oh, *not so nice.* They are beastly creatures … vagrants with no morals, surprisingly vain. They have terrible tempers. We try to avoid them whenever possible. They would steal the clothes right off your back. They are known for scavenging resources and stealing energy. They leave a trail wherever they go but never stick around for too long. They're always on the run and travel in packs. In the past, they used to introduce themselves when they entered another's airspace, but lately they've become paranoid about meeting new people. I think it's because they are afraid of being handed over to their enemies. They've created quite a list. They're notorious for consuming copious amounts of coti, getting buzzed up, and crashing their ships. Zaric and I have a bet going that they aren't going to get their drunken butts off one of their vessels one of these days and really blow their cover. "

"Lovely," I said sarcastically. I couldn't help notice the underlying pride he seemed to possess in having the ability to keep their ships undetected. He seemed to believe being seen was a weakness.

"Welcome to the galaxy," he said.

"Thanks. I think I've heard enough for one day." Just thinking about those reports and other alien visitors made me feel like a stalking victim. Talk about being watched. Then, there was Jack and his lies. Him not telling me the truth made me mad on so many levels. "Did you know about Leah and Jackson, too?" I muttered, trying to determine the extent to which my personal life had been violated. I thought about my family being the poster family for Earth. My temples started to throb from my rising blood pressure. I took in a slow, deep breath, trying to curb my rising anxiety.

"Not much. I only know that they are your children and that they are very bright. Jackson is a fine young man, a hard worker, and very inventive. You should be proud," he complimented.

"Thanks," I muttered. I wondered how much time he had spent working with him on the Space resort. I was comforted by the fact that Jackson liked Gaelan enough to invite him to lunch on the day Leah and I arrived at the resort. It seemed like our lives were intertwined in more directions than one.

"Don't worry about the reports. They are just a formality."

I shook my head in disappointment. "Noah, that little spy. He's lucky he is with Karis. If I could get my hands on him right now, I would tie him to a chair and make him tell me everything he ever said about me." I was sickened by his treachery. I considered Noah family.

"Please, Sami, this is hardly the time. I assure you, he has never said anything against you. His reports usually boasted your surprisingly quick advancements and his pleasing relations with you and your people. You have many admirers here."

"I just wish we were on an even playing field. It's not fair that you know more about me than I know about you." My face flushed with embarrassment.

"I will try to even my playing field if you tell me what to do," Gaelan nervously attempted to repeat my figure of speech, despite not understanding its full meaning. He reached out and held me by my trembling hands.

"I would just like to know more about you. I know that will happen with time. I'm just a little freaked out right now."

"Ask me anything. I will tell you whatever it is you want to know," he said openly.

"Hmm," I exhaled. I didn't speak. Would it be a completely unreasonable request to ask him what he had been doing for the past seventy years?

"I'm sorry I upset you. I hate seeing you so displeased. I'll find the reports and read them to you if that would help." He frowned while he gently smoothed the crease across my forehead with his fingers.

"No, it is okay. I'll be fine." I winced. "Maybe it's better if I don't know everything. I suppose we would have written reports on you as well if we were in your position. I just wish I'd known." I tried to regain my composure after I suddenly felt a wave of guilt. Gaelan's honesty on the subject made me love him even more. It also made me realize that he loved me back with the same fervor because he would eagerly tell me whatever I wanted to know. I knew I had to accept things as they were. If there was ever a time to be flexible—it was now. Leah always told me, "What's done is done, Mom." She had the amazing gift of going with the flow of life.

He gave me a reassuring look. "Thank you for your understanding. I am grateful that you're here with me." I consciously relaxed my face, trying to put him at ease.

"I love you. I'm glad I am here, too." I threw my arms around his neck. "It's nice to see your home and meet your family." I stroked my hand across his angular jaw and leaned up to give him a kiss. I could never stay mad at him. He was too precious a gift.

CHAPTER 25

VERDICT

The next morning came quickly. We prepared to defend ourselves to the council. Azil helped me to get ready as promised. She brought me a white shirt and long black skirt to wear for the day. She told me the colors are worn to represent the balance between light and darkness. She was so motherly to me at times. She could anticipate my needs and fulfill them before I had a chance to ask for help. Gaelan and I took one of the family's levitrons to the courthouse. It was a beautiful, sunny day. The sky was crystal clear, without one cloud in the deep blue sky. If someone told me I was back on Earth, I wouldn't disagree. The scenery felt so comforting and familiar. Along the way, Gaelan pointed out a large, beautiful, dark gray stone estate surrounded by lush colorful flowerbeds. The home was crowned by a circular wall of trees outlining the property.

"That used to be Noah's home," Gaelan said matter-of-factly. I quickly pressed myself up against the glass of my window in order to get a better look of the land sailing below us before it went out of sight. Our aerial view complimented the property's grand magnificence. I wondered if all of my friends from Kataria were incredibly wealthy.

"Really? You mean he lived *there?*" I was amazed at why he would ever want to leave.

"Yes, when he was young. Before his parents' accident." He grimaced.

"Did he sell it before he came to Earth?"

"No, he lost it," he paused, "along with everything else when his parents died. The court ruled the home and all of its possessions to be given to the closest living adult family member. Unfortunately, the only surviving relatives were so far removed, they had no true relationship at all. Instead of taking Noah in, they shipped him off to an orphanage and took over his family's estate. He was only thirteen. Katarian law dictates that only those who occupy a property can rightfully own it. They seized the opportunity to take control of his inheritance before he could legally claim it at the age of sixteen."

"That's tragic," I cried while I pictured my dear friend being abandoned. I felt guilty thinking that just yesterday I wanted to wring his neck. Now, all I wanted to do was to hold him in my arms and tell him how sorry I was for his hard life. I finally understood how Noah could leave Kataria and move to Earth. It was to escape from all the painful memories of his past. He came to Earth to start over and make a better life. "What was the orphanage like?" I had to ask.

"The orphanage or boarding school was established to take in all the children that didn't find homes and were left parentless after the disaster. There were thirty-five in all. My parents took in Azil and considered taking in others, but she proved to be more than a handful."

"*Azil?* Are you serious? I'm sure the grieving process must have been terribly hard for her, but I can't see her being a difficult child," I said, doubting him.

He raised one eyebrow. "*Oh no*, she was a *real* mess when we first got her home," he said emphatically. I remembered him telling me that he was fifteen and that Azil was already twelve when they had adopted her. I imagined that the stress of the situation with all those teenagers, and their raging hormones only made matters worse.

"I'm sure it was hard for her, adjusting to a new home and all," I acknowledged her loss.

"Not just her—it was hard on *everyone!* She was on a self-destructive warpath and trying to take the rest of us down with her. She would have outbursts and go into hostile rages. One time, when I was picking on her ..." he frowned.

"Not *you?*" I teased, interrupting.

"Yeah, I have been known to instigate for the fun of it. Anyway, she got really angry. She charged me like an animal, picked me up, and threw me through a closet door. I didn't even know it was possible for a little girl to be that strong. She scared the crap out of me. Things got so bad, we had to hide all the sharp objects in the house, fearful that she might hurt someone or herself." He took his eyes off the path in front of us and gave me a serious look, conveying his torment.

"Wow! What changed? How did she get over it? I mean, she turned out so well. She's one of the sweetest people I've ever met."

"Well, we were just *really* patient with her. My mother encouraged her to pursue her love for clothing design and taught her how to sew. It gave her a constructive way to channel her energy. My parents also enrolled her in defensive movement classes, to my dismay." He shrugged. "It's similar to your martial arts. I didn't agree with them at the time. Why in the world would you professionally train someone like *her* to spar? But, they were right; it worked like a charm. It became a therapeutic outlet for her. She and I became good friends, as well. I was happy to have someone other than Liam to hang out with. The two of us would team up against him. I guess we all just needed a little time to become a family. Now, I can definitely say I'm closest to her," he said, smiling.

I understood. The love they shared for one another was obvious.

***

We arrived at the massive building that hosted the welcome home gala. It looked shockingly different in the daylight. It wasn't glowing like it had been last night at the party. Today, it looked gray, dull, eerie, and downright haunted. It was amazing how the darkness could make something appear prettier than it actually was. The place seemed dead without all the commotion of people. The building's narrow windows appeared to have eyes that watched us approach the front steps. They gave me the creeps. We entered through a narrow doorway and found Tyden and Urit standing inside the otherwise vacant lobby, waiting for us.

"Are we ready to have some fun today?" Urit greeted us.

"There's nothing better to do," Gaelan replied sarcastically.

"Would you like to know who gave you away?" Tyden asked us.

"Enos," Gaelan and Urit answered in unison.

"It is no surprise. I imagine he wasted no time before he went rushing to his father to deliver his news," Gaelan surmised.

"Without a doubt." Urit groaned. "That is because you two showed him the most exciting affair he has ever seen in his pathetic, sheltered life."

"I knew he would try to sabotage our lives in one way or another," Gaelan scoffed. "He's lashing out at his father. This is his immature way of retaliating for being forced to go on the ship with us."

"You mean Enos never wanted to go on the trip?" I asked.

"No, it was *entirely* his father's idea. He wanted to broaden his perspectives," Tyden concluded.

"Sure, that's why," Urit retorted. "It was more likely a way of taking Enos off his hands for a little while. He needed a break from entertaining the spoiled runt."

"Come, Samantha, it's time. Let us clear up this nonsense," commanded Tyden, who then ushered me down the shiny marbled hallway.

"Thank you," I replied. I felt a wave of nervousness pass through me. I was dreading this. I hoped that the council would approve of my and Gaelan's relationship. I was prepared to fight for him if I had to.

"I've been on trial many times, Sam. We will set things right," Urit added. "Listen, do not volunteer any information. Only answer the question that is asked," he instructed. Gaelan and Tyden looked at each other and smiled.

"*You* would know," Gaelan teased, struggling not to laugh.

Urit shot Gaelan and Tyden an irritated glare before he turned to me. "I have had to defend most ... okay fine, pretty much *every one* of my inventions. It's difficult to explain life-altering medical breakthroughs to non-medical people. They cannot visualize the significance of anything without *blatant* proof staring them in the face," Urit quickly defended himself. "Just keep your answers simple," he said abruptly through pursed lips.

We entered the courtroom together. A man directed us to sit in a row of armchairs at the end of a circular pit. The room felt narrow and would be miserably claustrophobic if it was not for the high cathedral ceiling above. The council members were already seated in the bleacher-type seating that surrounded three walls of the room. There were at least fifty council members stationed throughout the rows. Aside from a panel of six men and four women seated together in the front row, each of them left empty seats beside themselves, as though no one wanted to be too close to one another. Their blank, unsmiling faces were upon us as we walked past them in order to take our seats. All of them were uniquely dressed, but all wore black and white clothing. I now understood Azil's wardrobe choice for me. The colors were a courtroom standard. The men and women looked as ancient as their surroundings and almost uninterested in being there. One man was so old or bored, he was actually napping while sitting up. Perhaps they didn't undergo Urit's treatment, or maybe they received the vaccine later in life. Knowing Tyden's extreme age, I couldn't help wondering how old some of them must be.

A man from the front panel stood. "Please give your attention for the trial of Gaelan Liitanen and our visitor from Earth, Samantha Bennett," he spoke in a loud voice. Gaelan whispered to me that he was the head councilmen. Unlike the others, he wore mostly white. I surmised that he was similar to a judge.

"Gaelan, it has been stated that you have gone outside of Katarian tradition and made this woman your companion. Please justify your actions for the council."

"I clearly state that my intentions are pure. I had not anticipated encountering my companion on this mission, but I did. I choose her. I do not see this as a problem, for we seek a long-term relationship with the people of Earth."

"You, Samantha, do you feel the same way?" his deep voice echoed across the room.

"Yes, I do," I replied.

"Witnesses, please verify what they say is true."

"They are devoted to each other. Gaelan has never taken this commitment lightly. It is the only time he has taken such a vow," explained Tyden.

"Did you approve the arrangement?" The councilman focused in on Tyden.

"Yes, I did freely," he answered firmly. There was a dragging moment of silence before either of them spoke.

"I know you would only approve those you believe in," replied the councilman. "But we do not want to interbreed like the Dreons have. We cannot commit such an atrocity in our society."

"There is no reason for such a fear," Urit interjected. "She is exactly the same as us. Our chromosomal make-up is identical." I wanted to chime in that Gaelan and I hadn't considered starting a family together but managed to keep quiet. I suddenly worried about my irresponsible behavior of having unprotected sex.

The councilman's eyes met Urit's. "This is true, but the Dreons are aware of her. It may uncover a trail revealing her true identity. It will fracture our excuse. Then what? The Dreons will break the treaty. They will take more than our DNA. They will start taking our people again. We could not defend our position that interbreeding is against our beliefs."

"Surely, this one girl cannot damage our arrangement with the Dreons," Tyden replied.

"It threatens our reputation," replied the councilman angrily. "Our peaceful world will cease to exist. They may be planning an attack. We will be forced into battle. Tyden Rigel, I do not have to remind you, of all people, of the casualties of war." Murmurs of discussion passed through the stands. I looked at the people, only to be met with unfriendly glares.

"Samantha, did you tell them you are from Earth?"

"No, but they kept asking," I answered truthfully. Voices of the council members exploded into an uproar. We looked around as the previously demure people came to life and started yelling and fighting with one another. Now I was really getting nervous. *Oh, please let them not have news on how the Dreons had implanted a tracer in my body.*

"Silence!" shouted the councilman with deafening volume. The group immediately obliged, and the room became uncomfortably silent. The councilman paced back and forth in front of us while he thought. His shoes tapped loudly across the hard floor. "Can you be *certain* you did not tell them of your planet?"

"I did not, sir," I answered weakly.

"Are you *absolutely* certain?" he said, jutting his face up to mine while grabbing both sides of the armrest of my chair, blocking my escape.

"Yes," I said defensively.

"Good," he said, slowly backing away. "Because if you are wrong, and I'm not saying you are, but if you *did* imagine your home, the repercussions are unforgivable. We need to be certain that your return to Earth will not cause your people to become the Dreons' next victims. I would insist you stay here rather than cause your people any undue suffering inflicted by the Dreons." I looked at Gaelan in terror. He looked back at me from the corner of his eyes and took in a deep breath, followed by a quick exhale. I was sure he was trying to control his temper. Suddenly, I worried the council would prevent me from returning home. My adrenaline surged, making my hands turn to ice and tremble on the armrest. I didn't want to be stuck here for good.

The judge continued his deliberate stride around the room as he collected a sheet of paper from the panel of men and women in the front row. Each of them wore a wide white scarf over their black robes. He stopped walking and carefully read each note. I waited for him to speak. The seconds slowly ticked by. Finally, he looked up from the pile of papers. "Hmm," he groaned to himself before he flicked the papers with the back of his other hand. "Samantha, are you planning on residing on Kataria?" he said, turning his attention back on me. Oh, thank goodness—it sounded like he was offering me a choice.

"No. I would like to return home. I have a family there."

"Gaelan, I do not understand. Do you plan to leave Kataria forever?"

"I would like the ability to return home at will," Gaelan replied. The judge gave Gaelan a hint of a smile. He seemed pleased by his answer.

"I see." He turned to face me. "Samantha, we will no longer burden you with our legal matters. You have given us all the information we need. We will make our decision after we discuss this matter further with Gaelan and Tyden," he said with a lighter tone in his voice. "You are, by the way, as I imagined. We have heard much about you from your friend, Noah. I hope that we will remain allies for years to come." His demeanor changed from terrifying to sweet. His dual personalities made me wary of trusting him.

"Yes, of course," I replied graciously, hiding the deep anxiety I felt about their reports.

"Urit, you may return to your responsibilities. Samantha, please allow Urit to show you the way out."

Urit took my hand to pull me from my chair and led me out of the courtroom. Tyden and Gaelan stayed behind for further questioning. Gaelan looked up at me with his piercing blue eyes when I walked by him. I didn't know if he thought it was going well or not. But judging by his expression, I knew he wouldn't back down from what he believed in. His eyes were bursting with determination.

"That's it. That's all we get to say?" I asked Urit once we got outside of the courtroom.

"Yes, sometimes less is more," Urit replied. I sighed. "I think it went well," Urit said encouragingly as he put his arm around my shoulder.

I shrugged. "I'm not so sure. I wish they would just say everything is okay and let it go."

"Don't worry, Sam. Some things take time. Be patient. You must have faith in Gaelan. He will do what is best."

"Thank you. You're a good friend." I smiled at him.

"As are you," Urit replied.

"Urit, has everyone here heard stories about me?"

"No, only people in our field and the council. It will be to your benefit, though. I am sure that their previous knowledge of you only helps your defense. In case you haven't noticed, they like to get into everyone's business. Now you understand why so many of us prefer to live on the ship, to avoid getting involved with this nonsense."

"Are your people considered free?"

"Yes, we are free to pursue our interests. The council only gets involved when politics are challenged. They want us to act in a morally acceptable manner and up-hold Katarian law. They serve to maintain order but tend to blur the lines to serve their own curiosity."

"*Gaelan*," I shouted excitedly when the courtroom door opened and he and Tyden stepped out through the door.

"Samantha, we need to talk." Gaelan took hold of my hand and led me briskly down the hall into the lobby. Tyden gave Urit a look filled with apprehension.

"What did they say?" I asked impatiently.

"Not here," he muttered. He rushed me towards the door. He seemed to be in hurry to leave.

***

We exited the building, walking directly into a mass of people awaiting us for questioning. There had to be seventy-five of them. Word of our trial had gotten out. Inquisitive people were yelling their questions at us once we walked out the door.

"Thank you all for coming," Tyden spoke out to the rambunctious group of people in a deep voice that over-shadowed the others. "This is Samantha Bennett, our visitor from Earth. I would appreciate it if you would allow her trip to Kataria to be a peaceful one," he said with authority.

"Gaelan, is it true that you and Samantha are together?" shouted a man from the crowd.

"Samantha, are you staying on Kataria?" a woman added. The murmurs of their voices were coming from every direction.

"No, I'm going home," I mistakenly answered her. They became thrilled at my response and eagerly fired more questions at us.

"Gaelan, are you and Samantha companions?" asked a young man walking beside us. He was close enough to notice a slight smile cross Gaelan's face. "You are! I knew it," he blurted out and looked back at Gaelan. This threw the group into a full frenzy, causing their yelling to escalate.

"Please, your questions will be answered in time." Tyden held up his hand to motion them to stop. His stiffened stance made him appear unshakable. We quickly made our way to our vehicles. Their shouting only became louder as we rushed to get away. It was unnerving to walk through the congested mob clamoring to get close to us. I hated crowds. Gaelan ushered me to the levitron. I clung tightly to his arm while Urit and Tyden acted like physical barriers.

Tyden leaned into the vehicle above me after he helped me with my door. "Sami, I will see what I can do," he said, ignoring the yells behind him. "Right now, I have to get home to Willa. She will wonder what's taking me so long." He pulled his body back, ready to close the door.

"Thanks, but who's Willa?" I asked curiously before Tyden shut the door on me.

"My companion," he answered, ducking his head back inside the vehicle.

"Tyden, *you're* married?" I asked, sounding surprised. I tried to ignore the chaos around us. "Why didn't you ever mention her to me before?"

"Well, I have been married … for 243 years. We decided it was best for both of us if we gave each other some time apart. She claims that I'm bossy and likes to complain that I'm difficult to keep entertained." He frowned. Gaelan was now sitting in the driver's seat beside me and caught the tail end of our conversation. He let out a small chuckle.

"Bossy, *huh?* No way, not you, Tyden." He smirked. Tyden shot him an irritated glare before nodding good-bye and slamming the car door shut. He didn't have time to stay around and argue. The commotion outside the courthouse was gaining momentum.

Once in the car, Gaelan told me that he'd filed a petition to the court's ruling and that certain things still needed to be worked out. I didn't understand the verdict. The suspense was killing me, but there was no time for questions. The following mob seemed to grow impatient in their quest to hound us for answers. Urit and Tyden flew away without a problem. We were what the crowd hungered for. People started pounding their fists on our windows and screaming their questions at us as they surrounded our vehicle. I was nervous that they might break in. Their voices were only slightly muffled by the glass and were downright frightening.

"We have to get out of here. Hang on," Gaelan huffed. He rushed to elevate the car from the ground. As he did, I saw a dozen other levitrons around us lift up as well. They had been sitting in their vehicles, waiting for us to leave.

"Who *are* these people?"

"Reporters, most likely. Strap up and hang on," he instructed me before we took off. Immediately, I flew back in my seat with the rush of body-crippling speed.

"*Ahh* ... Gaelan, don't kill us. Do you have to go *so* fast?" I yelled. We swooped in and out of the surrounding vehicles, barely missing them before reaching the clear blue sky. This was not the leisurely drive we had taken on the way to the courthouse. The swarm of cars followed our lead and circled in on us tightly. The niceties were over. Things had progressed into a full-fledged chase. I braced myself tightly against the door and seat with my sweaty palms. Gaelan quickly peeked over at me, meeting my eyes, before returning his gaze straight ahead. I was certain that he managed to see the panicked look across my face during his quick glance.

"I had no idea you *hated* flying so much," he said, sounding intrigued at finding something he had failed to notice before. He turned his eyes, holding them on my face instead of looking at where he was going. He appeared more interested in learning more about me than the chasing cars.

"I'm not crazy about it, if that's what you mean," I said lamely. "Could you *please* watch where you're going?" I demanded.

"Trust me, these guys have nothing on me," he stated with certainty. He then easily zipped above someone trying to block our way and shot past them without giving it a second thought.

The levitrons traversed our path from every direction and seemed to be dive-bombing us in order to pressure us to land. Gaelan tapped on a dashboard display. A holographic navigational chart expanded in front of us. It showed our position as well as the levitrons around us. I tried to decipher the foreign screen but struggled with its complexity.

"Watch out!" I screamed after another car tried to cut us off. It appeared to have come from nowhere. Gaelan swerved sharply to keep us from colliding.

"Damn—that was close," he said in a steady voice. I couldn't believe how calmly he reacted to the near miss.

"Here comes *another* one," I said, peering out my side window.

"Yeah, and he's persistent." Gaelan accelerated even more. He pushed the throttle of the levitron down to the dash. We thrust back in our seats with the sudden release of explosive power.

"What are we going to do? They won't go away!" My voice was rattled.

"We just need to get across the edge of our land. It is illegal for them to follow us there. They cannot cross over personal property without an invitation." He maintained his composed demeanor despite our limited options. Without warning, another vehicle cut down straight in front of us from above.

"*Gaelan*," I shrieked. He swiftly turned us to the left to avoid smashing into it.

"Just let me drive. I need to focus," he cautioned patiently.

"Sorry," I muttered. I couldn't help but be a backseat driver. I would rather scream than die.

"He's back," Gaelan muttered, looking at the complex digital screen in front of us. It showed the levitron coming up on our right. He seemed to rely more on the navigational technology than his own sight. I felt like I was living in a video game. Within seconds, I saw the car outside my window.

"Humph," I moaned. I stared at the determined driver's hardened expression at our side. "Is he *trying* to murder us?"

"Not today!" Gaelan assured me in a confident voice. He ducked underneath the chasing vehicle and changed our coordinates. The pursuing car wasted no time and came up on our tail.

"That guy's a maniac!" I huffed out of frustration.

"Mm-hmm." Gaelan angled us more to the right.

"*Ahhh*, he's too close." I peered out my side window to the car coming up on our side. "He's going to hit us!" I exclaimed angrily.

"Don't worry—we'll get rid of them," he stated convincingly.

"*Them?*" I gasped, turning back to look at the digital navigation screen.

"Yes, them." Gaelan pointed to the monitor, which now detected five more cars coming up directly behind us.

"Uh, where are we going? Isn't that the farm over there?" I pointed out his window in the opposite direction when the green fields came into view.

"We'll take a shortcut. Our property wraps around. We own the land down to the lake. We can take cover in the trees on a path I used to walk all the time," he reassured me.

"What path? All I see is forest." I gasped when I saw the thick rows of tall green trees before us.

"Right there." He pointed.

"You have *got* to be kidding me. We will never fit!" I demanded, looking ahead at the slight clearing.

"Sure we can. It's perfect," Gaelan said as if there were no other choice. He pulled us into a steep dive, lowering our levitron just above the ground before he turned us up on our left side and soared directly through the small gap in the trees.

"No, you can't. Jeez … *ahhh*, you're crazy! Oh my … I hate this!" I screamed while I held on to the dash and my seat. *That's it, we're going to die*, I thought. *We are going to hit a big tree and be dead on impact.* I became nauseous and found myself hyperventilating to keep from throwing up. I detested his flying us through the narrow forest path. Our extreme speed made the sunlight flash and flicker through the tall passing trees on our sides. I closed my eyes to hide from the sight. I heard the branches of trees snap and scratch across the body of the vehicle. I could feel us turning to maneuver through the course. My body jolted with every move. I braced myself tightly to keep from crashing into the side of the levitron. I thought it would never end.

"Sami." Gaelan touched my hand. I jumped with his gesture.

"Whoa?" I answered with a yelp.

"We're here. It's safe to open your eyes now. My goodness, look at you. Are you *okay*?" He sounded amused at seeing my petrified body glued to seat.

"Maybe. I … I don't know yet," I stammered. I was still in shock.

"You can let go now." He raised his eyebrows while looking at my hands. My fingers were locked down like a vise on the seat cushion and seatbelt. To my surprise, we weren't moving. I looked around to discover that we had already returned to the house and had landed. "You know, I have never seen anybody's knuckles get that white before." He shook his head in disbelief.

"Very funny," I muttered before I fought to remove my stiffened fingers from their grip. Gaelan jumped out of the levitron and walked around the front of the vehicle to open my door for me.

"I told you I would get you home safe and sound," he said, leaning into the air-car. He let out a chuckle at the pun before he picked up my right hand and laid a kiss across the top of my hand.

"You call *that* safe?" I shook my head in disagreement, unable to get up.

"Sure." He smiled. "You know I would never let anything happen to you. I adore you," he said seriously.

"Thanks, but you fly like a daredevil!" I poked him in the chest.

"I am taking that as a compliment," he said in a smooth voice. His lips turned up in a mischievous grin. He seemed excited by his ability to outmaneuver our aggressors.

"Do you have any *other* hidden talents you care to disclose?"

"I have plenty of skills I will reveal to you in time. I don't want you to grow bored with me," he retorted.

"*Impossible!*" I said with a smile. I admired him, even though his flying scared me to death. He possessed the ability to think clearly under pressure and act without hesitation. His plan to deter our followers had worked, and more important, he didn't kill us!

CHAPTER 26

DECLARATION

Silently, we walked inside the house. My body swayed. I was still trying to regain my equilibrium. We were greeted by Gaelan's family impatiently awaiting our return in the large living room.

"How was the hearing?" Colin asked eagerly.

"They suspended my flight privileges," Gaelan muttered weakly to the group. He looked like he had been hit with a truck. Why didn't he tell me? I felt a wave of pain sweep over me.

"*What?* How can they? That is absurd," Zaric huffed, sounding outraged.

"What about you and Sami?" Azil quickly asked.

Gaelan reached for my hand. "That is untouchable. Our commitment is honored." He gave me a half-smile.

Colin's forehead creased. "Did you petition?"

"Of course, but I only got four members to overturn it," he stated tensely.

"He needs the support of at least six of the ten senior council members," Miria explained to me after she saw confusion cross my face.

"Who was left?" Liam asked.

"Homic, Darion, Ryton, Planc, Surin, and Dilki," Gaelan said with contempt.

"Well, then—maybe there *is* something I can do to help," Liam said sinisterly.

"Liam, you must be reasonable here," Colin warned.

Liam looked at him smugly. "Father, I am the head of agriculture now. Remember, you signed it over to me."

"You wouldn't," Azil scolded.

"Son, you cannot withhold food. You do not plan on starving anyone, do you? Clearly, we can find another way," Miria warned.

"No, of course not. I have a much more effective solution." Liam hinted at an alternative resolution. He flashed us a wide, wicked grin. "Now, if you would excuse me. I have something to attend to." No one tried to stop him. I could tell that Liam's ambition ran at will.

"Gaelan, will they give you your flight privileges back before the ship returns to Earth?" I asked.

"Not unless something changes." He paused and pulled me into the foyer for privacy. "You have the choice to stay here with me until I am reinstated or to return home when the ship leaves. I can't be sure of when the next mission to Earth will be, though. I don't want you to miss out on your time at home." He lightly stroked the side of my face.

"Gaelan, you mean I have to choose between you and my life on Earth?"

"Only for now. You should return home. I want you to be happy. You will only feel trapped if you stay here with me. I will find a way back to you. I promise." He held both of my hands with conviction.

"The ship leaves in three days. You have to be able to go. They can't do this," I pleaded.

"I am so sorry. I never intended to hurt you. You never asked to be a part of this. *Please* ... you are not of this world. You belong more at home than you do with me. It is selfish for me to think otherwise," he insisted. He looked broken. I could tell it wasn't easy for him to tell me to leave him. It was as though the words scorched his lips when he spoke them.

"I can't just leave you. I don't want to live without you," I implored. He squeezed my hands and swung my arms. A glimmer of hope returned to his eyes.

"Hmm, what *are* we going to do?" He sighed.

"Why are they trying to keep us apart?"

"They said it was to determine my loyalty to Kataria and to prove my commitment to you." Gaelan looked at me tenderly but remained speechless for a moment.

I was about to ask what he was thinking when Zaric approached us with a determined step.

"Gaelan," he interrupted, "we should gather some support. The council needs some motivation to change their minds."

"You're right. Sami, I need to talk with some friends. I will get back as soon as I can. I think it would be better if you stayed home. The reporters won't bother you here. I can only assume the commotion out there has grown." Gaelan looked me in the eyes, trying to assess my reaction. I couldn't help but be relieved by his offer. I think he knew I would rather not step foot in that car again.

"I'll be happy to wait here, but why don't you just call people on the phone? You *do* have telephones, *don't* you? Don't you have voice communicators like you do on the ship? I can't believe you want to go back out there." I cringed, fearing for his safety.

"Of course we have communicators, but it is much better if we talk to our friends in person." He paused to search for the right words. "Most of us find comfort in old traditions. Our technology has taken away so many tasks that our culture looks for ways to maintain our human connection. It is one thing we can thank the Dreons for. They have taught us the importance of never taking our humanity for granted. We strive to preserve the balance with technology within our society," he explained.

I knew exactly what he was saying. In general, it had become too easy to avoid direct interaction with others. Who hasn't felt relief to have the luxury of leaving a voicemail message instead of having a conversation? Text messaging and voice dictation had practically taken over most of the communication on Earth. It was as though our society had become fearful of human contact and more comfortable relying on technology to interact. I shared his view. Humanity was something worth saving and even fighting for.

Gaelan gave me a quick kiss and soft stroke on the cheek before he headed out the door with Zaric and Colin. I stood in the large foyer, feeling crushed. I looked up at the light filtering through the round, domed skylight and prayed for divine intervention. I imagined the warm light filling me with the courage to persevere.

Azil walked over to comfort me. "Sami, he will be okay."

"I feel terrible. I have taken away his greatest pleasure in life." I was filled with shame and guilt. My eyes filled with tears. She gently laid her hand on my back.

"Shhh," she hushed me.

"I ruined his life," I whispered while I wiped my eyes.

"No, Sami. You have made him happy. He has never loved anyone the way he does you. Your relationship is just big news. No one has ever been brave enough to get involved with another kind and be so open about it."

"Azil, I can't lose him." I grimaced out of frustration.

"I know," Azil said quietly.

The day dragged on. Gaelan's mother showed me the rest of the house and told me stories about Gaelan growing up to keep me occupied. She was spunky and full of energy. We could easily become great friends.

"Sami, I have never seen Gaelan like this. I think he has been searching for you for a long time," Miria surmised.

"Thank you. That means a lot to me," I replied.

She seemed to be trying to make the most of our time together. I remembered Noah telling me about how people on Earth stifle their youth. Now, I understood. Miria explained how each of her children differed and that they each had many projects taking over the house when they were young. I really admired her. She loved each of her children deeply and possessed the ability to support each of their dreams without any reservations of her own. She possessed an inner strength and was extremely optimistic. It was as though she gave each of them wings to fly to their heart's content while never inflicting the fear of failure in them. I felt guilty when I thought about how I'd tried to sabotage Leah and Jackson's dreams to work on the Space resort. My selfish fear of losing them almost stopped them. I vowed to parent more like Miria when I returned home. I could see how she produced such strong children.

***

Noah came to the house later that afternoon. I was grateful to see him. It was as though he heard me calling out to him with my mind. Miria showed him to Gaelan's suite, where I sat obsessing about the events of the day over and over again in my head.

"Sami, I can't believe you. You haven't even been here a day and you are already on the news." Noah shook his head in disapproval. "You know, I was on Earth for over *twenty-five years* and never once caused a scandal," he teased. He approached the sofa I was sitting on.

"Noah, what have you heard?" I asked.

"Oh, that one of our commanding officers from the Space fleet has become *romantically* involved with a woman from Earth, and he has brought her here to meet his family." He plopped himself down on the sofa beside me, bouncing me up from the cushion.

"Is that all?" I asked fearfully.

"Well, they have pictures of you and Gaelan starting from the time you both stepped off the ship. Someone on board must have tipped the reporters off early. You're a celebrity."

"Oh, *great.*" I sighed.

"Hey, I was only kidding. It's not *that* big of a deal." He nudged my shoulder, trying to cheer me up. "Uh-oh, you must really be upset. You've completely lost your upper lip! What's wrong?"

"Noah, we were in court this morning. The council grounded Gaelan," I retorted.

"*What?* Are you serious? That's awful! What right do they have?" Noah's playful tone quickly became angry when he realized the gravity of the situation.

"Gaelan and his family are trying to get him reinstated," I said, making a wish.

"Now you understand why I left Kataria. I wanted to start a new life for myself away from those power-hungry morons. Our council makes some pretty bad decisions if you ask me. They butt their noses into places they shouldn't, trying to justify their purpose," he said, looking downward with resentment. Understanding his tragic past, who could blame him for holding a grudge? I put my hand on his and squeezed it firmly, conveying my support.

"I don't know what I'm going to do. Gaelan wants me to go home without him," I said solemnly.

"Hey, you aren't seriously considering staying here— *are you?*" he said, looking at me with widened eyes.

"Maybe. I'm not sure," I muttered.

"Sami, *No!* I know how you feel, but you have to think about Leah and Jackson. You can't stay here. They can't lose you, too," he said adamantly.

"I realize that. But if Gaelan has to stay, how long do you think it will be before I can see him again?"

"Well," he pursed his lips, "it might be a while. However, I am sure that you'll be able to pick things right up again when you are reunited," Noah said casually.

"Define a while," I groaned.

"Sami, I have to be honest. I'm *not* sure, but it might be a couple of years. But Gaelan is used to being separated from the people he loves. He wouldn't forget about you." He scrunched his face up, knowing that it wasn't the answer I was looking for.

"*Ahh*, I hate this. I feel like someone is tearing my heart in two. I can't handle it." I sunk my body down into Noah's side.

"Sami, please don't make it any harder than it is. Gaelan will understand," he urged. My eyes filled with tears.

"You think I can just leave him? Tell him good-bye and that I will see him again in a few years? It's just not that easy," I moaned.

"Yes, you can. It's the best choice. You will regret staying here as soon as the ship departs. Besides, I could stand in for him if you think it would help. I volunteer my services. I can assure you—you'll be satisfied. I know a thing or two about how to please a woman. You can use me for sex whenever you want. I can pretend to be Gaelan and look at you all ga-ga," he teased, trying to lighten my mood. He put his arm around my shoulder and gave me a shake.

"*Noah* …" I tried not to laugh. "What? *Now* you offer? After I find someone new to love?" Even though the thought of being with Noah made me uncomfortable, I couldn't say for sure if I would have turned him down in the last two lonesome years. Still, talk about awkward-ever-after.

"*Look*, what's not to love?" He held out his arms to show off his body.

"Could you *please* be serious for once? Besides, I'm not so sure Karis would approve."

"That's no longer a concern," he said flatly.

"Really? What happened? I thought you liked her."

"Yeah, I mean she's all right, a little clingy maybe, but I *can't* stand her family," he muttered. "Karis just informed me of her plans to stay here, and that is *totally* out of the question for me. Those people would smother the life right out of me. There's no way I could pal around with that group for an extended period of time. They see the bad side of everything and are always trying to top each other's misery. Two words sum them up: buzz kill! Just a few hours with them is completely *draining*," he moaned dramatically.

"You know you deserve better. You have so much to offer. Any girl would be lucky to have you."

"You think so, *huh?*"

"Oh, Noah, what am I going to do with you?" I put my hand under his chin and turned his face towards mine like he was a puppy.

"Sami, I'm not leaving here without you. I know you. You will become seriously depressed if you can't see your kids. Please, I don't want to think about you self-destructing. I demand that you come home. There, I made your decision for you. Now, pack up—let's go home," he instructed.

"When you say home, you mean Earth?"

"Yes, it's *my* home now, too, remember?" he said defensively.

"I can't do it. It hurts too much," I cried. Noah pulled my limp body in closer.

"You survived before; you can do it again. It's not forever, and it's the best decision." His voice was firm. I nodded in agreement before I leaned my head on his shoulder and fought to control my tears.

Gaelan, Zaric, and Colin returned home later that evening. They all were laughing and had full smiles plastered across their faces when they entered. I thought they were just exhilarated after outmaneuvering more reporters. I was right, but that wasn't the only reason for their happiness. Colin pleasantly reported his success in convincing another council member, Dilki, to change her vote. Dilki was an old classmate of Colin's. I became hopeful because now we only needed one more verdict to be changed. Liam returned home shortly after them. He told us he had set his scheme in motion and felt confident of its outcome. I was surprised that no one bothered to question what his plan consisted of.

"Gaelan, what is Liam up to?" I asked when we got to back to his suite.

"I have no idea. He won't tell us until he's ready, so it's no use to ask."

"Won't he at least give you a clue?" I asked curiously.

"Oh, you *highly* underestimate Liam's willpower. If we pressure him, he will stop talking to all of us and probably barricade the entrance to his suite and arm it with booby traps," he said like he was speaking from experience.

"Why is he so secretive?"

"He's afraid it will harm his plan. Liam thinks if he talks about something too early, it will not come true."

"You mean he's superstitious!" I laughed.

"Yes, that's what you call it. He likes to let everything *germinate* in peace, just like his plants."

"He really is different. They say real genius borders closely with insanity."

"He's bizarre," he said, raising his eyebrows. "Now you understand what I had to grow up with."

CHAPTER 27

ACCEPTANCE

The entire family seemed to put all of their efforts in helping Gaelan regain his flight privileges. Gaelan, Zaric, Azil, and Colin left the house early each day to rally as much support as they could gather. I stayed at the house and met many of Miria and Gallina's friends. They thought by introducing me to other Katarians, my presence would become more easily accepted. I couldn't help but feel like I was being scrutinized by the guests. I felt the weight of their penetrating stares every time I looked away. I thoughtfully answered their questions about Earth and how Gaelan and I met. Taking away some of the mystery seemed to appease their fears. Overall, it seemed as though I had won the group's acceptance. The women all claimed to be supportive of Gaelan and me before they left the house. My work was done. We waited for the rest of the family to come back.

"Any luck?" Miria asked hopefully when the group returned.

"No," Gaelan said flatly.

Colin walked over and took Miria's hand in his. "The council's ballot was swayed. Enos's father, Darion, managed to convince his closest buddies on the council that Gaelan has suffered poor judgment since meeting Sami. Apparently, his son has been having nightmares ever since landing on Decca. Darion wants Gaelan sit out on the next trip in order to regain his reason," he explained. Azil paced across the room.

"Darion thinks we endangered Enos's life and that Sami nearly cost us our treaty," Azil retorted.

"It's absurd," Zaric said defensively.

Gaelan looked at me in defeat. "Enos is accusing me of keeping us on Decca longer than necessary," he said. "He blames the delay on the Dreons not finding your Katarian registry. He believes the encounter could have been avoided if you stayed on the ship. He's convinced we would have left the planet before the large tremor awoke the Paramante. Like we can control the weather or when the planet's tectonic plates are going to shift."

"He has *no* place on a starship," Zaric scoffed. "What did he expect? A ride of leisure? A written guarantee?"

"They have no idea what you do," Colin added.

"Why *don't* they?" Gaelan huffed. "We go blindly into uncharted territory. No one could *ever* predict what we might encounter. Not to mention our lives are completely dependent on the integrity and operation of the ship. You don't have to be a genius to understand the risk!" Gaelan shook his head in disbelief. My suppressed fears resurfaced—validated by his accidental admission. For the first time, I really appreciated the fact that I wasn't the only one anxious about traveling in Outer Space. They were just as apprehensive about the unknown dangers of the universe as I was. Gaelan never revealed his vulnerability to me. He displayed an extreme confidence to overshadow his hidden reservations.

"Did he think he was sending his son to camp?" Zaric said sarcastically. "Maybe we should have had Darion sign a waiver releasing us from liability in case Enos got killed?"

"Oh, could you picture that? There would be *no* forgiveness if we didn't bring him home alive," Azil added callously.

"Sure seems like it," Colin added.

I looked up to see Gaelan's eyes glued on me. He looked at me nervously as though they had said too much in front of me. I acted unbothered by their eye-opening conversation. "So, they are punishing you because of me," I muttered.

"It's the perfect retaliation. They think by taking me away from what I love most, I will learn to act more cautiously in the future. It's an oppressive attempt to keep me in line," Gaelan said bitterly.

***

Gaelan and I left the house to visit Urit. He had called earlier to tell us he had something exciting to report on the Dreon tracer. Gaelan said he sounded like he made a breakthrough in deciphering the device. To my relief, he lived within walking distance … if you consider five miles walking distance. His home's lot touched the far north side of Gaelan's family's property that bordered the lake. I could see glimpses of the water through the trees the closer we got. We walked on a trail through tall wheat fields to get there. I'd longed to be outside. Just the sensation of my feet hitting the natural ground with each step was satisfying. A light breeze brushed gently against our faces, carrying the smell of clean, fresh air. It felt amazing to be on the open land. We strolled across the sunlit field, forgetting about the troubles of the day. The soft wheat strands reflected the glistening rays of sunlight in the most spectacular golden color. My stress seemed to melt away. I wanted to remember this peaceful moment forever. I made a mental picture of its glory, trying to freeze its beauty in my mind so I would never forget how wonderful it made me feel.

We arrived at Urit's modest log home. It was small and cabinlike. I asked Gaelan if Urit was well paid for all of his amazing medical contributions. He laughed. "Why? Because he lives in a shack?" he said, understanding the meaning behind my question.

"Yeah," I answered, despite sounding a little judgmental.

"Urit has more money than he could *ever* spend, if that's what you're asking."

"Oh, I wasn't sure."

"He spends everything he earns on supplies for his experiments. I've seen him trade sickening sums of money for minute amounts of rare ingredients or bizarre trinkets. He's not materialistic when it comes to normal things. He yearns for something bigger. He wants answers, solutions to life's biggest problems." We walked up the worn dirt path leading up to the house. Gaelan knocked on the red wooden door.

"Oh, hello," answered a pretty woman. It must have been Urit's daughter.

"Nia," Gaelan said with a smile. She gave Gaelan a friendly nod hello.

"You must be Sam," she greeted me kindly.

"Yes, it's nice to meet you," I replied. She opened the door widely and ushered us inside.

Nia was beautiful. She had long, wavy, dark auburn hair carelessly pulled back in a clip, green-blue eyes, and a flowing semi-fitted long pink dress. She was adorned with several long, eclectic necklaces and sandals. She would fit in perfectly if she were attending a party on the beach.

The home mirrored Nia's relaxed style. I smiled when I instantly spotted what looked like a knitting basket in the corner. We stepped across the creaky, worn, wooded floor into the overcrowded room. The place seemed to function as a lab, living room, and kitchen all in one. Four large, overstuffed chairs covered in mismatched fabric and a round wooden table filled the living room. Directly behind it sat the kitchen. Its entire back wall was made of several windows, providing a view overlooking the lake. They filled the room with natural light and let in a light breeze, swaying the curtains and the wrought iron ceiling rack that hung directly above the metal counter-top holding large pots and blue mugs. The greater part of the room was a full-blown lab. It had classroom-sized drawing boards hanging on the walls, tables covered with beakers under aquarium lights, and large machinery possibly used for scanning or producing things. I studied the equations written on the drawing boards to search for familiarity, but they were meaningless to me. I carefully entered the room so I wouldn't trip, break, or bump into something.

"Sam, Gaelan, any luck with the verdict?" Urit asked, coming around the corner.

"Nope," Gaelan answered bluntly. There was no explanation needed. His voice rang with sadness.

"I'm sorry," Urit said with sincerity.

"Thanks for all your help," Gaelan said graciously.

"Some help," Urit said in a serious voice. "I was hoping that the council would have come to their senses by now and we could all be carelessly on our way as soon as possible."

Gaelan looked suspiciously at Urit. "Is there a problem I'm not aware of?" he asked.

"We've run into a minor complication with the tracer," Urit explained with a frown. "We were contacted by Spaceport this morning to see if we knew a reason for the Dreon ship in our vicinity. They tracked a laser signal from them to our coordinates. Of course, we played dumb. Luckily, the Dreons claimed it was a misfire of their communication system and left on their own when Spaceport started questioning them. I just hope they're gone for good. Anyway, our good fortune didn't end there. Jed is the one who made the call," he said with a look of relief.

"Who's Jed?" I asked.

"My friend," Nia answered. "We work together when I visit Spaceport. He said he wouldn't report the news to the council since there was no threat of harm—out of professional courtesy. Jed likes to keep Spaceport matters on the station if he can," she explained.

Gaelan rubbed the corners of his mouth as he thought. "Great. They've come back to get what's theirs."

Nia interjected, "I can see why. The device has the most advanced relay-based software I've ever seen. It seems to be equipped with microprocessors capable of monitoring *everything*: visual, auditory, sensory, and spatial position. I am trying to figure out a way to decipher the information it gathers in order to control the instrument and reverse its maneuvers. But it won't be easy. It's a highly sophisticated supercomputer. It's even equipped with its own neural processor or tiny brain. It might be used to create the delusions the Dreons are known for. It's probably watching us right now," she joked. "No, don't worry. It appears to go into sleep mode and only comes to life every two hours. Then, it lights up for two minutes and fifteen seconds. A strong electromagnetic signal is released at the same time. I think it must beam information back to the Dreons. I am surprised that it can operate at such a horrifyingly far range. The device's internal guidance system and teleportation components seem so powerful, they might even be able to teleport someone off a nearby planet with it."

"I don't think it's quite *that* strong, Nia," Urit said to her.

Nia shrugged. "I guess you're right. Maybe I'm being paranoid. But either way, it's far more powerful than I'd originally anticipated. And the thing nearly scared me to death when it came to life at an unscheduled time.

I was in the middle of dissecting it to determine its capabilities when the Dreon ship came into our airspace.
I had it all in pieces, sprawled out across my workspace.
Without warning, the parts levitated off the table, self-
aligned, and snapped together!" she said with widened
eyes.

Urit scratched his head. "That's right when we
received the call from Spaceport," he explained, "inform-
ing us of the Dreon's signal. I was still on the communicator when the device started spinning and lighting up
the whole room. I hurriedly brought the communicator
outside to finish my conversation while pretending to
look for the laser beam. I thought we were done for."

Nia sat down on a chair in front of a table with the
tracer in front of her. It was now completely clean of the
red rubber substance Urit had used to disguise it while
on board. She had it positioned in front of her workspace
on a small, lighted platform, making it look like a precious lost treasure. "Come here. You have to see this."
She waved her hand, summoning us to join her. "Watch,"
she said. She leaned down across the table in front of the
ball to blow her breath slowly over the device. The tiny,
shiny ball lit up with a brilliant glowing orange light.

"Whoa, fascinating," I said, peering over her shoulder.
It looked like a little ball of fire. It quickly returned to
its solid, non-glowing, metallic finish when she stopped.
Nia smiled, seeming pleased in sharing her discovery.

"So, it's sensitive to changes in temperature?" Gaelan asked, sounding intrigued.

"Yes. Probably registers body heat. I'll find out after I take it all apart, *again*." She disappointingly leaned back in her chair.

Urit gave her a compassionate look. "Hey, you've already learned more about their tracers than anyone else has in the past. Be patient, my dear; you'll get it done," he encouraged her. He had to be the most patient, supportive man I'd ever known.

***

We spent the rest of the evening with Gaelan's family. It was unexpectedly enjoyable. No one wanted to ruin their limited time together by complaining. The family bantered playfully around the dining table, truly enjoying each other's company. They each possessed a charismatic wit of their own. The room was filled with laughter. It was delightful to watch. It was as though nothing could suppress their love for one another. I was sure I hadn't laughed that much at a family gathering since my parents were alive. It made me miss Jackson and Leah more than ever. I wished they were here. They would fit in perfectly with Gaelan's family.

I felt torn when thinking about leaving Kataria without Gaelan. Just the thought of the return trip home without him would be torture. The agenda outlining the ship's next voyage to and from Earth had the ship scheduled to return in two years. At least it wasn't forever. We all waited patiently for the *one* verdict that would reinstate Gaelan's flight privileges before the evening's end. It didn't happen. We were out of time. The ship was set to depart the next morning.

I told Gaelan of my plans to return home later that night. He told me he already knew. It had to be one of the hardest decisions in my life. He embraced me while we lay on his bed and gazed up at the constellations shining through the large wall of windows. The stars were much brighter here and gave off a soft, golden color that was visible with the naked eye. I imagined that their atmosphere was to blame, because everything seemed to have a yellow glow here. It was so peaceful lying beside him. It was a moment I would remember forever. It was, however, bittersweet since we both knew our time together was running out. Letting go was never easy for me. Part of me wanted to love him with all my soul—while another felt as though I should be weaning myself from him to ease the pain of my inevitable heartbreak.

"You're leaving tomorrow." Gaelan sat straight up in bed, sounding panic-stricken when he realized how relaxed we had become.

"I'm sorry." I exhaled breathlessly while I sat up next to him. "Are you mad at me?"

"Don't be ridiculous. I could never be angry with you. How could I be? Beautiful, intelligent, magnificent woman that you are," he said gently while he stroked my arm.

"Hmmm, I don't want to go so soon."

"We can't waste this time sleeping. Every minute with you is precious. I don't know how long it will be before I can see you again," he declared passionately.

"Listen," I pleaded. "You better not make it too long."

"I won't," he promised, but his face looked wounded by uncertainly. He stared at my face for an extended period of time. It seemed like he was trying to memorize it in case it was the last time he'd see me.

"I will sneak you aboard and hide you under the bed," I offered.

"Tempting," he mused.

"Yes, you want to try it?" I jested.

"I would be willing to break every rule for you despite the consequences. Unfortunately, I'm probably going to be escorted to and from the launch pad tomorrow with armed guards. I'd rather not get shot."

"It's not fair," I moaned.

"We will survive. *Trust me.* Unscheduled trips occur all the time. We didn't plan on returning home on this trip, but here we are."

"True."

"Besides, I think my friends will find some excuse to travel back before two years go by. I will get back to you, I promise."

We rested back down on the bed facing one another. He pulled me to him and ran his fingers through the back of my long hair and down my spine. It not only felt fantastic—but incredibly different. I touched the bracelet on my wrist and wondered if it was to blame. It couldn't be my imagination. This had to be what he meant when he said it would strengthen our connection. I felt extremely aware of his body next to mine. Every touch seemed to take on a heightened intensity. I let him explore my body freely while I relished his touch. He slid his hand up and down my legs, carefully slowing over every curve. I thought I'd explode in pleasure. He knew exactly how to touch me. Each stroke made me want him more. He didn't disappoint. He leaned up and gently kissed my neck before following an imaginary line down my side. I took the opportunity to glide my fingertips across his back, trying to savor every flexing muscle. Making love with this level of emotional bond was euphoric. There were no words to describe how badly I would miss him.

We talked and kissed for hours. Although I didn't want to lose one precious moment with him, I couldn't help falling asleep. It was already daylight when I awoke.

Where did the night go? I opened my eyes to the bright morning sunlight coming through the large uncovered windows. My eyes squinted to see Gaelan's silhouette painting beside the bed with his chair and easel. He was glancing back and forth between his canvas and me.

I sat up. "What are you doing?" I asked, puzzled.

"Come and see. It is my first portrait of a person." He grinned. "You are beautiful when you are sleeping. You look so peaceful." I slipped out of the sheets and got up to look.

"I can't believe it." I was stunned when I looked at the lovely painting he had made of me. It was glowing and soft-looking. The picture gave me the same surprised feeling I had if someone showed me a good photo of myself. Usually, I hated to see myself in pictures, but this was a very complimentary angle. "Is that *how* you see me?" I asked in disbelief.

"*Yes*, but you are much better in person." He pulled me in sideways by the waist, remaining seated in his chair.

"That's funny. I always sleep on my right side," I said, gazing at the painting.

"I know. I've had this image in my mind for some time now," he admitted.

"You're killing me. Could you make this any harder?" I felt weak and lost my balance for a minute. He held me up.

"Are you okay?" he asked, concerned.

"Yes, I just got dizzy." My emotions felt out of control. I think I forgot how to breathe.

"I hate letting you go, but I won't have you miss out on your life because of me," he whispered. "I will not hold you back. I will love you for the rest of my life." It sounded final, as though it might be forever.

I sighed and looked down on his weary face. It looked as though he had been up all night. "Don't forget about me," I said.

"No," he pushed my hair gently behind my ear, "I would never, ever forget you!" He pulled my body into his, enclosing me securely in his arms.

"I'm going to miss you *so* much."

"I will always be with you, wherever you are." He leaned back, looked up at me, and lightly touched my heart.

"Yes," I agreed. I closed my eyes, trying to find the will to uphold my decision to leave.

"Now, please try to behave yourself. Keep out of trouble on the way home. Nothing can happen to you. Stay away from the Dreons and anyone else you may encounter. Actually, don't leave the ship. I'm sure the Dreons aren't the only ones who would show an interest in you. They aren't the most dangerous things out there." He brushed his fingers across my lips softly. Whether he intended to or not, his warning scared the wits out of me. Perhaps he said it in attempt to help keep me safe. I could only imagine what he was referring to. I think we both felt incredibly vulnerable without him by my side to protect me.

"Yes, no trouble. I promise," I said in a silly voice.

"*Oh*, you are an ornery thing, aren't you?" He tickled my stomach while he kept me from getting away.

"Stop it!" I yelled between laughs. His serious demeanor returned. We looked at each other without saying a word. He pulled me onto his lap. I stroked his neck and back with my hands. I never wanted to forget the feeling of his strong shoulders and muscular body. How difficult it was to leave him. He had become who I yearned to see each day.

"Come here." He reached up and pulled me to his lips. He kissed me with such passion. I knew it was good-bye.

CHAPTER 28

PARTING

We arrived at the courthouse. The place was buzzing with the same bustling activity it had when we originally arrived. It was time to board the ship. My heart was still questioning my decision to leave. Truthfully, my agony meant little. Why did I even bother inducing such self-torture on myself? I had always known what my decision would be. It was to return to my kids. Their happiness overshadowed every personal choice I had ever made. I worried about never seeing Gaelan again. I couldn't bear losing someone I loved so dearly. Gaelan's family came to the launch pad to see the ship off. I said good-bye to each of them. They all expressed their desire for me to return to Kataria in the future. Everyone was present except Liam. Gallina told me he was running late but was on his way as we spoke. Azil and Zaric were elated that their son, Maric, was joining us for the trip.

"Don't worry, Gaelan. We will get her home safely," Zaric promised. He gave Gaelan a one-armed hug good-bye.

Azil smiled at Gaelan and me. "It will be okay, brother. I always take good care of my family. We won't let anything happen to her," she said convincingly.

"Thank you." Gaelan hugged her lovingly before she walked away with her family. Just then, Urit came rushing up to us. His face was stoic and uncharacteristic for him. Maybe he felt uncomfortable interrupting our good-bye.

"Gaelan, I need you to look after something for me while I'm away," he said in a serious tone. He shifted his body anxiously from side to side and handed Gaelan an envelope. Maybe he shot himself up with another dose of bottled hyperactivity.

"Sure, what do you want me to do?" Gaelan said reluctantly. He lifted the flap of the envelope and looked inside. There was a letter and a thin card. "What's *this* ... a key to your house?" Gaelan asked in a confused voice.

"Yes," Urit replied.

"What about Nia, can't she handle this?"

"Actually, I was hoping that you could help her with that thing we were working on," he said under his breath. "The letter will explain everything," he said without elaboration.

"Okay, whatever. I have nothing better to do," Gaelan said in a defeated tone.

Urit's eyes met Gaelan's. "Good. Thank you," he said firmly. He looked at me and opened his lips as if he were going to say something, but, instead, he turned away and quickly darted off.

"Great, I guess you know what I'll be doing while we're apart. I'm sure he has all sorts of experiments for me to tend to."

"Without a doubt," I agreed.

Gaelan walked me up to the ship's landing. It was as far as his escort allowed him. I looked him in the eyes and tried to fake a smile to hide my sadness. I didn't want to destroy his last memory of me. He reached for both of my hands and held them tightly in his.

"I love you," I said adamantly.

"I will be with you again soon," he promised. We were all prepared to say our final farewell when Liam came sprinting up the landing ramp out of nowhere.

Liam leaned over breathlessly. "*Gaelan*, here … I am sorry it took me so long." He propped one hand on his thigh and extended his other hand to hold out a small metal card.

"What is *this*, Liam?" Gaelan's face lit up with a wide smile.

"Your boarding pass. You are reinstated!" Liam shouted joyfully. He tossed the card in the air to Gaelan. Gaelan caught it with one hand.

"Really? *Amazing!* Liam—you're incredible! How did you do it?" Gaelan asked excitedly. Then he embraced his brother in a big hug, lifting him off the ground.

"Wait, I'll tell you in a minute." Liam snatched the card out of Gaelan's hand and walked over to show the guard standing nearby. With a rebellious look in his eyes, he held the pass in front of the man's face, waving it back and forth. "You may go now. He's been authorized to board," he said triumphantly, dismissing the man from his post. The guard just shook his head and left.

"Liam! How is this possible?" Gaelan asked.

"I spent the morning in the courthouse. I had to quell a vicious rumor about a ridiculously major price increase for our produce. I can't imagine who would have suggested such an atrocity. I explained to the council that some of the public may have been lashing out at our family in protest to your love affair. You know how people can get carried away."

"It sort of sounds like someone I know." Gaelan grinned.

"Yeah, I was a little disappointed when it did not travel as quickly as I had anticipated. Nonetheless, it finally got back to the right people. There was a public outrage at the courthouse this morning. How did you miss all that excitement when you got here? I told the council it was all due to your return, Gaelan. I said that the people just needed some time to accept your relationship. The council then agreed it was best for everyone if you left Kataria until things calmed down. I was able to obtain a unanimous vote for the return of your flight privileges," he said proudly.

"Wow, Liam, remind me never to mess with you. Clever, though! I owe you, brother," Gaelan said sincerely. He laid his hand on Liam's shoulder.

"Oh, and Azil packed your bags. I just handed them to the courier." He smiled.

"You're kidding? You mean she was in on your plan?" Gaelan shrugged.

"Yeah, but we decided not to tell you just in case it fell through."

"Great, she probably packed everything I own, knowing her," Gaelan joked.

"Thank you, Liam. You are the best." I reached for his hand.

"Come here, Sami." He grabbed me and hugged me tightly. "I do not know when I will see you again. Take care of him." He leaned away and kindly looked me in the eyes.

"I will," I promised.

"Oh, I almost forgot. I came to deliver you a present. It is nothing much, but it may help the trip go faster." He handed me a little box.

"Thank you, but you have already given me the greatest gift," I said, linking my arm in Gaelan's.

"Trust me, I am not completely selfless. I did not do what I did just for you. He would have been intolerable. Do you know how annoying his sulking around the house would have been? *Ahh*, talk about torture," he complained, as if Gaelan was invisible.

"Good-bye, Liam. May I find you and the family well when I return." Gaelan nodded at Liam.

"Well, off with you both. I am going to get out of here before this thing takes me with it. Take care, brother." Liam nodded in return. He turned and practically ran off the ship as though it was going to suck him up and hold him captive.

Gaelan and I stood on the landing, with our future together shining down on us brighter than ever.

"I can't believe it!" I cheered.

"I know." He smiled widely before he took me in his arms, lifted me off the floor, and spun me around.

"I didn't want to leave here without you."

"Well, now you're stuck with me." He gave me one of his sexy looks that rendered me speechless. I was struck with a wave of relief. I loved him so much. I was lucky to have found him.

"Gaelan, what did they give us?" I stared at the little box Liam had handed me before he sprinted off the ship.

"I don't know. Just open it." He smiled.

I opened the box to discover a tiny metal cube. "What is it?"

"Books," he replied.

"You mean there are books on here?" I asked, confused.

"Yes, I have a player in the room. It will show you the words and read you the stories. You can learn how to read Katarian."

"That's fantastic! How did he know? It has been driving me crazy not being able to read anything. Did I ever tell you how much I love your brother?"

"Hey …" Gaelan pulled me closer to him.

"Not like I love you, though." I beamed. I couldn't control my excitement. I threw my arms around him and kissed him passionately.

"Sami, you are my world. I will *never* let you go." Gaelan embraced me in his arms.

"*Never.*" I smiled while looking up into his eyes.

Although we had yet to survive the trip home, every day would be easier with Gaelan at my side. Gaelan took my hand and led me to the command deck to join him. He told me it was time for me to learn more about starship navigation. I watched as the crew prepared the ship for take off. It didn't matter that I was far away from home. I was so euphoric I could float on air. I looked forward to learning all I could about the Katarian technology. It was something I would be linked to forever.

I realized that the old adage proved true: if you want something bad enough and ask for it, it's as though the whole universe conspires to help you. I was on my way home, and Gaelan was with me. Soon, I would arrive back at the Space resort and be reunited with Leah and Jackson. I couldn't wait to tell them all about my trip. I felt ecstatic. I never could have pictured being in this position in my entire life. Despite being this far from Earth, our different worlds seemed closer than ever. The entire universe connected for me in that one moment. There were so many things that had led me to this point. I had to stop relying on the external forces around me for strength and pull from the power within myself. I realized that I already possessed everything I ever needed in order to survive this adventure. My life had prepared me for this journey. I understood the previous mistakes I had made as well as the wise decisions of my past. I was caught living in a stagnant pattern and had reduced life to a mere existence. Being fully alive meant going outside of my comfort zone and taking risks. Overcoming my fears had empowered me in ways I never dreamt possible. My newfound courage had given me the confidence that I could survive any challenge that arose. I'd been graced with a blessed life. I had never felt more grateful. This was absolute bliss!

We took our seats, and the crew initiated the ship's departure.

"What's this?" Gaelan said while he shifted uncomfortably in his chair. He reached in his hind pocket and pulled out Urit's crinkled letter.

"What's it say?" I asked. He unfolded the paper.

Gaelan's eyes widened. *"Tyden!* Get Urit—we've got trouble!" he shouted.

"What is it?" Tyden asked nervously.

"A change in course ..."

ACKNOWLEDGMENTS

Enormous thanks to my husband, Rich, for allowing my creative force to run at will. For my daughters, Jordan and Kendra, for teaching me more about life than anyone could. Thanks to my parents, Myrna and Tim, for making me believe anything is possible. To my brother and sister, Brian and Nikki, I value your friendship. To Shelby and Matia, my loyal dogs, thank you for keeping me company while I write. I love you guys!

Special thanks to Gene Meyers and Terry Martin of the Space Island Group for allowing me use of their name and for providing images used throughout the book. Although my characters employment was purely fictitious, the innovative company truly exists. Visit www.spaceislandgroup.com to learn more.

To Space.com and the History Channel for providing me continuous inspiration, and to hardworking minds everywhere helping to advance our existence for a better tomorrow.

Thanks to Adam Block for providing the space photo used on the cover: www.caelumobservatory.com/gallery/foxfur.shtml. Visit him at www.caelumobservatory.com.

Thank you to my editor and the staff at BookSurge for your support.

Thanks to Joshua Hudson of Dragonfly Digital Media for photos used on the cover and inside the book.

Thanks to all my friends at Alle-Kiski Medical Center for your friendship and support.

Coming soon:

The adventure continues …

Beyond the Stars

Ineo

Before Sami and her Katarian friends can happily depart Kataria for their return trip to Earth, she discovers her troubles haven't ended. Urit confesses to the crew about his study of the Dreon tracer. He explains how it is responsible for his daughter Nia's disappearance. With a broken treaty and risk of war, the crew embarks on a desperate pursuit of the Dreon ship before it's too late. Unfortunately, finding their vessel proves to be more than a challenge. They are forced to rely on the help of a superior race for assistance. Along the way, they inadvertently attract dark forces of the universe. Sami is not only concerned for her and her friends' safety but worries she will never get home.

If you wish to be notified of the upcoming book's release date, please register your e-mail address at www.beyondthestarsnovel.com.

Kelly Beltz has a master's degree in science with a concentration in nurse anesthesia from La Roche College, where she has taught in the anesthesia program. She is also an entrepreneur and holds one US patent. She lives in Pennsylvania with her husband and two daughters. Visit the author online at www.beyondthestarsnovel.com.